THE DAYMAKERS

GRACE MCGINTY

Cover Art by DAZED Designs.

Editing by Aubergine Editing.

ALSO BY GRACE MCGINTY

Hell's Redemption Series: The Redeemable / The Unrepentant / The Fallen

Damnation MC Duet: Serendipity / Providence

The Azar Nazemi Trilogy : Smoke and Smolder / Burn and Blaze / Rage and Ruin

Dark River Days Series: Newly Undead In Dark River / Happily Undead In Dark River / Pleasantly Undead in Dark River

Black Mountain Mates: Hunting Isla

Eden Academy Series: The Lost and the Hunted (Prequel) / Heart of the Hounded (Prequel) / Rebels and Runaways (Book 1) / Sweethearts and Savages (Book 2)

Shadow Bred Series: Manix / Frenzy / Feral / Crave

Stand Alone Novels and Novellas: Bright Lights From A Hurricane / The Last Note / Inside The Maelstrom Part 1 and 2 / Pay-Per-Heart

Penalty Box Players: Sticks and Stone / Break My Bones

Omega Lottery: Tryst In The Dark

PREFACE

This book may contain triggering content around the subjects of domestic violence, and emotional and physical abuse, especially in the opening chapter. If these themes are potentially detrimental to your mental health, please read with caution and take care of yourself.

This is **not** a dark romance, and the MMC's are marshmallows, so any triggering content comes from outside influences. This book also contains prostitution (of a sort) and wrongful arrest.

ONE

CHARLOTTE

"BABY, I'm sorry. I didn't mean it."

The sickly sweet tone of his voice made me want to vomit. Or that might've been the pain. Glass cut into the back of my thighs, but it paled in comparison to the throbbing in my face and ribs. It felt like he'd cracked a rib on the left. He'd been aiming for my stomach, but missed.

You know how much force it took to fracture a rib? I did, and it told me that Tom wasn't pulling his punches tonight.

He leaned down to pick me up, and I flinched away. His fingers tightened on my upper arms as he dragged me to my feet. "Don't do that. Don't flinch away, like I'm a monster." His voice had lost its crooning edge, and I did my best to open my one good eye and look at him.

I gave him a crooked smile, because my cheek

throbbed on the other side. "I know you can't help it. I'll do better."

At this point, I'd tell him anything to get him to calm down. To get him to step back and give me space. He'd snorted something in the bathrooms of the club, and whatever the fuck it was, it had turned him into a monster. Or at least, brought it to the surface. He'd lost what was left of the tenuous hold he had on his temper.

The wild darting of his eyes, with the burn of something crazy in their depths, told me that if I didn't move now, I was never leaving this alleyway.

I needed him to be calm.

I needed him to go back into the club.

I needed to get *away*.

He wrapped an arm around my shoulders, pulling me into a hug, and I tried to remain relaxed, but every instinct I had was screaming to get the fuck away.

"You're perfect, Charlie."

That wasn't what he'd been yelling when he backhanded me so hard, my vision went bright white. He'd called me a slut. A bitch. Slurred insults I couldn't understand as he cried and hit me.

It was the worst he'd ever been in public. He'd shoved me a couple of times at bars. Once, he'd thrown a plate at my head at a restaurant. But at home was when the real monster came out.

In the beginning, I'd written it off. He was stressed at work. I'd gotten in his face as we argued. He didn't mean it. He always stopped short of real harm.

Until he didn't. But by then, I was well and truly trapped. There were too many what-ifs and obstacles to leave. No money. No job. Nowhere to go.

Tonight, staring into his eyes as he swung at me over and over, I knew that girl—the one who'd always made excuses about why we couldn't leave—had been so wrong. There'd be no need for excuses after tonight, because I'd be cold and buried in the ground. Death was the greatest obstacle of all.

I rested my forehead against his shoulder, trying not to dry retch from the pain. "Let's just go back inside, Tom. I need another drink."

His hand dropped to my ass, and vomit slid up my throat as I felt his hard dick pressed against my stomach. He wouldn't. Would he?

"Maybe we should stay out here, and I can say sorry properly. You can show me that you weren't eye-fucking that cunt at the bar."

He meant the bartender. I'd been waiting for him to get back from the bathrooms, and the bartender had given me the vodka soda I'd asked for. That was it. That's what had sent him into a jealous rage.

I shoved gently at his chest. "I'm not feeling like that right now, Tom," I whispered, hating the shake in my voice, the way my spine curled to protect my organs. I needed to run, but where? I had no one anymore. My mom was gone. My dad had gotten picked up for cooking meth in our kitchen, and was currently in jail.

I was no one and nothing. All I had was Tom and

our shitty life. He'd loved me once. No one had ever loved me, and that's why I'd made excuses for him.

When his hand came up to grope at my tits, I thought about just letting him. I had nowhere to go, no money squirreled away. He'd be okay for a month or so after this; maybe I could make a plan in that time.

But then his hands pressed on my shoulders. "Get on your knees for me, Charlie," he grunted, and I wanted to vomit my vodka all over his shoes.

No. No, I couldn't. I'd rather be homeless and alone than assaulted in this dirty alley.

I pushed at his chest again. "I said no, Tom!"

He gripped the back of my head, his eyes narrowing, his face twisted maliciously. "What did you say to me?"

Decision made, I found my spine. "No! Are you stupid? N-fucking-o."

"You fucking teasing bitch." He yanked at my hair savagely, making me cry out. "You're nothing without me. No one wants your white-trash ass. When I say get on your knees, you get on your fucking *knees,*" he screamed.

I'd made a huge mistake. I should have made my stand somewhere with more light. Somewhere where I had a chance. But fuck it. I'd never thought I'd live until I was twenty-three anyway.

"Fuck you, you shriveled-dick fucking loser."

He pulled back his fist and pounded it directly into my face. The pain was… intense. I screamed as I slammed back into the wall of the club, banging into the dumpster with a dull thud. Someone yelled down the alleyway, and Tom turned toward the voice.

This was it.

Run. Now or never, Charlotte.

I scrambled to my feet and sprinted. I'd run track in school; I was fast. So fucking fast. I could have gotten a scholarship to a good university, if I hadn't been stuck at home with my dad. I could have gotten out, gotten a good job, a good life, if only I'd run.

I was going to do that now. I was going to run for my life and I wasn't going to stop.

"CHARLOTTE!" Tom screamed behind me. I could hear his feet pounding after me. I was fast, but so was he. He'd been a running back for his varsity football team, which made him fit. But I was fitter.

Faster. Faster. Faster.

I was so glad I'd argued that I could wear my sneakers with my black booty shorts and leather jacket tonight. I dodged around people in the street, the crowds slowing me down, but also hindering Tom. He was tall and bulky, whereas I could slip beneath arms and through small gaps.

The arena ahead of me was all lit up, filled with concert-goers and security. Whatever event that was on must have just finished, because grinning people clustered in large groups, their excitement palpable as they emptied from the stadium gates. I dodged between them, hoping to get lost in the crowd of black-clad teens.

My cheek aching and my ribs protesting with every

step, I tried not to make eye contact with anyone. I ran around the back of the stadium, not daring to look behind me. I needed to lose him. I needed to get somewhere safe. Somewhere dark and small where the boogeyman couldn't find me.

"CHARLOTTE!"

Tom's voice sounded frantic and angry, but also further away. Or maybe it was because the ringing in my ears had gotten so loud, I could barely hear anything but my own breathing and that high-pitched whine.

I looked at the eight-foot-high barrier fence around one parking lot, filled with trucks and buses, probably for whatever act was playing in the stadium. If I could shake him and get in there, I could hide until he gave up. I continued to run, hoping the security milling around in there just thought I was a jogger out for the night.

When I got to a blindspot around the back of a truck—hiding me from the crowds and hopefully security—I summoned every ounce of strength I had left and scaled the cloth-covered chain-link fence. It shook perilously, making a loud clanking sound as I flung myself up and over, my ribs screaming in pain.

My knees hit the asphalt, and I bit through my lip to swallow down the agonized cry that wanted to burst out. Quickly, I rolled across the pavement and underneath the closest truck. Scooching as close to the middle as I could, I lay under there, breathing through the pain, soaking myself in the darkness.

I held my breath as shiny black combat boots walked past, but they didn't stop near me. The guard's radio crackled on his hip, and he moved over to the fence I'd jumped.

"Move along!" he barked.

"Sorry, man. Just looking for my girlfriend." Tom's voice made me want to whimper, but I sucked it in.

Breathe. Breathe. Breathe.

"No fucking loitering outside the fence, asshole. Move along or I'll call the cops. This is private property, and no one is getting in here. I don't give a fuck where your imaginary girlfriend is."

I heard Tom rattle the fence. "Fuck you."

"Move!" the guy barked again. "Fucking groupies."

"I'm not even a groupie for your piece of shit singer, asshole," Tom screamed, sounding like an outraged child. He continued hurling abuse at the security guard, but I watched as his feet walked away. "Charlotte? Where the fuck are you?" he yelled, getting further and further away.

My body shook violently, the rough gravel probably scraping me up even worse. The security guard's feet moved away too, and the air whooshed from my lungs. I let myself release some of the tension in my body, and with it, came the tears through my busted-up eyes.

The pain rushed forth, and I moaned softly. I was in trouble. Every inhale felt like a dagger to the chest; I knew I'd done some damage. My face was throbbing, and everything ached.

But the day had been hot, and the pavement was

warm—if this was where I died, then so be it. I'd begun life in the dirt, and if that's where it ended, then it was fitting.

Closing my eyes, I let out a rattling breath and ran through my options.

I couldn't go home. Dad was in prison, and the bank had foreclosed on the house. I couldn't go to the hospital, because I had no insurance. I was a stay-at-home girlfriend, because Tom had always said I was his queen, and queens didn't work jobs at dingy nightclubs.

Everything I owned was in that apartment, though that wasn't much. It was all Tom's things: his furniture around the room, his memories on the wall, clothes that he'd bought for me to wear hanging in the closet. Nothing there was really mine. I didn't have anything left of the things I'd come into the relationship with. He'd told me that I was a butterfly, and I didn't need the things from when I was nothing but a grub in the dirt.

Man, so many red flags that I'd ignored. Just like a bull, I'd run toward them like I couldn't get enough.

I needed to get out of town. Tom was an associate lawyer uptown, and his firm was influential, even if he wasn't. He got paid well and had connections all over the place. I couldn't run to my friends, because they'd been Tom's friends first.

Stupid. Stupid. Stupid.

Tears leaked from my eyes, and I was so busy with

my pity party of one that I missed the boots stopping beside the bus. Missed the hand gripping my ankle and dragging me out.

I screamed as I looked up into the angry face of a security guard. "Please," I pleaded the best I could, now that my jaw had swollen considerably. It came out a slurred mess, but I was pretty sure my banged-up face got the point across.

I watched as the security guy's face morphed from anger to shock to rage, before settling finally on pity. "My guess is you're Charlotte. Your boyfriend is looking for you."

I rolled, grunting through the pain, trying to get on my feet. "No, please. Don't make me go back. I can't—" I choked out as black spots danced at the edges of my vision.

The guy caught me as my knees gave out. "Hey, hey, no one's making you go anywhere. It's okay."

My heart felt like it was going to beat out of my chest, and I was sucking in oxygen that had nowhere to go. It was like I couldn't get my lungs to function, and I began to claw at my throat.

"Ah fuck!" the guy cursed, scooping me up in his arms and sprinting toward an RV. He banged on the door, and a short, middle-aged woman answered.

"Shep, what's—" Her eyes took me in. "Holy shit. Bring her in. We need to call an ambulance."

I shook my head, sucking in air. "No. No." It was all I could say, but I tugged at the security guy's hands, trying to wiggle out, even though every movement was excruciating. He laid me gently down on a fold-up bed, the kind massage therapists used.

The woman came over and held my hands. "Be calm. No one's going to make you do anything you don't want to do. My name is Tricia; I'm a paramedic. I'm just going to check you out. No one will call an ambulance." Her tone was calm and reassuring. Her face was no-nonsense, and if she thought I looked like shit, she didn't show it. "First, I just need you to breathe." She grabbed an oxygen mask and placed it over my face. "Deep breath in. Deep breath out. That's it, nice and slow." She looked over at the big guy. "What the fuck happened?"

"Her name's Charlotte. Found her like that under one of the trucks. Looks like she's had the shit kicked out of her."

Tricia shook her head. "That much is obvious, Shep. Charlotte, can you tell me if you have any injuries besides those on your face?"

"Side," I coughed out, and she pulled up my crop top as I hissed out a pained breath.

The security guy, Shep, growled angrily at the sight of my injuries. "Holy shit."

"You're going to need x-rays, in case you've broken a rib," Tricia told me softly.

I shook my head. "No. No hospitals. No ambulances. I can't afford it."

"Fuck, kid. I'll pay, but you need some help."

I shook my head, trying to sit up. "No hospitals," I insisted. He'd find me if I went to a hospital. He had connections all over the place. I couldn't let him find me. I had to get out of town. Had to get out of the damn state.

Shep looked at Tricia, whose face had lost its professional edge, morphing into something more soft and compassionate. "Okay, let me just listen to your chest." She put a stethoscope to my chest and side, concentrating. "Can you take a deep breath for me?"

I sucked in as much air as I could, the pain making me cough, but then I did it again. The panic had started to subside now that I realized they really wouldn't give me back to Tom. All that was left was pain.

Tricia examined my ribs with her fingertips, frowning the whole time at the black and blue bruises on my torso, and I hissed as she prodded the tender spots. She listened carefully to the other side, then checked my pupils, her face a purposeful mask.

"I think the rib is just bruised, or maybe cracked at worst. I can't be more definitive without an x-ray. Your breathing sounds good, and I don't think you have a concussion, which is a minor miracle. I can tape your ribs to help with the discomfort, and you can ice it regularly to prevent swelling, along with your face." Using a key from around her neck, she opened up a small lockbox, pulling out a little glass bottle. "I'm going to give you something for the pain."

I eyed this perfect stranger, who said she was a paramedic but might just be some kind of organ harvester. Honestly, though, as long as the pain went away, they could have my organs.

She pushed something into the vein in my arm, and the world went hazy. As the pain drifted away, so did I.

TWO

CHARLOTTE

HUSHED WHISPERS DRAGGED me from the darkness.

"This is a problem for the cops. We have to roll out of here tonight. Just drop her off at the cop station and let's go."

There was an angry huff. "You didn't see how terrified she was. Didn't want us to take her to a hospital or call an ambulance. She looked *terrified,* Whitt."

"I understand that, Tricia, but this isn't our circus and she's not one of our monkeys. We've got a whole fucking menagerie without adding some battered girl. The police will protect her."

Fuck no, they won't. Tom's best friend, Armond, was LAPD and Tom had used him more than once to get an inside scoop on cases. If I went to the cops, he'd know. I may as well just give him my address and let him murder me.

Because I knew as well as I knew my name, that if

Tom got hold of me now, I'd either turn up floating in the ocean or go down as fish food. He'd always joked that a lawyer was only as good as his reputation, and if I went to the cops and pressed charges? It'd sink his career. He'd never let that happen. I knew it in my gut.

I whimpered as I sat up, the bed I was lying on creaking loudly. Everything *hurt.* I thought I'd known pain, but the way my face throbbed in time with my thundering heart introduced me to a new level of suffering.

Finding my jacket, I breathed a relieved sigh to see my phone and wallet still in my pocket. Not that I had any money. I might have to ditch my phone, in case Tom decided to get a little creative.

Hopefully, if I disappeared for a while, he'd know I wasn't going to sink his stupid career and just forget about me. But I needed money and to get out of town. If I took money from our account, he could have me charged with theft, meaning the cops would have a reason to pick me up.

I looked in my purse. I had a twenty-dollar bill and a bunch of ones. *Not enough.*

The door to the RV opened, and the paramedic from earlier appeared. "You're awake," she said softly, eyeing me as I held my jacket in a death grip while I looked for my shoes. "Before you go, let me check you out one more time?" She didn't push. Didn't argue that I should lie back down.

Nodding, I climbed back onto the bed.

She grabbed her stethoscope and penlight. "Your

pupils look even and reactive, so I don't think you have a concussion." She placed the stethoscope on my back. "Deep breath?" I took some big, even breaths in and out. It still hurt like a bitch. "Your chest sounds okay too. I've taped your side—hopefully giving your ribs some support will ease the pain." She stepped back. "Do you have somewhere to go?"

I considered lying to her, but what would I gain? Tears filled my eyes as I shook my head. "No."

"Family? Friends?"

Tom had made sure I had no friends. "No."

"Did your boyfriend do this?" I nodded. "Are you going back to an unsafe environment?"

I let out a shaky laugh. Had I ever known a safe environment? "I'm never going back there. He'll kill me."

Tricia looked relieved. "Good. Good. Shep can take you to the police station nearby so you can press charges."

I was already shaking my head before she'd finished. "No, I can't. Thank you for your help. I appreciate it." I climbed to my feet, hissing in pain as the cuts from the glass on the backs of my thighs stuck to the vinyl bed. I hesitated by the door. "Could someone give me a ride to the train station?"

I'd hop on the train somewhere. Even if they kicked me off at the next station, at least I wouldn't be here.

Tricia chewed her lip. "Are you going somewhere in particular?"

"Away. Anywhere but here." I hated how much my voice shook.

I couldn't look her in the eyes, hating the pity I saw reflected there. "Just wait here. I'll see if Shep can drive you," she said softly, her hand brushing my arm.

She stepped outside, and I could hear her whisper-shouting, probably at Whitt with the monkeys, whoever he was. "Just until the next town. She needs to recover a little. I made an oath."

"Tricia—"

"Just go in there and meet her, Whitt. Look at her fucked-up face, the beaten-down look in her eye, and tell me why we can't just take her to Vegas. Go on."

The door opened, and I flinched. An older guy, maybe in his early fifties, stomped into the RV. His hair was salt and pepper, and his jaw had a soft, gray beard. He would have been handsome in his heyday, and hell, he was a silver fox now. My daddy issues didn't run that deep, though.

The door rebounded shut behind him, and I jumped. The expression on his face softened immediately. "Ah, fuck. I hate it when she's right. I won't hear the end of this now." Sucking in a deep breath, he frowned, his jaw clenched. "You look messed up, kid. You need help?" Despite his frown, his voice was gentle. And something about that gentleness broke me completely. A choked sob burst from my lips, even as I shook my head.

Swallowing the emotion back down, I swiped at my eyes. "N-no. I'm okay. I'll be okay."

The guy looked at my tears like they were simultaneously made of acid and spread the bubonic plague. He leaned back out the door. "You were right, Tricia. Get your sexy ass in here, because she's doing *feelings* and I don't know what the fuck to do." He sounded panicked, and Tricia came in, glaring at him smugly, before her face transformed into a look of understanding. She wrapped me in her arms, though she was a good couple of inches shorter than me. I buried my face in her shoulder, and she patted my back.

"You're safe here, sweet girl. We'll take you to Vegas with us, then you can decide what you want to do, okay?"

I nodded, words trapped behind the lump in my throat. She stroked my back gently, and when I pulled away, she let me go.

The guy stood behind her, his face twisted with concern. "She stays in the med van and away from the damn band, okay? And the second we hit Vegas, we set her free," he warned Tricia, like I was a stray cat and not a person right in front of him.

She looked over her shoulder, love shining on her face. "Okay, Whitt."

He leaned forward and kissed her cheek, before spinning and stomping out of the van, shutting the door gently.

Tricia shook her head. "He's such a softie. Gotta be tough in this business, but the man is a marshmallow on the inside. A sucker for the underdog." She was gently nudging me toward a proper bed at the rear of the RV. "There's a bunk back here, and I want you to rest. I'll grab you an ice pack in a minute, and I want you to ice your face for as long as you can, and then your ribs for 20 minutes. You need rest, and try breathing as deeply as you can. I'll grab you something to change into, if you'd like?"

I chewed my lip as I whispered my thanks. I was safe for tonight, and if Whitt was to be believed, for the whole way to Las Vegas. I wondered what kind of music Whitt sang; I didn't recognize his face, but the arena had been packed so he had to be famous.

I turned off my e-sim so Tom couldn't track me when he came down off whatever the hell he'd taken in the restroom of that club. Then I powered the whole phone down. I needed to get a charger from Walmart or something. And hit up a thrift store to get some clothes, so I could get a job.

Tricia returned, and with her was Shep. The security guard looked me over with worried eyes, but didn't speak. Tricia handed me a hoodie, as well as a t-shirt. On the front was a bright pink skull with the words *The Daymakers* spewing from its mouth.

I didn't recognize the name of the band, though it tickled the back of my brain. Maybe I'd seen it on social media. I was a K-pop girl, though, or sometimes old country music from the eighties and nineties.

I gave Tricia a half smile, my jaw still too puffy and painful for anything more. "Thank you again."

She passed over a pair of yoga pants too. "These are mine, and they might be a little big, but they're better than nothing. You can keep them."

She was going to make me cry again, and I was all cried out. I just wanted to sleep away this nightmare.

"We'll all bump out soon and get on the road to Vegas. You're welcome to sleep through it. Shep will ride in this RV. He'll be just up there. Brian drives, but you probably won't see much of him. Shep can call me if you need anything. If you suddenly get a headache, problems breathing, nausea, anything like that, do not hesitate to call me, okay? I'll be in the car right behind you."

I nodded, my eyes darting to Shep.

Tricia frowned. "Shep's harmless. If he makes one wrong move toward you, I'll castrate him myself. He knows I'm good with a scalpel." She gave him the stink eye, but he looked amused at her threats. "You have my word; you're safe now. Get some rest."

She moved the curtain in front of the sleeping area at the back of the RV, and I heard her talking softly to Shep. When the door closed softly, I pulled off my blood-soaked crop top and slipped on the t-shirt. It was a soft vintage wash and was cute as hell. It also hit me below my ass. I kept my shorts on and climbed beneath the covers of the bunk bed.

A dry spot in my throat made me cough, then the pain in my ribs made me cough more, which then hurt my face. It was a painful cycle.

A knock on the wall had me peeking around the curtain. A bottle of water appeared in front of my face. Shep looked down at me, his face an impenetrable mask. I didn't know what he thought about me being here, and I didn't think he was going to give me any clues.

I took the offered bottle of water. "Thank you." I unscrewed it, though the idea of putting a bottle to my busted lip made me cringe on the inside. A straw appeared between his fingers, and I swallowed down the tears.

Shep's eyes ran across my battered face, before he looked into my eyes. I saw anger there, but I knew in my gut it wasn't at me. It was at Tom. "If I'd known, that fucker wouldn't have walked away from that fence on two legs," he said through gritted teeth. "Get some sleep. It's a long drive."

He turned and walked back to the front of the RV, stretching out on a couch, playing on his phone. I shut the curtain and climbed beneath the covers, and I was asleep before the RV even left the parking lot.

THREE

CHARLOTTE

I WOKE UP WITH A START, rocketing up in an unfamiliar bed. I'd been dreaming about the alleyway, and Tom's face kept morphing into a Chucky doll. Like the moment hadn't already been traumatic enough, my subconscious wanted to kick me while I was down. Panic sent bile surging up my throat.

Light poured through a tiny window beside the bed, no more than a hand-width wide, and I shoved at the sheets trapping my legs. I whimpered in pain as my conscious brain caught up with my flight response.

I was in a med van. I was not in LA anymore. I was in Vegas, maybe?

Someone knocked on the frame of the bed I was lying in. "You okay?" The gruff voice of Shep made my heart pound again, and I swallowed down the panic. He'd saved me. He was safe.

Hell, what the fuck did I know about who was safe or not? Tom had been perfectly fine for the first few months. Caring. Attentive. Love bombing the fuck out of me.

I had been hilariously naive. So desperate to be loved that I'd ignored every sign.

I cleared my throat. "I'm fine. Sorry, I just woke up confused."

There was silence, and for a moment, I wondered if he'd left.

"I'm heading for breakfast at a diner down the road. If you want to come. My treat." Then his footsteps moved away. I hesitated, but only for a second. I had twenty-seven dollars. I couldn't afford to turn down free meals.

Dragging on Tricia's yoga pants, I pulled the hoodie over my head, then slipped the curtain aside to find the RV was empty. I stepped over to the tiny bathroom, finally getting a good look at my face.

I looked like *hell.* The whole left side of my face was a swollen mess of angry black bruises. My lip was fat, and my eye was swollen shut. I had no makeup to make it less noticeable.

After peeing, I rinsed out my mouth and splashed my face, hissing at the sting of the water against my cuts. I finger-combed my hair as best I could, then pulled the hood up until it shrouded my face in darkness. I shouldn't go out in public like this, but how could I not? I needed to get myself sorted out, and it would be easier to do that with food in my belly before they booted me to the curb.

Going back to the bed, I pushed my feet into my

sneakers, their glittery black outer material standing in stark contrast to the rest of my outfit. I crept through the RV to the door, steeling my spine as I pushed it open. The lot where we were parked was another secure venue, fenced off from the rest of the area. Dozens of people bustled around, directing in big trucks, buses, and cars with campers attached to the back.

I looked to the left, and Shep was there. In the light, I realized he was a lot younger than he'd appeared last night. He had a thick, short beard, but no lines around his eyes. And he was big. Huge. No wonder Tom had run away.

I was a solid five-six, but Shep towered over me. He couldn't hold back the wince as he took in my face. "You look like shit in the daylight."

I frowned at him. "Thanks?"

He shook his head. "I should have killed the fucker."

Now it was my turn to look at him like he was a crazy person. "You don't even know him. Or me."

He pushed off the wall. "I don't need to know anything about either of you to know that any man who does that to a woman doesn't deserve to breathe precious oxygen." His tone was devoid of any warmth. "Let's go. Tricia and Whitt are waiting." He handed me a pair of sunglasses from his pocket. "Take these; it'll hurt less if you don't have to squint in the desert sun."

I took them gently. I didn't get this guy, but the sun was making my head throb and my face ache. Plus, I could use something else to hide behind. I slid them on, and the relief was instantaneous. Well, a little relief anyway. I pulled my hood further over my head, hiding the best I could from the rest of the people wandering around.

I followed along behind Shep, or more specifically, his boots, since I kept my head down. I could see a huge tour bus, bigger than the others, black and sleek. I wondered if that was where Whitt and Tricia stayed?

Finally, we came to an SUV. "Charlotte?" I looked up at Tricia, whose smile was soft and comforting. "How are you feeling today?"

"Fine. Thank you," I murmured, because manners had been literally beaten into me.

She raised an eyebrow. "Well, that sounds like bull-shit. How are you really?"

My lip twitched. "Sore, but okay."

Tricia stepped closer, taking off my shades to look at my eyes and the bruises around my face. "Any trouble breathing? Headaches or nausea?"

I shook my head, gently so that headache didn't become a self-fulfilling prophecy. "Only when I was staring at the sun. Shep gave me his sunglasses."

She nodded, sliding the glasses back up my nose. "That's good. Come on, I'm looking forward to Nutella crêpes. Honestly, they are to die for." Ushering me into the back of the SUV, she climbed in after me. Shep hopped in the driver's seat, with Whitt in the passenger seat.

The streets of Vegas were already busy, even though

it couldn't have been more than nine in the morning. Whitt was looking at his phone, his fingers moving furiously as he typed out an email.

Tricia smiled gently at me. "He works too hard. I don't think he's had a day off in his entire life, but do you think he'll listen to me?" she murmured softly. "Lucky I love him." Whitt huffed a laugh, which told me he was listening to our conversation.

"You and Whitt are together?" I asked politely. Whitt had to be at least fifteen years older than Tricia.

The look she gave the back of his head left little doubt that she adored him. "Coming up fifteen years now."

Shit, that was a serious chunk of time. I reappraised Tricia's age. I'd thought she was late thirties, but looking at her now, I wondered if she wasn't slightly older. If she was, I wanted to know the demon she'd sold her soul to for youth, because she didn't look it.

I couldn't imagine being with anyone that long. I didn't think I'd had anyone in my life who was so permanent. Not my parents. No siblings. Not a partner, or a friend. No one.

Fuck, I was worse than depressing.

I gave her a tight smile. "That's really sweet."

Shep pulled the car into the parking lot of a diner, but even from here, I could see it was packed. Everyone was going to see my face and judge me. I didn't care, though; I'd spent my whole life dodging judgmental looks. Still, I made sure my glasses were firmly on my face, and hid a little behind Shep's broad shoulders as we made our way inside.

The hostess chirped, "Table for four?"

When Whitt grunted his agreement, she moved us further into the diner. I kept my head down as she pointed to a booth by the window. Shep stepped to the side, indicating I should slide in first. I looked up at him and his impassive face, waiting for the worry about being trapped between this huge guy and the wall.

But it didn't come. My screwed-up brain seemed to think this guy, who was built for violence, was safe. I was broken, but going with my gut had saved me from some shitty situations, so why the hell not? If he wanted to drown me in a plate of maple syrup, surrounded by families, then I hoped they'd put it on my headstone.

He slid in after me, handing me a menu. "Get whatever you want," he grumbled, before leaning toward Whitt to talk about the security of the venue. There were waffles with crushed Fruit Loops and icecream on top, pancakes with lemon ricotta, and a breakfast burrito that looked amazing.

When was the last time I'd eaten something that wasn't a salad? Tom had insisted I be able to fit into designer clothes, which meant the gym six days a week and salads with protein for the sake of protein.

Fucking Tom.

When the waitress came over, she took everyone's order. "And you, love?" she asked softly. When I looked up at her, she gasped, before swallowing it back down.

"Just the fruity waffles please. And a coffee." The

waitress nodded, eyeing the rest of the table suspiciously. She was short, but she looked scrappy.

Whitt shook his head as she left. "Think she wanted to fight you, Shep."

Shep snorted. "Good. Gives me a little faith in humanity."

And that was the only mention of my face or how I'd ended up like this. The guys talked business, and they kept talking about the band. The band needed this. The band was doing that.

I tilted my head. "Aren't you the singer?" I asked Whitt softly. I could see him as some kind of aging rock-star, with his neatly trimmed beard and his silver fox good looks.

Tricia threw back her head and laughed. She had a contagious kind of laugh, somewhere between a heh-heh-heh and a hiss. Whitt gave her a sour look, but his lips were twitching too. "No, Charlotte. I'm not the main act. I'm the tour manager."

"Oh." Actually, that made sense. I couldn't imagine a singer who could sell out an arena having breakfast in some cute little diner.

Whitt's phone rang, and he excused himself. Tricia was still wiping tears of laughter from her eyes. "The man loves the industry, but when he sings, it's like an elk in mating season. Not even the punk rock kids can like that."

The waitress poured our coffee, still darting looks at my face, and I dropped my chin to hide the worst of the swelling from her gaze. She wandered off again, and Tricia turned back to me.

"What are you going to do now you're here?"

I had no idea. I had no money. Nowhere to stay. I chewed my lip, staring down into my coffee. "Find a shelter until I can get on my feet. Probably see if I can get a job as a waitress or something."

"Do you know anyone here?" she asked softly.

I shook my head. I didn't know anyone here, but that also meant no one knew me, or Tom. A fresh start. I wasn't scared of hard work.

"Got any money?" Shep asked, and I nodded. I had twenty-seven dollars. I didn't need his pity. I could adapt.

At least being fit, I could probably get a job at a strip joint, especially here in Vegas. I could dance well enough, and my body was good. I just had to wait for my face to heal up a bit more, then I'd be okay.

Shep's eyes saw too much, so I looked back down at my coffee. The waitress reappeared with our food, and when she put my waffles in front of me, my mouth instantly watered. It was a ridiculous looking meal—childish, even—with the colorful pebbles of breakfast cereal on top. I didn't care; it meant freedom to me.

I cut off a piece with my fork and put it into my mouth, making a noise that was embarrassing. Then another, and another, until half the waffle was gone in minutes.

Whitt reappeared, an annoyed expression on his face as he picked up his coffee and drank half down in a single chug. "Those fucking kids are going to be the death of me. Royal fucked some groupie backstage, and she took his fucking mask half off, enough that she made some pretty accurate guesses about his identity, so now the label's had to hustle to get her to sign a damn NDA. Including forking out an insane amount of cash to keep her quiet. If they could all keep it in their damn pants, it would make my job easier."

"They wear masks?" I asked, and Whitt nodded.

"They're a masked band. Completely anonymous. Stupidest fucking gimmick on the planet. Makes my life difficult."

Shep sighed. "My bad, Whitt. Normally, I'd keep an eye on them. They all need to get girlfriends or something. Make life easier."

Whitt stabbed at his home fries. "Fuck no. Four damn NDAs? Gotta keep it competitive too, because Knight's last girl almost got paid eight hundred grand to sell him out before the label squashed it."

Tricia shook her head, but it was almost fond. "They need to pool their resources and get one girlfriend. Then you'd only have to make sure one person didn't sell them out," she laughed. "God knows, those boys share everything else."

Shep huffed, but Whitt shot it down immediately. "Nah, can you imagine the fights if she loved one more than the other?" Shaking his head, he picked up his burrito, which was bulging with fillings. It made my mouth water, and I wondered if I could fit one of those in too. Shep had said to get whatever I wanted.

"You need someone you can watch, who they feel about as much for as a groupie," Shep added as he chewed.

Tricia frowned at him. "You want to get them prostitutes? That's a *terrible* fucking idea. My job is to keep them healthy, and hiring hookers in each city is a one-way ticket to an impressive STI collection."

Whitt chuckled. "A concubine, maybe? Then they could travel with the tour."

She slapped his arm. "Don't be fucking ridiculous, Whitt. This is the twenty-first century."

They moved on, but my brain churned over their problem. Their band wanted to be anonymous, which had to be difficult in this day and age. Now, when you could find the answer to every question on the internet, anonymity definitely added to the mystique. I mean, a lot of bands had done it over the years, but that was mostly back when you had to develop a roll of film and sell the story to a reporter in a dingy back alley.

There was that band that my dad had listened to while he cooked. Slipknot? Plus, I'd loved Gorillaz, and they were cartoons.

I ate my waffles more slowly, letting the idea bounce around in my brain. What better way to get lost than with a band who was always on the move, right?

Could I fuck strangers? Instantly, I knew the answer was yes. My body hadn't been mine for a while, and what was the difference between dancing on a stage mostly naked for dozens of men, or pleasing a couple of guys? I was in control of my sexuality, and for once, I wanted it to work for me rather than against me.

When it came down to it, I would do anything to be as far away from Tom as possible.

"I could do it," I said, cutting into the conversation.

They all turned to me, and Tricia took a sip of her coffee. "Do what, Charlotte?"

Clearing my throat, I lifted my chin, looking directly at Whitt. "I could be their concubine."

"Like fucking hell you can," Shep growled out, making me flinch. He softened his face and his tone immediately. "Sorry. I'm just saying, I can't raise my voice without you curling in on yourself like a kicked dog. It would be unethical to even contemplate it," he said, more to Whitt than me.

Tricia frowned. "I agree with Shep. You aren't in the right emotional state to agree to anything like that."

"Why, because I got banged up by my boyfriend?" I shook my head. "I hate to tell you this, but that's just par for the course of my life. I get kicked around and hope that I can drag myself out of the gutter. And if somehow I manage it, there's always someone there to cut the life rope I was clinging to, like my dad, or CPS, or my ex. I've never had enough to make something of myself. I assume a job like this would come with good pay?"

Whitt didn't confirm or deny, but I knew it would. If they were paying off ex-girlfriends with hundreds of thousands of dollars, then even a fraction of that would be enough to set me up for a while.

"I can have a foundation of my own making. I wouldn't be reliant on handouts for once in my life. No one could take it from me. I could get as far from LA as possible. And all it would take is giving my body, which is *mine to give*"—I directed that at Shep—"to some guys regularly. The other option for me here is stripping, or waiting tables for tips so I can just scrape by. Or prostitution, and not the ethical kind."

The silence around the table was so heavy, I could feel it like a blanket. Tricia looked concerned, and Shep looked like he'd sucked on something sour. But Whitt? He looked like he was thinking it over.

I leaned toward him. "You wouldn't have to worry about me getting attached. The only thing men have given me in life is pain. I'm done with your entire gender, to be honest. But this? It would change my life."

He was softening, and Tricia glared at him. "Whitt…"

Whitt pulled some fifties from his wallet and dropped them on the table. "Bring her back to the tour buses and let her rest before we boot her back to the streets." He looked at me, his brown eyes shrewd. I held his gaze with confidence. "I'll think about it. That's the best you're getting."

"Yes, sir."

We all stood and trailed after Whitt. I avoided looking at Shep, and when he strode out of the diner, my waitress watched him warily. She stopped me, with a hand on my arm.

"Are you okay? I've been there, and if you need help…" She waved a hand at my face.

I wanted to hug this stranger. "Thank you. But this wasn't him. He chased off the guy who did this. I got out, and I promise you, I'm never going back."

FOUR

CHARLOTTE

SHEP WAS STILL DISGRUNTLED as he walked me back to the med RV, Tricia beside him. "She can stay with me for now, Shep. Go do your job." With one final loaded expression, he turned and disappeared into the crowd of people working. She sighed as we both watched him go. "Come on then. I have to do inventory on our supplies and check in with a couple of people. Is there anything you need to do? Someone you need to call?"

I shook my head, but hesitated. "I probably need to get some more clothes at some point."

"We can probably find you a Walmart or something around here." Pulling out her phone, she did a quick search. "There's one just around the corner. Just ask to see Shep when you get back, and he'll get you through the security checkpoint. We keep it tight. You can't imagine the type of people who try to sneak in."

"Beat-up street rats?" I say lightly, waving a hand at my face.

She gave me a disapproving look. "You're a survivor, Charlotte. There is no shame in that."

I swallowed past the lump in my throat. "Uh, yeah. Okay, I'll be back soon." I got out of there before this turned into one of those teachable moments that inevitably just made me cry.

Weaving my way through the crowds, I kept my head down, hoping no one paid any attention to me. And they didn't. Whatever they were loading into the arena behind me had everyone's attention, and it looked like there were hundreds of people milling about.

I strolled straight out the security gates, no one even glancing my way. I guess they wanted to stop people getting in, not getting out.

I walked through the surprisingly quiet streets of Vegas to Walmart. There weren't a lot of people walking the sidewalks with me, which I appreciated. I could just let myself relax, even just for a moment.

When I reached the store, I smiled at the door greeter, who just gave me a sour look. Man, maybe they needed a new greeter. I should apply, because even a hobo would probably be more pleasant than that guy.

Rushing around the store, I grabbed some underwear, socks, deodorant, a toothbrush and a cheap hairbrush. That would have to do. I was making my money stretch, and that meant the barest of necessities to make sure I didn't stink too bad if I ended up on the streets.

I wasn't sure who was more relieved that I didn't want to make conversation, me or the cashier. "Nine dollars," she told me in a bored tone as she stuffed everything into a small paper sack. I handed her the money, not bothering with any kind of polite platitude. She didn't want it, and I didn't have it in me to give it to her.

I had eighteen dollars left. As she gave me my receipt, I chanced asking, "Is there a thrift shop somewhere around here?"

The cashier shrugged, but the woman behind me touched my arm. She looked frazzled and had a toddler strapped to her front, like a human shield. "Sure there is, sweetheart. Go straight out the doors, then three streets over, take a left. It's about halfway down the block."

I gave her a thankful smile and hustled out of there. Fortunately, her directions also led me back in the direction of the arena.

The hooded sweatshirt I was wearing was a couple of sizes too big, making it shapeless and baggy, perfect to hide from view in, but it also made me sweat like a whore in church. Even as a shapeless blob, a construction worker still catcalled me, making my heart pound and walk faster.

I gritted my teeth, telling myself off for being such a weakling. I couldn't jump at every shadow. Tom was at home; he didn't know where I was. I was tougher than this.

The woman's directions were perfect, because up

ahead of me was a Goodwill. It was quiet this early in the morning, and I spent an hour sorting through the racks. I needed something presentable, because I needed to get a job. But I also needed something cheap, so that I could get a few different options. If I spent ten dollars on clothes, I might still have enough for a couple of days worth of food if I just bought a loaf of bread and grape jelly.

I did sums in my head as I pulled out a pair of dark-wash jeans that were fifty percent off. When I tried them on, they fit perfectly. I also grabbed a couple of cheap black tees, plus one button-up white blouse. There was a rucksack in the clearance bin, and I grabbed that too. I'd need to carry my stuff around with me for a while, and I couldn't do that in a Walmart bag.

I took my tiny haul up to the register. The lady behind the counter gave me a happy smile, her eyes only briefly dipping to my fucked-up face. "Well, look at that. You've got a couple of bargains today." She scanned all my purchases, and when I counted out my ones, she frowned. "Silly me, I forgot to put in a discount code." She scanned her name badge, and it got another fifty percent off my total purchase. I had a feeling she'd just given me her employee discount, and I wanted to cry.

I gave her my change, and she patted my hand, loading all my purchases into the rucksack. "Thank you," I croaked out.

She waved a hand. "Oh, it's fine. You have a good day, okay? The sun is shining. You woke up this morning. Tomorrow is unknown. Only the right now matters."

I swallowed hard. "Yes, ma'am." Giving her another thankful smile, I hustled out of there before I broke down completely.

I took my time walking back to the venue, almost playing tourist when I made it back to the Strip. The flat, open expanse gave way to sprawling hotels and casinos, crowds and fancy cars. A glittering jewel of a city, surrounded by arid desert.

When I made it back to the checkpoint, security took one look at me, in my The Daymakers hoodie and looking ratty as fuck, and stopped me. "This is a restricted area, I'm sorry."

I gave him a tight smile. "That's okay. Can you get Shep for me?"

The guy frowned. "Who's Shep?"

Well, that was a good question. I should have asked what the hell Shep's job title was. "Uh, he's security for The Daymakers?" That was just a guess, but it seemed likely, right? I'd assumed he was security last night, but he was awfully friendly with the tour manager.

"Never heard of him. Do you have a pass?"

I winced. "No."

The guy's eyebrows went up. "Do you have his number?"

Fuck.

I shook my head, and the guy looked incredulous. "Sorry, lady. No one's getting in here without a pass."

I couldn't blame him; I wouldn't have let me in either.

He stood there at the gate, his arms crossed over his chest. Sucking in a breath, I nodded and walked back down the street, toward the back of the vans, hoping I could see Shep through the fence. There were so many people coming and going, I doubted I could get his attention even if I did see him. My ribs hurt, and I definitely didn't want to try jumping the fence again.

Walking back to the gate, I eyed the security guy again. "I'm just going to wait here until he comes to find me. Then I'll introduce you to your boss."

Sitting down in the gutter, I watched the traffic drive past. I tilted my face to the sun, letting the warmth heal me. But the Nevada sun was a harsh bitch, and soon enough, I was finding any scrap of shade I could so I didn't get sunburned.

Hours passed, and I was starting to drift off when an disgruntled voice shook me from my dozing state. "Have you seen a girl? Pretty, but with a banged-up face?"

Aw, he thinks I'm pretty, an oddly sarcastic part of me thought. I tried to climb to my feet, but every part of my body that had been sore before was twice as sore now from sitting on the pavement. My lips were dry, the scabs on the back of my legs cracked and split.

"Shep?" I called, and he stepped out into the street. When he saw me, his face folded into a frown of anger.

"Charlotte? What the hell? You're as red as a lobster. Why didn't you get someone to radio for me?"

I looked pointedly at the security guard, who was purposefully looking everywhere but at us. "I didn't have credentials. Or your last name. They were just doing their job."

Shep grumbled, wrapping a hand around my elbow and walking me steadily into the lot. He strode over to the big tour bus, the fancy one, and unlocked it. "The band's staying at a hotel, because we're in Vegas for a couple of days. Have a shower and cool off before you die of heat exhaustion."

He nudged me in the direction of the bathroom. I didn't protest. I was hot and sticky, and my breath probably smelled like ass. I looked around the bus, which was bigger than most apartments. There was a door to the right that probably led to the driver's cabin, and along both sides of the space were plush leather couches. A small dining nook sat across from a galley kitchen. Bunks lined the walls either side of a skinny walkway, stacked three high, and I could see charging cables and headphones strewn across the neatly made beds.

"Keep going. That's the main bedroom. The door at the back is the bathroom." I moved past the closed door and down into a lavishly large bathroom. "Towels are in that cupboard above the mirror. Take your time."

I nodded at Shep, then closed the door gently. I shed my clothes, hissing past the sting of open cuts. Turning the water on, I hopped in before it warmed up, yelping as the cold water hit my overheated skin. I let it run through my dirty hair, then used some of the fancy shampoo sitting in the alcove of the cubicle. Just a little bit. I hoped no one noticed.

Some of the soapy suds dripped into the cut over my eyebrow, and I hissed. Fuck, that hurt. *Fucking Tom.*

I made quick work of scrubbing down my body, happy to wash away the crusted blood that Tricia had missed. There was something rejuvenating about being clean. I didn't feel quite so much like a victim.

I stepped out, pulling open the cabinet above my head and grabbing a towel so fluffy, it was basically a blanket. I spent an inordinate amount of time rubbing my face on it, before grabbing some of the clean underwear from my bag. I would've preferred to wash it first, but I really wanted to be clean, and the idea of putting dirty underwear back on made me gag. I threw on my band tee again, along with the leggings.

Fresh socks and my shoes back on, I went to work on my face. But other than cleaning my teeth and dragging a brush through my messed-up hair, there wasn't a lot to work with. I looked at the bruises on my face.

This battered person in the mirror was me.

I'm not ashamed. I didn't cause this. I didn't bring it on myself. I deserve better than this. I'm worth more than this.

I repeated the mantra over and over. I mightn't believe it yet, but one day, I would.

Pushing open the door, I stepped back into the small hallway, moving quickly through the bunk area. It felt like invading the band's personal space if I lingered too long.

Shep sat back on the leather bench seats, his legs

straight out in front of him, ankles crossed. He had strong thighs, and his legs just seemed to go on and on. He looked up from his phone as I appeared, then pulled out a small tub of cream from the pocket of his cargo pants.

"Cream to help with the bruising. Also hemorrhoids, if that becomes a problem," he said with such a straight face that if his eyes hadn't been sparkling, I wouldn't have realized he was teasing.

I took the cream. "I appreciate it. Thank you."

He tilted his head at me, like he was trying to figure me out. "Do you really want to be some kind of sex doll for a bunch of strangers?"

I lifted my chin defiantly. He didn't get to judge me.

Finally, he shook his head, and stepped toward the door. "Come on. I'll get you back to Tricia." I followed along behind him, wishing I lived in a world where I could be respected by men like Shep and still survive.

I wasn't there yet. But I would be, eventually.

FIVE

ROYAL

KNIGHT STRUMMED his guitar where he sat on a couch by the window, his legs flung over the armrest. I played on my phone, answering some of the hundreds of mentions that flooded my socials every day.

A pretty blonde in my DMs was offering to suck my cock, and not going to lie, I was tempted. Hero was wrapped around Poet on the large queen bed, spooning him, but they were both asleep. Poet had his leg off, and even from here, I could see his stump was red. He needed to get his prosthetic adjusted, and I made a note in my phone to get Whitt to arrange time in the schedule to fit in an appointment with the specialist.

Knight was humming a melody, and it was catchy. Slow and lazy, perfect for a ballad. "I like it," I told him, but he wasn't really listening. He was in the zone.

Well, he was, until there was a knock at the door. Shep would normally be here to answer it, but instead,

Steve uncurled his huge body from the couch to get it. It groaned, and honestly, the guy was like six-nine and 370 pounds. I was surprised it could handle him at all.

I scratched beneath the skull gators we wore anytime we were around people who weren't in the inner circle. There were only a handful of people who were in that club.

As if I'd summoned him, Shep stepped inside. Knight lifted his chin in greeting, but we all kept our voices low so we didn't wake Poet or Hero. They needed the rest. Hero had gone hard on stage last night, and it had been a long set.

"And where have you been?" I sing-songed, like a disappointed mother.

He shrugged, shaking Steve's hand and sending him off on break. "We had an incident last night, and I was just cleaning up the mess."

I didn't ask what it was. Shep and Whitt dealt with the problems. I just caused them.

As if I'd thought his name too many times, like Beetlejuice, Whitt walked into the room just as Steve left. His phone was glued to his ear, but that wasn't unusual. "Are you sure? No, of course I'll get all the paperwork signed. You make it airtight, and if it goes through, I'll get it done. Yes. No, I'm pitching it now. What does it matter to you? You get paid either way," he snapped. "Yes, management approved it. They're getting sick of the payouts. Bad for business."

I winced at the word *payouts*. Yeah, I saw an ass-chewing in my future.

"Email it over when it's done." With that, Whitt hung up, and his eyes turned to me.

I ripped my gator down, and so did Knight. It was nice to breathe. Whitt was one of the few people who knew who we were, and Shep had been friends with us before The Daymakers were even a thing. He knew us inside and out. Tricia knew our real identities, and so did Helen in costuming, because you couldn't fit masks without seeing someone's face.

Whitt glared at me. "Can you not keep it in your fucking leather pants for *five goddamn seconds?"* he whisper-yelled, his eyes sliding to Hero and Poet. They slept pretty heavily, so I wasn't too worried they'd wake up with the noise of us talking.

I shrugged. I probably could, but I didn't want to. There was no high like standing on the stage at a gig, with thousands of people chanting your name. Rubbing one out after that just didn't cut it.

"I've got needs, old man," I teased, though I did feel a little bad. The girl last night—Sarah? Sienna? Whatever—had promised that she wouldn't sell the story, but I guess, some people's words were worthless. Besides, she hadn't seen me without my entire face mask. Most of the time, they wanted me to wear the full Royal mask. How was I supposed to know she was going to try and tear it off?

"Well, *your needs* went straight on the Gram to tell everyone that she fucked *the* Royal and that she knew your identity."

"By my dick?" I asked, arching my eyebrow. "Give

me a break. I'm not stupid enough to show my face to some random groupie, Whitt." *At least, not on purpose.*

"Yeah, well, management is fucking pissed about putting out these fires, Royal. They're about done. Anonymity is a key part of your contract, and you're jeopardizing it for everyone."

Knight was still hurting from Laura's betrayal and had basically become a monk. Hero and Poet had each other if they wanted it. I was the weakest link in this chain, because I was a manwhore.

"So, what, they want me to become celibate? Or would they like to geld me completely? I might be able to hit that falsetto better."

Knight snorted a laugh, and Whitt glared in his direction. Shep looked unusually sullen. I mean, to everyone else, he was a serious guy, but usually when he was with us, it was like we were all kids hanging in a rundown park once more. Making jokes and running our mouths.

Man, maybe Whitt was serious.

Whitt pinched the bridge of his nose. "Of course not, Royal. But I might have a solution." He cast a look at Shep, whose face still looked stormy.

Well, this was intriguing.

"Wake up Hero and Poet. This affects them too, in a way."

Shep stood and went over, touching Hero's shoulder softly, waking him up. I hated it. Touring always hit them hardest, but whatever Whitt wanted to say seemed important.

Hero slowly sat up, blinking at Shep, and then the rest of the room. "'Sup, Whitt?"

"Hey, kid. Sorry to wake you."

Hero yawned and stretched, and the movement jostled Poet awake. We didn't call each other by our legal names anymore. Didn't want to accidentally get caught out using the wrong name in public and fucking everything up. So we were just Royal, Knight, Hero and Poet, twenty-four seven.

Poet smiled sleepily at Shep. "Hey, Shep."

He was the softest of us all, and I wondered if it was because he'd lost his leg so fucking young. It could have made him bitter, especially considering the circumstances. Instead, it had made him see the world in a whole new light. He appreciated everyone and everything in it. He was the fucking light in our darkness, and it made us all protective of him, Shep included.

"Hey, Poe. Your leg looks rough. I'll get someone in Phoenix to check it out."

Poet just nodded, trusting Shep to take care of it, as he shuffled to the end of the bed to sit beside Hero. Those two weren't in an official relationship, but they needed extra support, and found it in each other. In us too, but not in the almost loving way they had with each other. They definitely fucked, but not a lot. Hero did it to feel grounded, when he felt like things were out of control. Poet did it when he wanted to feel desirable, or some shit.

"Okay, Whitt. We're all concentrating now. What's the problem?" Knight asked, always the impatient one.

"Not a problem, a solution. I get you guys are rockstars, and you deserve the lifestyle that comes along with it, but for reasons we all know, that's not really possible, especially when it comes to groupies. So, a solution fell into our lap, and I wanted to put it to you guys. It's entirely up to you, but I have to stress, you're on your final warning with Panama management. This tour has cost a fuck-ton of money, and keeping this gimmick alive takes a lot of manpower, when they can just get a K-pop group who'll fill the same stadiums with a lot less hassle."

Fuckers. We didn't really need Panama Records, but they were the only ones willing to take a chance on the gimmick of us being masked. Most others had turned down the pitch from our agent without even meeting us.

I growled in annoyance. "Enough with the foreplay. Spit it out."

"Just like your more average needs, like security and catering, I want to hire you someone to see to your other needs. Uh, your entertainment needs."

Shep snorted a derisive sound. "He wants to hire you someone as a fucktoy."

"You want to get us hookers at each stop?" Poet looked aghast, but I could see where Whitt was coming from.

Whitt was shaking his head. "No. I want to hire one girl who'll travel with the tour and will be locked into an NDA contract so tight that if she even sneezes and it sounds like your legal name, she will be broke for generations."

Knight scoffed. "That's insane. We don't even have the same taste."

He wasn't wrong. I would have rather stuck my dick in a cheese grater than Knight's ex. That wasn't even mentioning Poet and Hero's unique tastes.

Poet was shaking his head. "Who would even agree to that?"

Whitt sucked in a breath. "It was her idea, actually. She has her own reasons to want to do this, and I respect that she knows her own mind and hard limits."

I reared back in shock. "You've found someone already? Before even asking us?"

"She fell into our laps, coincidentally."

I rolled my eyes. "You're going soft in the head, Whitt. Some enterprising groupie talks you into getting unfettered access to us, and you just agree?"

Whitt gave me a hard stare. "Like I said, she has some compelling reasons. Besides, she has no idea who you fuckers are. She thought I was the headliner for this tour."

I wasn't conceited enough to think everyone knew who we were. We were big enough, but we weren't household names.

Hero, who didn't say much, shook his head. "I'm with Royal. This sounds kinda suss. I don't want some snake in our lives, getting all up in our business."

Poet tilted his head, looking over at Shep. "What do

you think?" Shep had had our back for so long now, I trusted him more than I trusted myself most of the time.

"I found her beat to shit underneath one of the tour buses in LA. Shitty domestic violence situation, I think. I chased off the boyfriend and took her to Tricia," he told Poet, who sucked in a harsh breath. "We let her hitch a ride to Vegas, and we were going to set her loose here. I was feeding her breakfast when management called about Royal's latest sexcapade. We were joking about solutions, and she put herself forward as an option. She wants money, and a free ride as far away from LA as she can get. I see what she gets out of it, and even why she'd suggest it. Doesn't mean I have to like it."

Although Shep unloaded all that completely impassively, I'd known him long enough to know what he was *not* saying. He liked the girl. Hated himself, because he wanted her to stay around. Hated the idea that I was going to fuck her. Wanted her for himself.

"I don't want to take advantage of some girl who has no other options," Hero snapped, and Poet nodded his agreement.

Whitt snorted a laugh. "Trust me, Charlotte's going into this with her eyes wide open. I don't think she's some groupie with good acting skills, and you know I don't trust anyone." It was true—he was a suspicious fucker. "Which is why you'll either be wearing your masks, or she'll be blindfolded when you're in each other's presence. Preferably both. There'll be no chance she'll know your identities at the end, even if she wanted to sell your information and the lawyers hadn't essentially gagged her with an NDA."

Shep's head whipped toward Whitt, his lips parted with incredulity. "Why the hell would she agree to that?"

"We'll see how bad she wants it, I guess." Sometimes I forgot how ruthless Whitt was. "She'll live on the tour bus with you, and because Shep appears to be so worried about her, he'll act as her go-between and keep her safe. I trust you boys implicitly, as does Tricia. If I thought there was even a tiny chance of her getting hurt in any way, I'd never suggest it."

He leveled us all with a cold look. "That being said, a single comment about her being used in a way she doesn't explicitly consent to, and Panama management will be the least of your problems. Tricia will make being gelded seem like the sunshine-and-roses option."

Knight sat up ramrod straight. "We wouldn't fucking do that." He looked at me. "Right?"

I frowned at my best friend, not liking what he was insinuating. "Fuck no. I don't need an unwilling hole when there are literally thousands of girls in my DMs ready to drop to their knees for me. If we agree to this" —I glared at Whitt—"and that is a *big* if, then the chick will be treated with respect. We aren't like that."

Whitt nodded. There was a small, satisfied smile on his face that meant we'd basically been toy poodles, who he'd told to jump, and we'd all leaped at his command. "Then I guess you should meet. Your tour bus before soundcheck."

Knight saluted him, and he left. I looked around at my best friends and wondered what the fuck we'd just agreed to.

SIX

CHARLOTTE

AFTER MY SHOWER, Tricia had introduced me to Helen, the costume designer. She was in her late sixties, and she looked like she'd been rock-and-rolling for far longer than I'd been alive. Her hair was a crazy puff of grey, with some purple streaks that made her look a little like a mad scientist.

Helen had taken me under her wing and put me to work, which had been a blissfully wonderful distraction. She was an artist, she told me, but even artists had to wash their brushes. She'd gotten a whole bolt of some kind of fabric that needed to be washed before it could be sewn, and Tricia thought I could use the opportunity to wash the clothes that I'd picked up from the thrift store.

There was a huge laundry room beneath the arena, which seemed like a weird addition, but Helen had informed me that this arena also transformed to a hockey rink for the season. Given how much the players must sweat, maybe a laundry room wasn't so weird.

While I sat on top of the industrial washer, my clothes in a smaller washer beside it, Helen told me about her life. She claimed she was the muse for the Prince song "Raspberry Beret" and that she'd once had a threesome with two very big name rockers in the eighties, though she wouldn't tell me who.

She talked about the band The Daymakers like they were her children. I still hadn't turned my phone on, scared that Tom would be able to track it, so I hadn't been able to google them or their music. I guess I'd see tonight, if Whitt let me stay that long. He hadn't reappeared since breakfast, and I had a sinking feeling he was going to boot me to the curb. But I'd take this safety for just a little longer, and besides, I couldn't find a shelter until the doors opened later.

"They decided they wanted to try theater makeup rather than masks while we were in Mexico City once, and I swear, it reminded me of that one tour with Alice Cooper. Lucky he liked the running guyliner look, but I have to tell you, Royal could pull off the look if he wanted to. That boy has a bone structure to make angels weep." She laughed, and I smiled at her happiness. She was hard not to be completely enamored with. I believed her about her eighties rock orgies, because if she'd been forty years younger, she would have been magnetic.

I also liked that she let me be silent, and hadn't asked me questions about the bruises or my fat lip. She accepted me as I was, letting me feel normal for a moment.

"But the others looked like they were an impressionist painting, and so I made their masks more breathable, which I think helped." She tilted her head at me. "They wear masks on stage. They're a costumed band, their identities a secret. Like that artist—you know, the one who does street art? It adds to the mystery, especially in this day and age. Everyone knows everything now. You can just become an amateur detective on the internet, and everyone's business is right there in front of your face. I think it brings back some of the thrill of music, personally." She pursed her lips. "You've really never heard of them?"

"Whitt told me that they wore masks, and their name rings a bell, maybe? But I can't picture them in my head. Or tell you what they sing." I shook my head, feeling a little like an idiot. "I'm more of a K-pop kind of person. The kind of music that builds you up. Though my dad liked eighties and nineties rock, so I know a few of the old songs. Including Prince," I teased her with a smile. "My ex listened exclusively to dubstep and he, uh, controlled the sound system."

And my entire life. Where had my personality gone? Had I ever even *had* a personality, or had I just been mimicking everyone else's? I really only liked K-pop because one girl in senior year had made us all learn a dance for prom. I'd been so honored to be invited to join that I'd binged it until I was convinced I liked it.

"They're big in their musical field, though I guess if

you aren't in that world, you might be oblivious to them. They're somewhere around post-punk, or maybe even prog rock. They like to vary it up, which I think is what makes them so good. The punk side lets you say fuck you to The Man"—she flipped the wall the bird—"but the soft rock ballads let the man fuck you," she said with a chuckle and wink.

I threw back my head and laughed so hard my ribs ached, and I coughed. I wanted to be like Helen when I got older. "They sound great. I'll look up their music."

She took the fabric from the machine and threw it in the dryer. "No point having dry clean only items, you know? I can make them amazing costumes that can be washed, because boys are sweaty as hell." She turned back to me. "Are you staying on the tour?"

She was fishing for information, but I had none to give her. "Maybe. I might stay in Vegas. I don't know yet."

"Charlotte?"

I jumped at the sound of a man's voice in the doorway, quickly ducking behind the dryer. Helen looked at me with a frown, then stared over at the door. "What are you doing, Shep?"

I heard his steps and cursed myself. *For fuck's sake. Stop it, stop it, stop it.*

Standing up, I pasted a smile on my face. "Shep. Sorry, I thought I dropped something."

The lie fell flat between the three of us. Shep's jaw tensed, but he didn't call me out on the untruth. "Whitt has a meeting for you with the band."

Helen's drawn-on eyebrows rose right up her forehead. I looked down at my outfit, made up mostly of tour merchandise. "Give me five?" I asked breathlessly, as I grabbed my clothes from the dryer. I could change into something more presentable.

Shep nodded and leaned back against one of the washers. I ducked into the bathrooms across the room, quickly changing into my crop top that I'd been wearing the other day. It was black with long sleeves, and stopped just above my navel. I made sure it hid the tape on my ribs well enough, and though you could see a little of the bruise, you'd have to be looking really hard.

The jeans I'd bought at the thrift shop were tight from being in the dryer, but I did some sumo squats to stretch them out a little. They clung to my hips, ass and thighs before flaring out into a gentle bootcut. They were low rise enough to show a good section of my toned stomach. I brushed out my hair again, until it fell in soft brown waves around my shoulders.

It would have to do.

I stepped back into the laundry to see Helen folding my clothes into a neat pile as she plucked them from the dryer. I opened my rucksack, and she placed the stack in carefully, so nothing would wrinkle. I was suddenly insanely thankful for the small oasis this older lady had provided me. Even if this meeting went badly, she'd given me a little pocket of happiness.

I hugged her quickly. "Thanks so much for the wonderful afternoon."

She gave a sharp nod, her eyes shooting Shep a fiery look. Whatever they'd talked about while I was in the bathrooms had pissed her off, but when she squeezed my arm, I relaxed. She was pissed, but not at me.

Shep herded me out of the arena, back into the private lot that held all the buses. "The guys agreed to meet you. Whitt gave them the basics, but there's no reason to progress further if you find each other abhorrent."

I didn't think it mattered much on my part. I'd be having sex with several strangers; by society's standards, that was probably pretty terrible. "Okay."

I couldn't judge what he was thinking from his expression, and I didn't know why it would even matter. He was their security, not part of the band, and he wasn't me. He didn't have to participate at all, so I couldn't work out why he'd be so uptight about it, his shoulders bunched with tension.

He stopped in front of the tour bus. Grabbing my shoulders, he carefully turned me so I was looking up at him. "Whitt will also insist you be blindfolded when you and them are…" He trailed off, like he was trying to find a politically correct word for prostitution.

"Fucking?" I offered helpfully.

He nodded, the muscles in his cheek jumping. "Yes. I'll be around to keep you safe, and I'd trust the guys with my life. But you should know before you go in there that there's a certain level of helplessness that would be expected of you."

I couldn't help it. I laughed in his face. "When I was

eight, I was making a peanut butter sandwich in the kitchen and knocked over a dirty pot of what I thought was water. It was meth. My father freaked out and beat me with the empty pot. Broke my nose." I pointed to the small bump in the bridge. "I still can't eat peanut butter." He looked horrified, and I knew the pity would come next, so I cut it off. "I've always been helpless, Shep. This is me taking back control. A blindfold doesn't scare me."

I knocked on the door, and Whitt opened it. He looked me up and down, his eyes catching on my ribs where he knew the bruises were. "Are you sure about this?"

I nodded. There wasn't an ounce of hesitation in me. "Absolutely."

He stepped back, and I straightened my spine, lifting my chin. This was the first step on the path of the rest of my life. I wouldn't go into it cowering.

I stepped into a room surrounded by dead men. Well, men in skull masks. Most covered their full faces, but one was a half mask, dipping down sharp cheekbones, but leaving full lips uncovered. That mouth gave nothing away, nor did the brilliant blue eyes behind the mask. It held a crown, black blood dripping down from it and pooling around his eyes until they looked like inky death.

Man, I was going to high five Helen if I ever saw her again. These masks were fire.

To his left was another guy in a black hoodie, whose skull mask had a silver gas mask running across where his mouth would probably be. His eyes were so dark, they almost got lost in the same abyss, like blackness around the eye sockets. The next mask had a warped face, the skull transformed almost into a demonic visage, with a rune burned into the forehead. He also wore a heavy black hoodie with the hood up, so it cast his face in an eerie shadow.

The last one was much like the other ones, long scrollwork up the sides of the mask, black teeth grimacing back at me, and across one skull eye was an ornate blindfold.

I turned to Whitt. "Holy shit. Helen needs a raise."

The one with the blindfold laughed. "They're pretty freaking cool, right?"

Man, I wasn't sure what voice I'd expected to appear behind the mask, but the soft, happy one was not it.

Still, I smiled. "Understatement. I could use one of those right now." I pointed to my bruised cheek. Though my eye was a little better today, it was still as black as the abyss around theirs. It was best to point out the elephant in the room.

The gas mask face lifted his chin. "Looks rough."

I cleared my throat, moving further into the bus as Shep gently nudged me toward one of the bench seats. "Feels rough too."

Whitt stood between the two sets of couches. "Let me introduce you all. Charlotte, this is Royal." He pointed to the guy with the crown half mask. "Knight." The guy beside him with the gas mask. "Hero." Demon skeleton guy with the rune on his forehead. "And Poet." The blinded skeleton with the happy voice. "Guys, this is Charlotte."

"The Sex Toy," Royal added, and I bristled.

I stared into those blue eyes that gave nothing away. "And you're the manwhore who makes everyone's life difficult. We're both whores, but one of us is nobler than the other. Which one is it, do you think?"

I could have slapped my own forehead. I'd fucked this up before I'd even begun.

SEVEN

HERO

I DIDN'T NEED to see everyone's faces to know that they were gaping at the girl in front of us. She hadn't flinched at Royal calling her a sex toy. She didn't shy away from her face, the bruises making me clench my fists.

I *hated* people who preyed on those weaker than them. I'd seen it so much growing up.

But she'd strode in here, proud as hell, and I had to admire that. Poet seemed tense beside me, and I squeezed his thigh. Her eyes darted down to where my hand was, but they didn't stay there, flicking back to look between us.

Shep growled at Royal. "Be nice. You don't have to agree with this"—his tone said he hoped we didn't—"but you have to be respectful."

Royal rolled his eyes, and I decided to jump in and save this meeting. "Have you heard of The Daymakers before? Are you a fan?"

Pink flushed across her cheeks—well, the one that wasn't banged up. Actually, she was really pretty if you saw past the fist-shaped marks. Anger at some unknown fuck bubbled in my gut, and I wondered how Shep was dealing with it. He was on a hair trigger when it came to violence against those weaker.

She had a pretty face, with light freckles across olive skin that hinted at time spent in the sun. Her body was absolutely smoking hot. Slightly curvy with a flat stomach, though if I stared too hard, it was almost more gaunt than flat, like she'd missed a few meals. I was trying not to be judgmental; it might've just been her natural shape.

She shook her head at me. "No. Your music isn't really my thing. Everyone I've spoken to says you're amazing, though."

Knight scoffed. "I find it hard to believe that you just stumbled into the restricted area of a band you've never heard of."

She shrugged. "Sounds far-fetched to me too, but it really was a coincidence. Or fate. Or something. I was getting the shit beaten out of me about four streets over from the arena in Inglewood. Things… escalated." Terror flashed in her eyes before she squashed it back down.

What the hell had happened that she could talk so nonchalantly about getting beaten, but whatever that memory was scared the shit out of her?

"So I ran for it. A crowd pouring out of a concert was the best cover, and when that didn't work, a fence between me and my attacker was the next best thing. I had every intention of sneaking back out before Shep caught me." She lifted her shirt, and I hissed out a breath at the sight of her bruised ribs. There was a perfect boot shape. "Trust me, I wouldn't scale a fence with a fucking potentially broken rib for anything less than safety. Especially not to land on some entitled asshole's dick," she snarked back.

Poet leaned into me. "I like her," he whispered, amusement in his voice. He liked it when people gave the others shit and didn't just fall at their feet. I knew he wasn't amused at her pain, though. I shook my head at him.

Whitt cleared his throat. "You can get to know each other later, but let's go over the expectations I have of Charlotte, and of you guys, too. I guess the first thing is that I expect everyone to act like grown-ups and be respectful. So you can put the claws away, the lot of you." He gave us all that disappointed father look he'd perfected. "Secondly, take a good look now, Charlotte, because if you're on the tour bus with the guys, you're going to be blindfolded. Just for an extra level of personal protection of the band's anonymity. All of you will have a full blood panel done to check for STIs, and you'll agree to have some form of long-term contraceptive placed."

She lifted her chin. "I've already got a contraceptive implant, but I'm happy for Tricia to check it out so you can be sure."

He nodded, then turned back toward us. "Charlotte

will live with you on the tour bus, but she'll get her own hotel room when we stop for overnights. Shep will also stay on the bus, as normal." Whitt looked down at my hand on Poet's knee. "Poet and Hero are in a semi-relationship, so if that is something you'll have a problem with, best to leave now."

I froze, my eyes watching her face for any fleeting signs of disgust or anger. Instead, she just shrugged. "I won't encroach on their relationship."

Poet tilted his head at her, and I knew he saw more than I did. He'd be able to tell if she was just paying lip service to get into Royal's pants or not. Whatever he saw, he kept it to himself.

"Lastly, this arrangement lasts for the length of the tour, then Charlotte will take her money and disappear. If even a breath of this arrangement makes it to the media, the deal is off." He stared her down, and she met his eyes without flinching. This chick had some serious brass balls. "You'll get a substantial weekly allowance, and the remainder of the money at the end of the tour when you cease contact with the band. Trust me when I say I can make your life so, so much worse if you decide to screw us over." His voice was steely, but she didn't flinch.

"I got it, Whitt. I'm not in a hurry to attach myself to another man. I want to know who I am before I let another guy fuck me over." She smirked. "Figuratively speaking."

A small laugh burst past Knight's lips before he

could swallow it back down. Royal nudged him with his knee, and he settled back down.

Whitt gave us all one more hard look, then dropped a boring-looking envelope on the dining table. "The contract. There are three copies in there. All five of you must sign every single one, or there's no deal." One more hard stare in Charlotte's direction. "If you don't sign, there's an NDA in there that you *will* sign that says you won't repeat anything that's happened here since the moment of your arrival." His voice softened, and he squatted down in front of her. I saw her face morph from badass queen to scared child. "I'll personally give you ten grand to start yourself off here in Vegas. Neither Tricia nor I want you entering this agreement with no other options. Free will is important around here."

She nodded, her eyes getting a little too large and watery before she blinked it back. "Thanks, Whitt."

He stood up, sending a loaded look in our direction. His muttered, "I've got shit to do," told us that his part of this meeting was over, and he left the bus.

Poet stood up, getting the envelope and pulling out the thick contracts. He handed one to Royal and another to Charlotte. "Holy crap, this is bigger than the Bible," she muttered.

Royal raised an eyebrow. "Spend much time in church on your knees?"

She snorted, still not looking at him. "I've spent my fair share of time on my knees, but not in church." She met his eyes unflinchingly. They were a soft blue, like cornflowers. "Last time I was in church, the preacher was telling me it was my fault the foster dad I was living with tried to touch me. Temptation and Jezebel, and all that. Home was better than that. At least I only had to worry about being raided by cops, and not have to watch my door every night."

She went back to the contract. "I don't understand any of this shit," she grumbled. She looked at Poet, like she could tell he was the softest of us. "Look, I'm going to be honest with you. Sometimes I feel like I was born to be a victim. My parents were shit. My homelife was shittier. My boyfriend and every boyfriend before him have all used me, like I was worth nothing. I'm doing this to get past that. If my body can pay my way, then I'm happy to use it. We'll discuss hard limits and soft limits, things you want. Things I want. And if it matches up, know that I'm going into this with my eyes wide open."

Shep stood up and disappeared to the back of the van, rage on his face. What was his problem?

Royal, as always, took control. "You're getting ahead of yourself, Toy. Contrary to what Whitt thinks, I don't just stick my dick in anyone. We are four very different men; there's no way you can be what we all need."

I wasn't sure about that. She was pretty classically beautiful.

She stood, sashaying toward him, and my eyes were fixed on her hips as they swayed. If she didn't do it for him, she definitely did for me. Though I didn't think I was the target of this fucked-up little arrangement.

She leaned forward until her nose was inches from Royal's, and her pretty, heart-shaped ass was right in my face. I wanted to bury my tongue right there.

"If life kicking me around has taught me anything, it's to be adaptable. To read what people want, their emotions, before those emotions burst out and hurt me. You're easy to read, Pretty Boy." She moved even closer. "You want someone to tell you no. Someone to chase. Someone to conquer, who'll bounce right back up and challenge you again. You want to work hard for something, for once in your life."

She ran a finger over his twisted lower lip. "I bet beneath this mask you're beautiful. An All-American dreamboat. I bet girls have been getting on their knees for you for years without so much as a word from you." She pressed her thumb into his mouth, and he growled.

Fuck, he might just bite it off.

"I bet you want someone to deny you. Someone to make you work for your release. Something more challenging than a warm hole to jerk yourself off inside." She stepped away, looking over her shoulder and winking at Poet as she sat back down on the couch.

Holy. Shit.

"Find me a fucking pen. I'll sign just to watch that every day. Man, I'm hard already." Knight's laugh turned into a groan.

Charlotte's face was serious again, but I could see the smug light in her eyes. She liked that. Maybe this would give her something more than cash.

She flipped over her copy of the contract. "Firstly,

we should talk terms. Is everyone interested in this… arrangement? From the way Whitt spoke, it was only Royal who was causing problems, but you're all rock-stars. I'm sure that comes with its challenges and temptations."

Knight leaned back, puffing out a breath through his mask. "I just broke up with a bitch. That being said, I could use some no-strings relief, and despite what Royal said, you're everyone's type. You're beautiful, but in an every-woman kind of way. No offense."

She raised an eyebrow. "None taken. Knight's in. Royal is thinking over his options." She turned to us, meeting my eyes. "I know you and Poet are partners, and I meant what I said to Whitt." Her voice softened, losing its businesslike tone. "Even if you don't want whatever this is, I'd like us to be friends. If me being here makes you guys uncomfortable, I'll bow out," she said quietly.

I looked at Poet, and his gray eyes were staring right back at me. We'd had enough silent conversations that I knew what he was asking. He was asking for permission, and I could never deny him anything, least of all when it was something I wanted myself.

Poet cleared his throat. "I'm in. I'm not sure if I want to have sex with you, but I'm happy to see where things go." He grabbed the bottom of his oversized black cargos he liked to wear. He dragged it up and showed her the prosthetic, and we all held our breath. People responded to his prosthetic in different ways, from sexualizing it to being disgusted by it.

Charlotte frowned. "You're an amputee?" There was no inflection in her tone. It was just a question without judgment. "Has it been long?"

Poet dropped his pant leg back down. "Over a decade. A car accident when I was eleven."

She nodded, and I saw the briefest flash of empathy in her eyes, but that was it. She looked up at him. "I don't find anything about you unattractive. Your body is yours to care for, and mine to please, if that's what you want."

He stared at her for a little longer, before his eyes darted back to mine. The relationship I had with Poet was born from necessity, but it didn't mean I didn't love him. Though he wasn't everything I needed, in the same way I couldn't be everything he needed. Sometimes I was just a warm body he needed to chase away the demons. Sometimes he was just someone I could save when the mistakes of my past crept up on me like a dark cloud.

Poet pulled a pen from the leg pocket of his cargo pants, signing his copy of the contract. He handed it to me. I looked up at Charlotte, her gaze bouncing between us. "I'm in, too." I scrawled my name on the dotted line.

At least I could help her get where she wanted to go, even if I never had sex with her. But the throb in my dick told me that I would definitely take her to bed, no matter what my moral high ground wanted me to do.

Knight took the paperwork from me, signing his name as well.

Royal and Charlotte were having some kind of posturing stand-off, and I knew that without Royal being on board, this was all for nothing. Just a case of blue balls and a taste of what could have been.

Once again, our fates rested in Royal's hands; it was Royal that insisted we be anonymous. Hell, it was Royal who'd insisted we form a band in the first place. And just like last time, I had to trust he knew what he was doing.

EIGHT

CHARLOTTE

ROYAL WAS FITTINGLY NAMED. All the other guys turned toward him, and I knew that he would make the final decision. I met his eyes and held them. I'd gambled earlier, with that stupid kittenish behavior. If I'd been wrong, this would all blow up in my face. But I didn't think I was wrong.

I could see the need to really work for something simmering there below the surface. And if he didn't respect me, then this would never work anyway. I wasn't escaping one abusive shithead to get trapped on tour with a bunch of other abusive assholes.

They didn't set off my red flags, but how the hell could I really know? I couldn't see their faces or read their body language. I was insane for making myself this vulnerable with complete strangers. They didn't give me sketchy vibes, though, especially not Poet. I wasn't sure how I knew he was smiling at me from behind that mask, but something in the crinkling corners of his eyes told me.

Royal held the bulky contract in his hand, tapping it rhythmically against his leg. I hoped Whitt wasn't screwing me. I knew that the terms would favor the band, because they were his priority. But as long as I didn't get screwed too hard, I couldn't be worse off than I was now.

"I'll get my lawyers to look this over." He stood, and I didn't miss Knight rolling his eyes in Royal's direction. "We have a soundcheck to get to, but Shep will give you a VIP pass backstage." He paused. "And ask Helen if she has any masks that'll cover your face. We don't need someone with a camera and a blog spreading rumors that we beat our girlfriends." He walked toward me, and I held my ground. He gripped my chin gently, turning my face up to his gruesome mask. His fingers were firm, but not painful. "The less I have to see your face, the better."

"Royal," Poet chastised, but Royal just shot a look over his shoulder at his bandmate. Poet huffed, but didn't say anything further.

I just grinned smugly at Royal. "Fine by me."

Squeezing my chin a little tighter, he spun on his heel and left, the rest of the band following behind him. I slumped back down onto the couch and huffed out a huge breath.

"That went well," I grumbled. Throwing my head back against the headrest, I tried to calm my racing heart. "I should just take Whitt's money and leave."

"You should."

I turned toward Shep, whose face was inscrutable once more. "I'm more stubborn than that."

He muttered something under his breath, then tilted his chin at the door. "Let's go get the mask that His Royal Ass requested."

I stood and tugged down the hem of my shirt. I felt exhausted from the exchange all of a sudden, or maybe it was just the fact the day had been long. One long-ass day in the series of long-ass days that made up my life so far.

I let my hair fall forward, already missing the privacy of my oversized hoodie. We moved through the lot to where Helen was directing roadies like she was the conductor in an orchestra.

"Shep. Charlotte. What can I do for you?" She seemed hurried, but still gave us a friendly smile.

"Royal wants Charlotte to have a mask to cover the bruises for the show tonight." Shep looked down at a message on his phone. "He, uh, also wants it to have a blindfold option."

She raised an eyebrow at me, but didn't comment any further. "I see. Any further instructions?"

I shook my head, but Shep wasn't done. "Make it befitting someone who'd hang with the band. I want to protect her identity as much as possible. And, uh, make it comfortable."

Helen waved a hand. "Darling, as if I would make anything that wasn't beautiful and wearable. What do you think I am? An amateur?" She looked down at her watch. "Give me an hour to whip up a prototype, but anything more detailed will need to wait, maybe a day or two."

"Anytime you can, Helen, that would be amazing," I said softly, and her eyes drifted between the two of us.

She gave us a tight nod, then shooed us away with a wave. "Come back before the band goes on, and I'll have something. I'll also put some stage makeup on that bruise to help hide it."

I nodded, and when Shep left, I followed behind him. He made it over to the med van, but the door was locked and Tricia was nowhere to be seen. Pulling keys from his pocket, he unlocked it.

"Grab your stuff. I'll take you over to the bus to get settled while the guys are doing soundcheck."

I went to the bed at the back, making sure it was still immaculately made. I wouldn't be a burden on the people who had thrown me this lifeline. Gathering up my meager possessions, I threw them all in the rucksack while Shep played on his phone by the door.

He still looked kinda pissed, but I wasn't going back on this. Besides, I hadn't insisted he play babysitter. That was all on Whitt.

"What about your stuff?" I asked, and he frowned sourly at me.

"My stuff is already there. I live on the bus."

Surprise made my eyebrows raise. "You do? Are the guys in danger on the bus?" I mean, there must be a possibility of someone sneaking in, and I don't know, murdering the guys, but surely it had to be slim.

He shook his head. "The band and I have been friends for a long time. Since we were kids."

Well, that was interesting. I couldn't see the faces of the band, but I'd guess Shep was around twenty-six. Did that mean the guys were all that age too? Royal held himself with such confidence that he could be eighteen or forty. Not that I cared either way. I didn't want to take them home to meet my father, so it didn't matter to me.

Shep pushed off the wall, and we went back to the tour bus. Unlocking it again, he led me down through the bunks, which seemed more spacious than I'd imagined.

He opened up the door just before the bathroom, showing me the main bedroom. When I stepped inside, I saw a double bed, with a large closet on the left. There was a mirror on the wall above a small floating vanity.

"Usually, Poet and Hero sleep in here. Sometimes the guys use it as a dressing room too, but you deserve your own space where you don't have to walk around blinkered like some chophouse horse," Shep grunted. "Put your stuff over there; I cleared out a drawer. We'll move more shit around as you need it."

I frowned at him. "When did you do this?"

"While you were trying to convince the guys that you'd be the perfect way to get their dicks wet."

My hackles rose immediately. "You don't have to like it, asshole, but you don't get to be a prick to me about it. I'm a grown-ass woman, and if this is what I want to do, so be it. If you're worried about babysitting me, I'll ask Whitt for someone else. Or hell, I'll just trust that you aren't friends with rapists."

His lip curled back over his teeth. "They aren't, but that doesn't mean they won't be assholes. Way worse than me. You've presented yourself as something with no value, and they'll treat you as such, because that's the way they've been raised—" His mouth snapped shut, and I got the distinct impression he'd said more than he intended. He sucked in a long breath. "I'm sorry. I think you deserve better, but you're right. You're all adults, and if this is what you want, I'll respect that."

I swallowed back my own anger. I needed an ally, and I wanted it to be Shep. I wouldn't let him walk all over me, but I wasn't going to hang on to a grudge either. "They haven't even all signed the contract, so you might have cleared out a space for nothing."

Shep shook his head. "They will. I've known them for nearly a decade. They will." He stepped back out of the room. "I'll let you get freshened up. Settle in, and I'll be back over to collect you for their set in two hours."

He strode out of the bus, the door shutting with a quiet click. I didn't put my stuff away, despite his confidence that I'd be staying. Instead, I resisted the urge to snoop through the room. The bed was made, and all the closets had latches to stop them swinging open as the bus moved.

I took a long shower, then spent some time fixing my hair into an elaborate updo—well, as elaborate as I could do with some clear hair elastics and a hairbrush.

But I'd never had excess money, so making do on minimal was basically my forte.

Spotting a charger in the wall, I grabbed my phone from my bag. Plugging it in, I waited a few minutes for it to load. It was immediately flooded with messages on the Gram from Tom, and just the ones I could see told me I didn't want to open and read the rest. I didn't delete them, as much as I wanted to, but I did go into his contact and block him from my socials.

On second thought, I screenshotted the messages, then deleted my accounts completely. I didn't need them for the next few months, and I couldn't post anything anyway. Besides, there wasn't anyone I wanted to stay in contact with.

Was that miserable? That no one would really care if I disappeared? Tom had alienated me from all my friends, though no one had tried very hard to stay in touch. His friends had become my friends, but they were never really mine. They'd just tolerated me for him.

There was something cathartic about suspending all my accounts, like I was wiping the slate clean.

A knock at the bus door had me looking up. Was I supposed to answer? Was that overstepping?

It wasn't like Shep would have knocked. When the knock sounded again, I decided to grow some ladyballs and answer. I'd ask for forgiveness if I committed some tour bus whore faux pas.

A dude with an irritated look held out a box to me. "Helen said this was for you." He thrust it in my arms and power walked away, talking to someone about spare quads.

I stepped back into the bus, making sure to lock the door again. Taking the box back to the bedroom, I rested it on the bed and lifted the lid. It was filled with packing peanuts and something covered in bubble wrap. On top of that, I saw some basic makeup. Concealer, and some tinted moisturizer. A lipstick in red. Mascara.

Man, when I saw Helen again, I was going to hug the shit out of her.

After carefully unloading the contents of the box onto the bed, I spotted the note on the bottom.

Charlotte,

This was a prototype I was going to use for Poet before we settled on his current piece. I've adjusted it for you and the requirements Shep mentioned. Just take out the insert to give yourself sight. The silk mask can go in for other times. I'll work on something more regal later. I have such ideas for someone with your facial structure, I'm practically giddy.

However, if you need ANYTHING, let me know. I once fought a death metal rocker for a chicken that was going to be part of an act. Pepe the Chicken lived a long life on my farm in Minnesota. The rocker never fucked with me or any live animals on his tour again.

If I'd do that for a chicken, don't underestimate what I would do for you if you need me, kid.

Helen.

I unwrapped the mask and sucked in a breath. It was beautiful, though having seen the ones she'd made for the band, I'd expected nothing less. It was a half mask, almost masquerade style, but it had skeleton hands coming in from both sides, palms down where my cheeks would be, its fingers linking over the nose. You could see by peeking through its skeletal fingers. Intricate filigree work sat beneath the bones, completing the mask.

It was fucking *gorgeous*.

Flipping it over, I could see a thin silk mask had been velcroed on the inside of it. Pulling it away, the scratchy velcro stayed on the eye mask part, leaving some kind of soft fleece material behind. She'd made it as comfortable for me as possible. The band of the mask was thick elastic, and there was a fastener for me to tighten or loosen as necessary.

Slipping the mask on, I tightened it and fluffed my hair around it. Then I slid on my leather jacket that had a hood, and pulled it up over my hair. My sight was limited, but I could still see. As long as I didn't have to cross a heavy stream of traffic, I'd be fine.

Holding my breath, I turned and looked at the mirror. A small gasp escaped my lips. I looked like a creepy goddess, arising from the ground to steal your soul, and probably your boyfriend.

I loved it.

"Charlotte?"

"In here."

I heard Shep's hiss, and I turned toward him. "Fuck me," he muttered. "You're their fucking wet dream." The darkening of his eyes told me I wasn't just *their* wet dream. Butterflies fluttered in my stomach, but I squashed them.

No men. No, that was a stupid rule, because I was legit hoping to ride this bus—and the men inside it—to a new life. I would let them inside my body, but not inside my walls. Because my heart had been obliterated over and over, and I had a feeling that if it happened one more time, there'd be no mending it ever again.

NINE

KNIGHT

NOTHING COMPARED to standing on stage in front of thousands of people as they screamed your name, singing your words back at you. It was a high like nothing else. Not like any drug I'd tasted, any girl I'd fucked, any thrill I'd ever tried. It was a beast that caressed your skin like a lover and devoured you alive.

I would never get tired of this, no matter how many shows we did, how many months we stayed on tour. This was my addiction, and I didn't want help.

We were coming to the end of the set, and Royal had the crowd right where we wanted them, all but panting for release. Sweat dripped down my skin from the lights, sticking my shirt to my body, and I got down on my knees at the front of the stage, my solo screaming through the speakers, my body rolling as my hands flew across the strings like they were born to be there.

The girls screamed as I fucked them, figuratively, and I grinned, though they couldn't see it. Royal walked over, gripping the back of my longish hair. We all kept our hair long to hide the ties for the masks, spraying it black so we looked uniform. No one would ever guess that Royal was so blond, it shone like gold in the sun. The only time the public ever saw him was with the black paint slicked through like boot polish, or with the balaclava.

As he pulled my hair, I let my body roll back in his grip, like he was indeed my king and I was just his adoring subject. It wasn't so far from the truth. There was little I wouldn't do for Royal.

He leaned forward and sang the ballad made for pure sex right at me, his tongue coming out and licking the side of my mask like it was my face.

The screams of the crowd were basically feral. We played up this fantasy the fans had that Royal and I fucked. Actually, depending on the day, sometimes he got handsy with Poet too. He oozed sex from every pore, and it was dark and violent and so damn sensual that I got a hard-on. I always did at shows like this. The thrill was like nothing else.

As the song ended, I climbed to my feet with no hands, making them scream again, even though my knees protested at the abuse.

"Vegas, you've been positively *divine.* What more could I ask from the city of sinners?" Royal purred, sending the crowd crazy again. "Mmm, yes… You've all been *very* bad, and maybe you need to be punished?"

The roar was deafening as Hero led us into "The Punisher," a song Poet had written about his recovery from depression in his teens, though it sounded like he was talking about a lover he wanted to put on her knees.

It was our most popular song, and I could probably play it in my sleep. Unlike the last ballad, this one rocked hard, and I jumped around the stage, sweat dripping down my face, chest and abs before it got caught in my wet-look jeans that shone under the stage lights.

Finally, Royal got around to the goodbyes, and the lights went dark as we scrambled off the stage. The roar was thrilling, and as soon as we were off the stage, I adjusted my dick.

Poet nudged me with his shoulder. "The fanfiction girlies are going to go wild with tonight's performance. If you aren't tagged in at least one fan video by tomorrow where they insinuate you're blowing Royal, I'll let you pick the food for the rest of the month."

I laughed. I wouldn't take that bet; there was no way I'd win. The fans were horny fuckers, and if that's what they wanted to believe, I wasn't mad about it. It sold tickets and albums, and honestly? Royal was hot as fuck, and I wasn't that picky.

I desperately wanted to take off my mask, but left it where it was. We'd get backstage, drink and eat the spread, then I'd go back to the hotel and shower off all the sweat and makeup.

Shaking hands with some of the roadies, I spotted Royal and Hero talking to the press. Dodging around them, I dragged Poet along. He hated talking to the media, and I wasn't a fan either. Both Hero and Royal had that schmoozing bullshit in their blood.

Pushing open the door to the green room, I stepped aside so Poet could go in first. We were all protective of Poet, though he really didn't need it. I'd seen him take a swing at a guy in a bar once, and he'd floored him with one punch. He was lean, but he was fit as hell. There was still something gentle and pure about Poet, though, and I didn't know about the other guys, but I wanted to protect that at all costs.

Shaking my head, I wasn't concentrating and plowed directly into Poet's back. "The fuck, man?" I stepped around him, then suddenly, I understood.

Charlotte was standing at Shep's side, a backstage pass around her neck, the bottom of the laminated tag brushing her exposed midriff. My already happy dick perked up again, throbbing as if to remind me that he'd very much like to be buried in this woman.

The mask she wore was fucking incredible, though I shouldn't have been surprised. Helen was a damn magician. Skeleton hands hid the top of her face, and somehow, that made her lips—stained crimson red—even more enticing. She had a pouty little cupid's bow that I wanted to see wrapped around my cock.

Poet recovered first. "You look amazing, Charlotte," he said softly. "The mask suits you."

She smiled at him, and god, I was so glad I could see it. "Thanks, Poet." She'd remembered who he was, and I could feel him light up with joy. "You guys were…" Her voice trailed off as she shook her head, searching for words. "Just, wow. I can't believe I've never heard of you before."

I laughed. "There's not a lot of synchronized dancing, so we probably weren't on your playlists."

She grinned, laughter in her eyes. "Probably not, but you will be now. You've converted me. You guys play like you were born to be on stage."

My shoulders tensed at her words, but I shook it off. "Feels like it sometimes." Shep raised an eyebrow, but I ignored him. "Did you eat? Drink the booze?"

She leaned forward. "Those cookies are *really* fucking good."

Poet laughed. "Hero always requests Everything But The Kitchen Sink cookies in our rider. He has a serious sweet tooth."

"It's a wonder he doesn't have diabetes," Shep muttered, shaking his head.

We all knew that Hero could eat his body weight in cookies, and he'd burn off the extra calories night after night. He was pure lean muscle, and he needed the energy after a ninety-minute set.

As if we'd summoned him by thought alone, Hero swaggered into the room. I smirked at Charlotte. "Lottie's been eating your cookies, Hero."

He tilted his head, which must have looked disconcerting to her in his mask. We were so used to them now—it didn't matter that I couldn't see his face, I could tell he was raising an eyebrow at her.

"Oh? Does that mean I get to eat your cookie later?"

A flush traveled up her neck and cheeks at his

words, and I watched her throat as she swallowed hard. The sex kitten from the tour bus was nowhere to be seen as he stalked toward her, swiping another cookie from the platter on the table. He lifted it to her lips, and she nibbled the edge. He watched her mouth as she ate her bite, her tongue flicking out to collect a crumb from the corner of her lips.

No shit, it was hot as fuck.

He looked down at her. "Asked you a question, sweetheart."

"Yes," she breathed, like there was any doubt. Everyone in this room knew if Hero had asked for it, she would have climbed on the trestle table in the middle of the room and spread her legs wide so he could eat her out. Actually, I wondered if I could request that, because my dick was now throbbing again in my pants.

One look at Shep's disapproving face had me holding back the question, though. Maybe not tonight, but soon. I wanted what this girl was offering, just so I could end my dry spell with the most deliciously soft curves.

I felt the vibe in the room shift, and I didn't need to turn to know that Royal had arrived. He had a way of making the air feel more electric. And more dangerous.

His eyes traveled over her, over Hero hovering close to her, and stopped at her mask. "Good."

Ugh, he was going to be a control freak about this, just because the girl had him totally pegged. Royal had spent his entire life in control, since his upbringing had been a chaotic mess. He desperately wanted to give up that control, but he couldn't in his day-to-day life.

She could give him that. I hoped he took the opportunity.

"Do you have a blindfold for that thing?" he asked, walking to the ice bucket and grabbing a beer. "I want to take this fucking mask off, because I'm sweating like a fiend, but I can't without breaking Whitt's fucking contract."

Charlotte pulled what looked like a piece of silk from her pocket. She pulled off her mask, and I noted that she'd concealed the bruise. My fingers flexed with the urge to beat the shit out of the guy who'd done that to her. Not because I felt anything for her in particular, except lust, but I hated men who beat on women. Especially when they were supposed to protect them instead.

She stuck the silk inside her masquerade mask, then put the whole thing back on. I saw her transform now that she was blind. Her spine was ramrod straight, her chin raised.

I drifted closer to her, lifting my hand to brush my knuckles along her delicate jawline. "Can you see anything, Lottie?" I whispered softly. The heady rush of this pretty little thing having to trust me completely was like another boost to my high. I ran my thumb over her bottom lip, swiping away the crimson. "How many fingers am I holding up?"

Her breaths puffed against my thumb as I pushed it into her mouth. She nipped the end, and I groaned.

Sucking it hard, she pulled back until it popped out of her mouth.

Her lips curled into a cocky smirk. "One," she teased, and I was a goner.

I looked over my shoulder at Royal. "Sign the fucking contract, asshat. I'm going to teach Lottie how to count, one appendage at a time."

TEN
CHARLOTTE

MENTALLY, I'd prepared for the fact that I'd spend most of the next few months blind when it came to these guys. But you couldn't truly prepare for the darkness, with unknown hands touching my jaw, fingers pushed into my mouth. Only Knight's purred, "Lottie," let me know who was touching me.

Surprisingly, I found I didn't hate it at all. I felt almost free. I could hide behind the mask, not have to control my eyes, or my expression, for once in my life. If I looked at anyone too long in my old life—before my ex—there'd been a good chance of getting a beatdown. Either from some girl at school, or my dad.

Not having to govern my face was like losing a shackle I hadn't even known I had. When Knight pressed his thumb in my mouth, he couldn't see my eyes widen. Couldn't see the lust in my expression. I'd taunted Royal about giving over control, but maybe I was the one who needed to give it up.

Shep's steadying hand on my spine was reassuring, though I didn't know how I knew it was him. His scent, maybe?

Knight's body disappeared, and I could feel the cool from the air conditioner swirl around me. "Sign the fucking contract, asshat. I'm going to teach Lottie how to count, one appendage at a time." His words flowed over my skin like a caress.

I could hear plastic hitting the table, so I figured they'd taken their masks off. "Why is it so fucking *hot* in Nevada?" Poet grumbled, sounding further away. I knew it was Poet, because his voice was softer than the other guys.

I didn't know what to do. Did I just stand here like a piece of furniture until one of them decided they needed me?

A hand touched my wrist. "Come and sit down, sweetheart. No need to stand there like a sexy floor lamp." The slightly rough voice meant it wasn't Poet or Knight, but it wasn't as deep as Royal's. So it had to be Hero. Gently, he led me across the room, my steps hesitant. Definitely Hero. I didn't think Royal would be so gentle. Holding my shoulders, he spun me slowly. "There's a couch right behind you. Poet is sitting down to your left."

Man, Hero was in the running to be my favorite. I gave him a thankful smile and sat down gingerly, breathing out a sigh when my ass hit the cushions. Hero's hand disappeared, but slightly cooler fingers touched my arm. Those fingers slid down my arm until they intertwined with mine, lifting our hands to his face.

"You can't see our faces, but you can feel them, right?" Poet's soft voice was close to my ear. He pressed my palm to his cheek. I lifted my other hand to the other one, cupping his face. It was long, filled with sharp edges and soft skin. I ran my thumbs over his high cheekbones and then back toward his nose, learning its shape. There was a slight bump on the bridge, like it had once been broken.

I gently pressed my fingertips into the hollows of his cheeks and down to his lips. I traced their lines, hitting a slight roughness on the top—a scar, maybe?—and then the full lower lip. My fingers continued down along his sharp jawline and up to his hair, which was long, but not so long that he was in the running for an eighties hair band lookalike.

"Helen makes us leave it long, so it doesn't ruin the effect of the masks."

I nodded. "Makes sense." My hands ran down the column of his neck, and I felt more scars along his collarbone. "From the same accident that took your leg?" I asked softly. "You can tell me to mind my own business."

I felt him shrug. "Yeah. There's a few scars from the crash." I had a feeling he meant both physically and emotionally.

Humming gently, I ran my hands across the breadth of his chest. "They make you interesting. Perfection is for those who can't see past the surface." I breathed him in. His cologne was something woodsy and sweet. I committed that to memory too.

I felt more than heard the soft noise that Poet made, as my hands rested over his chest. "I like that."

Someone brushed a hand down my spine. A cold bottle rested against my arm, and I instinctively reached over and grabbed it, the icy exterior on my overheated skin making goosebumps rise. "Water." I heard rustling, followed by Poet's muffled thanks. "And one for Poet. Hard work out there being a rock god," Hero teased.

Someone made a disgusted noise; there was no doubt as to who that was. "She's meant to be here serving you, not the other way around."

Knight laughed, and I could still hear how riled up he was from the show. "Hard for her to serve when you've got her blindfolded, Royal."

"And technically, *you* haven't signed, so she's not obligated to do anything but sit there, be happy and eat cookies," Hero added, and suddenly, there was a napkin-wrapped cookie in my hand.

I stifled a laugh at Royal's pissed growl. "Where's the fucking contract? Actually, no. Shep, get her out of here so we can do the meet and greets, then we'll meet you back at the tour bus."

There was a loaded silence, and I really, really wished I could see what was happening.

Finally, Shep responded. "What about the hotel room?" The words were forced out through gritted teeth.

"She stays on the bus. That was the deal. We'll see you on the bus."

With that, a hand lifted me to my feet, a gentle arm around my waist leading me through the darkness. I heard the door open and close, before Shep was pulling down my mask, yanking the blindfold insert out. Securing the mask back on my face, he led me through the back corridors of the venue, the bustle of people and black-clad workers almost rivaling the sea of people on the floor.

I could hear whispers as people took in my outfit, my mask that complimented the guys' ones, and the fact I was with Shep. I kept my head down and my hood pulled firmly up, determined not to make eye contact. Let them think I was an errant fan being escorted out.

I was still clutching my water and cookie, and I ate it hungrily. When was the last time I'd actually eaten? Breakfast? Jesus, it felt like a lifetime had passed today. I chewed on my cookie, unable to wait any longer.

I was exhausted. "Are the hours this long all the time?" I asked, double-stepping to keep up with Shep.

"No. Today has been unusual. Normally, we'd have a day's break, but we have two shows here in Vegas, so everything was expedited to make sure it was ready for tonight." He looked over his shoulder. "And you, of course."

I shrugged. I hadn't asked him to babysit me. He needed to take that shit up with Whitt or Tricia. "You think it's been rough for you? In the last forty-eight hours, I've gone from a battered ex-girlfriend to a masked band's glory hole. It's been a wild ride for us both, buddy."

Shep stopped dead, spinning to face me and grabbing my shoulders. I couldn't help but flinch away, waiting for the strike. He immediately dropped his hands, like my skin burned, and sucked in a deep breath.

"I'm sorry. I startled you again. I would never, ever raise a hand to hit you. I'd rather cut off my own limbs, starting with my balls. Same goes for the guys—but if they ever do, I'll chop their balls off myself." He cleared his throat. "I don't want you to talk about yourself that way, though." He dropped his voice so the dozens of people around us couldn't hear. "You aren't just a glory hole. You're a person worthy of their respect. Don't be afraid to demand it."

I nodded, but words couldn't get past the lump in my throat. Satisfied with my response, he walked me silently back to the tour bus, where he opened the door and ushered me in. "I have to go get the guys from the meet and greet, and walk them through the crowd. They'll be back soon. Rest. There'll be plenty of time to overthink things later."

I pulled off my mask, so he could see my face. "Thanks. I know you're only looking out for me, and that's more than I've ever done for a near-perfect stranger."

He didn't say anything, just shut the door. I made my way to the back of the bus, past the bunks and into the bathroom. I took off all my makeup, letting down my hair with a sigh. Maybe I'd take Shep's advice and rest for a little bit. My ribs still fucking ached, no matter how many painkillers I took, and my face didn't feel much better.

Shuffling into the bedroom, I slipped my jeans off my legs, flopping down on the bed in just my shirt and underwear. I'd be able to pull them on quickly when I heard the guys get back.

But as soon as my head hit the pillow, I was out.

I didn't wake up until the following morning, my hair a nest around my head, and my copy of the signed contract on the pillow beside my face. One day in, and I was already failing.

I finally looked at the dollar amount beside the dotted line and let myself dream of a future where I had the power and resources to be whoever I wanted to be. To have the luxury of a dream that I could work toward. I had a few months to work out what it was I actually wanted out of life, and I wasn't going to waste a second.

Because the moment this bus rolled into its final destination, Charlotte Lochrin was dead. This tour was my cocoon, and at the end, I was going to be unrecognizable.

ELEVEN

SHEP

AS I'D ESCORTED the guys back to the tour bus last night, emotions had burned deep in my gut. Guilt and lust had churned around, fighting for supremacy, and it made me short-tempered with these guys who'd been my best friends since we were kids.

Once we'd arrived, I'd found her passed out, sound asleep. I'd hovered slightly longer than necessary, just to make sure she was breathing.

Poet had come up behind me, oddly silent for a man with one leg. He'd taken one look at her and shipped everyone back to the hotel. He could be pretty authoritative, considering he was the softest spoken of the bunch. When he spoke, we all listened.

Even when Royal had grumbled that we should just wake her up, Poet had given him a surly look, making him shut his trap. Knight had thrust the contracts in front of him, and he'd begrudgingly signed them without the theatrics that I'm sure he would have preferred.

I'd had Steve drive the guys all back to the hotel, then crawled into my bunk and slept like the dead. It had been a hell of a long day.

Unfortunately, I'd only gotten about five hours of sleep before I had to be up to take the guys to a range of TV performances and radio interviews here in Vegas. Some days, they got to sleep all day while on tour, but because we were here for more than two days, the label had decided to cram in as many PR stunts as possible.

Checking on Charlotte once more, I found she was still asleep. Royal had put the contract on the pillow beside her like some kind of figurative horsehead, but at least he hadn't woken her.

Pulling out some money from my wallet, I left her a note saying Whitt had dropped off an advance, and put the cash on the breakfast nook table in the main section of the bus. She needed more clothes and personal items. A couple of hundred dollars would cover that, especially in Vegas. I didn't think keeping her financially chained to the tour was even remotely ethical. I also grabbed the security pass, so she could come and go as she liked, without a repeat of yesterday.

With that, I scrubbed my face in the bathroom and headed out. I'd shower at the guys' hotel, which was way easier than wedging myself into the tiny shower here.

I waved to some of the roadies as I grabbed my bike. It traveled on the tour with us, and me and the guys all knew how to ride. Sometimes you just needed to get away, and a heavy helmet and leathers definitely hid you from the paparazzi. It could be suffocating for the guys, with eyes on them almost all the time.

Hell, it was suffocating for me, and no one really gave a fuck about me.

Driving through the early morning weekend traffic was easy, and I made it quickly to the five-star hotel the label had put them in. Scanning my keycard, I parked in the underground lot near the elevators. I stopped in the lobby, grabbing pastries and coffee. Double shots in each, because I needed them alert and alive, and since last night's show had run over, it would be hard.

I smiled and tipped the barista, then hopped in the elevator, happily ignoring everyone else in there. When I reached the penthouse, I let myself in.

Unsurprisingly, it was silent. The guys were bunking two to a room in the suite, and I laid out breakfast before I even considered waking them. Opening the blinds, I looked out over the Strip, with the hustle of people stumbling from casinos and that unique skyline which was one hundred percent Vegas.

With a sigh, I looked down at my watch. I'd start with Royal; he always took the longest to get ready.

Wardrobe had already brought over their outfits and the masks that they wore to interviews. They had spandex balaclava skull masks, which Helen had screen-printed with their tell-tale pieces. The gas mask for Knight. The crown for Royal. The eyepatch for Poet. The rune *vegvísir* burned into a skull for Hero. The balaclavas helped them remain in character, but were less oppressive than the full stage masks. Plus, it meant they didn't have to wear the hoods in the desert, which everyone appreciated.

Opening the door, I saw Royal sprawled out on top of his blankets. He was thankfully alone, which was always a bonus. I couldn't count on two hands how many times I'd walked into his hotel room to see him and Hero wrapped up in girls. Knight had had his girlfriend, Laura the Bitch, for way too long. She'd been a leech—in love with the lifestyle, not my friend.

But Hero had once upon a time been as much of a manwhore as Royal. There'd been a couple of years there where I'd felt like I spent most of my time escorting eyelash-fluttering groupies from hotel rooms.

I wasn't exactly quiet as I strode across the room, and Knight's eyes snapped open. He'd always been a light sleeper. "Go away, Shep. I'm not ready," he groaned, rolling onto his stomach and burying his head beneath the pillow.

I nudged Royal as I stole Knight's pillow. "Sorry, brother, but you have an interview with some drivetime radio show in, like, an hour, and we still have to make it across town to their studio."

He let out a string of muffled curse words and a yell.

Royal opened his eyes and gave me his bitch look. Luckily, I was immune. "Time to wake up, sleeping beauty. We gotta be out of here in forty minutes, and we both know your hair takes that long." He flipped me the bird, making me chuckle. "Don't be sour. There's coffee in the living room."

I moved to the next room, where the sounds behind the door told me that Hero and Poet were definitely awake, but weren't exactly ready to get out of bed. I'd walked in on them fucking once, and it wasn't a mistake I wanted to make again.

I knocked on the door roughly. "We have to go. Quit fucking and get out here," I shouted through the wood.

"Fuck off!" Hero shouted back, and I grinned.

By the time I made it back to the living room, the shower was running, and Knight was sitting by the window, sipping his coffee. "How's Lottie?"

I shrugged, like I didn't give a shit. "Still asleep when I left."

Knight snorted. "Cut the shit, Shep. How long have we been friends? A decade or more? I know when you've got a hard-on for a girl, and you want Charlotte."

I rolled my eyes at him, but if he knew, then it wasn't long before everyone would know. Knight was the biggest gossip in the band—hell, maybe on the tour. I handed him a chocolate croissant to shut him up.

Knight just gave me a shit-eating, know-it-all grin that made me want to rearrange his face. Lovingly, of course. "I'm cool with it, you know? Adding you to the agreement. Or not, if you want to pursue her after the end of the tour. But I have to say, if you're going to be territorial, you might be in trouble. Either learn to share or wait your turn."

I gritted my teeth at him. "She's not a piece of meat, Knight. Watch your mouth."

He just smirked and ate the croissant as he looked out over the Strip.

Poet and Hero finally stumbled out of the bedroom, looking disheveled. Poet gave me a happy smile, and why wouldn't he be happy? He wasn't walking around with a giant case of blue balls. "Morning, Shep." He grabbed his coffee, passing the other one to Hero.

Slumping down on the couch, Hero raised a brow at me. He also looked perky this morning. "How'd you sleep? Sorry you got stuck on the bus again." Normally, I'd sleep at the hotel with the guys. Not in a room quite as fancy as this, but still in the same building.

Shrugging, I scrolled through my phone, answering texts and emails about mundane shit, which people knew how to do but just wanted me to hold their hand or pat their head about it. So irritating. "Fine. I don't care about sleeping in the bunks."

The guys' bus was better than the roadie buses, that was for sure. Some of those were like sleeping in a coffin, with eighteen guys on a bus and all your shit stored in that tiny little space with you. Absolute hell. But the guys had some decent head room, and there were only six bunks, plus the artist suite that Charlotte was occupying. I could deal. I'd lived most of my life with not much. Being on the road was a cakewalk.

Royal emerged from the bathroom, wrapped in a towel, and swiped the remaining coffee from the table before striding into the bedroom and shutting the door.

Poet moved to the bathroom, and Hero stood to follow him.

"Separately, you two. We're in a time crunch."

Poet smirked at me. "What do you mean?" But he walked to the bathroom and shut the door, his laughter drifting through the thin walls. Jesus, it was like dealing with horny teenagers sometimes.

I went over the day's events with Knight and Hero, including when the publicist would arrive downstairs, and what time they had to be back at the arena tonight.

Royal appeared, dressed in a black silk shirt, unbuttoned halfway down his chest to show bronzed skin. Hero disappeared into the bathroom, while Knight headed back toward the bedroom. "I spent about forty minutes in the shower rubbing one out last night. If I get any cleaner, my balls will shrivel up," he grumbled, and I screwed up my nose.

"Too much information, asshat." I threw a pillow at his head, and he slammed the door shut, giggling like a schoolgirl.

Sometimes it was hard to remember they weren't dumb kids who couldn't even grow a mustache anymore. I'd met them when I prevented them from being robbed in a shitty part of Coney Island. They'd been pushing a still-broken Poet down the boardwalk in a wheelchair, looking as upper class as you could get, a big neon sign that basically invited you to mug them.

I'd dusted them off, bought a crying Poet an ice cream and asked what the fuck they were doing there without their parents. They'd been, like, thirteen or so. Royal had told me to fuck off.

It had been Hero who'd given me his cell number and told me that he owed me one and to call if I needed anything. Getting an IOU from a thirteen-year-old had been wild—what was he going to give me, a box of cookies and a Playstation?

But the gravitas with which he'd handed me that card made me keep it. And then use it, three years later, in the worst period of my life. On the street. Beat to hell.

Maybe that's why Charlotte's situation was getting to me so bad; I'd *been* her once upon a time. Before I grew into my body. Before I'd lost faith in the world. Before I'd had these four guys.

Fuck it. I owed them everything, and if that meant I couldn't have the pretty brunette with the big blue eyes filled with secrets and pain, then so be it.

TWELVE

CHARLOTTE

WHITT HAD LEFT three hundred bucks on the dining table of the bus and told me to go spend it on myself. I couldn't even remember the last time I'd *held* three hundred bucks. Maybe when I was ten, and a local gang had bought a big batch of meth from my dad and paid for it in dirty money? My dad had let me hold it, and I'd spent an inordinate amount of time flicking through it, thinking it was the most money I'd ever seen in my life.

Of course, my dad had then bought coke with it and I'd gone hungry again, but still. For a while, I'd been able to find all sorts of change lying around, which I'd pilfered to buy food and another pair of shoes from the thrift store.

Soon, that would all be over. I wouldn't have to scrabble in the crevices of life for change ever again.

Changing into another black tee and my jeans, I headed out and over to the thrift store once more. Three hundred bucks somewhere decent would get me half a wardrobe. But at a thrift store? I could buy pieces that would make up an entire closet and then some.

I needed some decent heels, though. I loved my Converse, but I needed something better. Mentally setting aside a hundred bucks for emergencies, a hundred for toiletries and makeup, fifty for the thrift store and fifty for shoes, I set out for the day. I ducked over to see if Tricia was around, but I didn't think she stayed on the lot either when she didn't have to.

Making sure my lanyard was tucked inside my shirt, I retraced my steps from the day before. I ducked into Walmart and grabbed some cheap makeup, as well as toiletries I might need over the course of a few months. I mentally tallied each dollar in my head, because old habits died hard.

When I arrived at the thrift store, I smiled at the cashier who'd been so damn nice to me last time, and she gave me a wave. As I flicked through the racks, I gravitated toward items that were black. I found myself smiling as I loaded things into my basket, creating a black rocker wardrobe that would make Joan Jett envious. Vintage tees, tartan skirts, torn jeans, pretty lace tops—it all went in there. A few hoodies and sweats too, because no one wanted to be fancy all the time. I even found a little rolling suitcase and snagged that.

But the real winner was the shoe section. Some worn-in chunky boots would go with almost all my outfits, especially if I went back and got some tights from Walmart. A pair of sky-high dark purple heels were completely impractical and slightly over my price budget, but they called to me. Normally, I would resist, but I needed them.

Finally, I went to the book section. When was the last time I'd read a book? Reading had gotten me through so much of my childhood. Tom had ridiculed my taste in books until I never bothered anymore, just to save the embarrassment. What was wrong with reading romance? A little bit of fantasy never hurt anyone, especially when men like the heroes didn't exist in real life. I knew that firsthand.

I spent thirty minutes picking out some well-loved paperbacks. I liked to think that these books had seen so much, they'd had lives of their own. Tears had soaked into their pages. Laughter had ruffled their leaves. People had gripped their covers so tightly that they'd crinkled the cardboard. Corners had been dog-eared to remind the reader of moments they wanted to reread over and over again.

Finally, I settled on a stack of six books. Any more than that would take up too much room in my suitcase. Maybe I could donate them and get new ones at the next stop.

Dragging my haul up to the checkouts, I smiled at the cashier.

"Ah, it's good to see you again. Win big on the slots?"

I shook my head. "Nope, just finally got what was coming to me, you know?"

"Girlie, do I know or do I know," she cackled as she rang me up.

We packed it straight into the suitcase. I'd stop at a laundromat too, just to get it all washed and dried.

"Seventy-two even today," the cashier said, and I handed her eighty bucks.

"Keep the change for your kindness," I told her softly. "Or give it to the next girl who needs help." Eight bucks wouldn't get you much, but it was better than nothing.

"Bless you, love. Have a good day."

I saluted her and headed back out into that dry desert heat. I'd passed a laundromat on the way here, and that was how I intended to spend the rest of the day.

The laundromat was wonderfully air conditioned, and I threw my new clothes into a machine and sat on the hard plastic chair. Cracking open the first book, a romcom, I curled up and read. Peace washed over me like a wave, and I finally relaxed as I was pulled into a world of vampires and small towns.

Five minutes later, someone touched my shoulder. Startled, I swore, then slapped a hand over my mouth as I saw a young mother with a toddler on her hip. "Shit, sorry."

She just grinned. "Your machine has been done for fifteen minutes. Thought you'd want to know, so you weren't stuck here longer than necessary."

Looking at the clock on the wall, I realized I'd been reading for an hour. "Damn. Thank you." Hustling over, I moved my clothes from the washer to the dryer and settled back into my book.

Twenty minutes later, I checked my clothes, but they still needed a little more. The mother and toddler were the only people remaining in the laundromat with me. The kid was playing on the floor, while the mother had a little notebook out that she was staring at intently. It looked like she was doing a budget, and I felt a kinship with her. If I hadn't religiously replaced the implant in my arm every year since I'd turned sixteen, that might have been me with a toddler in too-small clothes, trying to make every penny stretch.

The toddler pointed to the juice in the vending machine, and the mother just shook her head. "Not today, Mellie. Here, have your water." She pulled a sippy cup of water from the diaper bag at her feet and handed it to the little girl, who promptly tossed it across the room, straight at my feet. The mother just looked annoyed and overwhelmed, lines around her eyes creasing deeper, even though she was probably only my age. "Go and pick that up."

The toddler's lip jutted out, tears pooling in her eyes. She started crying so loud, I was pretty sure dogs down the block could hear her and were barking in solidarity.

The mother threw me a frantic look and rushed over to pick her up, patting her back as she squirmed and grumbled. "Shhh, shhh. Maybe next month, I'll buy you a big tub of ice cream and juice, baby. Would you like that? Be good now and stop crying, okay?" Reaching down, I picked up the sippy cup and handed it over to her. She looked embarrassed. "I'm so sorry. Normally, I let her have juice while the clothes are washing, but the store jacked up the price of her formula because there's some kind of stupid shortage, and there's nothing to spare this month, not even a couple of dollars."

I waved away the apology. "Don't even stress it."

Hesitating, I reached into my purse and pulled out my hundred in emergency cash. She might have been taking me for a ride, scamming me out of money, but honestly, I'd rather help a mother who might be scamming me, than ignore a mother who was in genuine need. Besides, a laundromat was a weird place to try and scam someone.

"Take this."

The woman gave me a wide-eyed stare. "What?" she whispered.

I held out the folded fifties to her, pushing them into her hand. "The money. It'll help while the month is hard. A little buffer never hurts anyone." I probably should've taken my own advice and not given away my own buffer, but at least I only had to worry about me. I didn't need to worry that I couldn't afford to feed my kid.

She shook her head and tried to hand it back. "Is this one of those things where they record it and put it on the internet for views, then people judge me as a mother just because I can't buy my kid juice?"

I frowned. "People do that?"

She looked at me like I was nuts. "All the time."

"No. I don't even have a social media account anymore. I've been where you are, kind of, and I don't want you to have to feel guilty that your kid's going without, just because of something outside your control."

My parents had never cared if their child starved, but this woman obviously did.

She stared at me a little longer, then burst into tears. Big, ugly sobs that made the toddler stop crying to stare at her. I looked at the little girl and she looked at me, and it was clear neither of us knew what to do, really. Taking my cues from the movies, I reached over and patted the woman's back.

She pulled away, wiping her eyes on her arm. "Sorry. It's just a lot, you know? Thank you." Carefully, she tucked the money into her bra, and the toddler nuzzled into her neck. "My oldest wanted to go on a field trip, and I couldn't afford it, and I felt like a failure, you know? This was the miracle I was hoping for."

Man, a hundred-dollar miracle felt like such an easy thing to give. Still, her emotions were dragging up all sorts of trauma I wanted to keep buried.

"No worries," I said quickly, moving back to my dryer and taking my clothes out, folding them hurriedly. Placing them all in my suitcase, I watched as the mother took some change from her pocket and bought the baby a juice. Zipping up my suitcase, I walked toward the door. "I hope things get better."

The mother smiled, her eyes dipping to my bruised face. "For you too. Thank you again."

I gave her a tight smile. "They already have." I strode out of the laundromat, the sun's position in the sky telling me it was way later than I'd thought. I double-timed it back to the arena and winced when I saw Shep at the security gate.

First day on the job, and I was already fucking up.

Relief transformed his face, making me kind of feel like an asshole. But then the relief turned into annoyance, and I knew I was about to be spanked—proverbially speaking. Unfortunately.

"Where the fuck have you been?" His eyes flicked down to my suitcase.

I pulled back my shoulders, showing the security guy my badge. He waved me through, but his eyes were bouncing between me and Shep, like he was here for all the tea. Shep growled at him, taking my suitcase from my hand and ushering me further into the chaos of the lot.

"You need a phone."

I shrugged. "I turned off my old one. I don't have any money for a new one."

He looked at me incredulously. "There was three hundred bucks on the dining table this morning. You can't have spent it all."

Instead of telling him I'd given a third of it away, I just raised an eyebrow. "This is Vegas. Nothing is cheap."

Huffing, he led me back to the bus, stopping a roadie on the way. "Go to the store and get me a phone. Something decent. Get a receipt." He handed over a credit card, and the guy scurried away. Unlocking the tour bus, Shep handed me a spare key. "They're giving you a lot of trust, considering you're basically a stranger to everyone here. Don't abuse it."

He paused, and for a second, it looked like he wanted to say something else. Instead, he pushed his sunglasses back down to cover his eyes. "Royal said to miss the show tonight. They'll come around once it's done." He disappeared back into the crowd, leaving me alone on the steps of a bus that was half home, half prison cell.

Whatever. I needed a shower and to beautify the shit out of myself. I wasn't going to give anyone even a moment to regret they'd said yes to this, and if I was honest with myself, I was excited too.

THIRTEEN

POET

I COULDN'T WAIT for tonight's performance to be over. Not because the crowd wasn't amazing; they were fucking spectacular yet again. The energy was high, and the fans sang along to more than one song with so much soul, I was glad no one could see my face behind the mask. I would've looked overwhelmed by the crowd's devotion to The Daymakers, which wasn't very rock and roll.

No, there was only one reason I wanted tonight to be done, and she was sitting on our tour bus thinking fuck knows what.

Royal had made his decree that she should be there waiting for us, and ever since, my skin had felt too tight on my bones. It was the tingle of anticipation, even though I had no intention of actually participating. I'd gotten laid this morning.

But she was something new and exciting. Looking

around at the other guys on the stage, I realized everyone was feeling the same way I was. Like it was the night before Christmas, and you knew that when you woke up in the morning, there'd be something fun for you to unwrap.

Not that I'd be doing any of the unwrapping.

Still, we gave the crowd what they asked for. If it wasn't quite as electric as it was the night before, they'd never know. Royal came over and flirted with me on stage like he wanted to take me to bed. I'd never make a move on him, though; we were a delicate balance, and I wasn't going to be the one who tipped us over the edge.

Fortunately, we'd gotten most of the press bullshit out of the way last night, so all that was left were the meet and greets, then we could be out of here, on our way to the bus. Shep was there when we stepped off the stage, and I was disappointed to see that Charlotte wasn't with him.

Royal would be happy that she knew how to follow direction, though; that control freak shit had always been his thing. I mean, I understood it, but sometimes he needed to let go.

Shep ushered us into the dressing rooms, and I smiled at the cookies that were on the table with the rest of the hospitality rider. My leg ached tonight, but I gritted my teeth. Two big shows in a row, plus all the PR bullshit today, meant it hadn't gotten the proper rest it needed and the prosthetic was starting to rub.

Walking over, I ripped off my mask as I grabbed a

bottle of water and downed it in one go. Then I grabbed three cookies and wrapped them in a napkin, handing them to Shep. "For Charlotte later."

Shep gave me a look I couldn't quite decipher, but tucked the wrapped cookies in the pocket of his cargo pants.

I snacked on some fruit and Gatorade, trying to restore some of the fluids I'd sweated out under the stage lights. I could still hear the hum of the crowd as they excitedly left the arena.

Knight sighed heavily. "Let's go. I know the roadies want to get this place loaded out." He looked at Shep. "We'll try and make it quick."

Shep knew that meant he'd have to play bad cop and get the clingy ones out in their allotted time. Sometimes we let them hang around longer, chatting and taking more pictures, but tonight we were done.

We didn't have another gig until Phoenix on Saturday, which meant we had three days off, and honestly? I intended to sleep away at least one of those days. We were only a month into the tour, and while we'd gotten into the swing of it, exhaustion was trying to creep in.

The meet and greet was a blur of signing things and making conversation and smiling for pictures, but Shep hustled people through the line. I gave an exasperated shrug every time for the fan, like, *hey, I'd love to stay and chat, but what can you do?*

Shep didn't mind being the bad guy. It definitely satisfied his antisocial nature.

Finally, the last of the line was done, and I stretched

out my leg beneath the table. I was dying to get my mask off and stretch out properly, preferably naked.

Someone would have moved our gear under the bus, and we'd head down to Phoenix tonight. Normally, I'd be heading to my bunk and letting the motion of the bus rock me to sleep like a baby, but I had a feeling that there'd be a few fireworks before the night was over.

Shep led us out the rear entrance, over to the reserved parking lot. The whole place was buzzing. Trucks pulled up, with roadies loading crap on and off, and that gear would make it to Phoenix long before we did.

The lights were on in the tour bus, and I saw John, our driver, doing the last-minute checks on the vehicle. He straightened when we arrived, a broad grin on his face. "Good show tonight, boys?"

Knight nodded, shaking his hand. "Great show. The Vegas crowd never disappoints. Find any good food?"

John wasn't much for rock music, being more of a country music fellow—direct quote—so he spent most of his days off trying all the different foods each city had to offer.

"Kid, I had street corn that'd make your ears steam and your taste buds sing. It was coated in hot Cheetos and queso."

Considering John looked like Santa, with his gray beard and big, round belly, complete with suspenders, I was a little worried he'd drop dead from a heart attack one day.

"It's going to make your arteries sing, John," Knight teased, and the guy just waved a hand.

"Only live once. I'm going to make sure I live it deep-fried, then dipped in butter."

I snorted a laugh. "Amen to that."

"We'll be pulling out in about forty minutes."

I gave him a nod as I climbed onto the bus, my leg now on fire. Hero rested a hand against my spine, steadying me. I hated feeling weak, but I hated falling down the bus steps more.

I moved into the living space, then stilled.

Charlotte sat on the couch in an honest-to-god tartan skirt and a torn Rolling Stones shirt that didn't cover her midriff, her legs crossed as she ate dumplings from a takeout container with chopsticks, the television blaring in front of her. She had makeup on for the first time, mascara making her long lashes thick and dark, framing those pretty blue eyes.

She looked over at us, chopsticks still to her lips. "Shit, you're back! I thought you'd be another hour yet." Pushing the box away, she got to her feet, slipping stocking-covered feet into fuck-me heels. She grabbed her mask to slip it on, but Royal stopped her.

"Wait. I bought you one for the bus." He walked over to a boutique bag I'd completely missed near the door. The guys moved past me, and I shook myself from my stupor.

Pulling out the tissue paper, he grabbed a black silk mask. It had a layer of lace that was a little wider, and it would decorate her creamy skin. Charlotte eyed him as he handed it to her, as if he were giving her a rattlesnake.

"This will be more comfortable. Thank you," she said softly, her eyes still suspicious.

"Don't want to impale my dick on a skeleton hand while I'm face-fucking you," he grumbled. "Put it on. I want out of this damn mask."

She gave him a look, like she was imagining setting him alight with her mind, but pulled the elasticized mask over her face. It contoured perfectly to her high cheekbones and along her pretty nose, and just like I'd thought, the lace looked beautiful against her skin.

As soon as it was secured, Royal let his eyes wander down her body, raw lust overcoming his previously dispassionate expression. "How many fingers am I holding up?"

She flipped him the bird. "One?"

Knight laughed, flopping down onto the couch. "Close enough. Can you see anything, pretty girl?"

She shook her head, and everyone breathed a sigh of relief as we all shed our masks. I got that they were our key feature, our gimmick, but sometimes it felt like I was dying slowly behind it. I'd considered asking Helen for a half mask like Royal, but I appreciated how I could use the full one to hide from the world just a little too much.

Charlotte stood there, for the first time looking anything but self-confident. It would take time, I guess, but I could help make her comfortable.

Walking over to her—ignoring the searing pain—I

picked up the box of dumplings. "Sit down, Charlotte. Royal can wait to be an asshole until after you finish eating."

The man in question gave me a droll look. "I'm going to take a shower before the bus starts moving." He stepped around Charlotte, his eyes eating her up. Yeah, he might talk tough, but he was definitely going to rub one out so he didn't embarrass himself.

Turning back to Charlotte, I touched her hand softly so she knew I was there. "I'm going to feed you. Using chopsticks is hard enough when you can see."

She tilted her head at me, but nodded. Lifting the chopsticks from the box, I touched a dumpling softly to her lips. She bit it gently, her white teeth delicate. I watched the food slide past those crimson lips, and wondered if feeding someone was meant to feel like this.

She swallowed, then cleared her throat. "How was the show?" I tapped her lip with the dumpling again, and she took the rest of it. I wondered if I tapped my dick on her lips, would she take all of it too?

Hero answered, watching her just as intently as I was. "Good energy. Knight freeballed some of the guitar solo in 'Killer Machine.'"

Knight stripped off his shirt, like it was physically painful for him to actually not be naked. He wasn't a fan of clothes at the best of times, let alone in this heat. "Can't let Royal have all the glory, right?"

I looked at the elaborate spread of tattoos up and

down his torso. He was forced to keep his tattoos covered, because fans online were basically Sherlock Holmes these days. It was a shame, because the artwork was glorious. Basically a homage to where we came from, who we were, and who we wanted to be. Even my car crash had made it into his sleeve, an indelible moment in not just my story, but all of our stories.

The shower turned off, and Knight was on his feet, heading toward the back. "I smell like ass crack. I'll be back."

We'd always used the room where Charlotte would sleep as a space to change, because no one loved getting dressed in that tiny bathroom. Luckily, none of us were shy, because I guess we'd be spending a lot more free time walking around basically naked.

I continued feeding Charlotte, and she started to relax a little bit. "This is going to take some getting used to," she murmured, and for a moment, I wondered if this was the right thing to do.

Apparently, Hero was on a similar wavelength. "If you want to pull out at any time, just say the word. I'll smooth things over for you with Whitt and the rest of the band."

That's what I loved about Hero. He really lived up to the name.

Her lips curled into a small smile. "Thanks. Can I, uh, feel your face?"

He didn't even hesitate. He got down on his knees in front of her, picking up her hands and resting them on his face. "I'll be easy to identify. I'm the one with the shorter hair," he joked, and her fingers moved up and over his skull, scraping her nails along his scalp and making his lips part.

"I'm sure that isn't all that makes you different," she said softly, her fingertips sliding down to his ears, then along his jaw. "Your face is squarer than Poet's. You have stubble and softer cheekbones."

I had my mother's Nordic cheekbones, so she wasn't wrong.

Her hands roamed down his nose and over his lips. "Your bottom lip is fuller," she whispered softly, and I saw the moment Hero broke.

Leaning forward, he kissed her softly, sucking her bottom lip between his teeth. He pulled back, his eyes flicking over the parts of her face he could see and then over to me. I raised an eyebrow, but didn't hide how much watching him kiss her was turning me on.

Her tongue darted out to run along her lip. "You kissed me."

"I did," Hero whispered back.

She tilted her head in my direction. "I didn't think…" She sucked in a steadying breath. "Is Poet okay with that?"

I leaned forward and kissed her as well, swallowing down the little gasp that tumbled from her lips. She tasted like soy sauce and strawberry lip balm. It shouldn't taste good, but it did. "I'm fine with it, sweet thing."

She nodded. "Good. That's good. I don't want to cause drama."

I could see Hero's eyes soften as he watched her. "Poet and I are solid. If anything, I think we'd both enjoy sharing you." He brushed his lips across hers again. "Is that something you'd like?"

I could see her frown. "I'm here to give you what you'd like."

Turning her face toward me again, I leaned in so close that my lips brushed across hers as I spoke. "What we'd like is to bring you as much pleasure as you bring us. That means that we won't do anything you aren't one hundred percent on board with." I deepened the kiss. "If you want to please me, sweet thing, then I want you to please yourself. That will make me happiest."

She swallowed hard. "Then I think I'd really like to be"—she cleared her throat—"shared by you both." A red flush highlighted her cheeks, making me want to kiss the darkening skin.

So I did. I traced one cheekbone with my lips, then the other. The whole time she sat there, her lips parted, heaving in breaths.

Finally, I pulled back, trying to get myself under control. "It's a plan then."

Hero kissed the side of her jaw. "But not tonight. Soon." He rolled to his feet, tilting her head up and kissing her once more. "Sleep well, Charlotte."

He held out a hand to me, and I took it, needing the assistance to stand, both because my leg felt like it was on fire, and because my dick was so hard, it was going to explode.

I leaned down and kissed her cheek. "Goodnight." I looked past her, up into the molten gaze of Royal. "Give him hell," I whispered in her ear.

FOURTEEN

ROYAL

WATCHING Hero and Poet murmur soft things to Charlotte pissed me off. Not because I was feeling territorial or anything. I'd shared nearly everything with the four other men on this bus for most of my life.

No, I was pissed because they'd put that flush on her face—even made her lips part on a sigh—just by being gentle with her. They were soft and caring; I had none of that in me. It had been burned out of my soul early on in life, and I wasn't sure I could ever get it back.

Doubt crept in, filling my chest. It was the first time I'd felt inadequate in such a long time. That shit was making me grumpy.

I met Shep's eyes where he stood in the corner. I wondered if she knew he was still here, creeping on the moment like a silent gargoyle. He held my eyes, a challenge in them that I couldn't help but rise to meet.

Stepping further into the living section of the bus, I

rested my hip against the countertop of the galley kitchen. "On your feet, Toy."

Her head snapped toward the sound of my voice, but she didn't hesitate as she stood. She'd slipped the heels on, which gave her four inches of height, bringing her nose almost up to my chin and making her legs look incredibly long. The skirt sat mid-thigh, and it wasn't overtly provocative, but rather hinted at seduction. Still, I yearned to run my hands up the backs of her thighs and under that skirt more than I was willing to admit.

She'd cut the Stones shirt really short, and I knew that if she raised her hands in the air, I'd see more than a little of the underside of her breasts. Her shoulders were back, her chin raised, and gone was the uncertainty she'd displayed when we arrived. Maybe she felt a little of the freedom behind the mask too. Except she wasn't performing for the crowd.

She was performing for me.

"Walk toward me." I didn't move closer. I wanted her to find me, using nothing but my voice. I wanted her to know that she was at my mercy.

Shep's eyes were intense, but he didn't utter a sound. Let him watch what he couldn't admit he wanted.

There was only a little hesitation in Charlotte's steps as she navigated the bus blind. Her fingers were slightly extended in front of her, the only concession she made to being without her most vital sense.

She bared her teeth at me. "You could say something else, asshole, so I could find you."

I chuckled darkly. "And where would the fun be in that, Toy? You're mine to play with, and I make the rules."

She stopped in front of me, and I took my time looking her over, from her pretty dark hair that I was definitely going to wrap in my fist tonight, to those pouty little lips that liked to talk shit, back down the long column of her throat to the heaving of her breasts beneath the distressed band tee.

I gripped both her wrists and spun her with my body, until she was pressed against the counters. Shoving her arms above her head, her little gasps of desire—or maybe shock—were like the sweetest music.

I pressed her wrists into the overhead cabinets, holding them both in one of my hands. Just as I thought, her breasts were spilling out from beneath the crop top, and as I made her stretch to her full height, I saw one dusky pink nipple slip free. I slipped my other hand down to her hip, sliding my fingers slowly up her side and watching her shiver. Wrapping a hand around her unbruised ribs, I brushed my thumb across the underside of her breast.

"Mmm, I thought this tiny little shirt might be too small to hold those luscious tits," I murmured beside her ear. "Are you trying to be my manic pixie dream girl, Toy? Dressed up like a rock and roll princess?"

"You think too much of yourself," she breathed, and I smirked. I was glad she couldn't see my response, because I didn't want her to think she was even close to having the upper hand.

Dropping my lips to her neck, I scraped my teeth across the soft skin there, making her shudder. "Nothing about my reputation is exaggerated." Pulling back, I took a step away from her, only my hand around her wrists keeping us connected. "One last chance to bail on this, Toy. You can walk out of here right now, no hard feelings." I leaned close until my breath made the wispy hair framing her face flutter. "Do you want to play with me?"

I knew Hero would have given her the same speech, because, well, he was Hero. It was how we'd come up with his moniker; it suited him perfectly.

But I needed to make sure this was what she *really* wanted. She had options, and I'd be damned if she got to the end of the tour and regretted anything that happened. So every time, I'd ask.

"Just touch me already, Royal," she snapped, and I watched her chest heave, like she couldn't quite get enough air.

I pressed my body closer, until my thigh was between hers. "That didn't answer my question, Charlotte. Do you want to play with me?"

She hissed an annoyed breath. "Yes, fuck you. Please, touch me."

I cupped her tit, rolling her nipple between my thumb and forefinger, and she squeaked out a satisfied noise. My mouth back on her neck, I tasted her skin, right down to her shoulder, then pressed more tightly against her wrists.

"Keep your hands here, Toy. Don't move them, or

you won't like the consequences." Honestly, I was hoping she'd drop them so I could redden that pretty ass in that little outfit.

But she was a good girl, holding them above her head, giving me a free hand to explore down her body. Stroking my hand up the back of her thigh, I slid it under her skirt, hissing as I came hand to bare ass cheek.

I felt further over and traced my fingers down the line of lace that was her thong. Suddenly, I wanted to see it more than anything. Gripping her hips, I spun her until she was pressed over the countertop, her hands propped against the wall to catch herself. I flipped up her skirt, and her creamy white ass was right there, the bright pink thong disappearing between those round globes.

"Fuck me," I groaned, squeezing them, because how could I not? "This is the most perfect ass I've ever seen."

Someone let out a strangled sound, and my eyes drifted over to Shep. His jaw was so tight, it was a wonder I couldn't hear his teeth grinding. I raised my eyebrow at him, getting a scowl in return. I knew he wanted to storm out, but I also knew he was a chivalrous bastard and wouldn't leave, just in case I decide to go full BDSM and give her the wooden spoon or something.

I turned her slightly so he could see me dip my fingers down the crease of her ass, following her thong further south to her wet cunt. "So juicy for me. Do you like this, Toy? You like being my plaything?"

Her moan was frustrated. Yeah, she clearly didn't want to be enjoying this quite so much. "Who doesn't like their pussy being touched? I wish you talked less, though," she snarked, and I laughed.

Mouthy. I secretly liked that.

I pushed her panties aside and thrust a finger inside her. Leaning over her back, I put my mouth next to her ear. "Is that so?" I curled my fingers inside her, making her whimper a little more. "You don't want me to tell you how hard you're gripping my fingers right now? How I want to slide my cock inside that pretty pussy and fuck it so raw that the shape of me will be forever imprinted inside you?" She pulsed around me, and I knew that she was full of shit.

Dropping my voice low, I whispered, "You don't want me to tell you that Shep's watching me finger-fuck you with so much envy, I don't know if he wants to pull his dick out and stroke it, or come over here and break my jaw?"

Her whole body shuddered as I ground the palm of my hand against her clit. Her hips were moving as she rode my hand now, her moans turning into breathy pants, and I could tell she was so damn close. I hadn't enjoyed fingering a girl this much since I was fifteen.

I ground my cock against her ass, which was a dangerous game because I was going to come for sure. She needed to get off *now*, or I was going to be forever shamed.

"Come for me like a good toy," I growled, and she did. She milked my fingers, like her pussy wished it was my dick. Soon, it would be.

The moan that came out of her would definitely wake the dead, and I hoped like hell John's driver cabin was soundproof, because I intended to work that sound out of her over and over again.

"Holy fucking shit." Knight's voice behind me had me looking up with a smug-as-fuck smirk. He was in just his tight boxers, tenting those fuckers like his dick was about to punch a hole straight through.

I stroked my hand down Charlotte's spine. "We've got a real audience now," I crooned. "Maybe it's time for a little audience participation. Do you want to suck Knight's cock while I fuck you?"

She was nodding, her lips still parted, like she couldn't get enough air. Wouldn't matter in a moment, since Knight would be filling it right up.

I spanked her ass reasonably gently. We needed to talk about limits, but not right now. Now, we'd have plain old vanilla sex, and I'd still come just as hard. "What did I say about using words?" I growled, withdrawing my fingers. She let out a pouty little whimper at the loss, and honestly, I felt like I was the king of pussy right now.

"Yes, I want to suck his cock while you fuck me," she breathed, though she still sounded a little bratty about it.

Knight might be a joker, but I'd been in the room while he was fucking enough times to know that he was catnip to pussy. His eyes flashed, and then he was bending down, lifting her chin so she was arching up toward him, like she was a sunflower and he was the only light in the sky. I pressed down on her spine, making her bend even more. He took her lips in a savage kiss, plunging his tongue into her mouth like he owned it.

I slipped my hands around to play with her clit as he plundered her mouth, until she was making these mewling sounds that made my dick throb. I peeled her thong down her legs until it snagged on her ankles. *Perfect.* I looked at her pretty pink cunt, my mouth watering. One day, I would eat that, but I was too desperate to be inside her to wait.

Shep appeared beside me, pushing a condom into my hands. I picked up the whole strip I'd already thrown on the kitchen countertop, waving it in his direction. Rolling my eyes, I slipped on the protection. She hadn't been to get checked out by Tricia, and I didn't trust anyone's word.

As I slid in, I thought that might actually be a good thing, because if I'd been in her bare right now, I knew I probably would've busted. The sound she made as I seated myself inside her was purely pornographic, and I screwed my eyes shut.

Fuck me.

"Open up, Lottie. I'm going to fuck that pretty mouth."

She obeyed so sweetly, and I watched as Knight fed

her his dick. Finally, I pulled back and thrust, making her bounce on his cock, and making him growl at me.

"Should have done this on a bed," he muttered, holding her gently around her upper arms so she wasn't jammed forward on his cock with every thrust.

Yeah, this was a dick move, but if he thought I was stopping, he was crazy. He dragged her back up so she was pressed tight against me, her back to my chest, and my dick hitting places that made my eyes cross.

"So fucking *tight,*" I grunted.

Knight grabbed her hand and wrapped it around his dick, helping her jerk him while he played with her clit. This wasn't our first time having a girl between us, and I doubted it would be the last, now that Charlotte was here.

"That's it, baby. Your hand feels perfect on my cock." He was whispering dirty shit in her ear that I could hardly hear, probably because the only sound in my head was the pounding of my heart as my balls pulled up tight. Knight grinned at me, though his own jaw was tight. "Uh-oh. Royal's about to blow. You going to come with him, Lottie? Milk the release right out of him with that perfect pussy."

His words had the desired effect, and she clamped down, dragging me along with her release. "Fuck!"

Laughing, his head dropped back as he stroked his dick harder and faster, coming all over her stomach and tits. Her knees shook, and as they buckled, I banded an arm around her waist. Not because I cared if she ended up on her knees. She was just covered in spunk, and I didn't want to get it on the furniture.

I stepped back, pulling out of her and Knight picked her up, grabbing her ass as she wrapped shaky thighs around his waist. "Come on, pretty girl. Let's get you cleaned up and put to bed." He headed back toward the bathroom.

I washed Knight's fucking jizz off my arm, avoiding the burning gaze of Shep. "Enjoy the show?" I didn't miss the look on his face or the bulge in his pants. He stomped off the bus, and I hissed out a sigh through my teeth.

This was going to be fun.

FIFTEEN

CHARLOTTE

I WOKE UP SORE, in all the best ways. The ache in my core told me that Royal had fucked me so hard, I'd probably feel it all day long. I stretched and sighed. The bus was rocking gently, telling me we were still on the road. The early morning light told me that it wasn't quite dawn yet, but it was close.

True to his word, Knight had stuffed me in the tiny shower, then left. Obviously, I couldn't shower in a blindfold. As soon as I was done, he'd bundled me up in a fluffy towel, given me a bottle of water, and sent me to bed.

I'd thought for sure he'd want more, but he'd surprised me. If I was honest, the whole night had surprised me more than I thought possible. I knew sex. I'd had sex. A bunch of it, since before I probably should have. At one point in my life, any attention had been good attention, even if it was from people who should have known better, who'd taken advantage of my naivety.

But I'd never had sex like *that.* Even just thinking about it made my skin tingle with pleasure.

Dragging my ass from the bed, I picked up the over-sized The Daymakers tee I was using as a sleep shirt and slipped on some clean underwear. I stepped out into the quietly rocking bus, walking softly down the aisle to the kitchen. There were soft snores coming from the curtained-off bunks, and I wondered who slept where. My mouth was so dry that my throat was sore, and I had a feeling it was because I hadn't exactly been silent with my screaming.

Fucking Royal. Of course he knew how to fuck. He had the upper hand now, but I was determined to take it back.

"Good morning," a voice said, and I slapped a hand over my eyes.

Dumb, dumb, dumb. "Can you pass me the mask please?"

There was a low chuckle, and the sound of rustling around. "Don't worry. I pulled mine on."

I parted my fingers slowly, testing to see if he was decent. Poet sat on the couch, a soft fabric balaclava pulled over his face. I could see one eye, but that was it. The other was covered with a screen-printed eye patch. I knew it was Poet, because he wasn't hiding his prosthetic. He had nothing on but boxers, and the way his abs popped as he sat there made my mouth water.

The skull balaclava hiding him from view was as creepy as it was artistic. "More of Helen's work?"

Poet nodded. "These ones are more comfortable than our performance masks. The fabric is super breathable. We've worn them so often, sometimes I hardly notice it's there."

I knew he was just being kind so I didn't have to navigate the moving bus while blind. Filling a glass with water, I walked over to where he was sitting and pointed to the cushion beside him.

"May I?" He nodded, and I sat down gently beside him. "Thank you. I know you said it's nothing, but I'm sure wearing anything over your face is annoying. I appreciate the moment."

He shrugged, and I noticed a battered little notebook on his lap. "It's a small thing. How did you sleep?"

Breathing deeply, I relaxed into the moment. Poet just had that aura about him. Calm. Peaceful. Kind. "I slept like the dead. The rocking of the bus and…"

"Getting dicked down hard?" he suggested with a laugh.

"Yeah, that. It was pretty tiring."

He chuckled. "I can imagine. It sounded energetic." He tilted his head. "No regrets?"

My first instinct was to brush off his question without thought. Never admit weakness of any kind. But in the quietness of pre-dawn, with the softly spoken Poet, honesty poured from my lips. "For the first time in a long time, I felt powerful. Like I was in control of my life." Honestly, I couldn't remember the last time, but I didn't want to sound pathetic. "So nope, no regrets." My lips curled. "I found it very enjoyable."

Poet threw back his head and laughed softly. "So I heard."

I folded my legs beneath me. "What are you doing awake so early anyway?"

Our whole conversation so far had been barely above a whisper, and it felt like we were telling each other secrets. It was nicer than it had any right to be. Then I remembered what Shep had said about my room.

"Shit, is it because I kicked you and Hero out of your bed? I can move into a bunk, if you want it back? I'm small. It would probably be more comfortable anyway." Given how sweet they'd been to me last night, I felt kind of awful.

Poet squeezed my knee. "It's fine, Lottie," he said, using Knight's nickname for me. I kind of liked it. "I'm usually awake this early. It's when I write new lyrics, or just think."

Well, now I felt like shit for interrupting his quiet time. Something in my chest ached, but I gave him a lopsided smile. "I'll leave you to it. Pretty sure there'd be a hoard of fans who'd come for me if I prevent you from creating new music."

He watched me as I stood and stretched, trying not to let the loneliness seed in my chest. I stepped back toward the bunks when his soft voice stopped me.

"Lottie?"

I glanced down at him, wishing I could see his face, so I could know what he was thinking. "Yeah?"

"Do you need a hug? No strings attached?"

As the words left his lips, emotions surged up in my throat like a lump, and my eyes got watery. I wanted to say no again. But at that moment, more than anything, I wanted someone to hold me for no other reason than giving me the human contact I so desperately needed.

So I swallowed hard and nodded. He opened his arms, and I climbed into them, straddling his thighs as he enclosed me, his big hands resting on my back. I buried my face in his chest, my cheek pressed over his heart, his chin resting on the top of my hair.

I held myself stiffly at first, but soon, the gentle circles he was making on my spine, along with the rocking of the bus, made my whole body just let go. Air rushed from my lungs, and my body melted into Poet's. His skin was soft and warm, the light sprinkle of hair tickling my cheek.

He didn't speak and didn't ask me to speak either. He just held me safe in his arms, and I let the tears I'd been bottling up for so long pour from my eyes like rivers. I bit back the choked sounds, my shoulders shaking with the force of the emotions.

When was the last time anyone had just hugged me just for the sake of hugging me? The self-pity was back, and he began to murmur things in my hair, but I couldn't hear it over the emotion burning its way through my veins, a poison desperate to squeeze free.

Poet held me tighter and tighter, like he could hold

me together as I fell apart. We sat like that for what felt like hours, until his chest was wet with my tears and I was so exhausted, I couldn't lift my head. I just buried my face in his neck and breathed him in, shutting out the light and the world.

I could feel his throat vibrate as he spoke, his deep voice soothing. "She just needed to be held." I stiffened, suddenly realizing there was someone else there with us.

A hand stroked down the back of my head. "Take her back to bed so you can both be comfortable."

"Hold on, sweetheart," Poet murmured in my ear.

I held tight to him, wrapping my arms around his neck and holding on with my thighs as he hoisted himself to his feet. I didn't lift my head, praying everyone else was still asleep. Poet's limp was noticeable as he carried me. I wiggled to get down, but he held me tight.

"It's fine, Lottie. Hold on," he whispered. I heard the door open, then he flopped down onto the bed, both of us bouncing softly on the mattress, making me huff a small laugh. I rolled away from him, but he kept a hand on my hip.

"I'm sorry. I swear, I'm not normally like this. I don't think I've cried this much since I was, like, ten."

"It's been a rough week, we know." Hero stood in the doorway, his mask on too, though he was also dressed only in boxer shorts. He was covered in tattoos, just random ones sporadically placed all over his body, like a picture book.

I shook my head. "That's not what I'm here for, though," I reminded him, and I raised an eyebrow as he climbed into the bed beside me, squishing me between their bodies. Not going to lie, it was nice.

"We'll decide what you're here for, Lottie. Us, and you too. It's good for us to think of someone other than ourselves occasionally." He spooned himself around my back, pushing his arm under my pillow and reaching over me to put a hand on Poet's hip. "Now, go back to sleep, you crazy kids. There's still a couple of hours before we get to Phoenix."

I felt Poet's soft chuckle, but he rested a hand on my hip, his thumb rubbing little circles. Soon enough, the pressure of their two bodies, warm and safe, and the rocking of the bus lulled me back to sleep.

I woke up alone, but that was hardly surprising. My eyes felt gritty, my nose slightly stuffy.

Fuck. I couldn't believe I'd cried all over Poet. The embarrassment was real. I wondered if I never mentioned it again, would he forget it had happened?

I didn't like my chances. Not making the same mistake as earlier, I put my mask on and felt my way to the door. I was glad for the mask, because it meant no one had to see my big, puffy red eyes.

Poking my head out, I used my right hand to guide myself to the end of the hallway, then pushed open the bathroom door. Stepping in, I tugged my mask up. No need to pee blind. Taking the chance to freshen up, I quickly brushed my hair and teeth. I maneuvered the door open a fraction before I put my mask back on, then navigated my way toward the front of the bus. It was fortunate that the spaces were so small, and that the aisle ran straight from one end to the other. It made it easier to get around, that was for sure.

I could *feel* their eyes on my skin, though I didn't know who was there. "Hello?"

"Lottie, baby, you're looking wonderful after your snuggles." Knight's light tone was easy to pick, and I grinned back at him.

"Thank you, Sir Knight."

"You can just call me Sir," he purred, and it had a visceral effect on my lady parts.

Someone huffed, and a hand gripped my hip, dragging me down into the booth beside the kitchen. "She just woke up. Give the girl a break," Shep muttered. "Any allergies?"

"No, but don't worry, I can just eat later—"

But he was already putting what felt like a muffin in my hand. "Apple and cinnamon. I'll put some fresh berries and cheese on the plate in front of you. The passenger van got a flat an hour out of Vegas, so we'll be stuck here for at least another hour before it collects us. So eat."

I rolled my eyes, but took a bite defiantly. "Bossy," I grumbled, but man, this muffin was nice. "Who else is here?"

"Knight and Royal. Poe and Hero have gone out to check out a vinyl swap place on the other side of the city," Shep said, now sounding farther away. "Tricia wants you to come to her hotel room so she can check on your ribs and your, uh, general wellbeing."

Guess she wanted to make sure her boys were treating me right, and that I wasn't having cold feet. "Sure thing. I'll need a lift, though."

"You can ride in the van with us."

Royal muttered something that I missed, but Knight snapped, "Get the fuck over yourself."

I guess I was going too.

SIXTEEN

SHEP

EVERYONE WAS in their masks as we maneuvered from the tour bus into the van with heavily tinted windows that would give us a little privacy. Charlotte had covered the bruise on her face with concealer, and it was at a putrid yellow stage of healing, so she just looked a little jaundiced in certain lights.

The skeleton mask covered most of it, though, and I told my dick to calm down when she emerged from the bus in baggy jeans with shredded knees, the cuffs rolled up over chunky boots. She was wearing another vintage band tee that she'd chopped into a crop top, showing off the flat lines of her stomach. Her hair was in a messy bun on the top of her head, with the mask across her face.

That goddamn mask. I dreamed of fucking her mouth with it on.

Grinding my teeth, I hurried them along. "Let's fucking go."

Poet and Hero had already returned, a stack of vinyl between them. The bus had an amazing sound system, and a love of seventies and eighties music on vinyl was what had inspired their love of music anyway. Well, that and Royal.

Music was in Royal's blood, and you couldn't be friends with him for a long period of time without getting caught up in the magic of making music. I'd never wanted to join the band—I didn't want the limelight, plus I was completely tone deaf—but I loved the culture around it. The passion in the creative process. The challenge of moving from place to place, album to album. I loved supporting the guys, and I knew that what I did was important, even if I didn't get any of the glory.

I climbed into the front beside Steve, looking at the guys as they all lounged around in the back of the van. "Put your seatbelts on."

"Yes, Dad," Knight quipped, and I saw Charlotte smirk. Still, she buckled up.

"Whitt will meet you guys in your room later to go over the crap you need to do this week for tour promo. I argued that you needed a day off, and he agreed, so tomorrow, you're free and clear to do whatever the hell you want. But the rest of the week in the lead-up to the concert will be business as usual."

Charlotte frowned. "I thought you were their security? You almost sound like their manager."

Royal scoffed. "He's both. He started out as our

security, and then we had trouble keeping managers, so the label strongly suggested he step into the role."

What Royal *wasn't* saying was that he was an almighty asshole, and every manager had quit. The label had decided I was the only one he remotely respected, so I got a promotion, and he got to ditch the babysitters.

The guys talked over the setlist, while Poet wrote in his notebook, ignoring them all. He seemed focused, which was good. They'd have to do another album after this tour, and they all worked better when they bounced off each other. Sometimes Knight would come up with a tune, Poet would come up with lyrics, and Royal would make them work. Hero made it all come together and not sound like absolute shit. Though they all tried their hand at the different parts, they definitely had their strengths.

Charlotte's eyes bounced around them all, taking it all in. It was probably fascinating from the outside.

I groaned when we arrived in front of the hotel, seeing there was a small crowd of fans on either side of velvet ropes. Someone at the hotel must have leaked our stay here. The driver pulled up, and I could see the panic in Charlotte's eyes.

"Should I stay in the car?"

Royal snorted, sliding the door open. "Get out of the van, Toy. They're going to see you eventually—may as well be now. Just don't embarrass us."

I jumped out of the car and came around the side as Royal grinned at the crowd, making conversation and taking photos. He was made for this shit, for the adoration. I stood sentinel at the steps of the van, making sure no one face-planted on their step down.

Poet shuffled out next, holding out a hand for Charlotte. She took it gently and climbed down, her spine ramrod straight. I could hear the whispers in the crowd, and knew this would be a thing all over social media within an hour. I'd have to call the publicists and give them a heads up.

Knight came out and moved toward the crowd too, as people shouted his name. No, not people. Women. So many fucking women, throwing themselves at the guys.

In the early days, back before they were The Daymakers, they were a garage band called Little Bite. They'd played shitty bars where they couldn't even drink yet, and grown-ass women had basically stripped down for them in back rooms, begging to be fucked. That had been before they started wearing masks, before they played under fake names. It wasn't until they caught the attention of a label exec that they'd had to come clean about who they were, and they'd come up with the idea of being anonymous.

It had been the best and worst thing for them. It hadn't stopped the groupies, though—if anything, it had made them more rabid. The mystery was like catnip for pussy.

Even Poet began to sign some things for the crowd, and I guided Charlotte into the foyer. "Stay here."

I let the guys mingle for a few more minutes, before I started dragging them away. I started with Royal, because some of the fans were starting to get frenzied in a way that I knew meant violence would follow.

Gripping his arm, I gave the girl he was talking to a tight smile. "Sorry, ladies. Royal has to go."

She leaned closer, gripping his lapels with two hands. "Let me come. I can make you come too… if you know what I mean?" She winked, and you'd have to have been stupid to not know what she meant. She was pretty, in that contrived way. Pornstar pretty.

I groaned, because she was exactly the type of girl that Royal would have fucked in the stairwell and then made me politely ask to leave.

Royal grabbed her hands from his lapels and lifted one to his lips. "Sorry, beautiful. I have all the toys I need at the moment." With that, he stepped away, out of her reach.

I looked at the girl's surprised expression, and knew she was connecting the dots between Charlotte's appearance and Royal's words. *Fucking Royal.*

"Really, dickhead?" He just laughed and strode into the hotel like he owned it.

A girl was giving Poet a tiny knitted doll of himself, and he was grinning as he held it up so the girl could take a photo of them all together. Poet's fans were my favorite. They were an unproblematic bunch. He thanked her again, and she flushed so red, I wondered if she'd pass out.

Knight and Hero saw him move toward the hotel and quickly cut off their interactions too, waving and being friendly until they made it to the safety of the foyer. I stepped over to the concierge desk, sorting out everything we needed to check in.

Ushering them all over to the elevator, I hit the button for the right floor and breathed a sigh of relief. I'd get Whitt to chew out the hotel for the breach of security later.

As soon as the door closed, Royal grabbed Charlotte, pinning her to the elevator wall. She yelped in surprise. He kissed her hard, and she gripped his shoulders as if she was holding on for dear life.

Soon, she was letting out tiny moans, and like he was waiting for them, Royal dragged his lips away. "I just turned down a quick fuck in the lobby bathroom for you, Toy. At least Whitt can't bitch about me holding up my end of the bargain." He dropped her back to her feet, and she gaped at him.

The elevator doors opened, and he strode out. I just shook my head. *What a dick.* I gave Hero the door keys. "I'll take Charlotte down to Whitt and Tricia's room."

He kissed her cheek and stepped out. As the door slid shut on us, Charlotte huffed out a breath. "Regrets?" I asked once more, and she shot me a look that was pure venom.

"No. Stop asking. I'm not going to change my mind."

I shrugged. I didn't even know if I wanted her to quit anymore. It was just a reflex. "Just doing my job, firecracker. I'd encourage you to wear a mask outside of the tour bus from now on. Royal just threw you onto the map. People will deep dive into your life, so keep your face covered. I'll see if I can't get Helen to make you a mask that's more comfortable."

She slumped back against the wall. "I know he's your friend, but he's also kind of an asshole."

A laugh slipped out, and I swallowed it down. "You're not wrong. It's only a few months of hiding, and then you can do whatever the hell you want with your life. There are protocols in place that we use for the guys, so we'll just implement them with you too. Stay on the bus as much as possible otherwise, especially if you find the mask claustrophobic." I sighed, because this whole situation had the potential to fuck up her life, and she didn't even know it. "If they find out who you are, you'll always be linked to these guys."

Some women wanted that, but I got the impression that Charlotte wasn't like that. That could've just been wishful thinking on my behalf, though. Because I wanted her too.

Fuck me.

SEVENTEEN

CHARLOTTE

I WINCED as Tricia poked at my cheekbone. "It seems to be healing up nicely. Any headaches, distorted vision, ringing in your ears?"

I didn't point out that I'd spent a disproportionate amount over the last couple of days blindfolded. "No, I'm fine. My face isn't even that sore anymore, though my ribs ache at times."

"You were lucky," she tsked, checking my eyes.

I wasn't lucky. She didn't know the full extent of what it had been like to live with Tom. "I was desperate."

Tricia nodded, sitting back to look up at my face. "Are you adjusting okay? Whitt's offer of a ten grand severance still applies. Phoenix is probably far enough away for you to start again."

Phoenix was probably far enough away, but ten grand wasn't nearly enough. I needed to create a whole new life, and I was going to need way more than that.

Maybe I could fly to Canada, or Costa Rica. Get out of the States altogether and start fresh somewhere nicer. Or somewhere with snow. I'd never seen snow.

"It's fine. The guys are lovely."

Tricia raised an eyebrow. "No one has ever called them lovely. Except maybe Poet. He's a sweet kid."

We talked about contraception, in the world's most awkward conversation, and she checked the contraceptive rod in my arm. She also drew some blood to send away for an STI panel and casually dropped into conversation that she'd done the same for the guys.

Was it against the rules for her to tell me that?

I huffed a bitter sound. This whole thing was probably a little illegal.

As if to make my point, Whitt appeared. He looked harried, and his thumbs were flying across his phone screen. Noticing me, he looked up. "Everything okay?"

Tricia nodded, putting a small circle bandaid where she'd just removed the needle. "Fine. Just finishing up. Charlotte's healing well."

He nodded, as if he gave a fuck. "Good, good." He pulled an envelope from his back pocket. "We thought it might be best to pay you in cash, as you left the field with your bank account details blank."

I felt the flush on my cheeks rise up, but I took the envelope of money. "I've always worked for cash. My father said paying tax made you a communist," I joked. My father was an uneducated meth head, and that was probably his least politically incorrect opinion.

Tom hadn't believed I needed money, let alone a

bank account. He'd promised he'd provide everything I ever wanted. Unfortunately, he couldn't give me the one thing I wanted more than anything but had never had: safety.

And love. But mostly safety.

I didn't tell these people that, though. They looked like they were well off—upper middle class, for sure. They wouldn't understand at all.

Whitt rolled his eyes. "Get a bank account, kid. You can't keep that much money under your pillow."

I nodded and stood. Tricia rose too, leading me to the door. "I'll let you know the results. If anything shows up positive, I'd encourage you to tell the guys. If you don't, I'll be obligated to do it, and no one wants the sex talk from someone old enough to be their mom. If there's nothing bad in there, I'll also let you know, and then it's up to you what forms of extra contraception you choose to use."

Man, talk about awkwardness. I grabbed my mask and pulled it back into place, glad to hide the flush of my cheeks once more. Nodding at the two of them, I took the room key Whitt handed to me.

"You're the room two doors down. Shep is next door, if you have any problems. The room is paid up for the next two days, so enjoy it. Shower in a full-size bathroom. Sleep on a full-sized bed. Have some privacy. Someone will bring over your bag for you, if you'd like."

I chewed on my lower lip, breathing through the sensation in my chest. Relief. "Thanks."

When I got to the room, I stepped into the silence and flopped down onto the bed. Pulling my mask off, I set it down beside me. With shaky hands, I opened the envelope. Immediately, all the air in my lungs hissed out. A fat stack of hundreds looped in a rubber band sat nestled in that yellow envelope. Pulling it all out, I counted it.

Not because I thought Whitt would screw me, but because it just didn't feel right. It felt like Whitt was going to knock on the door and ask for it back, like he'd given me someone else's wad of cash. He'd just handed me three thousand dollars, like it was lunch money.

Laughter bubbled up from my chest and echoed around the room. I laughed and laughed, and I knew it sounded hysterical, but there was no one here to care. No one to tell me to shut the fuck up. No one to glare at me disapprovingly. No one to take my money and buy coke with it. And all I had to do was have the best sex of my life.

I wasn't sure if this was something I was supposed to thank God for, but man, I was throwing out my thanks all over the place.

Dear Jesus, thank you for putting me in the way of a band of kind, somewhat degenerate men who'll give me money to blow them.

Amen.

Whitt was right, though; I needed a bank account, because there was no way I'd feel comfortable carrying around this much cash. First thing tomorrow, I'd find a bank and take my first steps toward independence for good.

After taking a long shower and napping for a solid three hours, a knock at the door woke me. Looking through the peephole, I saw it was Shep. I was dressed only in a t-shirt and underwear, but whatever. The guy had seen me visiting the "Eiffel Tower," so he'd probably get over seeing me in my underwear.

Opening the door, I stood to the side. "Hey."

His eyes dropped to my legs, then quickly back to my face. "I brought you some stuff, and also a phone. Having to come down here like your bellboy is annoying."

Leaving the door hanging open, I moved back into the room. "Thank you. I appreciate it."

Kill 'em with kindness. I'd like to say that my grandma had always said that, but she hadn't. She'd smoked so much, she sounded like a chainsaw, and the only thing she'd ever said to me when she was alive was, "Get out of the fucking way. I can't see my shows!"

Shep's eyes snagged on my face, and I felt like he was trying to drink in my features. He lingered in the doorway, and I quickly found my pants and dragged them on so he'd stop being weird.

"I know you just said you don't want to be my bellboy, but I was wondering if I could ask a favor. Just a little one." He raised a single eyebrow, but didn't shoot me down immediately. "I need to open a bank account, and I don't feel right carrying around that much money by myself. Could you, maybe, take me to the bank please?"

His jaw tensed. "How do you get to what, twenty-one? Twenty-two? And you still don't have a bank account?"

I shook my head. I didn't want to explain how I'd relied on Tom for money. How he used to give me an "allowance." Before that, I'd simply had no money, so who needed a bank account? It was all so embarrassing now; I didn't want to admit it out loud.

"I just don't. Don't worry about it. I'll go myself." I didn't need him. I didn't need anyone. I'd stuff it down my bra or something. It would be fine. I turned away from him and moved toward the only window. It overlooked a brick wall, but I'd pretend there was something interesting out there until he left.

A hand on my arm had me spinning back toward him. "Don't turn away from me and pout. Just *tell* me I hurt your feelings. Use your words, because no one will stop to try and figure out what you want. Not in this life." He was so close that I could see the flecks of gold in his brown eyes. "I'll take you. You're right to be worried about carrying around that much cash. My number is programmed in that phone. It's got a pay-as-you-go sim in it, but you can switch it out at the end, if you want a clean break."

I could buy a hundred phones at the end, if I wanted. My current phone was several models below this, so it was already an upgrade.

"Thanks. Again," I whispered, because he hadn't stepped back. His warmth was seeping into my chest, and I couldn't drag my eyes away from his face.

Rising up on my toes, I brushed my lips across his. It was stupid. My brain screamed that I was being an idiot, but I couldn't help it. Maybe it was some kind of savior worship. Maybe it was purely attraction, but when he kissed me back, I melted into it.

I just wanted this moment of no expectations. His lips were soft and full, and his hands hovered just above my cheeks, like touching me would make this something more. We didn't touch anywhere else but our lips, and he was kissing me like wanted to catalog every moment.

I was helpless to resist. He was strong and safe. He made me *feel* safe. It didn't even matter that trying to find safety in men was the reason I was in this situation to begin with.

I wanted to wrap myself around him, like poison ivy curling around a solid oak. The problem was eventually I would cling to him too hard, dragging him down with me, poisoning everything I'd worked for and everyone who'd helped me in the process.

"Charlotte," he breathed, stepping back when I couldn't. He straightened to his full height, and I watched the emotions run across his face. Desire. Guilt. Need. Anger. Like an old-fashioned silent film, he was unable to shield his emotions from me as they played over his features.

He took a shuddering inhale, and the walls seemed

to immediately snap back down on everything. A blank expression looked back at me, and I mourned the loss of the Shep who had kissed me. Because I knew that he'd never let himself get into this position again. I'd have this small taste and no more.

He turned toward the door and left silently, the soft snick of the lock feeling more devastating than it should.

EIGHTEEN

KNIGHT

"MAYBE WE SHOULD ADD bagpipes to the next album," I told Hero quietly, but he just raised an eyebrow at me. "It worked for AC/DC."

We were at the Musical Instrument Museum as just us. Not as masked band members. Not as part of the tour. Just because we wanted to go. Well, Hero and I had wanted to go. Poet and Royal were at a baseball game, probably dying in the heat. I didn't like sports much, but I'd heard amazing things about this place, so I'd wanted to check it out.

Hero was playing the theremin, and I could already see him trying to figure out how to shoehorn it into the current setlist. We both loved experimenting with new sounds.

"We aren't AC/DC," he replied. "I don't look good in schoolboy shorts."

We'd been at this museum for hours, and I was

pretty sure I could still spend a few more. We had to write a new album, and this place was basically a mecca of inspiration. My phone was filled with notes and sound clips that I'd take back to the others. We were established enough that we could be more experimental now, and the fans would come along for the ride.

I felt people's eyes lingering, and I gritted my teeth. We both had baseball caps pulled low over our faces. Even though I wasn't worried about being recognized as the rhythm guitarist of The Daymakers, none of us were without our own form of fame. Or perhaps infamy would be a better term.

Hero was the son of two of the most selfish socialites ever to be given a trust fund. His grandfather had run a lucrative meat-packing business, and had wanted to hand it over to his only son. Unfortunately, the son hated anything that even looked like responsibility. He'd knocked up the third daughter of a cosmetic company giant while on holiday in Belize. They'd been forced to get married, then pawned Hero off onto a grandfather who'd hated what he symbolized. Failure.

He'd shipped Hero off to boarding school, which was where I'd met him. Where we'd all met, except Shep. Hero's grandfather had started to groom him to take over the business, but had died before he reached twelve. So Hero's dad still got the business, but quickly sold it and spent every waking moment snorting drugs and throwing parties. Not like the parties my parents had thrown—far more detrimental to both their health, and Hero's.

And for me to think it was bad, you know it was seriously fucked. My upbringing wasn't sunshine and roses, but it wasn't filled with neglect either.

It had been a big scandal for years, and even now, the tabloids liked to put him in articles about the world's most attractive nepo babies. Occasionally, someone recognized him from this magazine or that. But we generally tried to stay out of the public eye, which was way easier when you spent every night in a mask.

We moved through the exhibits, up to the modern music displays. There was one there for Royal's dad's band, which was probably why Royal hadn't wanted to come. Royal hated his dad, though not enough to give up music.

I paused, watching the small movie of his dad performing. You couldn't deny genetics. Royal looked like his dad and moved like his dad—hell, he even sounded like his dad. Fortunately, he wasn't a cunt like his dad. Not often, anyway. The guy had been an A-grade selfish prick back when Royal was younger. He'd mellowed a bit now he'd retired from the music scene, but the damage was done.

I looked over at Hero. "Should we set it on fire?" I murmured from the side of my mouth, and he chuckled.

"Tempting."

We stayed another couple of hours at the museum, before catching a rideshare back to the hotel. I wondered what Charlotte was doing. I'd had dreams about her every night since spit-roasting her with Royal. I wanted to be inside her more than anything—if it was half as good as her mouth, I was in for a treat.

"Are you and Poe going to fuck around with Lottie?" I asked Hero lightly as we sat in the back of the rideshare, keeping my voice down, though the guy in the front was blasting French hip-hop so loudly, it was a wonder he could hear anything.

Hero shrugged. "We talked about it. We're both open to the idea. Me and Poe aren't exclusive or anything."

Yeah, maybe, but there was no doubt in my mind that they fucking loved each other. More than they loved us, anyway.

"Doesn't mean you're not interested in this girl," I needled. I wanted to know where he really stood, and Hero was a hard one to pin down.

He slid his eyes toward me, flicking them from me to the driver, before sighing. "I am. She's interesting. Different…"

"Hot as fuck?"

He snorted. "Exactly. The arrangement doesn't sit right with me, though." He shrugged again. "It feels like exploitation."

I heard what he was saying, but I wasn't sure which of us was being exploited. It had been her idea; we definitely hadn't manipulated her into it. Hell, if anything, Shep had tried to manipulate her *out* of it.

Why would I resist accepting the thing she was so freely offering? Or, not so freely I guess, given she was being paid an insane amount of money to fuck us. I'd had my lawyers look the contract over too, and the Cliffsnotes version was insane. Six figures for silence was a lot of money.

I spread my thighs wider, letting my head fall back against the headrest. "Yeah, but that's because you're thinking of her as some poor, unfortunate soul. She wanted this. She searched it out. She put forward the idea. You're infantilizing her just because she's a woman. If she were a man, and we were an all-girl group, would you still feel the same?"

"Infantilizing is a big word for you. Was it the word of the day on that phone app?" Hero teased, but he pointedly didn't answer my question. He looked out the window, and I'd known him long enough to know he was probably turning the question over in his brain. He was the quietest of us all, the being seen and not heard mantra still heavily ingrained from when he was a kid.

The rideshare tore into the drop zone of the hotel, and I pulled my cap down as low as I could without being conspicuous. There were The Daymakers fans loitering around, but none really paid attention to the two dudes pulling up in a Toyota Corolla. People expected black SUVs and super tinted windows.

We made it to our room without a hitch, and I sent a picture of Hero playing the harp to the group chat. Poe sent one back of Royal with a beer in his hand, and some pretty girl trying to chat him up.

The fucker couldn't go two steps without someone

trying to climb on his dick. Didn't matter if he was the masked singer or the damn golden boy. He was just stupidly attractive, meaning women—and men—flocked to him like moths to a flame.

Tell him to keep it in his pants.

POET

Pretty sure she might just hump his leg anyway.

I laughed and threw my phone down. Walking to the nightstand, I grabbed my mask.

Hero watched me, his face impassive. "You're going to visit her?"

His tone was disapproving, and I narrowed my eyes at him. I didn't need his judgment. "Yes. You're welcome to come and make sure she wants it as much as I do, though I'd like to think you have more faith in me than to believe I'd have sex with anyone if it wasn't one hundred percent consensual. She'll be a fucking *joyful* participant, and I promise to make her come at least twice before I even fuck her."

He blew out a breath, displacing his fringe, and I could see the temptation on his face. Finally, he shook his head. "Nah, not without Poet."

I rolled my eyes at him, flipping him off as I left. Yeah, sure, they "weren't exclusive." They were so much a couple, it was almost sickening. They spooned, for goodness' sake. You didn't spoon with a person overnight if you didn't have feelings for them. You hit it and quit it, just moved on to the next piece of ass who wanted a ride on your disco stick.

Taking the elevator down, I told the rest of the guys in the group chat, just in case she went full Carrie and murdered me in the bathtub to sell my organs. Or in case they wanted to join me later. That was something Shep had drilled into us, right back when we'd been angry teens. Always take someone with you; you're safer in pairs.

Especially Poet, though he hated the thought of being weaker than us. Still, we'd almost lost him once, and no one was willing to take that chance again. Though the threats were no longer getting our ass kicked by bullies or thugs on the boardwalk, and more like some girl stealing condoms or trying to unmask us.

Which meant I'd sometimes had to stand outside the dressing room while Royal nailed one or more groupies. It was also why we were so comfortable sharing, because we'd all had to get real comfortable with fucking in front of each other real quick.

Knocking on the door to Lottie's room, I put my finger over the peephole. I wasn't going to be responsible for her losing her money.

"Who is it?" she called through the door.

I looked left and right, leaning closer to the door so I didn't have to yell my name so loud. I already missed being on the tour bus, which was unusual. If we didn't have to sneak around with masks and bullshit, this would be much easier.

Maybe we should abandon the need for masks and

just let her see our faces. The NDA would still hold, and I could watch her face as she came on my tongue.

A moment later, she flipped open the door, the silk mask from Royal over her eyes. It annoyed me more than it should. She was in another little skirt, this one tight and black, with a band tee tucked into the front.

Stepping into the room, I closed the door and pulled my own balaclava on. "Take yours off. I want to see your pretty face as I fuck you, Lottie."

She removed the silk mask, and I could see her smile. "What, no small talk? I'm shocked, Knight. Woo a girl first."

I knew she was teasing me, but it did make me feel a little guilty. Watching her ass as she moved into her hotel room, I noticed she had paperwork spread out on her bed.

I sat in the armchair by the window. "What's that?"

She grinned, and it hit me in the chest like a thunderbolt. "Bank account details. Shep took me to get a bank account and deposit my first paycheck."

I tried not to think about the fact she was getting paid to have sex with me, not because she wanted it. Though, I didn't think she'd been faking the orgasms we'd given her the other night.

Kicking off my shoes, I propped my feet on her bed. "You know, it's an unwritten rule that you have to blow your first paycheck on frivolous things. I bought a bike and way too much cocaine."

She frowned hard. "You guys do drugs?"

I mean, this was rock and roll. Everyone did drugs.

Well… "Not anymore. One of our support acts died a few years ago in a freak accident. Walked out in front of a car, right in front of his heavily pregnant girlfriend. Died right there on the scene. It shook us, and we all got clean. Life is so fucking short—you could lose it in a blink of an eye, you know? I don't want to spend it in a numb haze."

That shit had fucked us all up at the time. Even now, I still thought about Jackson Harper and his girlfriend. She'd had the baby, I knew that, but then she'd kind of disappeared off the face of the planet.

Charlotte chewed her full lower lip, making me want to do it too. But she was right. She deserved conversation before sex, and maybe I also wanted to know her a little.

"I don't know. I've never had money before. I'll probably save it."

I scoffed. "Boring. Come on, Lottie. There has to be something you want to buy. Something you've always wanted, but it seemed too frivolous? Or something you want to try? Collect? A dream? An interest? Something!" Her cheeks flushed. Oh, there *was* something. "Okay, spill."

"I'd like to make book nooks."

I blinked. "What?"

She went even pinker, and I wanted to bend her over and spank her until her ass went that same pretty shade of pink. It might be my favorite color now. I dragged my thoughts back to what she was saying.

"It's stupid." She slid her eyes away from me, and something clenched in my chest.

"It's not stupid. Show me."

She pulled out her phone, bringing up a shopping website. I mentally added buying her a tablet onto my to-do list, because how could you see anything on this thing?

Poet kept saying I needed glasses, but those weren't very punk rock.

I moved over to the bed and sat beside her, looking at the different kits. Fairyland ones, library ones, ones like little laneways. There were nooks themed to particular book series, like Sherlock Holmes, and ones that were just little glimpses into everyday life. I had to admit, they were kind of cute.

"But what do you do with them once they're done?"

Her tongue dipped out to wet her lips. "One day, I'd like to have a home with a library. I'd put them in there."

"You like books?"

"It was a way to escape. Pretend to be someone, anyone but me."

Fuck me. This girl.

I wrapped an arm around her shoulders. "One day, you'll have the best library, with all your favorite books and these fiddly little nook things, like tiny wonderlands." I rested my cheek on the top of her head. "Show me more. The garden one's my favorite so far. Do you think they have any music ones?"

That was how I found myself scrolling through a bunch of craft projects, instead of fucking the beautiful woman beside me. I couldn't even bring myself to regret it.

NINETEEN
CHARLOTTE

KNIGHT WAS STRETCHED out on my bed, with me next to him, propped up against the headboard. He'd already convinced me to buy two book nook kits. One was a library, with tiny bookshelves and a curling set of stairs. A cat and an armchair sat in front of the fire. It was sweet. The other one was a music room filled with guitars and a piano, band posters on the walls and a gramophone with records in the back. It was really cute, and Knight had insisted he'd help me with that one.

He had his phone out, scrolling through the Gram. His shirt had ridden up his stomach a little, showing me the light trail of hair that led down to a dick I knew intimately.

I wanted to kiss him.

"Knight?"

"Mmm?"

"I'm going to kiss you, but I promise I won't take your mask off all the way."

He sucked in a breath, his fingers tightening around his phone. "Okay."

I moved down the bed, throwing a leg over his body until I was straddling his waist. Resting my hands either side of his face, I pushed up the clinging fabric, revealing a strong jaw with a shadow of facial hair. A small dimple in his chin that I swooped down and kissed. Parted lips in the softest pink.

Holding his mask in place with my hands, I leaned forward and kissed him. It felt almost forbidden to see him like this, to taste him like this. The kiss started sweet, but as his hands moved to my thighs, it got more heated. I thrust my tongue into his mouth, and his tangled with mine.

I was in control, but I had a feeling I wouldn't be for much longer. Even now, he was digging his hands into the back of my hair, holding my head firmly to his as he took over the kiss, fucking me with his tongue until I was grinding against his abs. I tried to move down the bed so I could taste him, but he had other ideas. Breaking our kiss, he started to drag my body higher, up toward his face.

He must have seen my panicked look, because he smirked up at me. "I want you to ride my face, baby girl. I promised Hero I'd make you come at least twice before I get to bury myself in that wet little pussy. And I'm a man of my word."

With that, he held me up as he slid down the bed,

until I was kind of sitting on his chest, nothing but his head poking out between my thighs. "Knight, I've never…" Guys had hardly ever gone down on me, let alone wanted me to sit on their face. They hadn't exactly been there for my pleasure.

He grinned up at me, hooking his fingers in my underwear and pulling them down my legs. I shuffled off his chest so I could remove them completely, and as soon as I was done, Knight pulled me straight back onto his chest. "Were you ever one of the girls who wanted a pony?" I shrugged, because who wasn't? "Call me Seabiscuit and just ride me."

I couldn't help but giggle. "That's an oddly specific kink, Seabiscuit, but… giddy-up?"

His laughter puffing against my wet center made me gasp. Then he dragged me forward, placed me over his mouth and jammed his tongue inside me. He rocked me until I was literally riding his face. Well, it felt like it anyway.

His nose kept nudging my clit, and his tongue speared me, swirling and stroking until I was lost to everything but the sensation. If he suffocated and died, he'd made his own decision to do so.

He moved my hips down so he could suck on my clit, making me slam my hands onto the wall just so I didn't faceplant into it. *Holy shit.* I felt like we were working together, both of us chasing those gasps of pleasure, my thighs tensing and shaking as I ground down harder and harder. His fingers were definitely going to leave little bruise marks on my ass.

I threw back my head and came hard, gripping the headboard so I didn't fucking pass out. He sucked my soul out through my clit, and I wasn't sure I was ever going to be the same.

Sliding out from beneath me completely, Knight ran a hand down my spine, kissing my shoulders and back. Further down he went, until he was biting my ass, hard. Then he sucked the spot gently, and I moaned some unholy noise.

"We aren't done yet, angel. I promised Hero two."

He pushed down my shoulders, so my ass was in the air and my face was buried in the pillows. It was my turn not to care if I suffocated, as his talented tongue slid its way back inside me. His hand moved between my thighs, and he began gently tapping my sensitized clit in time with the motions of his tongue. My back curled as the pillow muffled my cries. He hummed low, and that was it, I shattered once more.

Fuck me. I wasn't ready for this. This pleasure. This much sensation.

"Look at that beautiful cunt, fluttering just for me." He curled back over my body, lifting me slightly as he notched his cock against my entrance. He kissed the back of my neck, then slid home, and the relief I felt was a full-body release. My head fell forward, but Knight kept his arms around my waist as he moved in and out of me. "You're going to give me all your orgasms, aren't you, good girl? Look at you, trembling in my arms, all that pleasure just for me."

He finally let me slump forward as he gripped my

hips, rolling his own until he was hitting places inside me that I didn't even know I had.

"Knight. Fuck... *Please,*" I begged. I didn't want him to stop. I didn't want this to *ever* stop.

He wrapped his hand in my long hair again, close to the scalp, and the tug was the perfect amount of pain to push my pleasure so high, I crested right over the edge, down into a puddle of pleasure.

I screamed his name as my orgasm coursed through me, and he rode it out. "That's it, baby. Such a good girl." He gripped my hips. "Now it's my turn." He pounded into me, his hands on my hips the only thing keeping me upright. He slammed home, the wet, slapping sound echoing around the room until he came hard, emptying himself inside me.

Finally, he let me fall to the bed, my muscles losing all ability to hold me up as I turned into a bundle of happy endorphins. He rolled to the left, flopping down next to me.

"Lottie, that was a fucking biblical experience."

I put my fist up, and he bumped it. "Hallelujah."

We'd lain there beside each other until I went to clean myself up. Knight was snoring when I finally made it back to the bed, and I just curled up beside him, appreciating for a moment that I wasn't alone.

Even with Tom, I'd always felt alone. He'd stay out late at work, though sometimes, he'd smell like perfume, which I'd write off as one of the female associates. When he was home, he still wasn't really there with me. He was working, or playing videogames with his friends, or on his phone, ignoring me. At the beginning, I hadn't cared; I was just happy not to be by myself anymore. To have someone else to rely on.

Until I couldn't rely on him anymore.

At least with Knight, it might not be forever, but there was an ease in that. I knew what he wanted from me. I knew my expectations. I knew my expiration date. All of those things I could control.

"You're thinking way too hard for someone I just did my best fucking with," Knight grumbled, and my lips curled into a smile.

I rolled toward him, tucking my knees up toward my chest. "Not even your skills can shut off my brain, Sir."

He groaned. "Don't call me Sir, unless you want the consequences, pretty girl," he warned, and as much as I wanted to call him out on it, he was a girthy guy and had just fucked me like he owned me.

I winked saucily at him instead, making him rumble a deep laugh. I wanted to bathe in that sound—let it wash over my skin and cleanse my soul from all the muck I'd wallowed in.

He bumped my foot with his. "What are you thinking about?"

I shrugged, too embarrassed to actually confess my self-pitying thoughts. "Wondering what I'll do when I reach the end of the tour."

"It's enough money to last you a couple of years, if

you're careful with it." He stretched, rolling his shoulders. "Enough time to give you a chance to chase your dreams. Or find something you want to do with your life. Other than making book nooks, is there anything you wanted to be when you grew up?"

Well, looks like the pity party was coming out to play, whether I liked it or not.

"Not poor. Not hungry. Very basic things." I didn't look at him. I didn't want to see his face. "I wanted to work at the Post Office, because the idea of getting packages every day was exciting. I don't think I ever really had a dream that mattered. I don't have many skills outside of cleaning and waitressing. I never went to college. I'm starting with nothing, but I don't care. I can figure that stuff out later."

He grabbed me up in his arms, pulling me onto his chest. "You have time. You have fire in your heart. You deserve to do whatever makes you happy."

I huffed. "You don't know anything about me, except what I can do naked."

He stilled, and his hands landed on my shoulders. I thought for a moment he'd push me off, but he just lifted me off his chest a little. "You're right. Come on, we'll go hang out with the guys and you can tell us all about Little Lottie Lochrin."

"That's a lot of alliteration."

"Like all good superheroes, babe." He kissed my neck. "Or the best villains." He kissed across my collarbone. "Maybe you're my kryptonite, because you make me feel weak."

My laugh at his bad line turned into a moan as he sucked my nipple into his mouth. He looked up at me, his eyes laughing. Letting go of my nipple with a pop, he waggled his eyebrows at me.

"One more?"

I grinned, my heart doing a weird flip-flop in my chest. "Just one more."

TWENTY

HERO

POET AND ROYAL arrived back at the hotel, half-drunk on watered-down ballgame beer. They ordered pizza and slumped around the room, talking shit. I loved seeing them so happy and carefree. This freedom wasn't something we got often on tour. It was usually all publicity and shows, personas and fantasies.

I helped Poet get his prosthetic off, because he was tipsy enough that his fingers were clumsy.

"Where's Knight?" Royal asked, slumping back on his bed. Unlike Vegas, we had two queen beds in this room, and we had to share. The label had been resistant to getting us two rooms, mostly because of the expense, but also for security. Us moving between rooms opened us up to being seen and outed.

I shrugged, avoiding Poet's eyes. "He went down to visit Charlotte." Even saying that made me feel gross. Like we held her in some form of sexual slavery.

Poet ran his fingers through my shortish hair, but I

couldn't help but feel guilty about the way I'd considered Knight's invitation to join him.

Royal huffed and stared at the ceiling. "Guess she's earning her money."

Poet snapped his head toward our fearless leader. "Don't talk about her like she's a hooker, Royal."

"Why do you even care? You don't know her. It's basically what she is anyway, so why be politically correct about it? It's the oldest profession in the world—isn't that what they say? Maybe she's honored to participate in such a tried and true career."

He was being a smarmy fuck, but I'd known him long enough to know he was only a prick when he was conflicted. When he didn't care about someone, he treated them much the same way you treated a piece of furniture. There for a purpose, but not something to give a fuck about.

We usually called him on his crap, and normally, it was Poet who'd say something. He tended to act as the conscience for us all. The beating heart of the band. Plus, he could say shit to Royal that would have gotten me punched in the face.

"Why are you practically neon green with jealousy if you don't care?" Poet snarked back. Royal didn't answer, and Poet smirked down at me. "How was the Musical Instrument Museum?" he asked softly, and I smiled up at him. This was what I loved about Poet. He made you feel like everything you did mattered, like your opinion was the most important one in the world.

"It was amazing. Next time we're in Phoenix, we

should go again. Also, how do you feel about adding the mandolin to a track or two?" I teased, and he chuckled.

He was saved from having to learn the mandolin by the sound of laughter in the hallways. I paused, and I could hear the thump of someone banging into the wall.

Then I heard Knight's booming laugh. Shit, was he drunk too?

I moved to the door and pulled it open to see a giggling Charlotte, blindfolded, and a sparkling-eyed Knight behind her, holding her shoulders as he directed her down the hall and toward our door.

"Left, Lottie. Left. No, your other left," he said on a gasping breath. "Grab her. She can't tell her left from her right."

Charlotte huffed as I reached out and grabbed her hand, pulling her into the room before they drew a crowd. "I can so. It's just disorientating being blindfolded."

"Babe, just because you can't see doesn't change the direction of left and right," Knight teased, wrapping his arms around her waist and carrying her further into the room. "Lottie is coming to hang out with us, no strings attached." The challenge was clear on his face as he waited for someone to protest. "If she's going to be with us on tour for the next three months, then we should get to know each other."

Poet, as always, played mediator. "Luckily, we just ordered pizza. I hope you like meat."

"Anecdotal evidence would say she does," Royal remarked snidely, but Charlotte just laughed.

She flipped the bird at him—well, at the wall to the left of him—and grinned. "Lucky for you, asshole."

Moving her to my bed, Knight dropped her down near the pillows. I hated that she had to be blindfolded. Or that we had to be masked. It was annoying as fuck. I was sure we'd figure it all out, but until we trusted her more, she'd stay blind.

There was an awkward silence, until Royal, of all people, broke it. "Shep said you opened up a new bank account?"

She rolled her eyes. "You guys gossip like old ladies. Yep, I'm finally a legitimate member of society, with a bank account and everything."

"Lottie needs ideas for what she can do once she's finished touring with us. Other than settle somewhere and be boring."

She took a swipe at Knight, missing completely. "Boring would be *nice.* I don't think I've ever experienced boring."

Knight just made a disapproving noise and wrapped his arms around her waist, pulling her close. He was a lot like Poet in the sense that touch was his love language, but he wasn't normally this hands on. I looked between them with a frown; they'd obviously fucked. Charlotte's hair was still a little wild, and she had a beard rash on her chin. But maybe Knight was holding her a little tighter than necessary?

If he got possessive, then we had trouble. A lot of it.

No one wanted a woman to come between the band. No one wanted their band to be Yoko Ono'd.

The beer was still making Poet smiley. "What do you like doing?"

"She wants to make these weird little book nook things. Actually, they look pretty cool," Knight said, his cheeks flushing as he smirked.

Royal hadn't missed any part of Knight's new demeanor, and his frown told me he wasn't nearly drunk enough to forget about it. *Fuckity fuck.*

Poet rolled onto his side, his eyes roaming over Charlotte. "So you like crafts and you have a pretty cool sense of style. Maybe you could help Helen out in the costuming section. I can't imagine sitting around the tour bus will be fun for eleven weeks. She's one of the best in the business, and she told me she likes you."

Actually, Helen had threatened to chop off our balls if we hurt Charlotte, like she had to Elwood Spire in 1973 when he got too handsy with one of her friends. The way she'd creepily smiled and whispered, "Elwood sings soprano now," in a monotone was probably going to haunt my nightmares.

Charlotte tilted her head, her lips slightly parted, and I wanted to kiss her so badly. "You think she'd agree?"

I shrugged, then realized she couldn't see the gesture. "Couldn't hurt to ask."

I'd ask Helen too. She was technically employed by the label, but we had a little sway with her. The wardrobe Charlotte had pulled together from thrift shopping was actually pretty impressive.

The pizza finally arrived, and we spread the boxes out on the beds. We put the TV on low, while Royal strummed Knight's guitar. Normally, Knight would be plastered, but he was too busy feeding Charlotte bites of his pizza. I wasn't sure she realized they were sharing, but if they'd done what I suspected they'd done earlier, sharing a little saliva was the least of their issues.

"How did you guys meet?" Charlotte asked between bites. "You know each other so well." Her thighs parted, meaning I could see up her skirt to her silky purple underwear. I wanted to crawl beneath it so bad, my dick literally ached.

Instead of giving in to the impulse, I answered her question. "Boarding school. Poet and Knight were roommates. Royal and I were in the same classes, and I was the only one who could tolerate his pompous ass."

Charlotte grinned, like she could see the unimpressed look Royal was giving me. "You mean he wasn't Mr. Popularity? I find that hard to believe."

She wasn't wrong. Royal deserved his moniker. He'd held court over the cafeteria every day, a whole sea of sycophants trying to get closer to him and therefore his dad. In a world of banker brats and minor royalty, Royal had one thing that most of them wanted badly: celebrity status.

I suspected he'd been drawn to me because I legit didn't give a fuck who he was. I had seen what celebrity could produce, and it wasn't something I wanted for my life.

Thoughts of my parents dragged the rage I felt about my childhood to the surface. I took some deep breaths to push it back down, into the little box where it belonged. I wasn't that rejected little kid anymore. I wasn't rattling around a mansion with an old man who hated me and parents who pretended I didn't exist.

I had a family now, people who loved me, in the three guys in this room and Shep. I didn't need anyone else.

I tuned back in to hear Knight answering her. "Oh, Royal was popular all right. He got his dick sucked so many times in boarding school, it's a wonder it hasn't been worn down to a nub." He chewed his lip. He clearly wanted to say more, but held it back. We could only give her the vague backstory we told everyone. We met in school, started a band in Poet's garage, and that was it.

We couldn't say Royal's dad was a Rock & Roll Hall of Fame member.

We couldn't say Knight's parents were a famous actor and actress from the seventies.

We definitely couldn't tell her that Poet's dad had been a famous Formula One racer.

I never wanted her to know that I was the heir to a multi-million dollar trust fund fuelled by a meat-packing and luxury cosmetics company.

To her and the rest of the world, our friendship didn't exist. To the rest of the world, we were Royal,

Knight, Poet and Hero. The people we were before, and would be after, were ghosts until we were done with The Daymakers.

We all needed to remember that this wasn't a fairy-tale. The pauper couldn't get the prince. The ghost can't keep the girl in the end.

But as I watched her laugh while Knight told her a highly edited story about Poet stumbling in on Royal in the bathroom writing a teacher's phone number on the toilet door, promising a "good time," I found myself resenting my own advice.

TWENTY-ONE

CHARLOTTE

AFTER THE NIGHT in the hotel, eating pizza and pretending we were actually friends, I didn't see any of the guys for two days. They had a bunch of promotional stuff, including nightclub visits, intimate jam sessions for some charity, and morning show appearances.

I didn't really mind. The book nooks I'd ordered had arrived overnight, and I spent hours stooped over the small desk in the corner of my hotel room, patiently putting one together.

Patience was something I had. Poet also bought me his favorite fantasy series, and I was slowly binge-reading it. He insisted that I text him my blow-by-blow thoughts, and we'd been discussing different plot points.

It was nice having a friend, and I realized that I'd been missing uncomplicated friendships for so long. I'd never gotten close to anyone in school, because the whole town knew my dad cooked meth. Obviously, I hadn't realized that everyone knew until high school, but I never would have invited anyone over to my house to play anyway. Embarrassment wasn't something you grew out of when your dad was a bad guy.

Knight had created a group chat with the band and Shep, and added me in. It was reasonably quiet, but I appreciated the fact they were trying to make me feel less lonely, especially Knight and Poet.

Hero was standoffish, but pleasant enough. Royal was a dick, but I kind of liked that. I liked butting heads with him, and I suspected he did too. I would never admit that to the asshole, though.

The night of the Phoenix show came around all too fast, and soon I had to pack up my hotel room to move back onto the tour bus. I'd enjoyed the small reprieve of having my own space, but the trip from Phoenix to San Antonio was a long one, so we'd be on the tour bus for at least two days, probably more. There were three shows back to back in San Antonio, so at least we'd be there for a while. Shep had told me to leave my bags in my room, and a bellhop would have them shipped back to the arena.

Standing in the bathroom, I looked down at my outfit. I had sheer black tights under my cut-off shorts, chunky boots and my oversize The Daymakers shirt, tied with a hair tie at the back and tucked up into my bra. Dark red lipstick looked like blood on my lips.

The mask went back on, and I stepped back to look at myself. I'd transformed myself, and that would have to do. Grabbing my rucksack, I filled it up with what I could, leaving everything else packed in the tiny carry-on size suitcase.

A knock on my door told me I was out of time to second-guess my outfit. Tucking my hair behind my ears, I answered the door. Shep stood there, looking harried. His eyes took me in, and I could see them darken. I watched his throat bob, wondering if he was remembering our kiss too. He'd distanced himself since then, and I'd let him. I was already in enough trouble without falling for the forbidden fruit.

"Ready?"

I nodded, doing one more visual sweep of the room, before stepping out and handing him my room key. He led me back up to the guys' room silently, and the urge to make small talk rode me hard.

But I didn't. Shep was comfortable in the silence, and I wouldn't betray my nerves by being the one to open my mouth first.

A couple got onto the elevator with us as we went down, and the girl did a double-take at me, taking in my mask and my band shirt. They flicked to Shep, then back to me. She leaned in and whispered something to her boyfriend, and I didn't miss them subtly raise their phones to take a photo. Shep stepped between them and me, his body language telling them to fuck off without even having to look at them.

The doors opened on the guys' floor, and as the doors closed, I distinctly heard the girl say, "Was that Toy?"

My eyes darted to Shep. "*What* did she just say?"

He shook his head, striding down the hall, making me walk twice as fast to keep up. "We'll talk about it later. We have to leave now—the transport's almost at the front doors." He knocked on the door, and the guys all appeared.

Now I'd spent a little extra time with them, they could all be wearing completely different outfits and masks, and I'd know exactly who they were, even from a distance. Hero was the tallest, his body wide across the shoulders and narrow at the waist, but he wasn't muscley so much as rangy. Royal had the most conventionally attractive body, which he showcased in just tight enough clothes. Knight and Poet were close to the same height, but Knight was more solidly built than the rest of them. Thick thighs. Thick arms. Wide chest. That ass. I knew it all intimately now.

Poet wore baggy pants and was the most pale, but he was still fit as hell. He also walked with a limp, though it wasn't obvious unless you were looking for it.

"Let's go," Shep huffed, herding us all down the hallway, back into the elevator. Fortunately, no one else hopped in, and we rode it to the lobby. I hung back, but Hero pushed me so I was forced to walk in front of him.

"Don't want you getting lost in the crowd," he said softly into my ear, and when we stepped outside, I understood. Hero's hand stayed on my back, and Shep maneuvered us all into the van again. People yelled and screamed, but the guys just waved this time instead of stopping to talk to the fans.

The paparazzi were there this time too, and I could hear their shouted questions. "Who's the girl? Hero, is that your girlfriend?"

The rest of the questions blurred together, and soon I was in the van, Hero blocking the cameras with his large body behind me. Shep slammed the door shut, climbing into the passenger seat as Steve, the other security guy, pulled out into traffic.

"Seatbelts," Shep ordered.

I grinned, remembering Knight's quip on the way there. "Yes, Daddy," I purred back, and the groan that echoed around the van made me smile.

Shep's shoulders tensed, but when he looked over his shoulder at me, his face was alight with desire. "Do as you're told."

I winked, but did what he asked. Knight was laughing his ass off, and I grinned over at him. The mask made me bold, that was for sure.

The arena was about ten minutes away, which meant no one could escape my question. "So, a girl in the elevator called me Toy. Does anyone want to tell me why?"

They all looked at Royal. I should have known. "What? It's not my fault. Someone took photos of you going into the hotel with us, and the die-hards wanted to know who you were. Some girl said that I called you a toy, and here we are." He gave me that cocky damn smirk I wanted to slap right off his face. "So now you're Toy. We needed a moniker to protect your identity—may as well be this one, right?"

"Wrong!" Man, I was kind of pissed. I didn't want to be known as some band's toy, even if it wasn't really me. "Is it too late to change it?"

I looked at Hero, who shrugged. "Maybe if we formally introduce the idea of you. Some will continue to call you Toy, though, or whatever else." I had a feeling the other names wouldn't be quite so polite as Toy. "We'd have to pass it by the tour management, and probably the label. I don't know, Lottie. It might be easier to lean into it."

Poet had his head leaning against the wall, but he passed me his phone, open to the Gram. *#Daymaker-sToy* was trending. I gritted my teeth. There were pictures from cell phones of me being herded into the lobby by Shep. Others of just the guys and the captions speculating who the girl with The Daymakers was.

Some were guessing Knight's ex-girlfriend, posting a photo of the ex to compare. She was fucking beautiful. Had she gotten to see his face? Had she seen the other guys too? Obviously, since they'd had to pay her off not to talk.

Inadequacy rose up in my chest. God, if he was used to girls like that, he must have felt like he was slumming it with me. I didn't look anything like that. I couldn't do my makeup like that. I wasn't golden and beautiful, the way she was. She looked like sex personified.

I scrolled a little more, then passed the phone back to Poet. "Fuck."

He reached between the seats and squeezed my shoulder. "It's okay, Lottie. Shep will talk to management about it. If you're going to be around for three months, it's in their best interests to take control of the narrative."

I sucked in a deep, calming breath. Poet was right. I couldn't change this, so if it didn't go away, I would lean into it. I was already thinking of outfits I could wear to play off the Toy persona.

Knight reached over and gripped my hand. Having seen his ex, I firmly told my heart and my head to not read into the gesture. I was going to finish this tour without a broken heart, thank you very much.

I was also clearly delusional.

He squeezed gently. "If you could pick your name, what would it be?"

I shrugged. I had no idea. Honestly, Toy fit just as well as anything else. It was better than other things I'd been called in my life. Trash. Whore. Scum. Redneck.

"What about Dreamer?" Hero said softly. I turned to look at him, though all I could see was the soft hazel of his eyes behind the mask that was the scariest of all four.

Dreamer. Hadn't I always dreamed of something more? Dreamed of happiness and security? Big dreams that were finally coming true.

I gave him a lopsided smile. "I love it."

Shep looked at me over his shoulder again. "Dreamer it is. I'll talk to Whitt and the label."

Gratitude threatened to make me cry. The worst night of my life had set me free. Fate really did work in strange ways.

TWENTY-TWO

DREAMER

THE GUYS WENT off to do soundcheck, and I went down to visit Helen in costumes. Hero had insisted I should at least ask if she would mentor me. Lottie was a scared little baby, but Dreamer was someone braver than that.

She dared.

I found Helen in the back of one of the vans, muttering to herself as she ran fabric through the sewing machine. I knocked on the door. Racks of clothes ran down one side of the van.

"Hello, sweets. I see you're still in the mask."

I waved. "Hey. It's surprisingly comfortable. Thank you. Shep thinks I should wear it whenever I'm out of the bus."

Her lips tightened, and her eyes ran over me. "I see. And are you feeling okay about your situation? Because if not, I know a guy who knows a guy. Well, Vincenzo was a strongman for the mob in the sixties, but some skills don't age, you know. Including breaking the knees of little boys who don't show a lady the proper respect."

I blinked at her, because... the fuck? Then I shook my head vigorously. "No, they've been fine. I promise. Vincenzo can stay in retirement."

"Oh. Well, good. Never doubted them for a moment. What can I do for you?"

I shifted from foot to foot, because asking for help had never been something that sat well with me. "I was wondering, and it's completely okay if you say no, because I *know* you're super busy and honestly, it wouldn't help you at all—"

Helen raised an eyebrow. "Spit it out, girlie."

"Could you use someone to help out in the costume department? I mean, I have no experience, and if I get in the way, you can definitely tell me to get lost, no hard feelings, but I have steady hands and I'd really love to learn. And I don't want to be paid or anything, just the skills you could teach me would be amazing. And maybe, after the tour is over, I'd have something to show on my resume other than unskilled labor. Not that there's anything wrong with that." I personally thought hospitality and custodial work was woefully underpaid.

Helen waved a hand. "Of course not. When you work in the business I do, getting to know the house-keeping staff in hotels can be a lifesaver." She eyed me up and down. "Can you sew?"

"I was poor as shit. I can mend holes in just about

anything. But I've never made anything from scratch. I'm no seamstress."

"Can you follow direction?" I nodded. "And you don't want to be paid? Because there's nothing left in my budget for another person. Goodness knows I would've hired someone already if there was."

"No, ma'am."

"Free help? Sign me up." She thrust a black shirt at me. "Here, start by sewing the buttons back on this shirt. I swear on Hendrix's guitar that boy rips open his shirt every concert. If I have to sew one more button back on, I'm going to start stuffing them up his nose." She gave me a pin cushion and a little box of thread, then went back to sewing, muttering about viscose.

I sewed each button meticulously, tight enough to keep his shirt on, but if Royal ripped it open on stage, there would be no damage to the material. When that was done, she had me mend a hole in Poet's shirt, where he'd gotten it caught on a nail backstage in San Francisco.

As we worked, Helen talked. Her stories were all fantastical, but somehow they didn't seem improbable. From sleeping with a rockstar in the seventies and traveling around with his band like a muse, to when she'd traveled across Europe on a bus filled with choral nuns on some kind of exchange, after she lost her passport in Frankfurt.

Before I knew it, I was sitting at a little bench in front of a wall of tiny drawers. A blank half mask was placed in front of me.

"I haven't had time to make you your own mask, rather than Poet's cast-off. But now you're here, you can make your own. I suggest you start with the half mask, though I'll teach you how to make a full resin mask also."

I looked up at her. "Really?"

She patted my back. "What kind of mentor would I be if I didn't give you the full scope of the job? First, you're going to want to do a rough draft of what you want. Do you have any ideas?"

Excitement I hadn't felt in so long filled me as a design flew from my fingers, like it had just been waiting for the opportunity to be free.

My laminated pass tapped against my stomach as I moved backstage, past the security holding back the hordes. I was in my tight jeans and my long-sleeve crop top again, though if I sucked my stomach in, I didn't look quite so skeletal anymore. I guess that's what happened when I could eat what I liked and didn't have to work out for hours a day. I liked the soft curve of my hips, now that my hip bones didn't jut out viciously.

A murmur followed me through the crowd, and I kind of hated it, but at least I had the mask to hide behind. Maybe I'd try and do a full-face one sooner rather than later, so I could hide completely.

I spotted Shep arguing with one of the roadies, and I moved toward them. "I mean it, Bergman. If you hand him that guitar on stage, he'll hit you over the head with it. Find his Fender asap or there'll be a riot." The roadie, Bergman, rolled his eyes but talked frantically into his walkie-talkie.

I stopped in front of a stressed-looking Shep. "Need help?"

He shook his head. "No, Vegas fucked up the load out, so now nothing is where it's supposed to be. They can't find Knight's goddamn guitar, and he will absolutely throw a shit-fit. Musicians," he grunted, putting a hand on my lower back and propelling me forwards. "I'll take you out where the guys are."

His hand was firm and warm against the skin of my back, and I tried hard not to shiver. I saw the support act rushing toward the stage, looking harried. Roadies ran around like chickens without heads. Fans screamed as they filled up the arena.

It was alive in here, and I could see why people would become addicted to touring.

Shep knocked on the door quickly, before striding in. A girl I'd never met was there, putting skull makeup on the lower half of Royal's face. She sat on a small fold-up stool in between his thighs, and I resisted the urge to growl at her. Jealousy wasn't an emotion that I had the privilege to feel right now.

Knight bounced to his feet. "Dreamer, baby, you look like all my wet dreams all rolled into one. The name definitely suits," he purred, gripping my hips and dancing closer to me. It didn't even matter that Shep was at my back, Knight just wedged me between the two of them.

What a fantasy come to life that would be.

Only Royal was in his stage mask, the other guys just lazing around in what I liked to call their leisure masks—hand-painted spandex blend, according to Helen earlier today. She'd been explaining the differences between all the different masks the guys had. Apparently, they all had half masks, but none of them wore them except Royal.

Knight didn't let something as pesky as a mask stop him from burying his nose in my neck and nuzzling me softly. The makeup girl's eyes burned as she stared at us. Well, until Royal cleared his throat, and she went back to work.

"If you take the mask off, I could definitely do this more easily," she whined, and I rolled my eyes. Not that she could see. I must've made a soft noise too that gave away my feelings, if Knight's chuckle was anything to go by.

"You know the rules," was all Royal said, and the girl clucked her tongue.

"Fuck the rules. I've already signed an airtight NDA. What am I going to do?"

I wanted to tell her I was fucking them, and even I didn't get to see their faces. I held my tongue, though. I already didn't like the catty way she was staring at me, and while I wasn't here to make friends, I also wasn't here to make enemies.

Royal gave her a haughty look. "Run your fucking mouth."

She gave a fuzzy giggle that made me grind my back teeth. "As if I would. Does Knight's girlfriend get to see your faces? What are they calling her? The Toy?"

My lip curled, and Poet popped in front of me before I opened my mouth and told her what I thought of her. "Nah, that's just what Royal calls her when they fuck. Her name is Dreamer."

Shep ran a hand down his face. "For fuck's sake, Poet."

The girl leaned back, looking between us all. "Seriously? She's your girlfriend?" I wasn't sure why she seemed so angered by the concept. Her eyes ran up and down my body, and judging by the look on her face, she didn't see what all the fuss was about.

I trained my eyes on Royal. He was a fucking wild-card at the best of times; who knew what he'd say right now. His eyes flicked between the two of us, looking like the bored, insouciant god that he was.

Finally, he pursed those perfect lips. "That's none of your damn business. Just remember that NDA you were so quick to bring up." He looked around her in the mirror. "You done?"

"Umm, yeah," the makeup girl said, pushing back and swishing her pretty blonde hair over her shoulder. "We're done." She stomped out of the dressing room, and I looked at Poet.

"He fucked her, didn't he?"

He threw back his head and laughed. "What do you think?"

Royal crooked a finger at me. "Come here and kiss your *boyfriend,* Toy." There was a challenge in his tone, but I wasn't going to shy away from a little verbal sparring. I sashayed toward him, my eyes daring him to make this my fault.

I stepped between his knees, where the girl had just been, but instead of sitting on her stool, I straddled his thighs. The buttery softness of his faux leather pants squeaked, and I ran my fingers down his buttons, the very ones I'd sewed on this morning. I leaned forward, brushing my lips against his, and the pupils of his deep blue eyes were blown wide. He gripped my ass hard, and I tested the structural integrity of his chair by rolling my hips over his.

"Here I am, Your Majesty. What are you going to do with me?"

He growled low in his throat, his hand coming up to wrap around my ponytail. He bent my head back and ran his tongue in a stripe up my throat, making me moan. "Not a goddamn thing. I just got my makeup done." He picked me up by my hips and lifted me off his thighs.

Rejection burned in my gut, but I pushed it back down. I could see the bulge in his pants, the way his eyes were hooded as he stared back at me. He wanted me as much as I wanted him.

"Tonight, though, you're mi—"

"Dibs!" We all turned to Poet, who had his hand

raised, gesturing between himself and Hero. "We call dibs."

"We do?" Hero asked, and I laughed as Poet elbowed him in the ribs. "I mean, yeah, we do."

Royal frowned. "You can't call shotgun on a person, Poe."

Poet hooked an arm around my waist and dragged me between himself and Hero. "Just did. Don't be a sore loser, Royal," he teased. "They made a TV series out of the books I loaned her, and we're going to watch it."

"Can't you do that after—"

"Nope. If it has to be sexual for it to be approved time, we'll watch it naked. I'll eat Milk Duds from between her tits. Whatever it is, she's with me and Hero tonight."

I grinned, because as much as I enjoyed whatever crazy game Royal and I were playing, it was nice to be wanted. Just to hang and watch movies.

Somehow, that seemed more perilous to me than whatever Royal had planned.

TWENTY-THREE

POET

I SHOWERED in the dressing rooms, because trying to shower on one leg in a tiny-ass bathroom on a moving bus was always a physical challenge I tried to avoid. We'd done the meet and greets, Royal and Knight were doing the media interviews, and I was just appreciating the cool water running over my overheated body.

I was excited for two days on the road. Not because I enjoyed traveling—honestly, it sucked being trapped on the bus, but it meant we didn't have any work commitments. We could jam a little maybe, binge-watch movies and shows, get lost between the pretty thighs of Charlotte.

I mean, Dreamer.

It was a great name, because Knight wasn't the only one having dreams about being inside Charlotte. I wasn't completely on board with this arrangement, except to help Charlotte out, but the more I got to know her, the more she slipped her way under my skin.

Hero stepped into the bathroom with me, closing the door softly behind him. He pulled off his mask, and I took in the sharp angles of his face and his brow that was in a perpetual frown.

"We should talk," he said solemnly, and I raised an eyebrow at him.

Turning off the water, I stepped out into the cold, gray room. "You can't break up with me. We aren't even a couple," I teased, and he handed me my towel, his eyes drifting down my body. He'd seen it hundreds of times in our lifetime. Before my accident and after, though not in the same way he looked at it now. Back then, we'd been little kids at school, or hanging out at Knight's house, playing in his pool on holiday breaks.

Now, when he looked at me, it was sometimes with lust in his eyes. Sometimes it was with concern. And sometimes, like right now, it was with a seriousness that meant we were going to have one of *those* conversations.

Wrapping the towel around my waist, I hopped over to the toilet and sat down on the lid. "Okay, hit me with it."

"I want to have sex with Charlotte."

I blinked. "Okay…? I don't blame you. I do too."

Hero frowned again. "I love you, Poet."

It wasn't the first time he'd told me he loved me. The first time had been when we were seventeen and had sex for the first time. He'd held me in his arms, promising he'd love me forever.

I'd run away as fast as my crippled body could carry me. Eventually, though, we'd had to talk about it in a conversation that sounded a lot like this one. We'd worked out that we loved each other, but we weren't enough. No matter what side we landed on, with girlfriends that came and went or with just each other, it always felt like the grass was greener on the other side.

When I'd had my last serious girlfriend—who hated Hero—all I had wanted was to feel his arms around me again. Then, when Hero and I had decided to be monogamous with just each other, I'd missed that softness that came with being in love with a woman. We were both too prickly, and with Hero, I found myself becoming the softer one. The submissive. I didn't want to be that all the time, no matter how fun it was occasionally.

So we dipped our toes—and dicks—outside our relationship, but we always came back to each other. Knight had called it an open relationship, and if anyone would know, it would be Knight.

"I love you too." I reached out and dragged him toward me. "Where are you going with this?"

Hero sighed, resting his head on top of mine. "For the first time in a long time, sleeping with anyone else feels wrong without asking you first. We aren't getting any younger, Poet—"

"Hey, you're twenty-four, not sixty-four," I protested, and he hushed me.

"And I feel like I owe you more than I've been giving you. If you asked me not to see anyone else, I wouldn't. So I guess, what I'm saying is that I'm interested in Charlotte, more than I thought I'd be. The whole contract thing makes me feel..."

"Ick?" I supplied, because I got it. It made me feel kind of weird too. "Don't worry. How about, from now on, if we pursue anything with Charlotte, we do it together. I know we'll both treat her with respect. We'll give her choices. She's sweet, and I don't want her to fuck me out of obligation." Or pity, which had happened more than once. "Tonight, we'll make it clear that she holds all the cards. We can be friends. We can be more. It all rests with her." I pulled back, so I could see his face.

He looked relieved as he nodded his agreement. "Okay. Okay, yeah. That's what we'll do. And if she just wants to hang out and watch romcoms, we can do that too."

I finished drying myself, pulling on my boxer shorts, and Hero handed me my sock. We'd done this dance so many times now, I was pretty sure if I ever went permanently lame, all of the guys could put on my prosthetic for me.

"Agreed. Now, get out of here so I can get dressed and we can go home. Actually, box up some of the stuff from the rider. We could use the snacks for the road."

And the booze. Man, I was going to need the booze.

. . .

When we made it back to the bus, everything was quickly loaded. Charlotte—I mean, Dreamer—was already on the bus, dressed in a pair of shorts and an oversized band hoodie.

She was blindfolded again, but it didn't slow her down as she told Knight and Hero all about her day with Helen, sewing buttons and patching tears, then making her own mask. She told them her plans for it, which sounded amazing.

It was easy to see that she had the soul of an artist. There was already a finished little book nook in a rarely used cabinet beneath the kitchen counter. It was a tiny little library, glued together carefully, with working lights and everything. It was pretty cool.

We didn't know much about her history, but what she'd dropped in conversation told me she hadn't had a great upbringing. If she'd been given the same opportunities as us, would she be where we were now?

Rich-person guilt was such a fucking cop-out. All I could do was insist we kept the ticket prices to our concerts affordable for everyone, and give the woman in front of me a chance to do whatever it was she wanted.

"Sounds like it's going to be beautiful, Lottie. I can't wait to see you in it and nothing else," Knight purred, and her whole body flushed. Her lips parted as she leaned into the warmth of his body.

I was on my feet and had my arms wrapped around her waist. "Uh-uh, we called dibs. I have snacks and a laptop filled with three seasons of a glorious man encased in leather, with a big sword," I told Knight, who just laughed at me, lifting his hands.

"Okay, okay. Man, you're like a dog with a bone there, Poet. Or should I say, a dude with a boner." He chuckled at his own joke, which was such a Knight thing to do.

Spinning Dreamer around, I hustled her toward the bedroom. Royal was in the shower, and I could feel the bus start to vibrate, telling me they were getting ready to roll out.

"Hero, grab the snacks! It's party time." Knight pouted, but I shook my head at him. *Fuck off,* I mouthed, and he laughed again. He made a rude gesture with his fingers, and I flipped him the bird in return. "Hero and I will wear our masks so you can watch," I told Dreamer, as I led her to her room, grabbing my laptop from my bed on the way past.

She kept her space incredibly clean, her bed made, her clothes tucked into the drawers. Pulling my mask from my pocket, I slipped it on.

"Okay, you're free to see," I murmured to her, pushing down the residual guilt that she had to be sightless for most of our interactions. "I meant what I said earlier, though. We're just having a chilled-out night—nothing more is expected from you, unless that's what you want." I winced, glad she couldn't see my face. Man, there was no good way to say *I wouldn't be opposed to you riding my cock, but don't want you to feel obligated,* without it sounding like I didn't want to fuck her at all.

She crawled up the bed toward the headboard, and my eyes snagged on that ass. That perfect, perfect ass. Man, I wanted to sink my teeth into it, leave my mark so anyone else who saw it would know she was claimed.

Hero pushed into the room, and I took a moment to appreciate how damn hot he was. He'd lost his shirt at some point, and his tattoos were all on display. He collected them like someone might collect Boy Scout badges.

It was the thing that Knight and Hero really bonded over, a tattooed chronicle of their lives. Though stylistically different—Knight's were a cohesive artwork, while Hero's were a random quilt of neo-traditional tattoos—they each got one after significant life events. I could find my accident on both their bodies. Knight had a twisted wreckage of a crash. Hero had a small fine-line tattoo of the earth exploding.

I snuck a look at Dreamer and spotted her ogling Hero, like she wanted to write a thesis on the hard lines of his body. I mean, I got it. I looked at him like that too.

He gave me a cocky smirk, dumping all the snacks at the end of the bed. I streamed the show from my laptop to the TV on the wall, queueing up the first episode while we all got comfortable.

I pulled off my shirt and lay down beside her near the headboard, sitting up slightly so I didn't choke to death on my Twizzlers. "Ready?"

She nodded, taking the cookie that Hero offered and snuggling further down into the bed. He climbed in on the other side of her, and I saw her muscles tense. Man, maybe this was a bad idea. We should have eased into this level of familiarity.

Hero just leaned back against the headboard, not touching her, seemingly completely unaware of her tension. I knew him better, though; he was letting her figure out her own level of comfort. If she asked him to move, he would.

Still, I watched her from the corner of my eye, just in case. Eventually, she relaxed as the extended opening sequence played. I slid further down the bed and wrapped her up in my arms, content to just hug her. She snuggled into my chest as an action sequence with a lot of grunting and more than a little decapitation flashed across the scene.

The airbrakes signaled we'd rolled out, and I settled in for a long couple of days on the road. We'd stop occasionally to eat and stretch our legs, and the driver had to have mandated breaks.

I fed her Twizzlers, and this close, I could see that her bottom teeth were slightly crooked, and that she had a slight scar below her bottom lip. I wondered what it was from, but didn't want to ruin the moment by asking. You didn't have to be an empath to know the story of her life had been fucked up.

I hoped this wasn't just the newest chapter.

TWENTY-FOUR

HERO

POET WATCHED her with heart eyes. I wasn't sure if he even realized how smitten he was, but when he fed her an entire Twizzler bite by bite, I resisted the urge to laugh. She'd been tense when we started the first episode, but now we were on episode three, and she'd relaxed into me. Her knees touched mine as she curled on her side, her head near my elbow. She looked more relaxed than I'd ever seen her, and I relished the moment.

This little bubble of peacefulness wasn't something we found often.

I'd been getting tired of the road. We'd only been on it for a few weeks, but I felt like we were stuck in a loop of record, release, tour, repeat. It had been years since our first headline tour, and few more since we'd first started touring as support acts. Normally, I loved it. But lately, it felt stifling.

We'd needed something new, and in had flown a

breath of fresh air in the shape of a battered girl with a proposition and a set of brass balls. I eyed the nearly completely faded bruise. When she put makeup on, you could hardly see it anymore. But I knew it had been there, and the anger that burned in my gut only intensified, the more I got to know her.

A hand reached up and touched my chest. I looked down at a frowning Charlotte. *Are you okay?* she mouthed at me, and I nodded.

I stroked her face, because I couldn't help it. The soft curve of her cheek was made for cupping. "Just thinking."

"About?" Her voice was still pitched low so we didn't upset Poet, who was immersed in the story of the show now.

"The tour. The rockstar lifestyle. You know, the usual," I teased, and she grinned back at me.

"Practically an everyday Joe," she quipped back, her brow raised.

I ran my finger over her cheek, tracing the edges of the bruise. She watched me with eyes that were pale in the darkness. "Be honest. Are you really okay with this? With being here?"

She bit her lip, dragging it between her teeth. "I know I shouldn't be. I know that I should be disgusted with myself, exchanging sex for money. But I think about what my life would be like if I hadn't had this opportunity, and feel nothing but gratitude. Happiness." She gave me a lopsided smile. "It's not like it's a hardship. You're all pretty nice to look at."

I made a small hum of agreement. You didn't have to be bisexual to appreciate the guys. Poet was beautiful, his fine features making him look like a high-fashion model. Royal was fucking sex and sin rolled up in an asshole package, and any person, no matter their orientation, would be drawn to him. Especially on stage, where he was the embodiment of sensuality. The fucker. Knight was handsome in a devilish kind of way too; his personality was so big, you sometimes missed the fact he was classically attractive, in a very rock'n'roll way.

Yeah, I could see how fucking the guys wouldn't be a hardship if you were attracted to them.

Charlotte—I couldn't think of her as Dreamer just yet—reached up and touched my face. "I promise if my feelings change, you'll be the first to know." She ran her thumb along my jaw and over my lips. "Now kiss me, because I've been dying to do it all night."

I groaned softly, leaning forward to capture her lips with mine and quickly realizing my mask was in the way. I wanted to roar in frustration, but she just laughed, pulling my mask up my neck, over my jaw and lips, until the entirety of the bottom half of my face was exposed.

It was bullshit. I wanted to bury myself inside her, lose myself in the softness of her body and taste every inch. How could I do that in this damn mask?

My frustration must have shown, because she brushed her lips across mine. She tasted like sugar, and her lips were pink from all the dyed candy. I wanted to suck the color from them, kiss her until she was breathless.

"I'll put my mask on, so you don't have to worry," she murmured between kisses, her teeth nipping the point of my chin.

"Wait." I grabbed her hand as she reached for the silk mask. "I want to see your face as I make you come. Just once."

"Me too," Poet said behind her. "I want to know what color your eyes go when Hero makes you scream his name." He stroked fingers down her spine. "I want to watch you watch me as I bury my face in your delicious pussy." He let out a shuddering breath, curling himself closer. "I've been jerking off to the thought of it for days."

I felt her body tremble between us, and the sense of rightness was almost overwhelming. This was how it was meant to be with Poet and I. We were meant to have a woman between us. Or Poet between me and Charlotte.

This was what we had been missing all this time. A soft counterpart to our hard edges.

I gripped Charlotte under her chin, tugging her face closer until she could see nothing but me. "Is that what you want, sweetheart? You want Poet to tongue-fuck your pussy while I fuck your mouth?"

I wasn't sure what Poet was doing with his hands, but she was already panting soft breaths against my face. "Yes! God, yes!"

"Good girl," I purred. "Now get naked and show Poet his feast."

We all stripped out of our clothes in what must have been world record time, and she crawled up the pillows, flashing her pussy, making me palm my achingly hard cock. She rolled onto her back and spread her thighs, and Poet groaned.

Hell, I groaned too. It was such a blatantly vulnerable act, showing the most hidden part of yourself to someone, and she'd done it for the both of us with desire in her eyes. There was a little bit of anxiety too; I was just going to have to show her that she had nothing to worry about with us.

Poet was naked except for his prosthetic, and I knew he wanted to take it off. We never had sex with it on, because honestly, that thing was a weapon in the bedroom.

He hesitated, his eyes darting between Charlotte and me, and I hated the look of uncertainty in his eyes. He'd been who he was for so long now, I honestly didn't even think about it. But there was always a small worry that flitted across his face. Worry he'd be rejected. Worry he wouldn't be seen as a real man anymore. All these things had come out in his therapy sessions when he was a teen, and conversations late at night when he was wrapped in my arms.

I hated that I couldn't ease that for him, but this next bit was between the two of them.

Charlotte's knees closed, and I held myself taut.

"What's wrong?" Worry flitted across her own face, and maybe a little self-consciousness.

"I'd like to take my prosthetic off for this."

Her eyes dipped down to his leg. It was the best prosthetic money could buy, and his surgeons had been amazing at the time. He'd been young enough when he had his accident that his recovery had been fairly easy, all things considered. If he'd gotten the same injury now, or in ten years, it would have been a lot harder.

Charlotte was still frowning. "Okay?" she said hesitantly.

Poet's cheeks burned red. "I just don't want you to freak out."

Understanding crossed her face in a wave, quickly followed by incredulity. "Oh my god, Poet. I swear on fucking Bowie's memory that if you think I'm anything short of one hundred percent attracted to you right now—regardless of whether or not you have a left foot—then I'm going to put my clothes back on and come over there to smack you silly," she grumbled. "I want you to do whatever makes you most comfortable. And then I want you to climb up this bed and tongue-fuck me like your life depends on it."

"Yes, ma'am," he breathed with a laugh, sitting down on the end of the bed and taking his leg off quickly.

"Well, while you're waiting, I might just have a little taste." I bounced onto the bed and pushed her knees apart, diving between those juicy thighs like I'd dreamed of doing. Her fingers gripped onto my hair as if she wanted to pull it from the roots, making me groan.

"Holy…" She lost the ability of speech after I sucked her clit between my teeth, then laved the flat of my tongue over it. Her thighs clenched around my head, and it was *perfect*. I sucked, licked and stroked, until her wetness spread across my mouth.

"Excuse me, I think you're eating something that belongs to me," Poet huffed from beside me. I pulled away, and Charlotte whimpered, her hands reaching out to drag my head back to where it belonged.

Poet grinned down at her. I knew that look. *Oh, shit's about to get real fun.*

"Here's what's going to happen, little Dreamer. Hero here is going to fuck you so hard, the whole bus will rock from side to side. Then he's going to pump you so full of his cum that it's going to leak down those pretty white thighs." He reached out and stroked the aforementioned thighs, where they were still flung over my shoulders. "Then I'm going to eat his release right from your pretty cunt and fuck what's left all the way back inside you until you're filled to the brim with us." His voice was pure sex, and my dick was so hard that if he didn't stop the dirty talk, I might just come all over the sheets like an amateur. "Do you want that, baby?"

Her eyes were big and wild, her pupils blown wide as she breathed heavily through parted lips. "Yes."

Poet's grin made me remember why I fell in love with him in the first place. Pure devilment wrapped around the softest center.

"Open for me, sweetheart, before I embarrass myself," I told her softly. "If you want to stop at any point, say the word, okay?"

She looked at me like I was crazy. "Did you *hear* him? Why would I want to stop any of that?"

I laughed, but it quickly turned into a groan as she spread her thighs for me, and I could see just how wet his words had made her. Climbing between them and up her body, I kissed her, the rough fabric of my mask scraping against her cheeks and nose as her lips devoured mine.

I centered my throbbing cock at her entrance, and as I pushed inside her, I was glad for the mask, because my eyes rolled right into the back of my head. It had been almost a year since I'd been with a woman. The way she was gripping me was fucking *heaven.*

Grabbing her calf, I pushed one leg up over my shoulder so I could get deeper. I wanted to forget where I ended and she began. I wanted to bring her so much pleasure so fast that her head would spin. Mostly because I knew I had, like, thirty seconds to make her head explode before I came.

I sucked one of her nipples into my mouth, biting it gently until she chanted my name with pleasure. It was a heady goddamn feeling, and I knew as soon as I blew, I was going to want to be inside her again.

Addictive, that's what she was. A drug that I wanted to shoot directly into my veins.

I went hard and deep, grinding my body against her clit with each thrust until she was panting my name on moans so loud, I hoped the other guys could hear it. Hell, I hoped the driver could hear how good I was fucking her.

"Oh fuck... *Oh fuck.* I'm so close, *please,* Hero." I didn't know what she was begging for, but I reached around and pinched her clit. She shattered around me like a bomb, her pussy milking me like it was sucking the very soul from my body.

I came right after her, my thrusts stuttering as I blew pulse after pulse of my load inside her. Panting, she lowered her leg from my shoulder, and I collapsed on top of her until I could feel my thighs again. I was careful not to crush her, though. I wasn't a massive guy, but I was still a solid weight, and she was a tiny little thing.

My mask had crept up my cheekbones, with only my eyes and the top of my head hidden from her now. She kissed along my jaw, then pulled my mask down hesitantly. I hated it. I wanted to rip it off, fling it across the room. I wanted to see the look on her face as her eyes trailed across my features. I wanted to stare into her eyes, read her emotions, and have them read mine right back.

I kissed the side of her face, up over her cheeks and the lids of her eyes. She was breathing heavily, her chest heaving and a small smile curling her lips.

She really was beautiful.

"I hope you aren't worn out yet, sweetheart, because we aren't even *close* to done." I rolled off her, and Poet was there. I couldn't see his face either, but every line of his body was straining toward us. A smirk curled my face, and I wanted to laugh at the pure contentment I felt right then. "Hope you're ready, because I think this is about to get wild."

Poet knelt on the bed. "Roll her onto your chest, Hero. I'm hungry."

TWENTY-FIVE

DREAMER

HERO HAD MELTED MY SYNAPSES. My core was still clenching with aftershocks, pleasure making my limbs feel heavy. Poet stroked a hand down my spine, and goosebumps trailed after his fingers. My skin felt too tight, too filled with pleasure. But I wanted more. I wanted everything they'd give me.

Poet's hands pushed me higher up Hero's body, until his face was buried between my breasts. Hero pressed them together and sighed happily as he spread his thighs, forcing my knees further apart. I could feel Poet's hot breath on my overheated folds.

"Look at him leaking from you, baby," Poet cooed as his tongue dipped inside me, and he hummed happily. "You taste so good together." His voice was muffled as he lapped his boyfriend's cum from inside me.

I forgot how to breathe.

His talented tongue pressed deep inside me, like he was chasing the taste. While my logical brain would be horrified, the wanton hussy I'd become thought it was the hottest fucking thing I'd ever participated in. I thrust my ass further in the air, giving him better access, and Hero took the opportunity to suck my nipple into his mouth, the long pulls going straight to my clit.

Tension burned through my body, and the pleasure climbed higher and higher, pooling deep in my body. I realized I was moaning incomprehensibly, but mostly, I was begging.

Begging for more.

Begging for release.

Begging for him to fuck me into his best friend.

Poet's hand slid down, finding my clit quickly. A slight pressure, a flick of his fingers, and I was exploding again. I could feel myself dripping my release—and Hero's—out, and Poet wasted no time lapping it up from my thighs.

His hands gripped my hips, and he dragged me down until my face was between Hero's pecs, his nipple just beside my mouth. I could feel Hero's dick—once again hard—pressed tight to my stomach. Lifting up, I looked back over my shoulder as Poet nudged Hero's knees together, tilting my hips up slightly. "I'm going to fuck you into Hero now, baby girl, until I fill you so full with my cum, your little belly will bulge with it."

My whole body lit up with pleasure at the idea. *Well, that's new.* I suspected Poet might have a breeding kink. I also suspected I might have one now too.

"I have to take my mask off. I want to taste your

skin as I bury myself inside you. Don't lift your head from Hero's chest, Dreamer. Do you understand?" His dick nudged at my entrance, sliding up and down my slit, the fleshy head hitting my clit and making me pant with need. "Are you going to look?"

I pressed back into him, trying to get his cock exactly where I needed it. "No, I won't look. Please, Poet," I begged, my eyes screwed shut.

The noise of pure satisfaction was the only warning I got until he was burying himself deep inside me. I'd seen his girthy cock earlier, and as it stretched me, it bordered on too much. Holding my hips tightly, Poet stretched along my back, his arms either side of my shoulders and he fucked me in short, quick strokes right into the hard body of Hero.

I took it back. It wasn't too much. It was *perfection.*

We all groaned. Being sandwiched between the two of them like this was something else. Something that set all my senses on fire: the pressure of Poet on my back, buried deep inside me; the salty taste of Hero's sweat on my lips; the puffs of his grunted breaths against my sticky forehead. The soft words of praise Poet was whispering in my ear with each thrust.

It was transcendent. And I knew that this was going to alter me.

I came hard, my teeth biting into Hero's fleshy chest muscle, screaming until my voice was hoarse. Poet didn't stop, switching angles and fucking me down into his boyfriend's torso, harder and harder as my clit ground against Hero's thigh.

"One more, baby girl. Come on, Lottie, give me one more," he encouraged me with a strained voice. I shook my head, but even as I did, I could feel the orgasms stacking, chasing the aftershocks of the last one with the crest of a new wave.

I screamed Poet's name so loudly, they probably heard it back in Phoenix. My body trembled and shook, black dots dancing in my vision as he followed right after me, Hero's release splattering across my stomach.

Rolling to the side, Poet kept me sandwiched between them as he kissed my neck, my shoulders, every part of my oversensitive skin. "You're so goddamn amazing," he breathed, his voice reverent. I wanted to desperately see his face. I wanted to kiss him with as much heat and raw passion as he was showing me.

I felt perilously close to crying and I had no damn idea why, except that the whole thing had been intensely pleasurable.

Hero reached over to the nightstand and grabbed the blindfold we'd discarded. Slipping it gently over my eyes, he rolled me so I was on my back, then brushed his lips over mine. I was grateful in that moment for the masks, because it meant when the tender kisses were pressed on my lips, the fabric caught the tears leaking from my eyes.

A kiss pressed to my right cheek, the brush of Hero's stubble across my oversensitive skin feeling like too much. "I'll get something to clean you up." He moved from the bed, and I shivered at the cool air that replaced him.

My back to his front, Poet pulled me closer and tighter, his arm around my waist, anchoring me. "Are you okay?" he whispered softly.

A smile curled my lips, even as I shivered. "So okay."

He nuzzled my nape. "Thank you."

"You just gave me, like, five back-to-back orgasms. I think I should be thanking *you*." My body felt languid in a way that only cats and ooze could feel. Like there was nothing holding me together except my skin.

His chuckle reverberated against my back. "I think it was only four, but the night's still young."

Hero returned with a washcloth and a couple of bottles of water. My throat was parched; clearly, I'd been more vocal than I thought.

Poet kissed me as Hero ran the washcloth over my thighs and my core, cleaning me up. It made me flush bright pink, but luckily, they probably couldn't see in the dim light.

Swearing softly, Hero muttered, "I don't know why it's so fucking hot to see your cunt dribbling Poet's cum, but I swear it does something primal to my brain."

Poet chuckled, his hips flexing against mine. How was he fucking hard again already? "I think it's time for orgasm number five."

I wanted to protest, but my pussy clenched in anticipation. I wanted what they were promising me, more than I should. How was I ever going to go back to ordinary guys, now that I'd had The Daymakers?

The bus was moving by the time I disentangled myself from between Poet and Hero. I needed to pee. Climbing over Hero, I groaned when he gripped my hips and ground himself into my stomach.

"Where are you going?" he whispered, his voice roughened by sleep and so fucking sexy, I wanted to purr.

"I have to pee. No one wants a UTI."

He kissed my shoulder as I sat on the edge of the bed and got my bearings. I'd made myself practice over and over getting to the bathroom with my eyes covered. I knew where every obstacle was, how many steps it was from the edge of my bed to the door, then from the door to the bathroom.

I followed the memorized path down the hallway, and once I'd firmly locked the bathroom door behind me, I peeled off my mask and turned on the lights. Hanging my mask on the small hook behind the door, I did what I had to do, then stood in front of the mirror, washing the sticky sweat from my skin. I looked thoroughly, one hundred percent fucked.

My lips were swollen, and my chin was red from Hero's stubble. There was a hickey on the upper swell of my breast, though I couldn't remember which one of them had done that. My body was achingly, deliciously sore.

The smile on my face threatened to crack my cheeks.

Dammit. I was getting attached. It was hard not to when Poet was so fucking sweet and Hero was so damn caring; I felt like the only girl that either of them had ever looked at.

Have you ever had an orgasm so good that you start to wonder if you can keep the person giving them to you forever?

Love at first O. Now multiply it by two.

I was so screwed.

I pulled my hair up into something no longer resembling a rat's nest that had just hosted an orgy, and brushed my teeth. Pulling my mask back on, I unlocked the door and stepped back into the hallway. Five steps back to the door.

I made it three before I ran into something solid and warm. Putting my hands on the chest in front of me, I tried to guess who it was. I ran my hands over their hard chest, up higher to their neck. Too tall for Knight, so that left me with Royal or…

"Are you all right?" Shep's low voice was close to my face, like he was stooping down to talk to me.

I hadn't seen him before we left, and I'd wondered if he was even going to travel on the bus with us. I guess him standing here answered my question.

Smiling, I gave into the urge to run my hands up to his face. "I'm fine. I don't know why everyone keeps asking me that. It's not like I was a blushing virgin before we left LA." I kept my tone light, though I wished I could see his face. "Is there anyone else around?"

"No, Royal and Knight are asleep. They stayed up… late."

I guess we'd kept the whole bus awake with our shenanigans.

I pushed up my mask so I could see his face. His jaw was tense, the dim strip lighting of the bus casting shadows in the hollows of his cheekbones. His eyes were impenetrably dark as he stared down at me, closer than I realized.

"I think I should apologize."

He shook his head, leaning in closer until his forehead rested on mine. In the still of the darkness, time stopped. I breathed him in, and all too soon, he was pulling back. "Get some sleep. We'll stop in a couple of hours for something to eat and so the driver can rest."

With that, he slid my mask back down, and I felt the wall of his body disappear. I stood there dumbly, trying to figure out what the fuck had just happened.

Finally, I felt my way back to the room and climbed back between the sleeping bodies of Hero and Poet, but my whirling brain wouldn't let me drift off again.

TWENTY-SIX

SHEP

WE'D PARKED near an overlook just outside of Las Cruces in New Mexico. The rollout had been later than I'd hoped, but John had noticed a check engine light on in the bus, so we'd had to get an emergency mechanic out to have a look. He'd patched up whatever was wrong, but when we got to San Antonio, it would have to go in to be repaired. So the bus just had to take it easy until then.

We all sat outside while the driver slept, the band with their hoods pulled up and gators pulled up over their noses. "This is fucking impractical," Knight ranted. "There's no one else out here, and if it wasn't for that stupid contract, I could actually breathe in this heat, rather than sweating through a damn mask."

I didn't miss the flash of hurt on Charlotte's face. "I can always go back on the bus? Or put on the internal section of mine?"

Knight reached out and gripped her hand. "I'm not

blaming you, Dreamer." They'd all done a good job of using her new code name in public. "Just the stupid clause in the contract. You shouldn't have to be blindfolded just so we can be comfortable."

"Why the fuck not? She signed up for it." Royal had his face tipped toward the sun, soaking in the warmth like the cold-blooded creature he was.

Hero reached over and punched him in the arm. "Don't be a dick. Technically, we signed up for it too."

Royal made a rude noise. "That's why you don't hear *me* whining about it."

Charlotte rolled her eyes as she played with her phone. I knew for a fact she'd removed all her social media, and I was confident that she wasn't going to waste an assload of cash to post that we were at some shitty desert overlook. I also knew that she had a hundred thousand good reasons not to out the guys after the tour ended, making the masks redundant, but we hadn't gotten this far by being trusting.

The guys continued to bicker back and forth while I looked at the very real missile that was perched up on a pedestal right beside us. According to the infographic boards that no one but me would read, they used the basin below as a missile range. It was pretty, in a wide-open kind of way.

If I was honest, I was a city boy at heart, and this much space always gave me a touch of anxiety, like I really didn't matter. Existential angst, as Poet would call it.

Charlotte sucked in a breath beside me, and I looked

over at her casually, as if I wasn't watching her religiously every fucking day, like a stalker.

She looked terrified right then, though, and all my security instincts went on high alert. I looked around, but there wasn't another car in sight, except those driving on the interstate beside us.

"What's wrong?" I strode over to her, taking in her pale complexion. "Are you in pain?" Fuck, maybe she'd fractured her rib or something else that had been brewing there in the background, waiting for us to be complacent and in the middle of fucking nowhere.

She shook her head, but the scared look never left her face. Her knuckles turned white where they were clutching her phone. I pried it from her fingers, looking down at what was on the screen. Had the press gotten photos of her? Released her name? Taken long-range photos through a hotel room window of them having sex? That had happened more than once. The whole world had seen a masked Royal fucking a girl against a hotel window in New York once.

Instead, it was an email. Pure vitriol was written on the screen, telling her that she was worthless, that if she ever spoke a word of what happened, he'd destroy her and her reputation until she'd end up giving blow jobs for five bucks. An unconscious stream of threats and insults followed for an entire page, from what I could tell was a burner email address, given the random combination of words.

It got more and more unhinged, until that stopped

right before the end. Then it sounded so calm, it could have almost been a formal request.

Return home, and we'll forget this ever happened. I will treat you the way you deserve. I love you, Charlie. However, if you don't, you'll force my hand, and you won't like the consequences.

- *T*

That fucker. That absolute fucker.

She was shaking now, still deathly pale, and I wondered if she'd pass out. The guys had now noticed, and Hero was in front of her immediately. He tilted her face up to his, searching her for injury. She sucked in lungfuls of air, but continued to wheeze. She looked up at him with frantic eyes, like she was trapped in a nightmare.

Poet nudged Hero gently out of the way. "She's having a panic attack." He gripped her hands, squeezing them tightly. "Charlotte, baby, you're having a panic attack right now. I'm here. I've got you, and you're safe."

"Can't. Breathe," she choked out, and I started to worry it wasn't a panic attack, but something worse.

Poet just hummed softly, his hands never letting go of hers. "It's hard; I know. But try for me. Deep breath in"—we all took a deep breath, like we could physically compel her to join us—"and then out. One more time. In, two, three, four. Out, two, three, four. You're safe. You're with us. Look around you. Tell me three things you see right here."

Her eyes darted around, like she couldn't see anything around us, but then they stalled on the missile. "Missile."

"Two more."

"Bus," she croaked out. Her eyes flicked to me. "Shep."

"Three things you can hear?"

"The cars." She let out a shaky breath. "A bird. You."

He stroked her face softly. "That's it, baby. I'm right here. Now, lift your head and look at me with those pretty eyes, so I can see you're okay." She lifted her chin, and he smiled down at her while I stood there feeling completely, utterly helpless. "Now, touch my face. Know that I won't let anything happen to you. None of us will."

Even as he said the words, I knew it was true. This was temporary, but it was hard not to let Charlotte slip beneath my skin. Impossible, even. I was going to find out everything I could about that fuck and then I was going to make him wish he'd never been born.

Poet pulled her to her feet and wrapped her in his arms, while we all hovered around looking uncertain. Even Royal had lost that shit-eating confidence he seemed to possess twenty-four seven.

He drifted back toward me, raising an eyebrow.

We'd been friends long enough that I knew what he was asking. I handed him the phone, and he read the email, his brows getting lower and lower until his eyes were filled with molten rage.

"We're going to make this go away," he said to me, his voice pitched low. I nodded. I was already thinking of people from the old days I could call to figure this shit out. Royal slid his eyes to me, and they were blazing hot with fury. "Find out what you can and I'll take care of it."

He wasn't without his own connections, and while they mightn't all run on the less savory side of the law, that didn't mean they weren't terrifying.

I nodded again, my eyes drifting back to Charlotte, who was finally breathing normally. Knight's hands rubbed circles over her back, and the look on his face was devastated. Apparently, I wasn't the only one who'd suddenly found Charlotte Lochrin deep under my skin.

We were back on the road, but the bus was unusually quiet. Knight was strumming the guitar as he worked on music, with Poet at the little dining nook, writing in his notebook. Charlotte lay curled up on the couch with her head in Hero's lap, as they watched a movie about robots.

Her breakdown had affected us all, and I wasn't immune. I made a list of things I wanted to know; as much as I wanted to give her space, parts of that email had me worried. They were violent, bordering on psychotic. That wasn't some spurned lover with anger issues—that was someone with far greater problems than I had even contemplated.

I sat down across from her, which drew her attention from the television. Her gaze shuttered as she took in my expression. She was a smart woman, despite her lack of formal education. She knew what I was about.

"I'll ask you these questions now, for your safety and the band's. You'll only have to talk about it once, and then we'll never mention it again, unless you bring it up first."

She nodded her agreement, and Hero buried his fingers in her hair, stroking his fingers through the dark lengths.

"First, what's his full name? Just so he's on the no-fly list anywhere we go."

She chewed her lip. "Thomas Granville Junior."

"What's he do for a living?"

"He's a junior associate at a law firm. Helena, Perlman & Carlton. They're a firm in LA."

Well, shit. That was either really good or really bad. Guys like that had shit to lose, which could either make them more pliable or more unhinged. I had a feeling he'd end up in the latter category.

She was still in Hero's arms, but I could see her pressing her head further into his hands. Knight was still playing, but it was the same chord progression over and over again, so I knew he was listening to the conversation while pretending he wasn't.

"And the night we met, was that the first time he'd hurt you?"

She shook her head. "No. Not the first. Or the tenth," she said bitterly, and I wanted to reach out and bundle her up in my arms. "He wasn't like that at the beginning. Only after he knew I had nowhere else to go. No escape." A tear rolled down her cheek, but she didn't lift her hand to brush it away. She just let it run its course.

Hero curled over her, lifting his mask enough to kiss her temple. "You did escape. He's just throwing a tantrum, because you're smart and resourceful."

I agreed, but I had to continue with my questioning. "Did you take photos of any injuries?"

She nodded again. "Every time. I'd store them in the cloud, then delete them from my phone. He checked my phone all the time to make sure I wasn't seeing other guys."

Hero smiled down at her. "See? Smart and resourceful."

I continued to grill her until I had an entire picture of Thomas Granville Junior. Firstly, he had sway. He was friends with cops, plus the partners in his firm were well connected. He was also a narcissistic sociopath who'd likely beaten her down because her home life had been worse, probably figuring she wasn't someone anyone would miss. I wondered if, eventually, the beatings would have gotten bad enough that he'd have killed her.

"How you want to proceed is up to you. We can

ignore the email and hope it goes away." Well, not completely ignore it. I'd have backup plans waiting in the wings, but Charlotte didn't need to worry about any of them. "Or we can involve the cops and press charges, get ahead of it."

She was already shaking her head. "I just want to forget he exists. I want to start fresh. We just need time and distance, and then he'll forget about me…" *And move on to someone else.* The unsaid words hung in the air between us, and I could see that didn't sit well with Charlotte.

Hell, it didn't sit well with me either. But I wasn't going to force her into anything. Maybe one day she'd bring him down, but right now, if she just wanted to hide and heal? That's what we'd help her do.

And maybe, just maybe, I could arrange for him to have an unfortunate accident along the way.

TWENTY-SEVEN

DREAMER

THE NEXT THREE STOPS—WHICH I thought of as venues, now that I'd been on the road for a little while—were a blur. The guys had been all super respectful and polite, but someone came to bed with me every night. Well, Knight, Hero or Poet. Sometimes a combination of both Hero and Poet, but the bed wasn't really conducive to a good night's sleep if there were three of us in there. It got hot and sticky really quick.

Sometimes Knight would just crawl in beside me after the show, wrap himself around me and go to sleep. Sometimes he'd fuck me until the only thing I knew was his name. The same with Hero and Poet, though normally, they made love to me together.

After I thought about it some more, that's what it had felt like, right from the beginning. They didn't *fuck* me. It felt like more than a mindless meeting of bodies, and I don't know why that scared the shit out of me.

The only thing that had changed since Las Cruces

was that Royal hadn't come near me. Oh, he chatted to me with the group while we were moving from place to place. But he kept his touches respectful, even if his tone was always imperious, then at night, he went to sleep in his own bunk.

I didn't know why it was frustrating, but it was. I'd asked Shep if he was fucking groupies again, because if that was true, then me even being on the tour was for nothing. That had been an awkward conversation, because no matter how monotone I said it, the words sounded jealous as hell.

Shep had assured me Royal wasn't fucking anyone, and the small spark of satisfaction in my chest was worrying.

However, despite all the worry, I'd finally finished my mask that I'd been working on with Helen in my downtime. The older costume designer had held it up to the light, moving it this way and that, before making an encouraging noise. "It's very good for your first mask, Dreamer. You're a natural."

I knew she wasn't just placating me, because I don't think that word was even in her vocabulary. Then she critiqued it, but I couldn't help the goofy grin on my face. Eventually, she smiled back.

"We'll make a costume artist of you yet," she whispered conspiratorially, and every part of me had been filled with pride.

Which was why I was going to wear it to tonight's show. I didn't go to every show, but most of them. I stood offstage and watched the guys play. It was almost like foreplay, because they were really something else under the heat of the stage lights. Sweat-soaked beauty.

The guys were already out of the bus by the time I made it there, and I pulled out an outfit I'd picked up from a thrift store in New Orleans. It was a short lace dress with tulle skirts, but had an embroidered bustier top with a sweetheart neckline, which cinched in with ribbons at the back. The top was trimmed with lace that spiraled up a sheer insert like vines, ending at my throat, with a collar wrapping around like a choker, a small snake charm at the center. More sheer fabric ran down my arms before it billowed out into more tulle, puffy sleeves ending at my wrists in tight cuffs. The dress was a lot, and I'd spent more money on it than I would have even contemplated a month ago, but I'd fallen in love with it.

Torn opaque tights and my boots finished off the ensemble. I curled my hair around my shoulders and placed my mask on my face. It was all intricate swirls and loops, more like silver lacework than my last one, dipping low down over my cheeks. Crown-like spikes of wire were wrapped around pink quartz crystals along the top, and a moonstone was set in the middle of my forehead. It was still a blind mask—you couldn't see my eyes—but I could see out of it surprisingly well.

I couldn't help the smile on my face as I took in the vision in the mirror.

I looked like an ethereal goddess. I loved it. I felt cute—beautiful, even. No bruises remained on my face from Tom. No part of beaten-down Charlie remained.

All that was left was Dreamer, who took her destiny in her hands and ensured that life worked for her.

As I walked through the security checkpoint, the guy on the gate looked at my laminated badge and raised a hand to stop me. "Excuse me, Miss, but we were told to escort you. Just give me a second to get someone to relieve me at the gate," he asked imploringly, like he thought I was just going to sprint across the road without him and get him fired. At this venue, the private parking lot was across a busy main road from the actual arena.

I smiled, and the way his jaw went a little slack made me feel good about myself. "No worries."

He turned and radioed someone, keeping an eye on me. Finally, he clipped his radio back to his belt. "You're Dreamer."

I raised an eyebrow, not that you could see it above my mask. "I am today."

An older man came to relieve the security kid, who had to be like eighteen, max. We walked to the pedestrian crossing, and across the road, there were hundreds of people milling in front of the arena. Some of those people stopped to stare, and as I walked across the road, I realized the low buzz of voices was now littered with the word *Dreamer*.

The label had okayed soft-launching my presence on the guys' socials, not officially, but dropping me in the background with some carefully curated photos, always in the mask. Sitting around in the dressing rooms, or candid photos at sites. They put me in the same class of people as Shep—a person who was always around the band, but not part of it. Some people had made the connection that Toy was Dreamer.

The conjecture about why I was also in a mask was wild, though, with some people speculating that I was the band's muse, others saying that I was trying to join them as a back-up vocalist, or that I was someone's sister/girlfriend/lover. A source close to the band said that Royal had called me his girlfriend. No guesses to who that source was.

Whatever it was, the mystery of my appearance had both perplexed the female fans and given the male fans something to put in their spank bank, according to Whitt. Shep had been extremely unhappy about that, hence the security guard accompanying me.

People began to surround us, the closer we got to the entrance, and the security kid was beginning to sweat.

"Dreamer?" someone called, and I looked over my shoulder at a girl who was probably too young to be at this concert by herself. Giving her a soft smile, I hoped she had a parent somewhere.

When a woman in her late thirties hovered a few feet back, I relaxed. "Yeah?"

"I like your new mask."

My smile turned into a full-blown grin. "Really? I made it myself."

The girl's eyes went wide. "Seriously?"

I nodded. "Yep, right down to hand-wrapping the stones."

She thrust a poster at me. "Can I have your autograph?"

Blinking at her, I was glad the mask hid some of my shock. "You want my autograph? I'm not part of the band. I can't sing a single note without sounding like a dying cow." I didn't want her to think I was joining The Daymakers, and then hate that my name was on her poster forever.

She shrugged. "I don't care. You're still cool."

Gah, I was going to cry. "Oh. Okay, sure." I took the sharpie from her and signed the poster down in the bottom corner. It felt weird, signing my name. I put a little moon and stars beside it, and a bubble of happiness settled in my chest. Giving her back the sharpie, I grabbed a wrapped rose quartz I'd hung on a chain around my neck and pulled it over my head. "Here. Have this for luck."

It seemed dumb, but this girl had given me something and she didn't even realize it. Giving her something small in return seemed like the least I could do. She took it, then launched herself at me, hugging me around the waist.

I blinked in shock, unsure what to do. I looked at her mom, who was holding back laughter as she nodded. So I hugged the girl back until her mom finally called her away. She waved and skipped off into the arena. She looked about fourteen, and that was a rough age, but I could see how she'd be all about The Daymakers. I wasn't sure they were overly appropriate, but hey, I wasn't someone's parent.

My parents had me carrying meth in my Little Mermaid purse back when I was six, like the world's youngest drug mule, so what did I know about acceptable parenting?

The security guard ushered me through the crowd, and I kept my head down until we were in the backstage area. This part was usually the same, no matter where the guys played, their roadies having it down to a fine art by now.

Some of them I knew by sight now, and I waved politely. Shep didn't let anyone get too close, trying to keep the chance of me blowing everything to a minimum. I'd missed seeing the guys before they went on stage, but that was okay. I was happy to stand off to the side and just watch. The vibe was good here tonight, and I knew that meant the band would feed off the crowd.

As soon as they stepped onto the stage, the crowd roared. It was deafening. A lot of the roadies wore earplugs if they didn't have earpieces in. I wasn't going to be around the tour long enough to develop long-term hearing damage, so I just sat back and appreciated the absolute rush of live music. I couldn't imagine how much better it would be from the stage, with the crowd singing my music back at me.

Shep appeared and lifted me onto the equipment case behind us. His eyes continued to roam around the back of the stage for people who didn't belong, but soon enough, the guys' set began, and you couldn't help but be transfixed.

They always started with one of their most popular songs. It had an upbeat rhythm and was very much a *fuck you* to modern society. It always sent the crowd into a frenzy. The moshpit started early, and I hoped to hell that the girl and her mom were in the seats, not on the floor.

I knew the band's setlist almost as well as they did now, and when they segued straight into their second song, this one slower and more angsty, about love and loss, I wondered who Poet had written it about.

There was so much I didn't know about them, or their lives, but I knew the sounds they made when they came. I knew the taste of their sweat on their skin. I knew the lines of their shoulders, and the sound of their laughter.

I didn't know their names.

Didn't know what their faces looked like.

Didn't know about their families or previous lovers, or if they had wives back home.

Holy shit, what if they have wives back home?

I turned startled eyes to Shep and grabbed his shoulders. "Do the guys have wives and families? Why didn't I ask that?"

Shep looked at me like I'd lost my damn mind. "You think I'd let this happen if they had partners at home?"

I shrugged. I didn't have much faith in humanity in general, though I had to admit, I had a little more faith in Shep. "That didn't answer my question."

He rolled his eyes. Even sitting on the equipment box, I was only nose to nose with him. I had the sudden thought that I wanted him to stand between my knees and kiss me silly.

Goddammit. Why did I want the one I couldn't have? I was my own worst enemy at times.

Huffing out a disgruntled noise, he shook his head. "None of them have significant others. Not since Knight and his ex."

"The beautiful ex," I grumbled, still feeling woefully inferior.

Shep gripped my chin. "She was pretty on the outside, but ugly where it mattered. She hated that Poet and Hero were in a relationship and had no interest in her. Hated that she had Knight and not Royal. Was disgusted by Poet's prosthetic, though we all shut her down the one time she mentioned it. She apologized later, blaming being drunk, but she was a vicious bitch. You're a hundred times the woman she is."

I swallowed hard at his words. It was the nicest thing anyone had said to me while not having sex with me. "You don't really know me."

"I know you more than you think." He scoffed. "Besides, a fucking rabies-infected raccoon would be a hundred times better than that demon."

I laughed, but it was muffled by the sounds from the stage. "This one is for all the daydreamers out there," Royal called, then went into their sexiest song. It was a song made for fucking, the bass line strong and slow, and Royal crooned out the words like he was trying to tempt the whole crowd into bed.

They'd all come willingly too.

When he walked over to Knight, the guitarist turned to face him, leaning back and playing that slow rhythm and rolling his body toward Royal like he was fucking him. Honestly, when they did this little performance, my whole body got hot, and I didn't think I was the only one.

Knight reached out and grabbed the side of Royal's button-up shirt between notes, tearing it open, making the crowd scream. Royal smirked, and as his eyes bounced to the side of the stage, they snagged with mine.

Tonight, I was going to bring that man to his knees, and he was going to beg me for it.

I blew him a kiss, and he grinned as he walked back to the front of the stage, his hand running down his body until he cupped his dick. Knight cast me a quick look and winked.

Fuck me. I was in over my head with these guys.

TWENTY-EIGHT

ROYAL

I LOOKED at the little girl in front of me, grimacing at the fact that Knight had practically dry-humped my leg on stage while this kid was in the crowd. Shouldn't she still be watching the cartoon channel? Instead, she was thrusting a poster at me.

"I think your band is just the best," she gushed. I signed my name over my body on the poster, but a small signature in the corner had me raising my eyebrows at the girl.

"When did you get this?" I asked softly, smiling to soften my words.

"Before the concert. Dreamer's so nice, and so, so pretty. I hope I'm as pretty as her when I grow up. And she gave me this!" She pulled a necklace from around her neck, showing me the gemstone on the end. "My friends are never going to believe me."

Her mother motioned her daughter forward to take

a photo, and I gave my trademark smirk. "Look, now you have photo proof."

The line was long, but when the girl leaned forward conspiratorially, I was too interested in her next words to shoo her along to Knight. "Is Dreamer your girlfriend?"

I shook my head. "Dreamer is the bravest person I know, but she's not mine. Prettiness is great, but you should want to be as tough and as loyal as her too."

The girl was nodding furiously. "I will! Thank you, Royal." She bounced along the line and was quickly replaced by another fan. Then another. I was riding the high of a great show, so I took my time talking to people. They'd been a great crowd. They deserved a little extra from us tonight.

By the time we were done, I was exhausted, and Poet's limp was pronounced. I needed a hot shower, a beer and sleep. I'd probably rub one out, because she'd been waiting for us when we got offstage and she looked…

I let out a shuddering sigh.

She made my heart beat faster and my breath stall in my lungs, and that wasn't something I was used to feeling. She was a temptation. She was a problem.

None of that mattered, though, because I still wanted her. I'd been so good the last couple of weeks after I'd seen her breakdown in New Mexico. Watching her struggling and terrified had shocked the hell out of me, and fucking with her now seemed wrong. She'd seemed so tough until that moment, so capable of taking my shit and throwing it back at me tenfold.

Now, screwing with her felt like kicking an already injured bird. One that you wanted to pick up instead. Nurse back to health. See spread its wings once more.

Watching her piece herself back together had made me respect her. Watching her laugh and play house with men I considered family made me look at her in a different light. However, logic was never far away, and it told me one of us had to keep our head, since the rest of them were smitten, all with one girl. Even Shep.

It was a disaster waiting to happen. I'd sat beside Poet's broken body in hospital when we were teenagers, and I told him that I'd never let him get hurt again. Charlotte was the first time I'd come perilously close to breaking that promise, because even if I got rid of her now, Poet was attached. So was Knight, and not just as a rebound. They'd be heartbroken.

Yeah, and you wouldn't exactly be happy either. Don't use them as an excuse just because you don't want to send her away yet. The voice of reason was an asshole sometimes.

We stepped onto the bus, and then she was there. She had beers in her hands, her blindfold on. A smile stretched across her face, and it was like the sun was shining on us, even in the late-night darkness.

"You guys were amazing tonight," she said enthusiastically, and I took a beer. The guys did too, the only difference being that they all swooped down and kissed her. One after another, like the fact they were kissing the same lips wasn't inciting even the smallest amount of territorial jealousy.

Bullshit. There was no way they could just be okay with it. It'd be one thing if she was just a convenient hole, but over the last few weeks, they'd treated her differently. They'd treated her like she was special, important.

Reaching out, she walked forward until she found the couch, sitting down softly. She'd changed from the dress she'd been wearing earlier into little silk pajamas which hugged her tight little ass like a dream. Though she'd been a dream in that dress too. She'd looked like all my black-cat, emo-girl fantasies come to life. It had been hard not to push her against the wall and bury myself inside her right there, backstage.

I didn't know why I was resisting the urge—it was her entire purpose on the tour—but after New Mexico, using her honestly felt wrong. I wanted her to come to me. Wanted her to *want* me.

I hated that she'd made no move to seek me out. Women threw themselves at me left and right, even my friends' girlfriends. Groupies. Music execs. My dad's friends' wives. The teachers at my boarding school. For as long as I'd been a man, girls had offered to get down on their knees in the hopes I'd give them a taste.

But not her.

She didn't ignore me. She talked to me like she wanted to know everything about me. I couldn't tell her anything big without giving away my identity, but I found myself telling her about the first song I ever wrote. When I realized I could actually sing. My favorite food. She had a way of dragging information out of me, and if she wanted to find a different career, she could be an interrogator for the CIA.

Knight sat down beside her, pulling her into his lap. "Thanks, babe. They were a great crowd." He nuzzled her cheek. "It helped that you watched us from the side of the stage. I might have performed a little better to impress you."

I rolled my eyes at my guitarist. To think there was a time he'd been as much of a manwhore as me, and now he was fawning all over her. We were going to have a band meeting soon where I reminded them all that this was a *temporary* situation, before they got in too deep.

We debriefed about the set, about the tour in general, and I noted the way Shep watched Charlotte from the side of his eye. The longing there was honestly painful to see.

Knight stretched, his arm tightening around Charlotte's waist. "I'm exhausted. Who's in your bed tonight, love?"

She chewed her lip, resting her cheek against his temple. "I thought, maybe, Royal would like to sleep in the bigger bed with me tonight?"

I swallowed hard as everyone turned to look at me. I opened my mouth to say something clever, but nothing came out. Her jaw was set in a challenging line, a little curl to her lips like she knew she had me. Like she thought I'd chicken out and foist her on one of the other guys.

This was what I'd wanted. I'd *wanted* her to come to me, but now I was flailing.

I was the lead singer in one of the world's biggest bands. I didn't flail just because a pretty girl wanted to ride my cock.

"Sure, Toy. Whatever you want." I kept my voice casual, like my heart wasn't pounding in my chest. She stood, sashaying straight down the hall as if she could see clearly. She looked over her shoulder and smirked, and I was transported back to the first day I met her—to the Charlotte who was full of bravado and sensuality, who'd put me in my place with a few sharp words and her thumb between my lips.

I felt like a dog, panting after her and coming to heel at her command, but my dick was already aching to be inside her. It meant nothing, just roleplaying. If she wanted to play dominant, I'd make her work for it.

I avoided the guys' eyes as I walked down the bus after her. Either they'd be laughing at me, or subtly threatening me not to do anything stupid, and I didn't want to acknowledge either of those responses.

Her room was the cleanest space on the bus. "Keep it tidy, don't you?"

She shrugged. "I need to be able to walk around in the mask without tripping over and breaking my neck. Besides, it's a holdover from my foster days. Easier to see when something's missing if you know exactly how everything goes."

Fuck me. There was a whole world between our lives up until this point.

She walked to the small closet and opened it with sure fingers. Finding the drawer she needed, she pulled out something wrapped in tissue paper. "I made you something. Well, I made you all something, but you get yours first."

She handed me a soft pleather mask, brass studs holding all the parts together. Other sections had been stitched, like over the nose. It curved up, and I knew it would sit halfway back on my skull. Small horns stuck up from the top, and it was honestly, really fucking cool.

"I used Helen's molds of all your faces, so hopefully they're more comfortable to wear around, so you aren't in full balaclavas all the time. Sorry it took me so long. There was definitely some trial and error involved."

They kind of looked like Daredevil masks, and Hero was going to lose his shit. He'd loved comic books when we were growing up.

"This looks great." I pushed it to my face, but my fingers failed to buckle up the straps at the back. They criss-crossed over the back of my head, holding it tight to my face like a second skin. It fit perfectly. "Can you buckle me up?"

She turned, sliding off her own mask. It was good to see her eyes. Not that I'd admit it. She stroked her fingers through my hair, and I resisted the urge to lean into her fingers. "Pretty." She buckled the two straps tightly, before I spun and kissed her. Hard.

She gasped against my lips, but quickly met my fervor with passion of her own. Her tongue battled with mine for control of the kiss, and it was hot as hell. Eventually, she tore her mouth away.

"On your knees, Royal," she gasped out, and I could see her trying to cling to her control. I smirked, giving her a moment to right the persona she was trying to portray tonight. "You might be the golden boy of the band, but tonight, I'm the one who needs to be worshiped. Can you do that?"

My first instinct was to battle her for control, but when she pushed on my shoulders, I found myself lowering to my knees. It put me nose to navel with her body, and she buried her fingers in my hair, pulling my head back sharply until I was forced to look up at her.

"You look so fucking good down there, ready to please me." Her words made shivers run along my skin. "You *do* want to please me, don't you?" She ran her thumb over my lip. "Tonight, you want to be my toy, isn't that right?"

God, I did. I wanted her screaming my name, telling me that no one else made her feel the way I could.

"Yes."

"Good boy," she purred, and my dick strained.

Was I into this? I didn't think I was into being praised, but I wanted to moan at her words.

She stepped backwards until her thighs hit the bed. "Come and undress me."

I went to stand, and she clucked her tongue at me. Raising an eyebrow, I *crawled* to her. Kneeling before her, I tugged down her silky pajama shorts, until she could kick them off her feet. Then I reached up and tore away her flimsy lace panties. She gasped, her pupils blown wide. Peeling off her own camisole, she stood above me for a moment, entirely naked. She sat on the edge of the bed, spreading her thighs. Her pretty cunt glistened, and I knew she was as into this as I apparently was.

"Make me come for you, Royal."

She didn't need to ask me twice as I dived between her thighs. I didn't go down on many women, the act way more intimate than sticking my dick into someone. But right now, I couldn't have resisted if I tried. I pushed her backwards on the bed, propping her thighs over my shoulders.

I showed her that my mouth wasn't just made for singing as I plunged my tongue inside her, then went back to torture her clit, alternating back and forth until she was panting my name, moaning about how good I was eating her.

"That's it… That's it; you're so good at this. You eat my pussy *so damn good*." She clutched my hair and pulled my head back so I was looking at her. "I want to see your eyes as you make me come," she moaned.

I growled on her clit before sucking on it hard, and that was all she needed to come all over my cheeks. The whole time, I held her eyes. My fingertips dug into the curves of her hips as I lapped up every little bit of her release. The way her lips parted, her eyes scrunching like it almost hurt to come that hard, was forever going to be burned into my brain. I wanted to do it again, right now, but she shook her head.

"So fucking good. So good for me," she said in a strangled voice. "But now I want you to show me what you can do with that beautiful dick. Take your clothes off for me. I want to watch you unwrap what's mine."

I wasn't hers, but I didn't want to stop her. Not right now. Right now, I wanted to be hers more than I wanted anything else in my life.

I shed my clothes so fast, it made her tsk again, but I just smirked at her. "Such a shithead," she chuckled. "So freaking beautiful, though."

I let her take in the body that I worked hard for. I ran every morning I could, sneaking out before dawn with Shep. I ran from my demons, from the noise of Knight or Hero or Poet making her orgasm as the sun rose.

Her eyes dropped to my dick, then that cute little pink tongue dipped out to wet her dry lips. I was going to suck that tongue into my mouth soon. I was aching to kiss her again. She curled her finger at me, and this time, I went willingly. Climbing up the bed, I gave into the urge to fuck her mouth with my tongue, hoping she could taste herself on my lips. She might think she was in control right now—and I might be enjoying it more than I thought I would—but soon enough, she'd be beneath me, saying *yes sir* as she pleased me.

She laughed, and it vibrated against my chest, before she slipped her hands up to my pecs and pinched my nipples *hard*. Throwing me off balance, she used the motion to roll me onto my back, until she was straddling my hips.

Honestly, if I wasn't completely transfixed by the

feel of her hot, wet core against my dick, I'd probably have applauded her for that power move.

Then she wrapped her hand around my dick, guided me to her entrance and sank down. Any thoughts, other than the feel of her wrapped around me, disappeared into the ether.

TWENTY-NINE

DREAMER

THIS WAS what people who took care of apex predators must feel like all the time. Like I had the beast on a leash, and one wrong move was going to end with me in pieces, but fuck me, what a way to go.

As I sank down onto Royal, the way he was looking at me—like I was some kind of goddess—was a heady experience. When he was balls deep inside me, we both groaned.

"You feel so fucking perfect inside me," I murmured, because forming words was a little difficult as he lifted my hips, then ground me back down. Soon enough, we were meeting in a rhythm that was just intrinsic. Deep and slow, we rolled against each other, and I whispered words of praise that made him shiver beneath me.

I wanted to tear the mask from his face, but I didn't. He fucked me in a way that I worried would be addictive. I *couldn't* become addicted to this man. However, anything close to logic disappeared beneath the pleasure as he sat up, wrapping his arms around my waist. I looped my legs behind his lower back and gasped.

Holy shit. Holy shit.

Then he kissed down my neck, nudging me backwards until my body was curled, hitting more places inside me I hadn't known even existed. His mouth wrapped around my nipple, and I moaned, gripping his shin as I rolled my body.

He cursed around my nipple and doubled his efforts, and that slow, creeping orgasm consumed me completely. I came hard, my whole body throbbing, like one big wave of pleasure. Then I was on my back with Royal on top of me, slamming into me with a chaotic energy that had another orgasm chasing the one I'd just had. I screamed his name as he chanted mine.

"Fuck, Charlotte… Fuck, *oh god*." He grunted as he came, the lines of his body straining as I held on for dear life.

He collapsed on top of me, catching himself on his elbows and burying his face in the pillow beside my ear. Nothing could be heard but our panting breaths and the sound of the television in the living area turned way, way up.

I stroked my fingers up and down his spine. "Holy hell. That was…"

"Yeah."

"You fucked me so good, I'm not sure I'll ever be the same," I purred in his ear. "My good boy."

He shivered on top of me with a groan. "Stop, or I'll get hard again." I felt his dick twitch inside me.

I snorted a laugh. "Not even the almighty Royal has that good of a refractory period."

He reared back, the look on his face telling me he was taking that challenge personally. "I'm about to ruin this pussy for anyone else, Toy." He leaned down and whispered in my ear, "It's my turn now."

"You can't just barge in here!" Shep's shout woke me from the warm cocoon of Royal's arms.

A gruff voice replied, "Yeah, this says we can."

The door to the bedroom opened, and a man in a suit stood there, silhouetted by the hall lighting. Royal sat up, his body between mine and the men in the doorway.

"What is the *fucking* meaning of this?"

It was in that moment I realized that outside of the band, Royal was rich as hell. Because when cops turned up at the door—and I had no doubt these were detectives, given the ill-fitting suits and the uniformed officers behind them—poor people got scared. Rich people got outraged.

"We have an arrest warrant for Charlotte Lochrin. Miss, you're going to have to come with us."

Royal pointed at the door. "Like hell. Get the fuck out of here so she can get dressed. Then you can show me your damn warrant. This is bullshit!" he yelled, but my whole body was shaking.

The detective looked at me, taking in my naked shoulders, and his lip curled. I could tell exactly what he was thinking, that I was some whore-groupie. In a way, he was right. That's exactly what I was. "We'll be right outside the door."

My lungs felt like they were locking up. I couldn't breathe. I couldn't *breathe.*

Royal gripped my face hard, and I flinched away. He removed his hands, like they were on fire. "No, Charlotte, I wouldn't..." He looked horrified. "I'd never hurt you. Never, you hear me? I need you to breathe and get dressed, okay? Fuck, I need Poet in here. Breathe with me, okay? Deep breath in..." He scrambled around for his jeans and a shirt, then found my band hoodie in the hamper. "Now out." I breathed out on his command. "Now in... Arms up." He pulled the hoodie over my head. "And out. Are you with me, baby? I promise, it's going to be okay."

I believed him. I did.

He let out a relieved sigh. "That's it. Good girl. Now, put on some pants and we'll go and get this all figured out, okay?"

I found underwear and some jeans, and quickly dragged them on. I put my hair up into a ponytail on top of my head, but my hands were shaking, so it took twice as long.

Royal held out his arms, pulling me into a tight hug. "I've got you."

He stepped out of the room, and then a detective was there, grabbing me and putting my hands behind my back. "Charlotte Lochrin, you're under arrest for grand larceny. You have the right to remain silent, but anything you do or say can be used against you in a court of law. You have the right to an attorney. If you cannot afford an attorney, one will be appointed for you."

My eyes went wide, and I felt like they were going to pop out of my skull. "What?" I breathed, but they were already marching me toward the front of the tour bus. "Royal? Shep!"

I looked between the guys and suddenly noticed no one was wearing masks.

They were so fucking beautiful. Their mouths were open, and they all looked horrified, but it still didn't dim their beauty.

"I didn't do anything! I didn't steal anything, I swear."

Shep stepped into their way, blocking the door. "That's bullshit. What the hell do they think she stole?"

"One point three million dollars."

My knees went weak. "*What?*"

The detective glared at Shep. "Move, or I'll take you down to the station too."

I shook my head, imploring him to get out of the way. I couldn't stand the thought of dragging him down with me. Knight reached out and gripped Shep's arm. His hair fell over his forehead, and I wanted to smooth it back.

"You're no good to her in lock-up. She'll be out by midday," he said firmly, but the promise was to me.

Hero had his phone to his ear. "I'm getting you a lawyer. Don't say anything to anyone, Charlotte," he told me as they marched me out of the bus. Thankfully, most people were still asleep, with only a few roadies and the security guards awake to see my walk of shame.

The officers put me in the back of a cop car, and I looked back at the bus. Shep was standing outside, watching me with a heartbreaking expression as we drove away.

No one talked to me on the ride to the police station, or as they booked me, taking my fingerprints. I could only imagine what would pop up when they ran those. By the time they interviewed me, they'd have formed a complete picture of me. Across the front of it would be *guilty as fuck* in big red letters.

They stuffed me into a holding cell with a prostitute, who was curled in on herself. She gave me a quick look, then went back to staring into space. That was fine; I didn't want to talk anyway.

I put my head in my hands and tried to breathe. I hadn't stolen *anything*. This had to have something to do with Tom, unless Jeanette from the Stop 'n' Shop had suddenly decided to charge me for stealing those peanut M&M's sixteen years ago. That had been the beginning and the end of my shoplifting career. I was a lot of things, but I wasn't a thief.

After several hours, they eventually came and put me in an interrogation room. Well, it said *Meeting Room* on the door, but the table was made of polished metal and one wall was entirely glass, so that seemed pretty interrogation-ish to me.

A cop came in, holding a remote and pointing to a camera in the corner. "We're filming this interview. Do you consent?"

I nodded, figuring that having this on tape was better than letting them make up whatever they wanted. I'd been on the bad side of the cops before.

After a few minutes, the detective from earlier came in to sit opposite me. "Miss Lochrin, you've been quite difficult to track down. It took an anonymous tip to work out you'd hitched a ride with The Daymakers. A fan?"

I shook my head. "I hadn't heard of them until several weeks ago." The last thing I wanted to do was incriminate the guys in something they hadn't done.

"Yet you're traveling across the country with them?"

Hero's words echoed in my head. "I'm not saying anything until my lawyer gets here."

The detective gave me a smarmy smile. "As a matter of fact, your lawyer just arrived."

Hero worked fast.

The door opened, and my relief turned to terror almost immediately. Tom stood in the doorway. His face was neutral, but his eyes promised pain.

My chair scraped back, and I shook my head forcefully. "No. No! He's *not* my lawyer."

The detective frowned between us, taking in my terror and Tom's impassive face. "Are you sure?"

"Don't worry, Detective. Miss Lochrin just has a fear

of lawyers from her childhood. We are working through it. I just need a minute with my client in private."

I looked at the detective, my eyes imploring him. "Please don't leave me here with him. Please." Terror was making my knees shake. "*Please*," I breathed.

The detective looked at Tom. "Seems she's revoking you as her lawyer, Mr…?"

"Granville. Thomas Granville Junior from the firm Helena, Perlman & Carlton out in LA." Tom looked around the interview room with disdain, like it was dirty.

The detective's voice turned icy. "As in, the firm suing Miss Lochrin for grand larceny? You don't think representing her might be considered a conflict of interest?"

"She was once my girlfriend. I feel an obligation that she be represented to the full extent of her rights."

He had an obligation to see me dead; that's what his eyes were saying. I'd fucked up and pissed off a psycho.

The detective looked back at me. "Are you waiving your right to a lawyer?"

"I want him gone," I squeaked out, panic stealing my words. "Please make him leave."

The detective looked at the uniform, tilting his head at the door. The cop ushered Tom out, but not before he got the last word in. He always needed the last word.

"I'm going. I'll stop and see The Daymakers instead. See if they have anything to add to your case. My private investigator was *very* thorough, so I'm sure I'll catch them before they move on to their next stop."

It was a threat in a pleasant tone. The cop shut the door in his face, and I let out a shuddering sob.

"Obviously you know him?"

I nodded, sitting back on the hard plastic chair before I collapsed. "My ex-boyfriend. He used to beat the shit out of me."

The cop's eyes turned flinty. "He seems like the type. When you've done this job as long as I have, the warning signs may as well be neon." He shook his head, looking down at the folder in front of him. "Honestly, looking at your history, you may as well be a textbook abuse case too. Drug addict parents who dealt on the side. In and out of trouble with the law. A report in your father's write-up says they had you carrying around bricks of methamphetamine in your Dora the Explorer backpack?"

I shrugged. "Yeah, they weren't stellar examples of parenting."

"Your mother, Sophia Lochrin, died of an OD when you were thirteen—"

I interrupted. "She left long before that."

"And your father, Henry Lochrin, died in prison earlier this year, where he was serving fifteen years for drug charges."

I jolted in my chair. My dad was dead? I didn't have any love for the man, but he'd been my last living relative. "Oh."

The detective frowned. "You didn't know?" I shook my head, and he sighed. "Look, Charlotte. If you have anything you want to say, you should tell us now. If you wait for this to go to court, they are likely just going to see another bad apple in a barrel of bad apples and throw the book at you. You have the hallmark of a generational criminal."

"I—"

The door burst open, and a harried-looking guy in a suit appeared. "My client is invoking her right to not incriminate herself. Tobias Lecter, attorney. Hero sent me." He shook my hand and side-eyed the detective. "If I could have a moment with my client?"

The detective looked between us. "This one is *actually* your lawyer?" he asked, and I nodded. If Hero had sent him, I knew he was here to help.

"Yes."

"You've got fifteen minutes."

Tobias Lecter scoffed, but didn't dispute his words. The lawyer was wearing a sharp three-piece suit in gunmetal gray, his hair combed back carefully, his eyes seeing everything. "Sorry I took so long. I had to get the private jet down from New York, which took longer than we would have liked." He looked down at the charge sheet. "Seems the firm of Helena, Perlman & Carlton has accused you of stealing a hefty sum of money from their holding accounts. I can't see why they would think you had anything to do with it. You aren't a known hacker or anything, are you?"

I shook my head. "I can barely work my phone."

"Hmm, their evidence seems… Oh. I see. They have your digital fingerprints all over it, and the account it was transferred into was... Charlotte Lochrin, LLC. Really?"

"It wasn't me! As if I'd be that fucking stupid."

The lawyer's lips twisted. "Well, that's true, but when you've been a lawyer as long as I have, stupidity isn't really that unexpected." He sighed, pulling out a tablet with an attached keyboard from his briefcase. "You better start at the beginning."

THIRTY

KNIGHT

I PACED UP and down the bus. Royal was on the phone to Whitt and the label, who were absolutely losing their minds at the press drama of cops turning up at the arena and dragging Lottie away. Luckily, it had been early, so there were no photographs from paparazzi, but still, there were enough first-hand accounts that rumors were now flying around wild and unchecked.

The label wanted us to make a public appearance somewhere to make it clear it wasn't the band personally, but none of us wanted to go on parade while Lottie was rotting in a cell.

Hero had called Sampson Rubio, who we knew from boarding school, to get the number for his criminal defense lawyer. Sampson had gotten into some trouble a little while ago, and his lawyer was a fucking shark. He had a reputation as the best, and we wanted the best for Charlotte.

Grand larceny... The hell? I'd thought Shep was going to punch Whitt when he suggested that maybe the charges were true. Luckily, Tricia had done it for him.

Whitt had been running interference with the label the best he could, but he wasn't as invested in Lottie as we were. The label wanted to cut her loose, move the tour on. Distance ourselves both physically and metaphorically.

I wasn't leaving her behind. *No fucking way*. It burned that I couldn't be there, but I couldn't exactly walk into a police station as fucking Knight, mask and all. And that was the crux of it—these made-up personas had no legal standing, but the real me? I could throw around some weight. But it would mean unveiling ourselves, which would breach our contracts with the label.

They weren't scared about threatening us with legal action if we didn't honor the terms of our tour contracts either. They'd used that stick to beat us several times in the last six hours.

Fuck. She'd been sitting in a cell for *six hours.*

I looked at Hero, who was staring at his phone. "Anything from the lawyer?"

He shook his head. "No."

The show had already loaded out to head to Nashville, and we were delaying. I'd walk off this bus if I had to, the tour be damned. When had Lottie become so important to me?

I looked over at Poet, who was staring at nothing, his thoughts obviously far away. I knew now that there was no way I was going to just wish her luck at the end of the tour. I wanted her to stay with me, without the promise of money at the end.

Shep was on his phone to god knows who, but judging by the language, he was trying to figure out where the bogus charges had come from. I knew the look on his face; I'd seen it all through our teenage years after he'd kind of adopted us. Feral protectiveness. He would have killed men for us—still would—but I didn't know when Lottie had become important enough to him that she qualified for that kind of loyalty too.

They hadn't even slept together, from what I was aware. Was there more going on with them than they let on? Was she going behind our backs?

Jealousy burned in my chest, but it was a bitter feeling from old wounds. When Laura had tried to fuck Royal, her cheating broke something inside me. That had been the moment I'd gone from trusting implicitly to wary of everyone's intentions.

Shaking my head, I pushed the negative thoughts back down. Now was not the time to start overthinking. Lottie needed us, and if that meant she got Shep too, that was good with me. I was already sharing her with my three best friends—what was one more?

Honestly, I'd thought it would be hard, but it felt almost right. Laura had almost torn us apart, but Charlotte had brought us closer together. Getting to know her, caring for her, having her care for us? It meant something.

A knock at the door had me leaping to my feet. Was she back? Had Hero's fancy lawyer shut this bullshit all down?

Shep opened the door to find one of the roadies standing there. "There's a lawyer at the gate," he said quietly. Alexi was one of our regular roadies, and I trusted him more than others.

"Dreamer?" Shep asked, his voice purposefully neutral.

Alexi shook his head. "There's just the lawyer."

"Send him up," Shep growled, and I could see the defeated feeling in my chest mirrored on his face.

We were silent as we all slipped our masks back on. They felt ridiculous right now, like we were playing dress-up while Charlotte's future hung on the line. I wanted to down an entire bottle of vodka, but I also didn't want to be drunk if she needed me.

There was another knock on the door, and Shep opened it. His face turned from pleasantly neutral to rage in the space of a second. He was out of the bus in a dive, laying into the guy in front of us until Hero and Alexi got him around the shoulders and pulled him off.

"How does it feel to be on the other end of fists, you *fuck?*"

Hero dropped Shep's arm as his words penetrated. The guy climbed to his feet, spitting blood, his face already blackening into a bruise.

"I'm going to have you charged with fucking assault," he spat back, and I was kind of glad to see there was a tooth in the blood on the ground. Because the guy wasn't any random person.

He was Tom. Charlotte's ex, Tom.

Abusive psycho Tom.

I growled low, and he held up a hand. "Before you attack me again, you might want to wait and hear what I have to say."

"I don't give a flying *fuck* what you have to say." I wanted to fucking wring this puny asshole's neck with my own two hands.

"You might want to reconsider that stance, Mr. Beck."

"I don't want to reconsider… What did you just call me?" My heart pounded in my chest, and my eyes went wide before I shut it down.

But that fucker knew he had me.

Had us all.

He gave me a smirk that made me want to rip his head off. "Why don't we go inside and talk—unless you want to have this conversation out here, among all your employees with their cellphone cameras and social media pages?"

I flicked my eyes to Alexi, who was gaping at us all. Using my last name had given nothing away to Alexi, but if this guy ran his mouth much more, the secret would be out.

Shep ground his jaw so hard, I wondered if his teeth might crack. He shook off Alexi's arm and stepped aside. The guy showed he had no actual self-preservation because he walked up the stairs like he owned the bus, showing his back to a real predator.

Shep looked at Alexi. "Not a fucking word." It wasn't a request.

Alexi shook his head. "I don't know what you're talking about." Then he walked away. Yeah, that was why Alexi had been with the band so long.

As we climbed the stairs, Tom and Royal were having a staredown. Royal looked like death, the mask making him look more ominous than his golden-boy visage would normally allow.

Tom gave him an effusive smile. "Ah, Rourke Stokes, infamous playboy son of even more infamous playboy Roman Stokes. Guess the apple didn't fall too far from the tree, seeing how you're fucking every whore this side of the Mason-Dixon line, my girlfriend included." He turned to Poet, who was standing behind him. "And Moss Aguilar, beloved son of Formula One driver Olivier Aguilar. Tragedy that he fucking drove like a lunatic into another car, right? Lucky you only lost your foot and not your life, unlike everyone else in that accident, including your dad."

Immediately, Hero stepped forward to pummel the fucker, because no one—especially not this fuck—got to poke at Poet's wounds. But Poet gripped the back of his shirt, holding him back.

"He's not worth it," he murmured softly to Hero, before facing Tom. "Yeah, I know who you are too, Tom fucking Granville Junior. Abuser. Piece of shit. Has just as much to lose as we do." Poet's voice was soft, but I could hear the rage beneath the words.

"Listen to your boyfriend, Curtis Hawkins. Not even your family's money could get you out of a murder charge." The asshole held up his hands in front of him. "Look, gentlemen, I have no argument with you, despite the fact you've been fucking my girlfriend. I just want my Charlie back. I've missed her so much, and I want these last couple of months to go away. I made mistakes, but I've gotten into anger management and I swear, I will make her happy again."

"Bull-fucking-shit," I snapped, but Royal held up a hand.

"And what do you want us to do about it? Charlotte's an adult, not a prisoner on the tour. If she wanted to go home to you, she would."

Tom snorted. "And leave the glamor of touring across the country with a famous rock band? She's always had a bit of a wandering soul, that one. Probably comes from being booted from foster home to foster home for seducing her foster dads. That one has serious daddy issues. I can't blame her. Her father was a meth addict who took as many drugs as he made, before he was sent to prison. Honestly, she's so fucked up, it's no wonder she stole all my firm's money, then skipped off to join a music tour to be a glorified prostitute."

I couldn't take it anymore. "Shut your *fucking mouth.*"

"Ah, Jessie Beck. This little setup should feel just like

home, considering the articles written about your home life. A family of degenerate deviants means you never stood a chance."

Yeah, my family were notorious swingers. *So fucking what.*

Royal gripped my arm. "Make your point and get the fuck out, asshole."

"She was amusingly easy to find, considering how hopped up on anonymity you are. My PI asked the right questions in LA and then Vegas, and this sudden appearance of Dreamer?" He snorted, like we were the ridiculous ones, then steepled his fingers beneath his chin. "Look, I'll make this simple for you. You kick Charlotte to the curb. Go on with your tour, keep your anonymity, and forget she ever existed." He rolled his eyes at me. "I can already tell by your faces that you don't believe me. I'll write up an NDA to sign, make it ironclad, as long as a few conditions are met—starting with you fucking off to Nashville and leaving Charlotte behind."

Shep snarled. "We aren't abandoning her to prison, you piece of shit."

Tom's eyes slipped from Shep, like he was inconsequential, and I guess if you judged power only by wealth and family name, he would be the least powerful here. But he was a child of the streets, and physically more dangerous than all of us combined.

Tom just frowned, nodding in a condescending way. "I see. I promise that I'll get the charges against her dropped completely. My colleagues are lawyers; they'll understand that when the money is returned, making it go away will be better for business than a drawn-out court proceeding." His gaze sharpened. "But only if you agree to my terms. It's simple. You leave Charlotte alone, and everything gets fixed. Your tour contracts won't be in jeopardy, your careers won't be in tatters, your anonymity stays in check and Charlotte's charges disappear. It's win-win. Think it over. I'll see myself out."

Shep was already moving after him, making sure he left the lot, and hopefully this fucking mortal coil. I slumped back onto the couch, ripping off my mask and looking around at the men who were my brothers. Everything we'd ever worked for was in jeopardy, but so was Lottie.

"What the fuck do we do?"

But no one had any answers.

THIRTY-ONE

CHARLOTTE

THE INTERVIEW that occurred after I offloaded my entire sordid history onto my new lawyer was nothing if not torturous. The detective from before, plus another I didn't recognize, returned and the cameras were turned back on.

Tobias sat beside me, a notebook in front of him. He'd told me to be honest with the cops, and that he'd watch for any statements that could be misconstrued, or if the police were leading me down a path that might sound incriminating. All the evidence they had so far was circumstantial, so without a confession, it was going to be a hard sell to the DA.

It had to be Tom, and that's what I told them. Repeatedly.

My tone was monotone as I explained about first meeting Tom at a bar where I was working. How he'd been charming and kind, buying me drinks and walking me to my car after my shift to make sure I wasn't attacked by random drunks. How he started coming to sit at my bar every Thursday and just talking to me, like he cared about what my dreams were.

I felt like such an idiot when I admitted that I'd moved in with him after only a couple of months. His pristine apartment with its shiny chrome appliances and fancy coffee maker had seemed like paradise. How, when the bar went belly-up, he'd told me that I didn't have to find another job, because I could look after the house and he'd look after me.

As soon as he had me cut off from everything, he changed. How it was just slowly at first, telling me we should eat better, go to the gym. How he'd call me fat and then restrict what I could eat, even when he'd eat fast food. How he'd complain about the way I loaded the dishwasher or vacuumed the floor. How the food I cooked was trash. How I wasn't as pretty as his coworkers' girlfriends. How I was lazy and using him. How he'd dress me for corporate office parties, fuck me in his office, then berate me for being a whore when we got home.

I told them about when he started hitting me. How he'd worn me down so much that I believed him when he said it was just because of a hard case at work, that he didn't mean it. That he'd never do it again.

Again and again. Until I was convinced there was nowhere I could go and nobody who would help me.

When I got to the part in the back alley of the club, how he'd beaten me and tried to sexually assault me, my words caught in my throat. It had been the best and worst night of my life. Tobias gripped my fingers tightly, a show of support from a stranger that I desperately needed.

"This is when you joined The Daymakers tour?" the detective from earlier, Detective Ball, asked, making his own notes.

I nodded. "I scaled the security fencing and hid under a truck. The band's manager found me and kind of took pity on me."

Detective Ball looked at his notes. "Manager-slash-security personnel… Grover Shepherd?"

I snorted a laugh, before slapping a hand over my mouth. "Sorry. I just call him Shep. I didn't realize his first name was Grover." If they ever let me out of here, that was the first thing I was going to ask him about. I cleared my throat. "Yeah, he took me to see the tour doctor, and she patched me up."

"So you never attended a clinic or the hospital? Made a police report about your injuries?"

I let out a shaky breath. "No. I just wanted to escape. I wanted to get away. They offered me the chance." I shrugged. "What was a hospital going to tell me that I didn't already know from having the shit kicked out of me for years? I've had broken ribs before, Detective, and I wasn't going to sit in urgent care for them to look at me with pity in their eyes and then tell me to ice it." I'd been there way too many times already.

Tobias tapped his pen on his notebook. "Can we get to the actual charges now? Because this looks like revenge to me, but you're the detectives." His sarcasm in his tone was so sharp, it was a wonder it didn't shred the cops to pieces.

Other than the shell company with my literal name, the firm had video surveillance of me looking at Tom's computer after an office party for someone's retirement. What they couldn't see was the screen.

I remembered the night clearly. I'd been looking at the time, hoping that I could leave. Tom had banged me against the door, his hand plastered over my mouth to keep me quiet, not caring that I could barely breathe. He'd finished and left, telling me to fix myself up. That fucker had known the camera was there too, because he'd looked directly at it at one point.

To complement that was Tom's statement that he'd caught me on his work computer at home, as well as the fact that I was listed as the only beneficiary on a huge transfer of money to the Caymans.

The detective gave my lawyer a droll look. "The evidence isn't inconsequential."

"All you have is hearsay and literal grasping at straws."

"Enough to charge her with larceny, though. Proving it wasn't her is a you thing, Mr. Lecter. Not a me thing."

Tobias sighed heavily. "We both know this won't go past preliminary hearings."

The other detective—Detective Michaelson—shrugged. "The firm seems intent, and they have friends in high places."

Putting away his notebook, Tobias fixed narrowed

eyes on the detectives. “I have a history of bringing those friends in high places back down to earth where they belong. I won’t let my client be railroaded by some piece-of-shit ex-boyfriend. I want her arraigned as soon as possible, so be a decent human being and put her ticket in immediately, if that’s the path you wish to take.”

Detective Michaelson just gave him a hard look, but didn’t comment. “We’ll give you one last moment with your client. Someone will be down to take her back to her cell shortly.” The detectives stood and left, and Tobias turned to me.

“Don’t worry about the bond. I’ll get the band to arrange it, and if they can’t, I’ll do it myself. I know a few people who’ve been in your position who wouldn’t mind helping you out. Trust me, you’re never going to see inside the walls of a prison.” He stopped short of promising me, though.

I let out a shaky sigh. “Thank you, Tobias. I know this isn’t what you wanted to do with your Monday morning.”

He gave me a pat on the back. “Still better than my morning commute. Is there anything you want me to tell your friends?”

I hesitated. “Tell them thank you. And that they need to go to Nashville for the next show. I think they might try and stay, but I don’t want them to get in trouble. So tell them that I said they have to go.”

A uniformed officer appeared then to escort me back to the cell. Trying not to look as panicked as I felt,

I waved to Tobias and walked back toward the lock-up.

Twenty-four hours later, I was transferred to the courthouse. I stood there in crusty clothes, my hair like a rat's nest on top of my head, probably smelling like asscrack. I wanted to cry.

Whitt and Shep sat on a bench at the back of the courtroom, and just looking at Shep had me close to losing it. His jaw kept flexing, like he wanted to race over here and bundle me into his arms, and I desperately wanted him to do it.

Tobias was there, and he smiled at me confidently. "Are you okay?" he asked in a low voice, and I nodded. I was okay. I'd been through worse. I wasn't some rich princess who had never been in trouble with the law. It made me tougher, but didn't make it any easier to bear.

The prosecution flicked through some notes, looking absolutely bored out of his mind. My eyes went back to Whitt and Shep.

Shep mouthed, *It'll be okay.* I just chewed my lip and nodded.

"Miss Lochrin, your attention, if I may?" The judge already sounded pissed. "This is my last case of the day, and I'd like to get home to a glass of scotch and my dog. Now, you're charged with one count of grand larceny. How do you plead?"

"Not guilty, Your Honor."

"Your Honor, we'd like to file a motion to dismiss

the case. The evidence is circumstantial at best, and at worst, it's a gross misuse of the justice system."

The judge read the papers in front of him, one eyebrow raised. "While I agree it seems… tenuous at best, there is a case there, Mr. Lecter. Whether it gets to the next stage or not is up to you to work out among yourselves. I'm setting the bail at three hundred thousand dollars."

I gasped, my eyes flying up to the judge. I didn't have three hundred thousand dollars.

Tobias patted my back. "Don't worry, Miss Lochrin. That's why Mr. Shepherd is here. They'll post your bail, and you'll be out within the hour."

I nodded, but as I followed the bailiff out of the courtroom, I couldn't help but look one more time at Shep. He was standing, watching me go, and I realized in that moment that maybe I had stronger feelings for him than lust.

He'd rescued me, twice now, and that was two more times than any other person in my life. I'd had a lot of time to think about all the guys while sitting around in my cell, and I'd come to the chilling conclusion that I might have feelings for them all already, despite my intent to keep myself separate. To hold my walls around me like a safety blanket.

They'd stomped right through them, and now I was going to be broken in a way I hadn't ever let myself feel. They would leave, and I would be alone again.

THIRTY-TWO

SHEP

WATCHING her walk away again killed me on the inside. I paid her bail as quickly as possible and now I was waiting around for her to be released.

I messaged the group chat.

Bail set at 300k. Judge wouldn't dismiss it, but said it looked weak.

KNIGHT

Fuckers. Does she look okay?

POET

You paid it, right?

ROYAL

300k. Who is she? Pablo Escobar?

I paid it. She looks rough and so damn sad. I'm waiting for her now.

HERO

I want to see her.

I sighed. It had taken all of Whitt's considerable negotiation skills to get them to Nashville, and I felt sorry for the crowds there, because they weren't going to get their money's worth, that was for damn sure. They had three cities in the next six days, so they had no time to run back and forth to Georgia.

Charlotte wouldn't be able to leave until the trial was done, and her preliminary hearing was set for three weeks' time. Must be a slow month for the Georgia courts, but I was thankful. The sooner this nightmare was over for her, the better.

The guys didn't know what they were going to do, but one thing was clear: no one was letting Charlotte go back to that dick, or get wrongfully accused of something that could get her fifteen years in prison.

Tom hadn't seemed like the kind of psycho who made empty threats, though. He'd come after the guys. I should have killed that fucker when I had the chance. I could take jail time; Charlotte couldn't.

Just play the shows. It'll keep everyone off her back for now, until you decide what you want to do.

The ultimatum was something that affected only the band, and it was a choice only they could make. I would be okay no matter what happened, and I hadn't told the guys this, but there was no way I was giving Charlotte up.

In fact, as soon as I got her into my arms again, I wasn't ever letting her go. I didn't care about what was right. I didn't care about the fact that half my friends loved her too. I certainly didn't give a flying fuck about some record label contract keeping her mouth shut. I was going to keep her, if she'd have me.

Suddenly, the door opened, and she was there. She stepped out warily, like she was unsure. I just opened my arms. She let out a choked noise, diving into them. I wrapped her up tight, kissing the top of her head. She sobbed in my arms, and I let her tears soak into my skin, fortifying my decisions.

She was my priority at the moment, and I hoped this situation with the band and the bullshit with the label all worked out, but it was time for me to be happy too. If she wanted me, I'd stay with her here in Georgia. I'd stay with her long after that, if she'd let me. She needed me, and the band had each other to lean on. She had no one.

I stroked her back soothingly, resisting the urge to pick her up and carry her out to the SUV I'd rented. She didn't say anything, just rubbed her face on her sleeve.

I'd booked us a serviced apartment, since I hadn't been sure how long we'd be here. I drove to the outskirts of the city, pulling up in front of a tiny row of townhouses. Parking just out front, I came around and opened her door.

"Let's get you something to eat and then into bed. I bet you're exhausted." I felt like I was talking to a wounded animal, rather than the fierce woman I'd gotten to know over the last couple of months. Jiggling the front door open, I led her inside, then to the bottom of the staircase. "Your room is the first one on the left. I've put your bags in there. Why don't you have a shower while I get you something to eat?" I kissed her temple, and she leaned into the embrace. "You'll feel better after a shower."

She still hadn't said anything, but I watched her wearily climb the stairs. She was breaking my heart right now.

I turned, heading over to the fridge. I'd had food delivered this morning, just in case we had to stick around, and I pulled her out a microwave meal. It wasn't great, but it'd do for now. I listened for the shower, and when the water shut off, I put her food into the microwave.

I didn't know what to do right now. I was half tempted to tell Hero to come down, to bring Poet. I knew those two would know exactly what to do and say, but I was out here, flailing.

She came back downstairs, wrapped in my hoodie, which was hanging to her knees. I fucking loved how she looked in my clothes. I must have been staring, because she shifted from foot to foot. "Sorry, I forgot to take my clothes into the bathroom. I saw this on the floor and borrowed it." Her eyes darted to mine. "And then I didn't want to take it off again."

I shook my head. "Anything I have is yours, Dreamer."

She sniffed again, and I ignored her red-rimmed eyes; I got the feeling she wanted to pretend she hadn't been crying in the shower. "You don't have to call me that."

"Dreamer?" Pulling the food from the microwave, I transferred it to a plate. "It's who you are now. Until you tell me to stop, you'll be Dreamer to me." Even if I had been the last one to get on board with the name, I wasn't going to strip this from her too.

I knew I had to tell her about the visit from her shithead ex, but not right now. First, she needed sleep and food and to feel safe again. I could give her that.

She nodded and came to sit on the stool at the counter. I put the plate in front of her, and she ate it like she was starved. I pulled out some bread rolls I had warming in the oven and slathered them with butter, placing them beside her plate.

When she finished eating, she looked up, slightly embarrassed. "Sorry. There's only so many salad sandwiches and granola bars you can eat." She ripped off a piece of bread and popped it into her mouth, chewing slowly. "Did the guys make it to their next stop?" Her tone was light, but I could hear the tremor beneath her words.

"They did. They should be on their way to Kansas City today." I reached out and gripped her hand. "They wanted to come back here, but the label put their foot down. Gave them an ultimatum. I'm pretty sure they would have told them to go fuck themselves, but the tour employs a lot of people who wouldn't get paid if they didn't go."

She frowned, waving a hand. "Of course, they have

to continue. They don't need to get caught up in my crap." She sucked in a breath, and I knew what she was about to ask, hating that I was going to have to be the bearer of bad news. "The label canceled my contract, right? I won't get the money?"

I nodded, clenching my jaw. "There was a code of conduct clause in there, which was violated as soon as you were arrested. Plus, you missed two tour stops and won't be able to leave the state for a while. There won't be any money at the end."

She nodded slowly, her lip wobbling, but she held it together. "I thought so. I would have felt weird taking the money anyway, considering—" She cut off quickly. "Whatever. It's better if they aren't connected to me." Her eyes dropped down to the counter, and she picked at a small divot in the wooden top.

Sliding a finger under her chin, I lifted her face toward mine. "Considering *what*, Dreamer?"

"Considering… Considering I might have developed feelings for them. It's better this way," she whispered, and I wanted to roar at the injustice of this bullshit. The fact she was going to get *nothing*, through no fault of her own. The fact I knew the guys wanted her too, but might make the wrong choice. The fact she'd said she'd developed feelings for *them,* and that didn't include me.

I swallowed down all that outrage. "I'm sorry." It was a useless platitude, but it was all I could give her.

She gave me a tight smile that didn't quite reach her eyes. "That's okay. I'll be fine." She cleared her throat. "So, when do you have to get back to the guys?"

I shook my head. "I'm with you for as long as you're stuck here. This place is ours for the next month at least, until Tobias Lecter gets this shit all figured out for you." Walking around until I was on the other side of the counter, I pulled her up until she was in my arms and held her in a tight hug. "They can't be here, but we aren't abandoning you. I know I'm not them, but I'm here with you until you tell me to leave. You aren't in this alone anymore."

She inhaled deep lungfuls of air against my chest. Finally, she looked up. "You aren't a consolation prize, you know. Not to me."

It made me an epic piece of shit, but I couldn't help myself. I bent down and brushed my lips across hers. She clutched my shirt in her fists, like she was worried I'd disappear too. The little part of my brain that worried that I was just what she'd said I wasn't—a consolation prize—crept up inside me, but I pushed it down. This thing between us had been bubbling for a while. I had to trust in it.

I stroked my thumbs over her cheekbones. "Go and get some rest. None of this bullshit is going anywhere soon, so you have time to recharge a little. Then we'll call the guys, okay? Your phone is in your suitcase, in the closet of your room."

She stepped back and nodded. "It'll be okay, right? Tobias says it'll be okay, but he doesn't know Tom. Doesn't know how persuasive he can be." She gave a bitter laugh. "He persuaded me that someone could actually love me, and I fell for it completely. Look where that got me."

I'd never heard her so defeated, so full of self-pity, but I couldn't blame her. I knew what it felt like to get kicked over and over in the guts by all the shitty things in life. Before I could tell her that she was so deserving of love, confessing something to her that I hadn't even admitted to myself yet, she was gone from the room.

I'd made a promise to Poet before he left that I'd take care of her—not just her physical safety, but her emotional wellbeing too. Honestly, he'd probably entrusted the wrong person, but in that moment, I wanted nothing more than to see her smile and laugh again.

We'd get there, even if I had to kill Tom Granville Junior to do it.

THIRTY-THREE

POET

WE WERE A MESS. It had been just under two weeks since we'd posted Charlotte's bail, and I missed her so fucking much. I hated that she wasn't on tour with us, and I knew I wasn't the only one. Knight had been so fucking sullen that it was a wonder the label hadn't started giving out refunds.

For the last three concerts, we'd gone out on stage and played, and Royal did his thing, engaging with the crowd, singing the songs, but the energy wasn't there. We were worried about Charlotte, and the threat of being unmasked hung over our heads like a guillotine. Didn't help that the guillotine was being controlled by a complete lunatic.

Which was why we were stuck sitting in this office in Chicago, the label execs in front of us, like they were our parents and we were just wayward teens. Royal already had his *fuck you* look on his face, which meant that whatever way they thought this meeting was going to go, they were wrong.

I missed Shep in these moments. He was the one who usually handled this shit. He was the unwavering barrier between what the label wanted and what we wanted. They'd sent two senior execs over to meet us, and maybe that should've made us feel special, but instead, it just felt like they thought they'd have more success if there were two of them.

They were wrong.

"I said this was a stupid idea from the beginning," Gino snapped at Whitt, who was doing his best to look completely unfazed by the fact they'd been tearing him to pieces for the last ten minutes.

Gino was an asshole. He was from the sleep-with-the-popstars era of music exec, and I was fairly sure that if they tested his blood, it'd be ninety percent cocaine and caffeine.

Oxo was the other exec, but he'd once been a musician himself. He was from the same era of sex, drugs, and rock'n'roll as Royal's dad, but he was all businessman now. He raised an eyebrow at Gino. "It did keep him out of trouble for several weeks."

"A few fucking weeks, and now we have a scandal with some little skank being dragged from the bus in cuffs."

Royal leaned forward, his hands gripping the edge of the conference table. "Watch your fucking mouth. What more do you want? We are performing, meeting our obligations. You can fuck off with all the dramatics. Charlotte is no longer your concern."

Gino sneered at us. "That's where you're wrong. Everything you do, every girl you fuck, every guitar pick you throw into the crowd is our concern. It doesn't help that someone's threatening to expose your damn identities—what are you worth to us then? *Nothing.* Your social value tanks overnight, and The Daymakers are just another band filled with nepo babies making mediocre music."

Oxo turned to Gino, looking like he wanted to punch him. "We both know that's not true. Stop pulling your dick, so we can get to the point of this damn meeting." He looked back at Whitt. "Have we neutralized this"—he looked down at the tablet in front of him—"Thomas Granville Junior?"

Whitt's jaw clenched at the mention of the man currently fucking with our world. And by our world, I meant Charlotte. I hadn't told the guys yet, not even Hero, but what I felt for Charlotte wasn't just casual affection. Watching her leave, not being able to see her, was killing me.

I was in love with her.

I probably had been from that first time I had her with Hero. She was kind, funny. She saw me as a man, even if I was half a leg off being complete. Our tour bus was still littered with those tiny little book nook things, even though we had no books. Her room was still her room; no one had even gone in there, because it felt wrong if she wasn't in there too. She'd been sunshine, even though her life had been one thunderstorm after another.

I loved her, and I didn't give a fuck what some narcissitic ex-boyfriend said, or the label, or even my bandmates.

Except Hero. If he said I had to let her go, I'd be seriously conflicted, because I loved him so fucking much. But I knew Hero felt the way I did about Charlotte, even if he wasn't ready to admit it to himself, much less me.

Whitt cleared his throat. "So far, we've given him what he asked." That might've been an exaggeration by Whitt, but even he liked Charlotte. "But we both know people like that aren't just going to give up their blackmail material, no matter what we get him to sign. He's a fucking psychopath."

I wanted to end him.

Gino scoffed. "The guy is a lawyer?" Whitt nodded. "I could tell. The NDA he sent over—signed, I might add, which is ballsy as fuck—very loudly declares he'll be silent if his terms are met. But the little weasel definitely put in some loopholes he hoped we'd miss, which would let him break the contract. He's good, but our lawyers are better."

He looked at me, then the rest of the guys. "Look, the guy is a fucking sociopath. The label gets that, but on the matter of Charlotte Lochrin, we are in agreement. You'll cut contact with her. She's a liability. You'll finish your tour and give people the performance they expect from The Daymakers. You'll haul Mr. Shepherd back to the tour so he can undertake his duties, or we'll assign you a new band manager."

Knight looked flushed, and he was definitely going to start throwing punches soon. "Shep does what he wants. He's not part of the tour, so if you need to replace him, go for it. He's not a dog to come to heel."

Gino gritted his teeth. "I mean it, you little shits. Finish this damn tour and keep your noses clean, or I'll personally see that you're dropped from the label completely." He stood and stomped out of the meeting room.

Oxo looked between us all with a sigh. "He's dramatic, but the masked singers concept is what sells out stadiums. You guys are good, but this gimmick? It's what makes you *great.* No woman is worth your career. Be smart," he said softly, before following Gino out of the room.

Whitt let out a long breath. In that moment, he looked ten years older. "Fuck."

I felt bad for him. I bet he felt like his good intentions were coming back to bite him in the ass. I squeezed his arm. "You did the right thing back then, by letting her stay. I know it doesn't feel like it now, but you did," I told him, and he raked a hand down his face.

"I know, kid. Sometimes doing the right thing has consequences, though, and that's something I'll have to deal with." He gave us a soft smile.

Technically, Whitt owned his tour production company and was only contracted to the label, but if he lost their good graces, it could have some serious ramifications for the rest of the business… forever. He'd managed our tours since we were just a support band for bigger acts. He knew us, and so did Tricia. They were almost like family, considering how much of our year was spent with them.

He was in a shitty position, and I felt guilty. But still, I had no regrets.

Whitt squared his shoulders and met my eyes. "Okay, what are you guys going to do?"

"I'm going to visit Charlotte. We can fly back to Indianapolis before the show on the weekend," Hero said, his tone daring anyone to argue.

Royal crossed his arms over his chest. "No, we aren't." I opened my mouth to protest, but he held up a hand. "We have to figure this out before we can give Charlotte what she needs. First, we have to go home."

I blinked at him. *Oh shit.*

Roman Stokes, Royal's dad, was music royalty in his own right. He was from a time when rock stars were messy anarchists, and that was all that was expected of them. They trashed hotel rooms, got into fist fights, did so many drugs they burned out their septums, and drank so much vodka, they lost whole years of their lives.

They had no responsibilities, other than to play

music and run around like sugared-up toddlers. The music scene had been a messy, chaotic business, and rock bands had been their best-selling product. They were like cigarettes; everyone knew they were bad for you, but damn, they looked cool.

Until people realized that second-hand smoke gave the people around you cancer too. That there were long-lasting effects to years of abuse. But for rockstars, it wasn't lung cancer—well, sometimes it was, but that didn't fit the analogy I was trying to make. No, the effects were that you ended up sad and alone, in your mansion, surrounded by pretty young things who sucked your dick for clout, but left you as quick as possible once they realized you were washed up.

The guys all hated Roman Stokes, but I saw him for what he was—a sad, lonely man who had only his memories of greatness to keep him warm as he aged. A man filled with regrets, even if he was too stubborn to admit them out loud.

Royal's mom had left when he was fourteen, after his dad had been photographed screwing some girl half his age in the back of an SUV. She'd never come back; and I thought that was worse than anything Roman had ever done. Who left their son to be raised by an alcoholic and a sea of nannies, knowing what Royal's home life had been like?

Selfishness knew no bounds with that one. It was a common theme among the show business elite, though. When you'd lived many years of people treating you like you were better than the rest of the world, you started to believe it.

We followed the sound of giggling toward the rooftop terrace of Roman's penthouse apartment. I wasn't even surprised to find him in the hot tub with three girls who'd be barely older than us.

One was grinding on his lap, and the other two were kissing each other. And Roman Stokes looked *bored*.

But when he noticed us, his face lit up. "Rourke! Boys!"

Here, we weren't Royal, Hero, Knight and Poet. We were the same boys who'd decided to shake off our histories and try to make it on our own. Rourke, Curtis, Jessie and Moss.

The girls in the tub looked over too, and there was no doubting their predatory gazes as they took in our group. One girl, who had big fake boobs, licked her lips in a manner that I thought was meant to be seductive. But her face didn't move as she did it, so it just looked like a worm popping out of a hole and flailing around.

Roman abandoned the girls and stood, naked as the day he was born. I wish I could say it was the first time I'd seen Royal's dad's dick, but honestly, after his wife left him, Roman had made it his mission to fuck a girl in every room of his new apartment, regardless of whether his son was home from boarding school with his friends.

"Put a fucking towel on, Dad," Royal grunted, turning away from the girls and moving back into the house. We walked into the kitchen, and Royal grabbed us all a beer. There was always booze in this fridge. Though I was surprised to see there was also some kind of green juice, along with prepackaged meals that had a lot more vegetables than expected.

Roman came inside, still smiling widely, a towel tucked tightly around his waist. “Son, it's good to see you. I wasn’t expecting you, though, obviously.” I could see the genuine happiness in his face, and if I had to guess, I’d think Roman had realized the only person who might be around for him forever was his son.

Too little, too late.

Royal passed his dad a beer, then leaned on the countertop. “I need your advice.”

Roman looked like he’d been slapped, before joy—the kind I hadn’t seen in all the years I’d known him—lit up his face. “Really?”

Damn, now I just felt kind of sorry for him. Maybe I’d encourage Royal to forgive his father. I was the only one of us without a dad and I didn’t think he knew just what he was throwing away. His dad had been a fucker for most of his life, but people did change occasionally.

Maybe it was time to give Roman one more chance. But that was a problem for after we’d solved our current issues.

Royal’s face looked like he was sucking on a lemon as he nodded. “Yeah. Look, you survived your fair share of scandals in your career, and I want to know what you’d do.”

Gone was the excited father in Roman’s expression, and out came the musician who’d had a career spanning generations. You didn't get there without a shrewd business sense, even if you'd been fucking everyone who moved and fucking up the world around you in the process.

"Tell me everything."

THIRTY-FOUR

CHARLOTTE

A MESSAGE POPPED up on my phone from the guys, and I swiped it away. Shep looked over from where he sat beside me on the couch, but didn't say anything. He just dragged me closer into his side, like he could see the hurt festering inside my chest.

After he'd told me about Tom coming to see them, about his ultimatum, I'd felt sick. It was one thing for them to be subject to bad publicity because of me, but it was quite another thing to possibly lose their entire careers.

If being subject to even a small slice of their fame for a limited amount of time had taught me anything, it was that their masks were a large part of their fame, even if the die-hards screamed they were there for the music.

Fucking Tom. I hated him so much.

Shep kissed the top of my head. "You should message them back. They miss you."

Not as much as they'd miss being on stage, singing to sold-out concerts. "It's better this way," I told him, stubbornly watching the movie on the screen. I'd tried to pull away from Shep too, tried to send him back to the tour, but he was just as stubborn. When he'd said he was with me until the end, he meant it.

I'd raged. I'd called him every name I could think of. I'd pretended to want nothing to do with him. He'd just stayed by my side. I'd been keeping him at arm's length, because if we took the leap that I so desperately wanted to make, then my heart wouldn't survive. Because eventually, he'd have to go back to the guys. They were his family. His best friends. I'd never come between them like that.

"You're overthinking again," he whispered. I snorted, because the truth was I was always overthinking things. Going through every possible scenario in your head was a recipe for anxiety, but sometimes, it also saved you from disaster.

I nudged him with my shoulder. "It's my default setting."

"Dreamer?"

God, I wanted to tell him to stop calling me that. That Dreamer had died viciously at the hands of someone who was supposed to love her, just like all of my dreams had. I wanted to tell him that, but I couldn't. I was clinging to who I wanted to be so tightly, that if I let go, I would slide into oblivion and never come out.

"Mmm?" I answered, because I had to.

"Look at me," he whispered against my cheek. I

dragged my eyes up to his, dying a little at the sympathy there. "They're coming back to you, sweetheart."

I shrugged, like I didn't care. Like my heart wasn't breaking in two. "They need to do what's best for them."

Shep wouldn't let me hide from my words, though. "And who does what's best for you? Because baby, this isn't it." He cupped my cheek, and I looked up into those eyes that had mesmerized me from the first moment, chasing the golden flecks in their depths. "Let me take care of you, Charlotte. Let me be the one who does what's best for you."

I stopped breathing as my mind tumbled around, trying to grasp his words. "But…"

There were so many buts, it could be a nudist colony. But what about the guys? What about his career, his life, his home? What about his reputation?

All that came out though was, "But I like them too."

I didn't need to specify who *them* was. The Daymakers sat between us like a wall.

He kissed my cheeks, one and then the other. "They are my best friends." His lips brushed my eyelids. "You make them happy. They make *you* happy. Watching you together makes me happy. I can share, if that's what it takes to get a little of your sunshine on me."

My heart was pounding at what he was suggesting. Was he seriously considering sharing me with his friends in some kind of messed-up poly relationship? This was redundant, because there was *no* way that four famous musicians would go for all being committed to one girl.

Ridiculous.

I wanted Shep, wanted what he was offering right now so badly, it was an ache in my chest that felt like a heart attack. But could I travel around with the band, watch them fuck groupies, fall in love, get married, all to girls who weren't me?

"Overthinking again?" Shep asked, and he kissed me hard. It was a claiming kiss that I felt down to my toes; I was helpless to do anything but return it. I wanted to know how he tasted, the noises he made, the way he felt inside me, in case all I had to keep me warm at night were memories.

He grabbed me around my waist and pulled me onto his lap, and I melted into this massive man like I was made for him. His whole body curled around mine. I wasn't sure I'd ever felt so safe in my entire life.

His hands stroked up and down my spine, then slipped under the bottom of my shirt so I could feel his rough hands on my skin. He made a happy noise in the back of his throat, and I wanted to laugh, for the first time in weeks.

We kissed for ages, learning the taste of each other. I found that he really enjoyed it when I bit his bottom lip, and he'd curl up into me if my thumbs brushed his nipples through his tight black shirt.

An eternity later, when I knew the taste and feel of his lips as well as my own, he pulled back. "Baby…" he panted. "Tell me this is what you want? If you want to stop here, I'll put you back down there on the couch and we'll rewind this movie twenty minutes and pretend it never happened. But if you want to keep going…" He trailed off, his voice light, like he didn't mind either way, even though I could feel the hard bar of his cock between my thighs.

I kissed my way down the strong column of his throat. "Do. Not. Stop," I whispered between nipping kisses, and he groaned happily, his hands tightening on my hips as he thrust up against me.

He slipped my shirt over my head, tugging me backwards. "God, you're so fucking beautiful. I've dreamed about this for so long." He leaned forward, sucking my nipple into his mouth. "You taste so good."

I captured his lips again, my hands tugging at his shirt until his huge chest was bare. He had a light dusting of hair across his pecs, and I scraped my nails down them as I got lost in his mouth on mine.

Every roll of my pussy over his hard cock, trapped in his pants, made my eyes cross. "Please, Shep," I breathed. I wanted this so much. I wanted to give in to the promises he'd made with his eyes, with his hands, with his mouth. I wanted to be owned and loved by this man.

His hands slid under my skirt and gripped my underwear. Pulling hard, he tore the fussy lace easily. His fingers slipped between us, and he slid them up and down my slit until he landed on my clit, his mouth never leaving mine. I moaned into him, and he inhaled my pleasure like a drug.

I pulled back, panting. "I want you inside me."

His head fell back, and he breathed hard through his nose. "Baby, if you knew how many times I'd imagined you saying those words to me." He shifted me back a little, tugging his sweats down until his fat cock slipped free. I grabbed it, like the greedy bitch I was.

As I stroked it, he swore and gritted his teeth. "If you keep doing that, I'm going to come all over that pretty hand." He lifted my hips, pulling me up his body to position me over his cock, then stopped. "You need to know that this means something to me. You aren't a glory hole, or a casual fuck. There's nothing casual about my feelings for you, Charlotte Lochrin. My Dreamer."

I swallowed hard, my eyes getting wet, but I didn't want to cry. He slid me down on his cock slowly, and I closed my eyes as the sensation washed over me like a wave of pure bliss. When I opened my eyes, he was staring up at me, his eyes tracing my face like he was committing the moment to memory. As he shifted me up and then back down, he continued to watch, his eyes filled with feelings I'd never seen in someone's eyes when they looked at me.

Shep was making love to me. It felt different when that person might actually love you. The whole thing felt… more.

I moved with him, the pace slow and leisurely, like he was cataloging every move that made me moan, every breath I took. He hit places inside me that just… I had no words.

The orgasm didn't creep up on me. It didn't hit me like a freight train. It was like a forest fire, burning through my body, laying waste to the person I was before, revealing someone new in the ashes.

"Shep!" I breathed, my whole body locking tight around his. He gripped my hips hard, bucking up inside me and prolonging my pleasure until he was coming right along with me. I collapsed forward, my world spinning.

He flopped back, his arms holding me so tightly to his body, I wondered if he wanted to make us one person. Breathing heavily, I rested my cheek on his chest. Emotions hung heavily between us, but it felt like too much to air them right at this moment. I needed to examine them myself, overthink the shit out of it first.

So I did what I did best. I deflected. "Have I told you that they let slip your real name is Grover?"

Shep groaned, his chest vibrating with the noise. "It was my grandfather's name. No one has ever called me Grover in my entire life, and I'm not making an exception for you, little Dreamer."

"Are you sure? What if I only shout 'Grover' while I orgasm? Surely that'd get me a pass, right?" I teased, and he slapped my ass. I squeaked, then giggled an offensively cute sound. "Okay, okay. No Grover. What about Grovey? My little Grovey-Wovey."

"It's like you *want* me to spank you," he warned, but I could hear the laughter in his own voice.

Well, now that he mentioned it…

My phone rang on the coffee table, and Tobias's

name flashed across the screen. Definitely a call I had to get. Stretching out, I clicked the answer icon.

"Hello?"

"Charlotte, it's Tobias Lecter. I've got news." My heart started thundering in my chest. "Are you sitting down?"

Well, technically I was lying naked across Shep, his arms wrapped around my waist, but that was close enough. "Uh, yeah?"

"The DA has dropped the charges. Apparently, on closer inspection of the case, there are some gaping holes in the evidence." He snorted. "No fucking shit. If the holes were any wider, it would be the Grand Canyon," he muttered, more to himself than me. "If they find more evidence in the future, they might reopen the case, but considering what we both know, I think you're free and clear."

My heart felt like it was going to explode from my chest. It might've been the post-sex endorphins and the relief all mixing together, but I wanted to scream with happiness. Finally, something was going my way. It was just this tiny thing—which should never have been a thing in the first place—but it was *something*.

"Thank you, thank you, thank you, Tobias. I owe you so much."

I heard a soft sigh from the other end of the line. "You've had it rough, kid. But take it from me, life doesn't hand you anything—you have to take it. You have to believe you deserve it too. Life is something that happens for you, not *to* you, so grab those boys with both hands—" I snorted, because that *was* kind of funny, considering. "And don't let them go if you don't want to," he finished, although he sounded amused.

I looked down at Shep, at the shining happiness on his face that echoed mine.

"I promise."

THIRTY-FIVE

CHARLOTTE

THE CHARGES BEING DROPPED WAS a relief that I felt viscerally, in every muscle of my body. It meant I could finally leave Georgia and go… where?

I was right back to where I'd started, when I crawled beneath a bus in LA. No money. No prospects. Nothing but a couple of thousand miles between me and the City of Demons.

Someone knocked at the door downstairs, and I froze.

"I'll get it," Shep yelled from the next room, and I went back to packing. Maybe I should stay in Atlanta? Or head over to Charlotte, or somewhere like that. A whole fresh start somewhere random.

I had a little more money saved up this time, my allowance from my time on the tour, and I'd noticed another ten grand had gone into my bank account from Whitt, probably severance money. So I could put a deposit on a rental and maybe buy a cheap car. It was enough that I could survive for a bit without panicking while I found a job.

I purposefully hadn't asked Shep what he was doing, because I was worried that it wouldn't involve me. So I was burying my head in the sand and fortifying my walls. If he went back to the tour, I couldn't go with him.

"Dreamer, it's for you!" Shep called up the stairs. Probably Tobias. I still had to fix up his bill. I wondered if he'd let me take out a payment plan.

I grabbed my phone and took the stairs two at a time, already shouting my questions to my lawyer. "Tobias, does your firm take—"

I stopped dead on the bottom step. Standing in the tiny foyer were my guys.

Without their masks.

Their faces were just there, for me to see, and I couldn't breathe.

Knight stepped forward first, his face twisted up into a huge grin. His eyes laughed at me, shining like onyx under the recessed lights. His nose had a little bump on it, and I could swear he had freckles. I wanted to kiss each and every one.

"Lottie." It was all he said, but the way he said it made my heart threaten to burst from my chest. He grabbed me up into his arms and kissed me so completely that there was no room for doubt. There were just his arms and me, and nothing else mattered.

Well, nothing else but the men behind him. My eyes searched out Shep first, but as I met his gaze, he gave me an encouraging nod. I let myself relax into Knight's hold and finally breathe. I wasn't going to second guess *why* they were here. I was just going to be happy that they were.

Someone shoved Knight, which resulted in us rocking from side to side, because he refused to loosen his hold. "I missed you so fucking much," he whispered in my ear, then grunted. "Not the kidneys, asshole."

He stepped back, letting me go, and then Hero was there. Poet, too. Fuck, they were as beautiful as I thought they'd be. Hero's broad face was stretched tight with a smile, his eyes shining as he looked at me. Poet had a longer, more angular face, with those high cheekbones that I'd felt beneath my hands so many times. They hugged me between them, and I melted into their warmth, their security, tears welling in my eyes. I'd wanted them so damn bad, and here they were.

"You aren't wearing your masks," I sniffed, and that was when I realized I was actually already crying.

Poet nuzzled my hair. "We don't need to hide anything from you."

Hero wrapped his arms around us both. "I'm sorry it took so long for us to get here. It won't happen again."

As much as the promise made butterflies alight in my stomach, I wouldn't hold him to his promise. How could I? They were some of the biggest names in the music industry, and I was a glorified street rat. A toy to play with, but not to keep.

My eyes met Royal's from between the bodies of his

two bandmates, and just the sight of him stole the air from my lungs. He was beautiful. He was…

"Holy shit," I breathed, because I knew who he was. Everyone knew who he was. He'd been on the covers of shitty tabloid magazines since he was a baby.

"Rourke Stokes. It's nice to meet you, Toy," he said softly, and the guys stepped back so I could make my way to him. He wouldn't come to me; I knew that. Royal wasn't the type of person to make the first move, or even the second. But some part of me knew that him being here, as the man he was and not the persona he played, meant more than taking three steps forward.

He'd already made a leap of blind faith on me. I put out my hand, grasping his. "Charlotte Lochrin. The pleasure is all mine."

He chuckled darkly, tugging my hand until I was pulled tight into his body. "It will be." He gripped my face and kissed me, his tongue pushing into my mouth like he was dying for the taste of me.

I was kissing Rourke fucking Stokes. Teenage me would be dying right now, if she wasn't already dead and buried six feet below. I had no idea how long he kissed me, but by the time we pulled away, the rest of the guys were gone from the foyer. I could hear them chatting in the kitchen, and I gripped Royal's hand as I dragged him after me. There was no way I was letting him go, now that I'd just gotten them back.

The guys were drinking the last of the soda in the fridge, taking up too much space in the tiny kitchen. My eyes feasted on them, like I'd been starving for far too long.

"What are you guys *doing* here? Don't you have a concert in..." I racked my brain for their tour schedule. "Baltimore?"

Knight nodded. "We do, but we've got a couple of days and we wanted to spend them with you." My heart did a little flip at that. "Plus, the time for masks and subterfuge is gone. The tour hasn't been the same without you. We want you to come back. No blindfold this time."

A ball of anxiety sat heavy in my gut. "Guys, I can't. What about the label? Your contracts?"

Hero leaned back against the counter, his eyes running across my face. "We got so caught up in ourselves—no one's asked if you even *want* to come back. Whether you feel... anything for us. I know you weren't looking for strings and commitment, and that's okay. If it's about the money—"

I shook my head vigorously. "Fuck the money. Honestly, I don't want a cent from you guys." I took a deep breath, because I was about to lay my shit bare for them all, and hope they didn't run the other way. "I'm not going to lie and say it didn't start out about the money, because it absolutely did. It was about the money for a long time; I wanted the security it provided.

"But if this whole fucking thing with the charges and sitting in a jail cell has taught me anything, it's that it wasn't the almighty dollar that had my back in there.

It was you guys. It hasn't been the idea of the money I've missed the last couple of weeks—it was you four." I looked over at Shep and winked. "Though Shep has been my rock through the whole thing, so if anyone has a problem with that, they can take it up with me."

Royal barked out a laugh. "Easy, Killer. We've known that Shep's had it bad for you for ages. We don't care. Shep is part of us. And so are you."

My chest felt so full, I was sure I was going to burst like an overfilled water balloon. Nodding furiously, I slid back into Royal's arms. Some things were worth more than money; this was one of them.

Getting to know the guys without the subterfuge and masks was a trippy experience. I realized how much I knew about their personalities, about their preferences, but it was all surface stuff. I hadn't truly known them at all.

Like the fact they all lived in Brooklyn Heights together when they weren't touring. Or little things, like the meanings of all their tattoos, which were so entwined with their histories that they couldn't have told me about them and kept the anonymity clause.

Or that Knight loved cats, so much so that they had three, who even had a designated babysitter while the guys were on tour, and he regularly Facetimed them. He showed me pictures, like they were his babies. I hadn't picked Knight as a cat guy; he had such Golden Retriever energy.

Or that Poet ran a foundation in his father's memory, helping underprivileged kids get into karting, so they could eventually pursue motorsports, which had been a rich person's sport for far too long.

Hero and Royal owned a bar in Brooklyn, though it was managed by someone else. It was known to host open mic nights that music execs sometimes frequented.

The whole band, plus Shep, even owned a couple of stud horses on a farm in Colorado.

But deeper than the superficial things was who they really were, which hadn't changed.

I did discover reasons for small quirks I'd already noticed. The reason Poet and Royal went to baseball games all the time was because Poet's godfather had been a professional ball player. He'd stepped up when Poet's dad had died in the car accident, becoming a male role model not just to Poet, but for all the guys, who'd had pretty shitty role models as a whole.

I found out that Hero had spent every holiday with Poet and his mom, ever since Hero's grandfather had passed away and he was no longer forced into going back to the "mausoleum of darkness." Direct quote.

They told me all this over pizza, lounging around in the living room, and I tried to mesh the idea of the masked men I knew with the very real people in front of me.

"So, do I call you guys by your real names, or do you prefer your stage names?" I sat on Hero's lap, and he kept rubbing his cheek against mine. Even though it was a little scratchy, I couldn't get enough. To be able to kiss every inch of his face and see it at the same time felt almost decadent now.

"Baby, you can call me whatever you want. Especially when you come." He grinned. "Oh, Curtis…" he said in a falsetto imitation of my voice.

I couldn't help but lean closer, breathing, "Mmm, Curtis, right there," into his ear, making him shiver beneath me. His arms tightened around me, and he growled.

Royal cleared his throat. "We usually just call each other by our stage names. They're basically nicknames now anyway, and it stops us slipping up in public. But I'm not sure that'll matter much longer."

All the good feelings eked out of me at the reminder of Tom and his threats. I mightn't be going to jail anymore, but he was still threatening the guys.

Hero's hand ran up and down my spine, doing battle against the tension suddenly stiffening my body. "I'm sorry. I promise, I'll keep it on the downlow. I was thinking about moving to North Carolina or somewhere under the radar, and maybe Tom will think you've kept your word." I tried to shake off the melancholy that threatened to swamp me at the thought that I might only see them every now and then. It was better than nothing.

Royal leaned forward. "Look at me, Charlotte." I met his ethereal blue eyes, and the intensity on his face made my chest tighten. "I mean it with every fiber in my body when I say *fuck Tom*. Fuck his manipulative, narcissitic, abuser ass if he thinks he's going to win. Because I would've burned this whole band down before I let a little weasel like that treat me and the people I love like puppets."

I warned my wildly beating heart that he didn't mean me. He meant the guys, who he loved like brothers. But the look in his eyes was screaming something at me that I didn't dare hope for.

Shep's whole body went taut. "What have you guys done?"

Knight leaned back against the couch, his arms crossed over his chest. "What needed to be done."

Well, that's ominous.

THIRTY-SIX

HERO

I CURLED around Charlotte in a hotel bed in Baltimore, and I knew at that moment that this was the right decision. Because I might be in love with Charlotte Lochrin. It was a seed of feeling in my chest, and if I examined it, it would be labeled with a capital L.

She'd protested for the last forty-eight hours about our plan, and occasionally, I'd see guilt creep into her eyes. She thought she was sinking our careers, but really, she was just a catalyst.

Exhaustion had been creeping in for a long time now. Before this tour had even started, the physical toll of keeping our identities hidden was a never-ending stress. We could never really relax, even when we weren't touring. I was done, and if it meant I got to keep the woman in my arms, then all the better.

Shep, surprisingly, had taken the whole thing in his stride, going into manager mode. He went over the contracts with the label, talked to the lawyers, liaised with an independant PR company to deal with the fall-out. Not once did he try to talk us out of it, even though it could possibly sink everything we'd worked for.

It had been Royal's dad who'd told us to chase happiness, because there wouldn't be bright stage lights to keep us warm at the end. He'd stared hard at his son when he'd said that, but Royal's jaw had been so tight, you could have cut cheese on the sharp edges. It'd take more than a few sage words of advice to mend the rift between those two, but this was a step in the right direction.

Roman Stokes had given us the number of his PR guy, and if you took into account that Roman was still a respected rocker after half the shit he'd pulled in his career, the guy was obviously the best.

Soon, I'd have to wake up and get ready for the interview that would change the trajectory of our lives, but for now, I wanted to spend a moment holding my girl, keeping her safe between my body and that of the guy I loved.

Poet was still sleeping softly, and I watched his lips twitch as if he was having an imaginary conversation in his dreams. He was so fucking beautiful, and I wanted to tell the world he was mine—Charlotte, too. The PR guy had suggested we should just do one career-altering revelation at a time, though.

It was fine. My relationships were no one's business anyway. The fans, the tabloids and the label could either get on board or fuck right off.

I was pretty sure Jenny, Poet's mom, already knew.

We hadn't overtly said anything, but she knew her son. She knew me. She'd definitely guessed. She was the only person outside of our group that mattered. She'd been the only decent parent we had between us, though Joseph, Poet's godfather, came a close second.

Joseph had proposed to Poet's mom as soon as he retired from baseball. He'd told us, when he asked for permission, that he hadn't wanted Jenny to be tied to another sportsman, waiting at home while the person who was meant to be her other half traveled the country, playing with his balls. He'd wanted her to have the chance to marry a nice accountant or something. But when he retired and Jenny was still single, he saw it as a sign.

That had been an awkward, kind of tense moment, when the man Poet had thought of as a father figure—his father's best friend—had wanted to marry his mom. But in the end, he was a soft soul who wanted his mother to be happy, and clinging to a ghost wasn't any kind of way to live life.

"You're thinking really hard," Poet said softly.

I nodded once. "Just going over things in my head."

"Reservations?" He didn't need to specify. We both knew what was going to happen today, and we'd prepared for it.

"None."

Poet's hand covered mine where it rested on Charlotte's hip. "Me either."

"Me neither," she whispered, her eyes fluttering open with a yawn. She snuggled further into Poet's chest, and he kissed the top of her head reverently. If I wasn't ready to name that kernel of feeling in my chest, Poet was the exact opposite. Love shone from his face like a beacon.

"Good morning, gorgeous," he whispered, leaning in to kiss her.

She gave him a chaste kiss back, then shook her head. "I've got morning death breath."

He rubbed his nose against hers. "I don't care." He kissed her deeply, pushing her back into my body, and I stroked my hands up and down her sides. I wanted to kiss every inch of her creamy skin, bury my cock inside her, or maybe inside Poet while he was inside her. Maybe with Knight or Royal there, too. I wasn't sure if Shep would be open to sharing, but we had time to figure that out.

This situation was absolutely batshit insane, but I knew that Sampson Rubio—who I'd called a couple of weeks ago about a lawyer—was in some kind of alternative polyamorous relationship. If he could do it, surely we could. I mean, those guys weren't as famous as The Daymakers were, or maybe even as famous as Rourke Stokes was individually, but they'd spent their own fair share of time in the tabloids. They weren't unknowns, and they made it work.

So maybe we could too.

Lottie started to make that soft noise that always went straight to my dick, and if I didn't stop this soon, we were going to be late for the biggest interview of our career. I kissed the back of her neck and tightened my arms around her ribs. Hoisting her up over my body and onto the other side of the bed, I ignored their protests.

"Save the celebrations for later, you two. The alarm's going off and it's time to get ready. Today's an important day." I felt like a dick, but one of us had to be. Otherwise, I'd be buried deep in one of them within the next twenty minutes.

Lottie smiled happily at me. Contentment looked good on her. It lit her up from the inside, making me just want to bask in it. Soon.

"I'll make coffee and make sure everyone else is awake," she said, rolling from the bed and stretching. I groaned as the lines of her naked body transfixed me. She looked over her shoulder and winked, the little minx.

Happiness bubbled up inside me, and laughter burst from my lips. "Get out of here before I spank that perfect ass."

She gave it a little shake, throwing on a hotel robe and disappearing into the suite's living room. I slumped back against the pillows and tried to breathe away my erection. I was going to have to paint the walls of the shower to get rid of this boner.

Poet was smiling softly, and I looked over at him. "Love you, Moss."

His smile turned into a beam of happiness. "Not as much as I love you, Curtis," he replied, and as always, hearing him say my real name made it seem like so much more. "I love her too, you know."

I kissed his cheek. "I know. How could you not?"

At this point, it seemed inevitable. Lottie had transformed us all.

I'd suggested that Lottie still wear her mask when we went out, but she shook her head. "No. I'm not going to spend the rest of my time with you guys hiding," she replied stubbornly.

Now, as we sat in hair and makeup on the set of a very popular morning show, we were putting on our masks for the very last time. Shep had made all the makeup artists sign NDAs, just so no one pipped us to our grand reveal. But in less than an hour, it wouldn't matter. We would be free of the masks, unless we chose to continue wearing them at shows.

We might also be free of our recording contracts, but it was a risk we were willing to take. All of us. The Morning Show had no idea what was going on, only that they were going to be the source of a really big band reveal. Rumors were swirling around that we were breaking up, that we were adding a new lead singer, that we were doing an international tour.

There were always the whispers that we were revealing our identities, but normally, those were dismissed pretty quickly. Who would abandon a million-dollar gimmick?

Turns out, the four of us.

Lottie stood beside Shep, her fingers entwined with his as he talked on the phone in a low voice. We needed all our ducks in a row, and that involved giving Whitt the heads-up.

Rupert Drip, the manager of the public relations firm we were using, was ready in the background for the information drop. It would be blasted across our socials almost immediately after we unveiled ourselves on the Morning Show. Clips of the show would be played throughout the day, explaining why we'd decided to unmask.

A showrunner appeared. "Six minutes, guys."

I pulled my mask up and walked over to kiss Charlotte. She returned it softly, squeezing me in a tight hug. "You've got this." She pulled my mask back into place, smoothing my hair around it.

The rest of the guys came up and kissed her, and she whispered words of encouragement to them too. We weren't doing this for her, exactly, but I didn't know how much longer we would have gone on before saying enough was enough. She hadn't caused it, but her situation had expedited it.

I didn't have it in me to care, though. I wasn't losing anything. What I was gaining instead was worth more than money or fame.

We filed onto the stage, greeting the gushing hosts. The female host ate Royal up with her eyes, and he ignored her completely. Knight was the flirt, and Royal was the unobtainable one, until he took you against a wall like a damn savage.

But today, neither of them flirted. Neither of them

gave the pretty blonde host anything more than polite greetings.

The guy beside the camera got our attention as we sat down on the couch opposite the hosts. "Going live in five, four…"

THIRTY-SEVEN

ROYAL

"WE'RE HONORED to have one of the premier rock bands in the world in the studio with us today—The Daymakers!" announced one of the hosts, Tony Tremaine, with teeth that were far too white to be real. "Guys, it's great to have you back in Baltimore. Your last tour here was over four years ago, correct?"

Hero nodded. "That's right. The Leave The World Behind tour. Though it feels like yesterday."

"Your concert is sold out, and by all accounts, you've never been hotter. But we are dying to know what your big reveal is today. There've been rumors of you adding a girl to the band's lineup." The host looked down at his notes. "Dreamer, is it?"

I shook my head. "No, The Daymakers will maintain their current lineup." I looked directly down the barrel of the camera. I really was born for this shit. "We've recently become victims of an obsessed individual, who's trying to blackmail the band. He's discovered our identities by hiring a private investigator and made demands that we can't—no, absolutely *won't*—succumb to. So we are removing his leverage today."

The hosts sat there with stunned looks on their faces as I lifted my mask. They audibly gasped; my face was easily recognizable, especially if you were the kind of person who liked to watch gossip on daytime shows.

"Wow… Rourke Stokes. Or should we still call you Royal?"

We'd discussed this. We'd decided we'd still go by our stage names in public, because it helped us maintain some of what we built.

"Royal. To fans of The Daymakers, that's who I am, and who I always will be. Just because I'm not wearing the mask anymore, it doesn't change that."

The other guys all took off their masks, and Molly Lemore audibly squeaked. "Oh my."

I looked at the men who were more like family to me than my own. "You might know Jessie Beck, better known to The Daymakers fans as Knight. Moss Aguilar, everyone's favorite Poet and bass player—"

"Hold up there, Rourke." So quickly, they'd reverted to my legal name. "Moss Aguilar, as in son of deceased Formula One racing legend, Olivier Aguilar?" Molly Lemore asked incredulously.

Tony wasn't to be outdone. "And Jessie Beck, of the famous—"

"Or infamous," Molly interjected.

"Infamous Beck family, Hollywood acting royalty?"

I nodded, my jaw going tight. This was why we had

the masks. Already, our parentage had overtaken our own achievements. "Yes." I wouldn't give them any more than that. They weren't entitled to our histories.

They both swung their eyes toward Hero, and I saw recognition dawn on their faces. "A regular gossip column of band members, because if I'm not wrong, this is Curtis Hawkins, heir to the combined Hawkins-Fiere empire."

Hero gave them a dead look, and I almost snorted. There wasn't going to be an empire or fortune left by the time his parents were done. Anything that Hero had, he'd earned himself. He'd donated most of his grandfather's inheritance money to food banks and homeless shelters, just to spite the old fucker.

"I prefer to just go by Hero. Or Curtis, if you must," he chastised with a smile on his face and disdain in his eyes.

The hosts were obviously completely oblivious, and whatever questions were hammering down their earpieces couldn't come out of their mouths fast enough. Did our parents approve of our careers? How did we meet? Was there truth to drug rumors about assorted cousins, fathers, friends?

We fielded all the questions and tried to come back around to the tour, our music, our fans.

Molly Lemore got a devious glint in her eye. "What about reports that you're all sleeping with the masked woman often seen at your shows this tour? The one called Dreamer—or is it Toy?"

I ground my jaw, but gave Molly the most impassive

look possible. "That has nothing to do with you or anyone. She's not for public consumption, and I know our fans will respect that."

They wouldn't. We sold the illusion that you could go home with a rockstar. The idea of one of us being in a relationship was palatable. But all of us, together, with one girl? We would lose fans and followers in the tens of thousands.

I didn't care. I wasn't going to be unhappy, just so the label could sell me as some kind of sex symbol and line their own pockets. If they weren't here for the music, they could suck my dick. Metaphorically.

Unsurprisingly, when we left the stage and headed back to the green room, we walked in on chaos. All our phones were ringing, vibrating like mad as Charlotte stared at them with bewilderment. Shep was also ignoring his phone, which I could see lit up and buzzing in his pocket.

"Let's go. We can handle this in private." He bundled us all out of the studio, our security around us trying not to gape at the fact we weren't wearing masks for the first time ever with them. We hadn't decided if, once we'd unmasked, we'd continue to wear them all the time on tour or not, but I was leaning toward no. It was liberating to feel the breeze on my cheeks for once.

My phone continued to buzz in my pocket, and I pulled it out. There were already hundreds of notifications on my Gram account, as people tagged me in every post. I scrolled through a few of them, looking at the post the PR firm had put out almost immediately after our reveal.

There was no putting the genie back in the lamp now.

> @MAKEMYDAYZ
> HOLY SHIT @ROYALDAYMAKERS IS ROURKE STOKES? I FEEL SO STUPID. HE EVEN SOUNDS LIKE HIS DAD.

> @CALLMEQUEEN
> DOES ANYONE ELSE FEEL A LITTLE BETRAYED BY @ROYALDAYMAKERS AND @THEDAYMAKERSOFFICIAL NOW?

There were quite a few comments under that one.

> @TURTLESDON'TCLIMBTREES
> I CALLED IT. IF YOU'RE HERE FOR THE MUSIC AND NOT JUST FOR THE SPANK MATERIAL, YOU CAN HEAR ROURKE STOKES IN @ROYALDAYMAKERS VOICE. IT'S ALL THERE ON THE TUBE, IF YOU DO YOUR RESEARCH.

There had been a few people who'd guessed correctly over the years, but we'd never engaged. It didn't hurt that there'd been millions of guesses, so the right ones had just gotten lost. Everyone from European royalty to criminals had been floated as possible band members.

A text popped up on my phone.

ROMAN STOKES

I'm proud of you.

I swallowed down the emotion that bubbled up; this

was not the time to unpack my daddy issues. He had come through for us, though. He'd also seemed a little different on our last visit. A little more reserved. More like my father and less like his Roman Stokes rock persona.

Swiping the message away, I looked up to see the guys were all equally as immersed in their phones. Charlotte was looking between us all, a worried look on her face.

"Come here." I patted the seat beside me, and she unbuckled herself, making Shep growl, but I pulled her quickly to my side and buckled her in to keep him happy. I didn't want anything to happen to her either.

When she'd been forced off the tour, and I no longer got to see her every day, it had made something ache in my chest. I wasn't used to that. Women had always been something fleeting in my world. Girlfriends. Lovers. My mother. They all came and went in a short period of time. So when we'd been forced to move on, I'd thought her absence would become less and less noticeable as the days passed.

But the opposite had happened. Every stop, every mile that separated us felt *wrong*. It wasn't even that the guys had been nagging Whitt to let them go and visit.

I'd missed her.

I hadn't missed anyone since my mom, and when she never came back, I'd promised myself that I would never miss a single person ever again. Which was bullshit, because I'd miss the guys if they were gone, but I'd *yearned* to just lay eyes on Charlotte again.

Who the fuck yearned anymore? This wasn't Edwardian England, and I wasn't some stuffy society girl.

But as she cuddled into my side, that yearning in my chest disappeared and was replaced with something else. Happiness, sure. That was what it was. Happiness. Not anything deeper and more life-altering. Nothing that would make me vulnerable again.

She looked up at me with her big blue eyes. "Are you okay? That was some heavy shit."

I laughed, so glad that she could just look at me like that, like she was consuming the angles of my face. The masks hadn't really inhibited us in our relationship, but it had still been a barrier between us. I'd caught Poet on more than one occasion just rubbing his cheek on hers like he was scent marking her, cat-style.

I understood the urge.

I shrugged. "I'm okay. The fallout will suck, but I have no regrets." Guilt flashed across her face, and I kissed the little frown line marring her forehead. "I mean it, Toy. It was time. The masks were wearing us all down. This situation just gave us a massive kick in the ass to shut down the label about the stupid anonymity gimmick." I kissed her lips, breathing her in. "They don't get to treat us like shit and expect us to roll over. Do they not know who I am?"

She giggled against my lips. "There's that ego I remember. You're fucking Royal, lead singer to the hottest, most talented rock and roll band to emerge in the last decade. You're Rourke Stokes; swagger is built into your DNA." She gave me a crooked smile. "You're my good boy, giver of the best orgasms of my damn life," she whispered, and I shivered at her words.

Damn, a couple of crazy sessions of praise and I was a certified whore for it.

She stroked my face. "You're their brother and best friend. Their leader. You're so much more than a mask on a stage, Royal."

This time when I kissed her, I poured into it all the emotions that I felt but wasn't ready to admit, all the words I wanted to say but was too scared to voice. I kissed her like I possessed her, but if I was honest with myself, she possessed me.

THIRTY-EIGHT

DREAMER

TO SAY the label was pissed would probably be an understatement. All their calls were being forwarded to the band's lawyers, which was probably pissing them off even more.

When Whitt turned up at the hotel room, I wanted to hide. He'd know this was my fault. That if it wasn't for me, the guys would have continued this tour and maybe several more before they imploded like this. He'd be well and truly off the hook with both the label and his own tour company.

Whitt had Tricia with him as he entered the hotel room, and she gave me a soft smile that was more reassuring than any words. She wouldn't be here if Whitt was going to wring my neck. Or maybe she was here to resuscitate me?

She walked over and hugged me tightly. "Are you okay, Charlotte? It's been a crazy few weeks for you."

I nodded furiously. "I'm fine. My lawyer said the

case was weak at best, and as soon as he started poking holes in the evidence, it collapsed like a paper mache dam. His words, not mine."

Tricia frowned. "Then why even try if the evidence was so weak? That makes no sense."

Whitt let out a noise that was suspiciously close to a growl. "He wanted to scare her. Or maybe scare us into just handing her back over, because without us, she'd have been on her own again, susceptible to that fuck's manipulation."

I pulled back at the ferocity in his voice, and Tricia rubbed my back. "You're a sweet kid, Charlotte. Both Whitt and I are fond of you. We treat the band like our children—even if they can be the spawns of Satan at times—and we feel protective of you too. No one comes for one of ours without unleashing the wrath of Papa Bear over there."

I blinked furiously, swallowing down the emotions clogging my chest. I went back over all my interactions with Whitt and Tricia, from them helping me when I was obviously going to be trouble, to ensuring I had money to buy things when I had nothing. They'd made sure I was involved in decisions; they'd made provisions for my safety on the tour. Whitt had even come to my arraignment.

Everything they'd done had shown they cared. "Oh."

Whitt patted my back firmly, clearing his throat. "You'll be all right, kid." He walked over to the couch and slumped down. "Now, you little fuckers are another story. The label is out for blood. They're trying to get you for non-performance, according to my sources, which will be a hefty chunk of money. There've been some ticket returns for the last few stops on the tour."

My heart sank. *Fuck.*

"But they've been picked back up immediately. Apparently, the fans think this might be an iconic moment in music history, and they want to be part of it. Have you decided what you want to do?"

The guys all shook their heads. Shep piped up from where he was sitting beside the window. "We haven't decided how to handle the rest of the tour yet."

Crossing his ankles, Whitt stretched out. "Well, if you don't mind taking advice from an old dog who's been in the business a long time…"

The crowd was a different kind of electric in Baltimore tonight. There was a wild edge to the ordinary enthusiasm, complete with loud squeals of surprise and outrage for people who'd been living under a rock and hadn't seen yesterday's big reveal.

The guys were playing the gig in their masks, as Whitt had reminded them they were contractually obligated to do. Anything outside of the arena and label-necessitated PR events, they were free to do whatever the hell they liked.

Oh, the label's lawyers were arguing otherwise, but

they were always going to be pissed. This seemed like a good middle ground.

I'd also heard the label was suing Tom's law firm, since it was someone supposedly representing them who'd tried to blackmail their artists to start with, so the label were arguing he'd acted on their behalf.

I was rooting for the label to nail all those old fucking lawyers to the wall, even if the label's lawyers weren't my biggest fans.

I stood on the side of the stage as Royal sang their hits, mixing up the setlist to include hits from their past albums, as well as their new stuff. They were reminding people why they were fans of The Daymakers in the first place. It wasn't for the masks. It was for the music.

Shep hovered behind me, his body curled around mine protectively. He didn't like me out here, not wearing a mask, like people who snapped pictures of me were suddenly going to magically know who I was. I was a little worried that the tabloids would find out my whole sordid history, but as Knight had said, who fucking cared?

The guys knew, and if the media wanted to spin my survival as something terrible, then we'd weather that.

The guys were playing for their lives out there, and they sounded amazing. Every one of them was a sweat-soaked rockstar, and when Royal lost his shirt, the crowd still went bananas. Maybe *more* bananas, because now they knew who he was. He flirted with Knight onstage, who was literally playing the guitar as he lay on his back. Royal had his boot on his chest, leaning down and singing in his face like some kind of kinky dom.

So fucking hot.

Hero's drum solo reverberated around the arena, and Royal pulled Knight easily to his feet. *Jesus.* This whole show was meant to make the girlies wet, and I was no exception.

Knight made the guitar sing, and they did a good job of showcasing everyone's talent in this setlist.

Finally, they were almost done, and Royal talked to the crowd softly before their final song. "Baltimore, we love you. I know the last twenty-four hours have been kind of a roller coaster for our Daybreakers"—that was what their fans called themselves—"but we want you to know that we're still here, making the music you love, and the music you want to make love to," he purred, grabbing his dick. The scream was deafening. "So if you know the words to this one, sing it loud, because I want to hear you *scream!*"

Poet opened the song with a killer bass solo, and I was lost in the music, watching the guys I had feelings for make the entire stadium fall in love with them again. Pulling out my phone, I recorded them from the side of the stage. They were electric right now. Maybe they could use it in their Gram posts or something, so the whole world could see how fucking talented they really were.

I zoomed in on each of the guys, getting their frenzied movements, their sheer stage presence, because it would be impossible to watch this and not fall in love with them.

An email notification suddenly popped up on my phone, making me freeze. It was from Tom's personal email. *Just delete it,* I told myself, but I found myself pressing the notification, opening my email app.

You think you're so fucking smart, don't you, bitch? I don't need the legal system to destroy you and those fuckers who think they are so much better than me. Have fun being crucified by the court of public opinion, slut.

There were several links at the bottom of the email. I recognized the web address of a gossip site immediately.

Oh no. No, no, no.

Feeling sick, I clicked on it and everything I feared was there.

Sex, Drugs and Rock'n'Roll: Meet The Daymaker's Secret Tour Concubine.

I scanned the text. Tom had told them *everything*. Every terrible thing that had ever happened in my life. My mom leaving. My dad being in jail. The shitty foster placements. The fact that I was a bartender. The amount of lovers I'd had.

Everything, except for the fact he used to beat the shit out of me.

Somehow, he'd found out about my contract, and

pieces of it were published, redacted except for sensationalized lines.

Oh god. Why couldn't he give me one good moment? One memory of happiness to hold onto when everything eventually turned to shit.

"That fucking *fucker!*" I shouted loud enough that several roadies turned.

Shep was in front of me in an instant. "What's wrong?" he barked, looking around for a threat. I thrust my phone at him. His eyes got stormier and stormier as he read, first the email, then each of the links.

Fuck, I hadn't even looked at the other links.

I turned and ran from the arena. I needed to run. Needed to get away. To think. I ran out into the lot where all the buses and trucks were parked, not really running anywhere in particular, just *away*.

Tears streamed down my cheeks, because there was no mask there to catch them now. Turning a corner between two of the RVs, I barreled right into Helen. I only managed to pull up at the last moment, grabbing her so I didn't knock her over and break her hip or something. That would be just my luck. I was a fucking curse to anyone who'd ever shown me kindness.

"Woah there. Where's the man buffet?"

"What?"

She raised an eyebrow at me. "The only reason to run at a speed like that is if the Chippendales decide to ditch the thongs and lay themselves out for my own private carnival ride, if you catch my drift."

Nothing dried up tears—and other things—like the

idea of a nearly seventy-year-old riding a stripper. I blinked several times, dragging in a shuddering breath. "Uh. No. No man buffet."

"Then why are you running like the hounds of Hell are on your heels, kid?"

"Not the hounds of Hell. Just one demonic ex-boyfriend."

Helen's eyes slitted. "I should have run that little asshole through with my fabric shears when I had the chance." She dragged me into the costume van with a spindly hand around my upper arm, and she was surprisingly strong. Pulling out a bottle of gin from between two heinous, gold-sequined bolts of fabric, she handed it to me. "Take a drink of mother's milk and tell me what's happened, and how we plan to make his body disappear."

I let out a choked laugh that was half sob, then sucked down a mouthful of gin and coughed. That shit was *rough.*

I let the whole sordid tale tumble right out. My white-trash childhood trauma. Finding out that my dad had died in prison while being questioned by the police. The feeling that I could never escape my history. The agreement the guys and I had. Tom. The tabloids.

When I was done, she stared at me with wide eyes. "Where's your etiquette, kid? Pass the dutchie." She made a grabby hand at the gin bottle and took a healthy swig.

I laughed, because the woman could down gin like it was water. "Isn't a dutchie meant to be a blunt?"

She raised a single penciled-on eyebrow. "Child, if I had some Mary Jane, do you honestly think we'd be sitting here drinking bad gin? No." She swigged another mouthful, then pointed the bottle at me. "Here's what we are going to do—a tried-and-true plan straight from the School of Helen." She stood and grabbed a scarf, waving it like a war flag we were rallying around. "We are going to stop crying. We don't cry over stupid men. You are strong. You are a warrior, and while sometimes warriors might cry, they might bend, they do not break. Do you hear me? They. Do. Not. Break." I nodded furiously.

"Good. Now, I am going to dress you up like you are a fucking rock and roll queen. Don't worry, if anyone can make you a goddess, it's me. Then you're going to stand in front of the paparazzi—because there *will* be paparazzi; there always is when there's a sex scandal." She rolled her eyes, like a sex scandal was so tedious. "You're going to stand there, with your boys at your back, and you're going to flip off those misogynistic pearl-clutchers. You're going to look down the lens of the closest camera, stick out your tongue, give them the two-finger salute and you're going to become an icon.

"Fuck Tiny-Dick Tom. Fuck the tabloids. Fuck the stuffy old label execs who think they know what's best. You are going to be a goddamn institution. The Daymakers' muse, Dreamer. Women might not know if they want to hate you or fuck you, but they'll all want to be you."

She was standing on the couch now, giving me her best impression of what she wanted me to do, and I saw it at that moment. The icon she had once been. The one who toured with bands, who was the muse to more seventies rockers than I could believe. I could see why they'd written songs with her name in them, begging for a chance to be her man. I could only hope to be half as badass as she was.

She pointed the scarf at me. "Now, what are you?"

"I'm a warrior."

"I said, what are you?"

"A survivor!"

"I said, what are you?!"

"An ICON!"

She grinned, downing more of the gin. "Too fucking right you are!" She winked at me. "Now, help me down, because I'm not as steady as I used to be, and healing from a broken hip is a real bitch."

I laughed, helping her down and then hugging her tight, no matter how much she grumbled about the mushy stuff. "You're the real queen, you know that, right?" I whispered. "Thank you so much."

She stepped back, patting my arm awkwardly. "We gotta stick together, Dreamer. Now, let me make you something that will slay them all." A smirk spread across her face. "I have just the thing."

THIRTY-NINE

KNIGHT

WHEN I GOT off the stage, I looked around for Lottie, but she was nowhere to be seen on the side of the stage. We walked through the roadies, who slapped our backs and congratulated us on our amazing performance, and I dodged the press, who wanted interviews. I'd come back for them. First, I wanted to find my girl.

I went back to the green room, but still no Lottie. There was, however, a furious Shep who looked like he was ready to commit murder. He had his phone to his ear, yelling at whoever was on the other end.

"I don't give a *fuck* about source confidentiality. Take it the fuck down or the label, the band, and the tour company will all sue the ever-loving shit out of you." He ripped the phone away from his ear and mashed the end button. "*Motherfucker!*"

I took an involuntary step back. I'd never seen Shep so angry. He'd always been our rock. The wall between us and the world. But right now, he was a volatile mess of rage.

I looked around for Lottie. I knew he'd never hurt her, just like I knew he'd never hurt us, no matter how much Royal annoyed the shit out of him. But if he was this mad, there could be only one possible reason.

"Where's Lottie?" I asked, searching the bathroom, behind the racks of clothes.

"She ran out of here like she was running for her life." He slumped on the couch and put his head in his hands.

"What? Get the fuck up. We have to go look for her."

He shook his head. "She's with Helen. She's okay." He showed me his phone.

HELEN

I've got your girl safe. She's a hot mess. Figure this the fuck out before you lose her forever.

I sat down opposite him, reeling, because what the hell was happening? "What's going on? Go and get her!"

Shep growled. "I can't, because I can't make this better. No one can—she'll have to weather it. I can't shield her from it."

I wanted to shake the big fucker. "From *what?*"

He grabbed the phone back and opened up the browser to a website article, a picture of Lottie in her mask right in the center.

The Secret Life of The Daymakers Live-in Sex Toy

The actual fuck? I scanned the article and everything about Lottie and her history was just there, for public consumption.

"There's a dozen more articles on a dozen different sites. I'm trying to get them shut down, but we both know it's out there now. There's no putting it back in the bottle."

I reared back, my brain whirling about what this would mean for Charlotte and the band, and our relationship. "I need to find her," I told Shep, and he stood, shaking his head.

"You need to do the damn meet and greets, so the label doesn't have a leg to stand on about non-performance. I'll go find her and bring her back to the bus."

"Fuck the label, and the meet and greets. Tell them I ate a bad burrito or something; I don't give a fuck. I'm going to find my girlfriend."

I pulled on a plain black hoodie and took off my mask, leaving it in the dressing room. Pulling on a cap, I probably looked suspicious as fuck, but at least my normal face would give me a little bit of anonymity in the crowd.

The irony.

I flashed my badge at the security guys and jogged through the back lot to Helen's van. I slowed as I heard music pumping from the RV. Not The Daymakers or anything. Was that… disco music?

When I got closer, I realized Helen was pumping "I

Will Survive" by Gloria Gaynor, and the singing from inside was enthusiastic. Not good, but enthusiastic. I leaned against the wall and listened for a moment.

"Sing it, girlie!"

"Oh, now, now go! Squawk out the door…"

Were those even the words?

"Just spin around now, because you're not fucking welcome anymore!"

Okay, they *definitely* weren't the words.

Helen cackled a laugh, and Lottie's giggle sounded almost hysterical. I knocked, not that they'd be able to hear me over the pumping music. Pulling open the door slowly, I peeked inside. Lottie was standing on a box in her underwear, a bottle of really shitty gin in her hand, while Helen draped her in black lace. It looked like an oversized men's shirt, if the shirt was entirely made of mourning lace.

"This shirt was meant to be for Royal, but the lace was too delicate. One tug during a show and poof, basically confetti," Helen said as the music ended, before moving into "Rasputin" by Boney M. Lottie drunkenly tossed her head from side to side, and I saw Helen wince as she stabbed her in the thigh with the needle, but I had a feeling that Lottie was too drunk to feel it.

A breeze from the open door swirled around the van, and Helen looked over at me. Her eyes asked me questions. Or maybe they were statements. Silent conversations were open to interpretation, I guess, but their meaning was the same.

Are you going to take care of her, or are you going to be a prick?

I did my best to convey the fact that I loved her with my expression. I must have done a half-decent job, because Helen nodded in satisfaction. "Kid, your Knight in shining armor is here. Take this off, so I can do some alterations without you wiggling around in it like a coked-up jellyfish. I'll send someone over with it tomorrow."

Lottie looked over at me, and her bottom lip trembled. But I saw her pull herself up, straighten her shoulders.

So fucking strong. "Hey, pretty girl."

She stripped out of the lace and handed it gently back to Helen. God, she was beautiful. Throwing on a hooded sweatshirt and some sweats, she still looked fucking beautiful. I held out a hand, and she walked over to me silently. What I'd give to chase away all the hurt and worry in her eyes.

Pulling her to me, I held her tightly to my chest. "Heard you had a rough night," I whispered in her ear. She didn't say anything, just buried herself deeper against my chest. I must stink like ass from being on stage for so many hours, sweating beneath the lights, but she didn't seem to care. "How about I take you back to the bus and we can cuddle?"

I felt her sigh, but the tension in her tiny body remained. *Thank you,* I mouthed to Helen over my shoulder as I led Charlotte out of the RV. I wanted to tell her that it was okay. That we'd get through this just like everything else, but I wasn't the one having all my deep, dark secrets plastered across the internet right now.

I mean, I had before—you didn't grow up in the public eye without having your name dragged through the dirt at least once or twice—but everyone dealt with it differently, and she wasn't used to this.

For a brief second, I thought about setting her free. Giving her money to start over, because god knows I had enough of it, and just letting her escape the limelight and the constant eyes and the bullshit that came with it.

It would be the selfless thing to do. Maybe even the right thing to do.

But I loved her, and I was a selfish fuck. There was no way I could give her up, not without tearing my heart in half.

I scanned my pass to open the door of our bus and led her up the stairs, straight through to the back, where we'd left her room exactly how she had it. Her suitcase was back in there and unpacked, but otherwise, it was still littered with small mementos of her. Her tour passes, a scarf over the window, the unfinished little book nook thing on the desk.

I stripped off my clothes and threw them in her hamper. I needed a shower, but I didn't trust her not to disappear. "I'm just going to have a quick bird bath. Don't go anywhere," I whispered, kissing the side of her face.

It took me two minutes to wipe myself down with a

washcloth and splash my face with water. By the time I got back to the room, she was burrowed beneath the blankets, her face solemn.

"Do you want to talk about it?" I asked softly, climbing into bed beside her. She shook her head as I pulled her to my chest, wrapping my body around hers. "Okay. I just want you to know that this changes nothing for me. I will stand on stage and tell everyone to mind their fucking business, if you want me to. You're important to me."

She sighed heavily. "I'm a dead weight. A drain on society, just like my high school counselor said. The last stop in a generational cycle that is determined to ruin the American way of life."

I pulled back. *The fuck?* "Your high school counselor said that?"

She huffed a bitter laugh. "Yeah, after I'd been caught fighting in the bathrooms. I was jumped by a bunch of girls, but it happened to coincide with rumors of someone dealing meth in the hallways. She decided who else would do it but the daughter of the local meth cook? I mean, I see her logic. It wasn't true, but I get it."

Fuck that bitch. "What was that teacher's name again?" Maybe I'd pay her a visit and give her a piece of my mind.

Lottie shook her head. "It doesn't matter. It's what everyone believed. And maybe they were right? Look at the mess I've landed you in."

"Fuck off," I snapped at her, and her eyes opened wide. I gripped her chin and tilted her face to look up at

me. "None of this bullshit is your fa
past is your fault either—well, may
brawl, but I'm sure those bitches de
down. I'm the son of rich swingers w
busted with cocaine more times than I ...unt, and
keep getting let off with a slap on the wrist. Your only burden was being born poor, and if those judgy fucks can't see the beauty that shines from within you, then that's a them problem, not a you problem."

I sucked in a lungful of air. "You've come to mean so much to me in a short amount of time, and I won't listen to you talk about the girl I… really like"—I winced, because that was awkward as fuck, and now was not the time for declarations of feelings—"just because some piece of shit threw a tantrum at being beaten at his own game."

My jaw ached from snapping my mouth shut so hard on the word vomit. Breathing out a calming breath, I kissed her lips. "Now, if it's okay with you, I'd like to eat your delicious cunt until we forget about anyone outside these four walls. There's me, and you, and the guys, and we are the only people in the universe who matter. What do you say?"

She gave me a crooked smile, her eyes shiny in the darkness. "I think I might love you."

My heart galloped in my chest. "I think I might love you too. Now, lie back, because I'm about to do my best work." I slid beneath the covers to the sound of her watery laughter.

I'd take that sound over her tears any day.

FORTY

DREAMER

I WOKE up the day after Tom's email, surrounded by bodies. Knight was still spooned tight against me, having passed out after he'd given me an impressive amount of orgasms. Poet was in front of me, his hand cupping my boob. Hero was at his back, an arm slung over Poet's waist and fingers touching my hip.

Shep and Royal were nowhere to be seen, but it made sense. This bed was definitely a four-man capacity, and they didn't seem like the "snuggle on the outer edges" type.

I did my best to wiggle out from between the guys, and by some small miracle, I managed to get out without waking any of them. Probably because they were exhausted. It was weird to walk around the bus without my mask, without kicking my toe on random crap.

I went to the bathroom and brushed my teeth, scrubbing off the stale gin from my tongue. Helen partied way too hard for me.

Tiptoeing back out into the main living room of the bus, I was unsurprised to see Shep and Royal there, both sweating and in running clothes. Royal's shorts were two solid inches away from being booty shorts, and looking at his long, tanned thighs did something to me. Shep wore longer ones with compression tights underneath, and his torso was bare, a shirt tucked into his waistband. His chest was broad and the sight of it made me want to bite his pecs.

"Are you done ogling there, Toy?" Royal teased, stepping toward me and kissing me solidly on the lips. He tasted salty, like sweat and man, and I couldn't help but run my hands down his chest and over his abs.

I raised a challenging eyebrow at him. "No."

He smirked, taking a step back. "Then by all means, continue."

I laughed, but stepped over to kiss Shep. It felt nice being able to kiss them whenever I wanted. He wrapped me up in his arms, like he wanted to absorb me inside himself.

Finally, he pulled back, his eyes searching my face. "How are you feeling?"

Ah, there it was. The shitty reality of my life was back.

I shrugged. "I'm doing okay. Knight took it upon himself to suck my soul out through my clit last night, and that does wonders for your existential angst." It also made it clear where he stood. I had no doubt that

Shep had told the rest of the guys what happened, and yet they'd all ended up in bed with me anyway.

I was going to take what I wanted, and if it ended badly, at least I'd have good memories and no regrets. Well, according to Helen anyway.

"I might have seen your soul pass over around the fifth orgasm," Royal teased. The smile slowly slid from his face, morphing into a frown. "What your piece of shit, diseased-dick ex-boyfriend did was shit, but you know it makes no difference to us, right? Most of the stuff in those articles you'd told us yourself, and those shitty things made you the Charlotte you are today." He caged me in between himself and Shep. "I won't lie and say it won't be rough, but eventually some trust-fund baby will get caught banging a stripper outside a bar, or snorting coke off her security guard's forehead, or whatever else passes as gossip, and everyone will move on."

He kissed my neck. "So we're going to stay at Ritz Carlton for a few days, soak in the hot tub, eat our weight in room service and wait for it to blow over a little. There's three days until we start the New York concerts, and I intend to personally catalog every single one of the freckles on your body."

Apparently, Royal did have a sense of kindness, because when he'd said it would blow over, he was being optimistic. Although we'd managed to sneak into the hotel without anyone knowing, by the time the last

New York concert rolled around, the paparazzi were swarming the entrance of the hotel. There was only so much Shep and the hotel security could do.

While I'd been hiding in the hotel for the last two NYC concerts, somehow the paps knew I had to leave eventually, and it was probably going to be for the last show. I didn't understand how the fact I had a shitty childhood was such big news.

Okay, I wasn't that naive. It wasn't that I had a shitty childhood, or that I was a poor girl from the wrong side of the tracks fucking celebrity royalty that had them all in a frenzy. It was the fact that we had some weird little polyamorous thing going on that they couldn't get their head around. The whole sordid tale had been a featured tabloid piece that had run every day for the last week.

I stared at myself in the full-length mirror, the lace dress Helen had made contouring to my body in a way that somehow covered most of my skin, yet left me entirely exposed. It was long sleeved and hit mid-thigh, but the lace she'd chosen was almost sheer, just deep black roses dancing across my flesh like tattoos. Tiny black boy shorts were the only thing I wore beneath it.

A solid black satin collar ran down into wide lapels, which hid my nipples from public view. There were no buttons until my navel, but the whole thing was taped into place, holding onto the fabric for dear life. I wore thigh-high boots that somehow made me look taller, and simple makeup, with eyeliner so sharp, it would hopefully shred the paps to pieces.

Even I could admit I looked absolutely fire. I looked

like the rock and roll goddess Helen had promised, and as I scrunched my carefully styled locks into waves, I hoped I wouldn't look like I was trying too hard. The guys' outfits all complimented mine—dark button-up shirts with lace inserts, though theirs had a lot more fabric.

When we emerged from the hotel foyer onto the street, the flash of a dozen cameras burning my retinas, I just focused on Helen's words. I was a warrior. A goddamn icon in the making.

I looked at a sneering pap, who was repeatedly shouting, "Are you fucking the guys for their fortunes?"

I didn't want him to get the money for this pic. He didn't deserve to make a dime off of my suffering. I saw a girl, maybe a little older than me, standing off to the side with her camera, away from the undulating mass of male photographers. Moving toward her, I met her gaze. Sure, she was still predatory; who else came and sat outside a hotel trying to catch photos of people just living their lives?

But it felt a little better that she wasn't being obnoxious.

"You want the photo?" I asked her, the guys spreading out behind me to block the cameras from the other side.

The girl nodded furiously.

"Guess what? Dreams do come true." Then I flipped off the camera with two fingers, a sneer on my face. The camera clicked repeatedly. I looked at the girl again, her eyes wide like she could see the dollars pouring into her bank account already. I gave her a seriously disappointed look. "Be fucking better. This is the twenty-first century. We should be past slut-shaming by now."

With that, the SUV pulled up and Shep herded us all inside. He stood behind me so the cameras couldn't get a shot of my crotch as I climbed between the seats. Once we were all settled, I slumped back. My heart was beating a million miles an hour.

"Is it inappropriate to have a massive boner right now?" Knight asked, breaking the tension as everyone laughed. "I'm serious. That dress. The attitude. Ummmph." He leaned over and buried his face in my neck, sucking the skin between his lips in a quick love bite.

Poet reached out and slapped him in the back of the head. "If you leave a big-ass hickey on her neck and draw attention away from that dress, Helen might actually murder you. And we need you for at least the next eight hours."

Knight sighed and leaned back, though his eyes kept drifting to my neck. I had a sneaking suspicion that it might have been too late.

The guys had gone out and done rehearsals and soundcheck earlier, which meant the car could drive straight through into the underground parking. Hero helped me from the car, and I shimmied my dress down, not that it would make it cover more.

Every inch of my back was visible through the lace, and he ran a finger down the coarse fabric, making me shiver. "Knight was right. You look beautiful right now." He kissed my temple. "You look beautiful all the time, but right now, you look like you could bring your enemies to their knees while they beg you to end them."

I grinned up at him. "The only person I make beg is Royal."

The man in question uncurled himself from the SUV, kissing me hard on the lips. "Only for you, Toy."

Shep rolled his eyes, but he was smiling as he shook his head. "Get up there. Masks on. We are literal hours away from being able to go home to our own beds and rest."

I held Shep's arm as we walked over to the elevator and took it up to the correct floor, arena security appearing to run crowd control as the people backstage swarmed closer. The guys had banned photography outside the meet and greet, but I still spotted a few people taking sneaky photographs until security got up in their faces.

We made it back to the green room, where a makeup artist was waiting to do the bottom half of Royal's makeup. This one had replaced the other girl from a few months ago, and loved his boyfriend Chadwick and his bichon frisé Brutus more than life itself. We weren't friends, but at least he didn't hit on my guys like they were an open banquet.

While we waited, the guys talked about the setlist and any changes they wanted to make. The excitement for the tour to be over was palpable.

Whitt appeared like a specter. He was grimacing, but I thought perhaps that was just his default face. "Okay, kids. The label execs are here. The pyrotechnics are arranged, so please be aware of them. Stay on your blocking marks and *don't catch on fire*. Show them why they invested in you complicated bastards in the first place."

He turned to me. "You!" I blinked rapidly in shock, thinking he was about to turf me out. "You look killer, Dreamer. Well done. You proved to those assholes that the boys are lucky to have you, not the other way around." He awkwardly patted me on the head, like he couldn't work out where else would be appropriate in this glorified lace curtain. "Let's finish this tour with a bang! But not a literal bang. Stay on your blocking marks and watch for the fireworks!" he repeated as he left.

The guys stood and came over to kiss me, one at a time. I hugged them tightly, because it felt like the end of something. For the whole time we'd known each other, we had the tour. The constant flow of traveling and arenas, concerts and buses, had given us a foundation for our relationship. Without it, what would happen?

Didn't matter. We'd figure it out. Or we wouldn't. But what we *would* do was try, because I wasn't dying in seventy years, wondering *what if*?

I was going to live and love hard, or die trying.

FORTY-ONE

DREAMER

ROMAN CANDLES LIT up the stage behind the guys as they played their fastest song. It galloped like a heartbeat, Knight's guitar howling like a wolf at the moon. Once again, I stood just to the left of the stage, watching them take the crowd and place them in the palm of their hand. They were so fucking good, and if the label lost them, I knew Shep would find someone to pick them up sooner rather than later.

Royal had mentioned that his dad was talking about starting his own record label, and if they didn't like what their current label had to say after this tour, they'd ditch. As long as they didn't have to pay any restitution, I didn't think they felt any particular fondness for their current management.

Shep was hyper-vigilant, as always, standing beside me as he mouthed the words to the songs he must have known as well as the guys by now. The crowd was electric, playing their own part in the vibe of the final concert, a mosh pit pounding at the front like an undulating wave, even as security dragged people over the barriers and into the void between the stage and crowd.

One girl reached up as she was dragged away, and Royal dipped down, gripping her fingers and crooning the words at her, like he was some divine being bestowing good fortune on his worshippers. The girl was crying, big screaming sobs, and honestly, if it wasn't kind of sweet, it would be terrifying.

A roadie came up and yelled something in Shep's ear, and Shep rolled his eyes. He pointed to the roadie, then to me, probably telling him to watch me while he went to put out a fire.

"I'll be right back," he yelled. Or at least that's what I thought he said. I could barely hear him over the sound of the music and the protective earmuffs, but I read his lips. It was either "I'll be right back" or "Alby's white sack." I was pretty sure it was the former.

The roadie lasted three whole minutes before he was called away for something else, making a set of elaborate hand gestures which I think equated to *mind yourself, you're a grown-ass human being.*

I waved him off and went back to watching the guys. They were onto a ballad, and I knew this was one of Poet's. It had such yearning and pain, and although Royal sang it like he was talking about a woman, I knew Poet had written it about the life he had before the accident.

They were winding down, and Shep still hadn't returned, so I decided to head back to the dressing room. That's where I normally met the guys, because they were swarmed with people once they came off stage. Roadies. Press. People with backstage passes. By the time they got back to the dressing room, they were all mine.

I waved to Whitt and Tricia on the way past as they schmoozed what could only be label execs, given the effortless designer wear and self-important expressions. I dodged them as quickly as I could; I wasn't looking to make shit worse for the guys, and I had a feeling I'd probably just put my foot in it.

I made it back to the dressing room and swiped the keycard that would let me in. Pulling off my earmuffs, I breathed a sigh. No wonder everyone who did this kind of thing regularly ended up with hearing loss.

I ate one of Hero's cookies and slumped down on the couch. It was over. Really over.

I wondered if I could convince the guys that a celebratory orgy was just the kind of end-of-tour celebration we needed. First, we needed to head to a party being hosted by the label, and I hoped that I could hide in the corner for long enough that people might forget I was there.

Someone knocked on the door to the dressing room, and I walked over. Everyone who should be in here would have a keycard, unless it was the makeup artist. I looked out the peephole to see two guys in suits.

Fuck. Guess I was going to meet the music execs, whether I wanted to or not. Opening the door, I plastered a polite smile on my face. "Hi, you must be from Panama Records. The guys aren't off the stage yet."

The two men in front of me were kind of average looking. I wasn't sure why I thought most music execs looked like Studio 54 rejects, but they did. The suit guys didn't come in, though.

"Charlotte Lochrin? You're a hard lady to track down."

My heart thumped in my chest. *Fuck. Fuck.* Had Tom decided to have one final, more permanent word? Were these guys here to kill me? They looked nondescript enough to be hitmen. I looked to see if I could run around them, but they were blocking the door completely.

Seeing the panicked look on my face, one guy reached into his jacket. I let out a scream and ran, jumping over the couch. "No, please don't! Whatever he's paying you, I'll double it. Triple it."

Jesus, what was the going rate for a hit these days? Ten grand? Nah, you couldn't even get a Toyota for ten grand now. A hundred, maybe?

"What? Miss, my name is Agent Bianchi, and this is my partner, Agent Briens. We are with the FBI."

The fuck? I poked my head back up. "The FBI?"

"Yes, ma'am," Agent Briens said, with a soft Southern accent. "Sorry for frightening you. We just want to chat about your ex-partner, Thomas Granville Junior. You're a hard person to track down, so we had to resort to crashing the concert of your, uh, paramours."

I'd seen movies where the dumb lead took the bad guys at their word and got shot in the head. "Can you show me your badges please?"

"Sure we can." Agent Bianchi pulled out a badge from his jacket. He stepped toward me slowly like I was going to bolt—which, granted, might still be a possibility. At least until I could find one of the guys. Or Whitt. Someone.

The badge looked legit, and when Agent Briens showed me his too, I stood. To their credit, their eyes never dipped below my face, despite the fact I was practically naked in front of the damn FBI. I grabbed Royal's hoodie and pulled it over my head.

"I have a feeling that this is a normal-people outfit conversation and not a rock'n'roll outfit conversation," I said lightly, and they both looked relieved.

Briens laughed. "You're probably right, ma'am, but I promise we won't take up too much of your time."

Well, it didn't sound like they were here to arrest me. "Uh, do you want a seat? Something to eat?"

Agent Briens politely declined, but Bianchi grabbed a strawberry. "Sorry, it was a long way from DC and I haven't eaten since breakfast."

Briens rolled his eyes. "As my partner said, we just have a few questions about your ex-boyfriend, Miss Lochrin. We are currently investigating him for a number of fraud and embezzlement crimes. Our notes say that you were recently pinpointed by his firm as a possible perpetrator of grand larceny?"

Shit, did I need to call Tobias Lecter? I was in no

hurry to end up back in jail because I said the wrong thing and pissed off the FBI, so I asked, "Do I need to call my lawyer or something?"

Bianchi shook his head. "Larceny isn't our thing, and if anything, our preliminary research further exonerates you. No offense, but we don't think you have the technical knowledge to pull off a scheme quite like this."

I blinked at the guy who still had strawberry juice in the corner of his mouth. "Well, that's the nicest way a Fed has ever called me stupid." I turned back to Briens. "What can I help you with? I haven't seen Tom in months, except for that one time he tried to fake being my legal counsel for a crime he had me framed for." I hated that fucker.

"A forensic accountant from the Bureau has gone over the evidence, and it's been discovered that far from the one-point-three million he accused you of stealing, he's actually stolen over thirty-seven million dollars from his firm, his firm's clients and a number of vulnerable people in the community. He seems to have been hiding money away for quite some time in offshore accounts. We were hoping you'd have something that could help us bring him down."

Holy shit. I'd known Tom was a piece of shit, but I wasn't aware he was *that big* of a piece of shit. "Is he in jail at least?"

Bianchi's jaw tensed. "We believe he was tipped off and has left the country and gone to Montenegro. If he comes back to the States, he won't make it off the plane without being arrested."

I felt both rage and relief. This fucker who was still ruining my life was living it up in Eastern Europe, and would likely never pay for the shit he'd put me through. But on the other hand, he was never going to appear behind me on a crowded street. He was never going to put hands on me again, and that uncurled a heavy tension I hadn't even realized I was carrying.

Still, I wanted to pick up the tray of fruit beside me and hurl it at the wall. "So he gets away with *everything*? What are you even gathering evidence for, if he's already fled the damn country?"

Briens gave me a sympathetic look. "I understand your frustration, Miss Lochrin. But it's much easier to gather evidence while it's still fresh than for him to return in a decade or two and the case is cold and memories have faded."

Fuck. I understood, but still, the injustice of it burned me. "I'm not sure what I can help you with. I'm not sure if you read my police interview, but Tom wasn't just a thieving piece of shit. He was also abusive." They both nodded solemnly. "He didn't share his plans for dinner, let alone ripping off his bosses. The first I even heard about it was when I was being arrested at dawn." I chewed my lip, trying to think back to when we lived together. He had to have some evidence, surely. I shrugged. "I'm sorry. I wish I could be of more help."

Bianchi gave me a reassuring look. "It was a long shot, but worth a try. We believe he might have hidden back-ups of his data somewhere in your apartment. Was there anywhere he was particularly protective of, something that seemed odd?"

Everything about that asshole had been odd. "I wasn't allowed in his office, of course, but I assume you've torn that apart." I thought back to all the red flags and signs that were there, which I'd ignored. *Actually…* "He was always tinkering with his vintage record player. The speakers always sounded buzzy, and he was always there with tiny screwdrivers 'fixing it' even though it never got any better."

Briens smiled so widely, it was a wonder it didn't send me blind. "That's perfect, Miss Lochrin. Just perfect." He gave me his card. "If you think of anything else, please don't hesitate to call me. But if not, I hope you find happiness. The Daymakers are a favorite of my wife's, so I'll be glad if they are all off the market."

Bianchi laughed, nudging his partner, and they left just as a disgruntled Shep slammed into the room. He looked at me, then at them, like he wasn't sure if he wanted to make sure I was okay, or track down the men who'd just left and beat the snot out of them.

I opened my arms, and he ate up the distance between us in two strides. "Who the fuck were they?"

"The end of a nightmare." I explained what the Feds had told me.

When we got back to the hotel that night, I fell into the first dreamless sleep I'd had in a long time, surrounded by men I had come to love, and who loved me, even if we weren't all ready to say it just yet.

EPILOGUE

DREAMER

HARD MARBLE CHILLED my ass but I didn't care, because Knight was currently eating me out like I was Thanksgiving dinner. I had the fingers of one hand curled tightly in his hair, the other slapped over my mouth to muffle the noises he was eliciting from me. He kept bringing me to the precipice and pulling back, teasing me, and I was about to lose my mind.

"Knight, I swear to god..." I threatened, which would have been way more scary if it hadn't been a breathless moan.

As he grinned up at me with that mischievous look in his eye, I didn't know if I should hit him or kiss him. Luckily, he finally relented, spearing me with his tongue until I came all over his face.

Leaning back against the mirror, I panted, and when he slid up my body, I kissed him hard, regardless of the fact that his lips were glossy with me.

"I love you, you know?" he whispered against my lips, and I couldn't help my smile.

"I love you too, but everyone we know is downstairs, and there's no way they haven't noticed us both missing."

We were at Royal's dad's mansion for Thanksgiving. Honestly, I wasn't sure who'd been more surprised at the invite, Royal or the rest of the guys, because when we arrived, we'd discovered Roman Stokes had invited Poet's mom and Knight's parents too.

He hadn't invited Hero's parents, because apparently even an aging, degenerate rockstar could tell they were epic pieces of shit.

Meeting Roman, and the guys' parents, was a little weird. They were faces that had stared out at me from TV screens and tabloid magazines for my entire life, but having met them, I realized they were just as fucked up as the rest of us. They were just fucked up in the spotlight with a whole lot of money.

Meeting the parents was hard enough. Meeting the parents when you were in a poly relationship and all those parents were famous in their own right was daunting as hell.

Except Poet's mom. Jenny was a sweetheart, and seemed to accept the alternative lifestyle we had fallen into since the tour ended four months ago.

Knight heaved himself back to his feet. "Fine, I guess we have to go and play happy families. But tonight, baby, you're mine."

I stroked my cheek against his. "I'm yours always."

Shimmying from the counter, I leaned up and kissed him once more before dragging him from the bathroom. I could hear music downstairs, as well as laughter.

It was nice to hear the guys laugh again. The weeks following the end of the tour had been stressful. Their label had dropped them, but Roman Stokes had been there to pick them right back up. Apparently, Royal's dad had been their Plan B. When they'd come to visit him after their meeting in Chicago with the Panama execs, they'd had to basically choose between me and their careers as masked rockers.

They chose me.

For the first time in my life, someone—several someones, actually—had chosen me.

So when Panama Records booted them to the curb, Roman Stokes was there to pick up the pieces, both of their career, and his fractured father-son relationship. Roman had been bored and thinking of starting his own label. Royal had needed a fallback plan, in case Panama dug in their heels.

And that was how Daydreamer Records had been born.

Walking into the living room, I saw Roman regaling Poet's mom and step-dad with some crazy story and smiled. I'd thought the guys had named the record label, but apparently, it had been Roman. He'd told me a couple of months ago it was because without me, he wouldn't have his son back, and this was the least he could do to recognize the fact that I'd healed something between them, even if it was by jeopardizing their careers.

Royal moved away from Knight's parents, excusing himself as Knight and I reappeared in the room. His eyebrow raised as he looked between us, and I felt my face flush pink.

"I didn't know using the bathroom was a two-person job, Toy." He kissed my lips gently, but nipped my bottom lip in reprimand.

I shrugged, trying and failing to hide my smirk. "What can I say?"

"Shep is going to spank that pretty ass pink later on," he warned, or maybe promised.

I just winked at him saucily and went to find Shep; maybe I'd butter him up first so he spanked Royal instead. I'd pay good money to see that.

"So damn cheeky," he muttered, leading me over to the wet bar and pouring me my favorite gin cocktail. We'd promised to visit Whitt and Tricia between Thanksgiving and New Years in Boston, and I was looking forward to it. Apparently, Helen was coming as well. I'd missed the old guard. They'd helped me escape more than anyone else, even the guys.

Royal poured himself some scotch that I was sure cost more than the average car, and held the glass out to me. "To good friends, and the great love of my life?"

"Music?"

He shook his head. "No, Toy. You."

My heart thudded in my chest. Somehow, those

small words continued patching all the broken pieces of my soul back together again.

I pulled him close and hugged him tightly. The music turned into a ballad, and he slow-danced with me, our drinks pressed tightly to our chests. "I love you, Rourke Stokes. I love you with all your different personas and masks, because none of them change who you really are deep down."

We danced a little more, before Roman called Royal over to talk about Daydreamers Records. I went in search of Shep. He didn't have any family at the gathering today, and in terms of upbringing, his was the closest to my own. But everyone here accepted that Shep was part of the guys. Like they'd all adopted the man the day he rescued them down on the boardwalk. Especially Jenny, Poet's mom.

I didn't find Shep, but I did find Hero and Poet, cuddled close together on a stone bench, watching the rain fall. They had a blanket over their laps and looked so much like a festive card, I couldn't help but step out there. They turned, and the smiles that lit up their face made me feel like I wasn't an intrusion—rather that I was the perfect person to complete the moment.

Hero lifted the blanket and settled me on his lap, and I leaned my head on his shoulder. Poet held my hand, his thumb stroking along mine. "Has Knight's mom started on the wine yet?"

I nodded. The senior Becks were an interesting pair. They were definitely stoned, and they were on their second, maybe third bottle of wine, but they were happy and jovial. The life of the party. I could see how they'd gotten the reputation they had, because I barely knew them and already I felt like they'd attended this party just for me.

They didn't seem to think that me falling in love with five guys was weird at all. In fact, Knight's mom had fistbumped me. *Insanity.*

I looked between them, my heart thumping in my chest. "Hey, guys?"

Hero nuzzled my hair as he watched the rain. "Mmm, yes, sweetheart?"

"You know I love you, right?" Admitting it out loud seemed terrifying. Like if I never said it, then they were never forced to say it back. There was comfort in the status quo.

Poet leaned closer, kissing me with a gentle brush of his mouth on mine. "I love you too. So fucking much."

Hero pulled me back, dipping me over his arm until he could kiss me absolutely breathless. "I love you as well. Both of you. I'm so damn grateful that luck, or fate, or whatever other forces control shit brought you into my life."

It was early days yet, and life with so many men and only one of me was going to be complicated. It was hard enough deciding whose bed I slept in each night, or who slept in mine. But eventually, I'd figure out how to juggle, and we'd find a rhythm. I just knew that everything was going to be okay.

We sat in silence, watching the rain and the traffic

and the huge rolling clouds. I just soaked them in. My guys.

Shep appeared, leaning against the door jamb. "Dinner's ready." The soft look in his eyes as he took us in made my chest feel full. Hero and Poet stood, kissing me on the cheek before ducking around Shep with a shoulder pat.

I watched them go with a raised eyebrow. "Well, that wasn't suspicious."

Shep grinned, leaning down to kiss me. "They know I wanted to tell you I loved you. When I think of the future, it has you in it, front and center. One day, I want to marry you and make you my wife. Start a family, maybe." My breath stalled in my lungs. He wrapped his arms around me and pulled me tight into a hug. "But not today. First, you get to live any life you want. If you want to travel, we'll take you. You want to go to college, we'll enroll you as soon as possible. The choice is yours now. The world is yours."

I burrowed my face into his chest, his smell so comforting, it was like a balm on my soul. "I love you too." I tilted my head up to catch his lips, and he didn't disappoint. He kissed me until I was breathless, and my body felt electric. "You know what else I love? Stuffing. Let's eat."

Shep laughed, wrapping a huge arm around my shoulder and leading me back into the living room, toward the men who were my present and my future.

ABOUT THE AUTHOR

Grace McGinty is eclectic. She has worked as a chocolatier, a librarian, a forensic accountant, and finally, a writer. Like her professional career, the genres she writes are chaotic and out of control. From contemporary new adult to smutty reverse harem novels of every sub-genre, if you like it, she's probably written it.

Except dark romance. She's a marshmallow, and somehow the mean guys always end up cinnamon rolls.

Grace lives in rural Australia with her crazy family, an entire menagerie of pets, and will one day be crushed by the giant piles of books that litter every room.

Head over to www.gracemcginty.com and join the mailing list for sneak previews into what she is working on and to stay up-to-date with new releases and giveaways!

Need more rich assholes? Check out INSIDE THE MAELSTROM

Need more music? Check out THE LAST NOTE on the next page.

The Last Note

GRACE MCGINTY

CHAPTER ONE

HARPER

I wasn't sure how long I'd been standing in the foyer, staring at the cat hair on my mother's favorite peacoat, but a loud knock at my front door startled me so badly that I nearly tipped over the coat stand.

The knock sounded again.

I clutched my mug to my chest. The coffee inside was now tepid, but it felt like a security blanket. Or maybe an anchor. I shuffled the few steps toward the door and pulled it open.

A handsome man stood on the other side, probably in his late twenties, dressed in a soft gray three-piece suit. He seemed out of place in my rundown apartment building, looking more like he belonged between the pages of GQ.

We stared at each other for a moment, his gaze traveling quickly over me, his eyes purposefully neutral. He stared at my favorite mug, which had the words *Marry the beast and get the library* emblazoned on the front in curlicue script. The corner of his mouth quirked.

"Miss Barry? Harper Barry?"

I continued to stare at him blankly, fighting my way through the haze clouding my brain.

"Yes, I'm Harper. I'm sorry. I'm just a little out of it. My mother just died. What can I help you with?" I sounded like a robot, and the man winced a little.

"Can I come in?"

My fingers felt numb. Maybe I was having a heart attack or something?

"Sure, come on in." I moved away from the door, leaving my mug on the hall table, beside three other semi-full mugs.

The man stood uncomfortably in the middle of my small living room. He didn't fit in with my thrift store furniture. He was luxury personified.

"Miss Barry, my name is Knoxfeld Long. I'm a partner over at Long, Long, Gallagher & Smith."

The obviously unhinged part of me laughed at the absurdity of his name. Only a rich, attractive, white guy could pull off a name like that with such quiet confidence. As it was, Knoxfeld Long looked at me like I'd lost my mind. He might have been right.

"Do I owe someone money?"

Knoxfeld Long shook his head, "No. My firm represents—er, represented, I should say—your mother. She had us on retainer for the last twenty-three years. We are the executors of her will."

Executors. Knoxfeld Long would probably still look

good in one of those black hoods that executioners wore. Hangman chic.

"My mother couldn't afford to have lawyers on retainer. I think you might have the wrong person."

He shook his head again, and gave me a soft smile, his eyes full of sympathy. "No, we have the right person. Your mother left you a Memory Reconstruction in her will, and I am afraid that time is of the essence. I am here to drive you to RecoMem. You have an appointment with the proprietor of the clinic, Doctor Desoto, in half an hour. Perhaps you would like to change?"

I looked down at my Deadpool onesie, a gift from my best friend for my birthday. I looked back up into the concerned eyes of Knoxfeld Long. I was repeating his name over and over in my head for some reason, but it was just one of those names that you had to say in its entirety.

"I'll go change," I mumbled, suddenly embarrassed.

"You have time to freshen up, if you like." His gentle tone probably meant that I looked like complete shit. But it had only been a handful of hours since the hospital had called, so looking like shit was my prerogative.

I walked into my tiny bedroom that was dwarfed by my king single bed, and grabbed a pair of jeans off the floor and an old band t-shirt from my drawer, before pulling my hair up into a messy bun. I wasn't going to win any fashion awards, unless 'unwashed hobo' suddenly came into fashion.

I walked to the bathroom, casting a furtive glance over at Knoxfeld Long, who was still standing uncomfortably in the middle of my living room, then shut the door. I couldn't even remember the last time I brushed my teeth. Gross. It had been a long week, filled with life support machines and bedside vigils. She'd waited until I left for the night to let go though. My mother, selfless until the end.

By the time I left the bathroom, I looked alive at least. I winced at the thought. Bad choice of words.

Knoxfeld gave me a once-over and then pulled a flask from his jacket pocket. "It's brandy. Take a sip. You still look a little shaken." He held out the delicately etched pewter flask like it was the cure for everything that ailed me.

I gladly took the flask from this perfect stranger, downing a huge mouthful of brandy. It was smooth, no burn, and I could tell it was quality. I handed him back the flask and he tucked it back into the inside pocket of his jacket. I'd always wondered what those inside pockets were for. I couldn't find a skirt with pockets, but guys got booze pouches in their suit jackets. The injustice of it all.

"Let's go," Knoxfeld Long said gently.

I was halfway across town in his Maserati before it occurred to me that I hadn't even checked his credentials. Mom would have been so disappointed that I was being this reckless, but I couldn't find it in myself to care.

By the time we arrived at RecoMem, I'd pulled

myself together a little. Maybe the brandy had helped, or maybe Knoxfeld Long had put some uppers in the flask. Either way, I was thinking more clearly. Which was good, because Doctor Desoto hadn't stopped speaking since we sat down in his office.

"Do you have any questions, Miss Barry?"

I had hundreds, but the good doctor didn't know the answer to any of them. He wouldn't know, for instance, how my mother could afford the expensive memory reconstruction that she'd gifted to me in her will. A memory reconstruction cost a bucketload of cash. It was usually reserved for trust fund kids who wanted to double check that Grandpappy Warbucks was actually in his right mind when he'd left all his money to his Brazilian housekeeper, or occasionally for the police to use the memories of high-profile murder victims to catch killers on the city's dime. It wasn't for a poor art teacher who'd barely made her mortgage repayments, and who'd clothed her only child in thrift shop dresses until she was sixteen.

"No questions."

Doctor Desoto continued. "As I was saying, when one of our clients passes"—he paused, clearing his throat loudly—"the hospital will call us and we send out a collection team as soon as we are notified, usually within forty-five minutes of T.O.D. That's time of death. That usually gives us a viable chance of recovering almost the full range of memory data. The longer it takes for us to receive the deceased, the fewer long-term memories we can recover."

He cleared his throat again. Either the man had a tic or the beginnings of a head cold. "You see, we view the brain like a roadmap, full of destinations, and the viewer—in this case you, Miss Barry—gives us an attraction to find. We then follow all the pathways of the map, finding little bits of memory and knowledge that relate to that attraction. But time is the antithesis of memory, and as soon as a person ceases to be, it is like someone has put a match to the bottom of the map."

Knox chewed his bottom lip in a super attractive, but not very lawyerly action. "How do you find these attractions? I mean, each person must have millions of memories."

Doctor Desoto nodded sagely, as if he were glad one of us was asking the intelligent questions. "Trillions, more like it. Probably an infinite number, in my estimation. But, to use my geography analogy, our clients—at least, the ones who come in with the specific purpose of leaving a reconstruction in their will—come in and complete an interview. We ask them questions, get them to think about important events, people, lessons, moments in their lives, and we map all of this. We correlate the particular brain activity with the corresponding topic, which gives us a rough topographical map, if you will."

I nodded, like everything that he was saying made sense to me. The doctor was obviously one of those map enthusiasts in his spare time. Cartophile? I shifted uncomfortably on the hard plastic chairs and stared at Doctor Desoto's forehead. It wasn't flushed, so he probably didn't have a head cold. Maybe he was just a nervous throat-clearer.

He caught my eye, pinning me in his gaze as if he knew my mind was wandering. "But please remember, we can only access the memories once. If we continue with my map metaphor, what we do is the equivalent of burning the bridges after we have crossed them. Therefore, you must be very certain about the topic you wish to pursue."

He was trying to instill a sense of urgency, but he was wasting his time. I felt nothing. I was entombed in ice. I sat in the doctor's office, with its warm yet neutral décor barely masking its clinical roots, and I felt nothing but a bone-deep chill.

The good doctor and my handsome lawyer were both staring at me, as if I was supposed to give a response. My eyes slid to the handsome lawyer in question.

Tall, with sleek musculature that told me he must have more than one conference call while working out, he fit into his suit with almost artistic perfection. A well-tailored suit was the lingerie for the modern man, or so Cosmo said. Looking at the way it stretched across his shoulders and hugged his thighs, I believed it. He had light brown hair, hazel eyes and a straight, white smile that only money could buy. He was enough to make any girl a little mushy in the brain.

"Miss Barry?" Doctor Desoto prompted again, bringing me back out of my sexy lawyer daydream. How inappropriate was that?

"Please, call me Harper. What was the question? Sorry, my head is a little tangled at the moment."

He gave me another of those sympathetic smiles, like he was talking to a crazy person. "It is quite alright, Harper. I just wanted to know if you have decided on a subject?"

I looked down at my hands as my mind whirled. My mother always said I had cellist's fingers. Long and supple, but very strong. She'd say this with a hint of jealousy. She'd had tiny hands, with squat little fingers. I must have inherited my father's hands, whoever he was.

It was an old argument between my mother and I. I had begged to know who possessed the other half of my DNA for years, from the time I realized that most of the other kids in the playground had both mommies *and* daddies. And that I wasn't like Clara, who had two mommies. But despite my childhood epiphany, Mom had refused to answer. When I was little, Mom would just change the subject to something fun, and I'd jump on it with the fickleness of a child.

As I got older, and more persistent, she would turn away and ignore the question, like she hadn't heard it. When I became an adult and demanded to know, she'd said he was a man she met in a bar, and she didn't know his name. I hadn't believed her then, and I didn't believe her now, not really. My mother hadn't been the kind of woman who had random one-night stands with strangers.

I had thought my mother was an open book. Just a

simple art teacher from Silver Lake, who taught decoupage to budding hipsters. Apparently, it took her death to prove me wrong.

Knoxfeld Long cleared his throat. "Perhaps Harper might need a few minutes alone to make her decision." His voice was deep and firm. The doctor murmured his agreement and stood, but I motioned him to sit.

"No, it's fine. I know the information I need. I want to know about my father. Everything about him."

This was my last chance to find out. The answers would die with her if I didn't ask. Maybe there was a clue, a hint that I could pick out of her memories to help me track him down.

He nodded as he scribbled down on his notepad. "Certainly, Miss— uh, Harper. Jeanette will bring you in some refreshments, while I get the techs to run this through the Memorix program. We will essentially download the images stored in the different memory centers in the brain, mostly from the parietal cortex. I don't want to bore you with the scientific details, but there is a booklet on the coffee table that goes into the procedure in more precise detail if you'd like to read through it. We will give you a call when your viewing room is ready. Or of course, you are welcome to view this at a later time, if you would prefer?"

I shook my head. I needed to know now. I felt like this was my first chance in twenty-two years to find out who I was. I wasn't going to waste a second.

Doctor Desoto excused himself and left the room, the door closing softly behind him. Knoxfeld Long stood up and motioned to the couch that ran along one wall of the room. I gave him a half-hearted smile. After all, my mother had raised me to be polite, if nothing else. "Thank you for arranging this, Mr. Long."

"Please, call me Knox. Mr. Long is my father." He mockingly quoted the cliché. "After all, Harper, I've known you since you were a baby."

I noticed that when he smiled, the little dimple in his chin disappeared, only to reappear in his cheek. "What do you mean, you've known me since I was a baby? I'm pretty sure I would remember if I'd met you before today." If only because he would have frequented my dirty dreams.

"I rocked you once in your capsule, on the floor of my father's office when I was six. You were a cute baby, and I remember I felt so important because my father and your mother had left me in charge of this tiny human. I spent so much time in the office with my father, I was basically a sixty-year-old in a six-year-old's body."

He sat down beside me, a polite distance away, but Knox had presence with a capital P. I was fairly sure I could be in a pitch-black room, blindfolded, and I'd know if he was in the room. It was far more than just his good looks.

"Anyway, you slept most of the time, but when you woke up, you started screaming something awful, like an injured cat. I basically had to do back flips, pulling funny faces to get you to stop." He gave me a megawatt grin then, all dimples and sparkling eyes. He didn't seem to pay any attention to my dazed expression, just continued his story.

"And when you started laughing, I felt the most immense pride. For a year afterwards, I was convinced that being a clown was my calling. Dad was glad when I grew out of my desire to attend clown college, though." He gave me a goofy grin, and I felt my mouth tug up in a smile. My first real smile since the hospital had called. "I see your smile hasn't changed in twenty-odd years either."

An odd warmth chased away the chill in my face. I coughed and looked at the floor. "So you knew my mother? Do you know how she's paying for this?"

His smile faded, and it was his turn to look uncomfortable. "Your mother was my father's client. I know he was quite fond of her, and he isn't fond of many people. He's a ruthless old bastard most of the time. But not with your mother. They caught up for coffee and went out for dinner quite a few times over the years, from what I remember. I'm pretty sure he did everything for her pro bono too. I know this is pro bono." His forehead creased, and he seemed as confused by that as I was. "However, they both agreed that I should be the one to look after your interests. They thought you'd feel more comfortable around me than Dad."

They were probably right. There was something laid back about Knox that set me at ease. Sitting in this waiting room with a guy old enough to be my father would have been uncomfortable. But it still irked me that some stranger had been sitting around with my mother planning what was best for me.

"You don't think your dad is my dad, do you?" If that was the case, I'd been having some very impure thoughts about my half-brother.

Knox roared with laughter, until he was coughing to catch his breath. He opened his mouth to say something, and another fit of man-giggles overtook him. He did some of those deep breathing exercises they taught you when you went to birthing classes, and wrestled his features back into a semi-professional expression.

I frowned. "You know, I'm not sure you are supposed to laugh at your clients, Mr. Long. Especially ones who are grieving." I couldn't keep the peevishness out of my voice. I didn't even feel bad I'd played the grief card.

Knox had the good grace to look a little apologetic. "I'm sorry. But the idea is pretty hilarious if you know my father. My dad is nearly twice your mother's age. The idea that he'd have an affair with one of his clients, who would have been all of twenty-three when they met, is really amusing." He looked like he was going to laugh again, but I could see him mentally try to rein it in. "No, the man still pines for my mother, twenty-odd years on. She was the love of his life, his one great passion. When she died, all that was joyful in the man died with her." There was no mirth on his face now, and I had the feeling I'd inadvertently poked a sore spot.

We sat in an awkward silence for a moment, and when the door swung open to admit Jeanette the secretary with coffee and sandwiches, I breathed a sigh of relief. Knox gave the secretary a warm smile. In return, the woman just blinked at him, her mouth slightly agape.

"Thanks, Jeanette. This looks delicious," I said, a little too loudly, feeling sorry for the woman who seemed to be stuck in the quicksand of Knox's handsome face. She dragged her eyes from Knox, and swallowed hard. Giving me her most professional smile, she unconsciously straightened her blouse.

"You're very welcome, Miss Barry, Mr. Long. Please let me know if there is anything else I can get for you." With that, she hustled out the door as fast as her practical, rubber-soled shoes could carry her.

I fell on the cucumber sandwiches with ferociousness. Apart from the nip of brandy Knox had pushed on me this morning, I hadn't eaten anything in nearly twenty-four hours.

When my mother's breast cancer had returned, the doctors had told her she had a month at most to live. I'd been prepared for her death, but the call in the middle of the night had still shattered me on a level I wasn't expecting.

Since then, I'd been walking around in a fog, never able to settle on one task, unable to sit still for a second, in case the memories bombarded me and brought with them all the feelings that I wasn't ready to acknowledge just yet.

Maybe a little part of me didn't care who Knox was when he arrived on my doorstep this morning. He offered a reprieve from the feelings that threatened to break through the walls I'd erected the day the doctor had first given my mother the terminal news.

I looked down at the empty plate of sandwiches in front of me, then sheepishly at Knox, who was sitting beside me on the couch, sipping a cup of tea. "Sorry."

"It's okay. You needed them more." He handed me a cup of tea too. "Would you like sugar and milk?"

I attempted to drink my tea with a little more decorum than I'd inhaled my sandwiches. Knox was flicking through the pamphlet of information on the memory reconstruction procedure. I hoped he could give me the condensed layman's version later.

Jeanette suddenly poked her head back in the door. "The viewing room is ready, Miss Barry. If you would like to follow me?"

I dropped my tea cup with a loud clink of fine china. This was it.

"I know it will probably be an intensely personal experience, and I'm happy to wait here for you, or I can give you a little support in the viewing room. Whatever you need," Knox said, his tone so earnest that it scared me a little. Like I was going in for surgery, or about to find out that my pet hamster had actually died when I was five, and not run away to join a huge hamster colony in New Mexico, like Mom had said.

I knew I should be brave and shoulder this alone, but I didn't want to. I wanted someone to hold my hand. I would have preferred someone a little closer to me, like my best friend, but a handsome stranger would do in a pinch.

"I would like you to come in, if that's okay?" My voice sounded small and uncertain. Pathetic.

In a very unlawyerlike move, he reached out and held my hand. "You got it, Harper. I'm here for whatever you need."

The warmth of his hand centered me a little more as I squeezed his fingers, and he squeezed back. He strode with purpose out the office door, like the lawyer version of Saint George, ready to slay my emotional dragons and save this damsel in distress.

We followed Jeanette down a professionally decorated hallway, and I couldn't help but notice her pencil skirt was wrinkled at the back. Something about that little fact reassured me.

Knox walked a little in front of me, ready to guide me around any obstacles that may pop up in an uptown doctor's office, like ninjas or court injunctions. Maybe he was expecting ninjas. Or Cthulhu. The thought made me grin; I could see why my mother had wanted him here. He was an Armani-clad security blanket.

The viewing room looked like a smallish cinema. On the wall in front of us was a white screen, hooked up to a projector. It reminded me of the little old home theater setup we'd had when I was a child. That was when we'd been living in the one room walk-up in Chinatown. We had a little second-hand projector that we'd shoot onto a sheet tacked to the wall, and we'd play classic movies from the eighties, or have movie marathons where we'd only watch movies with Audrey Hepburn or Julia Roberts.

But this viewing room was state of the art. A large designer couch was set back against the farthest wall, a small coffee table holding a box of tissues and a jug of water between the couch and the high-tech screen.

Doctor Desoto sauntered into the room, his earlier intensity gone. "Please excuse the wait, but we found far more information than we were expecting. It took a little longer to collate and translate than usual. However, we managed to go back to what we think were her earliest memories on this subject. Your mother was very specific in her wishes that we receive her brain as quickly as possible. She wanted to leave you as much as she could. She was my client personally. Such a wonderful woman," he said wistfully.

Yeah, so I'd heard. I'd wished I'd known this wonderful woman that everyone seemed to be raving about.

"Again, I'm very sorry for your loss," Doctor Desoto continued, patting my forearm. I gave him a polite smile, and willed him to hurry up. I was so close to knowing the truth. "We've organized it chronologically, from the earliest to the latest memories. There is several days worth of material however, and I'm afraid you are only booked in for a one-hour slot. I'll have Jeanette book you an appointment at this time for the next four days. That should about cover it, I think."

I felt my eyes widen. Five days of viewing my mother's most intimate memories. A cold sweat crawled over my skin, and I could feel my heartbeat thudding in my throat. It was too soon; I wasn't ready for this. But the logical part of my brain argued that this was it. This time I would have the truth, and my emotional well-being would just have to cope.

The lights dimmed, and the doctor pressed his finger to his nano-tablet. "Now remember, you'll see what your mother saw, and you'll hear her thoughts. We can't transfer smells yet—that science is a little more complex—but generally speaking, you should get an immersive experience. Thought, sights, sounds, body language, all these elements are tied up within memories."

The screen came to life, and my mother's hands appeared on the screen, running across the sidewalk in a movement so familiar to me that it made my heart ache. Knox's hand returned to mine, squeezing gently as we sat back to watch.

CHAPTER TWO

EVIE

He was back again. Stealing her audience, and most importantly, getting her tip money in his battered guitar case.

Evie pressed too hard into the sidewalk with a piece of chalk, and it snapped in half. She swore under her breath and sat back on her haunches, picking up the two broken pieces and putting one back into the dented cookie tin she used to carry her chalk. Silently apologizing to her supplies, she returned to the reproduction of *Whistler's Mother* on her little strip of the Venice Beach boardwalk.

A tourist hotspot, she generally made enough to pay her rent each month just from tourist tips.

At least, she did until yesterday, when the Kurt Cobain wannabe showed up in Old Wild Joe's spot next to her.

It wouldn't have been so bad if he was terrible, though that would have driven the crowds away too. If he was mediocre, Evie would have been happy. But no, the guy had to be fantastic. His soulful voice was gravelly, giving him a sweet tone that you could listen to for hours. And he drew the crowds alright. They emptied their full pockets into his guitar case, all the while walking right past her section, whispering how very good he was, ignoring the pavement art that she'd pored over for hours, the soles of their rubber walking shoes smudging the edges of her work.

Now, she was going to have to beg for more shifts at the bar just to make ends meet. All she could do was hope that he was one of those flighty musicians who stayed a week and then left. Maybe some music exec would walk past and love him so much that they'd sign him on the spot, and she could have a nice little street stall back. Maybe one of those hippies who sold crystals attached to leather thongs. Sure, they got a little high during their lunch breaks, but at least they always offered to get her a hot dog when they got the munchies.

She was going to have to up her game if she was going to draw the tourists back in. Maybe she'd do some of those 3D works that they loved so much. She was going to have to try to commandeer some more space. But she didn't think Juanita, who sold handmade *Día de los Muertos* skulls, could give her any space. Maybe the young Joe Cocker tryhard next to her would give up a piece of his real estate, seeing how he'd come and trampled all over her profits.

She huffed as she messed up a line, and decided it

was time to go home for the night. The sun was setting over the water, turning the surface a soft pink color. She loved Venice Beach at dusk.

She noticed the lame Bieber wannabe next to her was packing up for the night too, although she knew that the buskers got some good tips after dark, when the night crowd came out. Maybe he only came down so he could torment her during the day. It was a conspiracy.

Gathering up her little tip jar, she sighed at the measly amount rattling around inside it. She screwed on the lid and stuffed it into her beat-up tote bag. She had to hurry if she was going to grab a burrito from Manny's food truck before her shift at the club started.

She rocked back to stand, when a hand appeared in her vision. She looked up to see the subject of her internal rant proffering a large paw. Ignoring him, she raised herself up to her full five and a half feet.

"Hi, neighbor. I'm Jackson Harper. You rushed off yesterday before I could introduce myself." He held out his hand again, this time for a handshake, and Evie begrudgingly took it. His fingers were warm and calloused, probably from the steel strings of his acoustic guitar. He didn't look like he did much hard manual labor. His palms were dry, and his large hand encompassed her own like she was part of the lollipop guild.

"Evie Barry."

She removed her hand as fast as she could. She wasn't going to think about the broad, muscled chest which was conveniently located in her direct line of sight. Instead, she stared at him in the eye, which was an uncomfortable degree upwards when they were this close. She took a large step backwards.

The guy was hot—undeniably hot. Like, sex on a stick hot. He had hair shaved close to his head, but it looked like it had been blond, judging by the five o'clock shadow gracing the sharp angles of his jaw. He had broad shoulders and a slim waist. Full lips complemented electric blue eyes. A sleeve of tattoos ran from his wrist up under the edge of his tight black tee, and well-worn jeans clung to his thighs like a magnet.

Evie stared hard, searching for flaws. His nose was definitely crooked, and had a small cut across the bridge, like someone had punched him in his too perfect face. Maybe his forehead was a little high, but now she was just clutching at straws.

He cleared his throat, and Evie realized she'd been staring like a crazed fan. "Evie, that's a beautiful name. Your art is beautiful too. Like, stupidly good. I wouldn't have known the difference between yours and the originals if I hadn't been standing here all day watching you create them."

The thought of Jackson Harper—he even had a sexy rock star name, the asshole—watching her all day made heat flare in her cheeks. She gave a silent thanks to the fates that the sun had dipped down below the skyline, washing the vibrant colors out of the landscape. In this darkness, he wouldn't be able to tell that she blushed like a Southern belle. She just mumbled a half-hearted thanks.

"Wanna grab a beer or something? There's a little bar around the corner that's no more than a hole in the wall, but they stock this amazing Mexican beer—"

"I have to work. There's been a sudden downturn in tips, and I need to work another job to make ends meet." She was definitely feeling out of sorts, and this man was the reason. She hoped she wasn't being too subtle for this meathead.

His lips twitched. "I'm sorry to hear that. Maybe they aren't Whistler fans?"

"Or maybe the yodeling from next door is scaring everyone away. What happened to Old Joe anyway? Listening to you makes me long for his off-key country songs." Her hands balled on her hips. "Look, the street vendors and artists down here on Venice Beach are a community, and we don't really like it when some rock-star wannabe comes in and steals all the foot traffic. Most of us make a living this way. So if you're going to be a crowd hog, how about you throw around some recommendations to your groupies and perhaps direct them over to Juanita's skulls, or Jack's snow cone cart. Spread the wealth, Mr. Harper, and the community will stay a harmonious one. Step on too many toes, and you'll find that working down here can become very uncomfortable, very quickly."

Evie hadn't meant to make them sound like the Mob, and in all honesty, it was probably a bit of an exaggeration. But she so wanted to put this Ken Doll in his place, and he'd danced on her last nerve all day, so she let her tongue run away on her. Again.

He gave her a mock solemn expression. "Maybe everyone else's stalls just need to be better?"

She gave him a burning look, hoisted her tote onto her shoulder and strode away. Standing around making goo-goo eyes at Jackson had made her late, and now she wouldn't have time to brave the line at Manny's and scarf down a burrito. It looked like it was going to be juice and saltines again for dinner tonight. Just another reason to hate on Jackson Harper. Fueling the hate was better than recognizing the other burn in her gut.

Lust. She had a serious case of lust for the jerk.

She slammed through the employee entrance of Casablanca's ten minutes later. Casablanca's was a 1940s inspired dance club, and she waved to one of the security guys who was sitting on a stool, guarding the door to the back alley.

She went to her locker and found her uniform freshly drycleaned, still hanging in the clear plastic. It was a deep red dress, with short, capped sleeves and a sweetheart neckline that showcased the curve of her breasts. The long pencil skirt brushed just below her knees. The club drycleaned all the cocktail waitresses' uniforms, a service for which she was grateful.

She reached into the bottom of the tote bag, grabbing her garter belt and silk stockings, safely tucked away in their satin lingerie bag. She'd tried wearing pantyhose to work once, and in the hot California summer, she thought they were going to melt to her skin. So she allowed herself this one small luxury, and was all the more comfortable for it.

Heading into the employee bathrooms, which were unisex, she ran into Steve putting on his white suit jacket and fixing his black bowtie. She watched him struggle with the silk tie while she washed the chalk off her hands and forearms. When she couldn't watch him screw it up any longer, Evie handed him her dress, and reached up to straighten his tie for him. Steve had been working here for as long as her, and he still hadn't mastered it.

"Thanks, Evie. I wish the big guys would just let us wear clip-ons and save my sanity," he said with a sigh. It was the hundredth time she'd heard him say it, in his slow Southern drawl. This was a familiar routine for them.

"You could always try wearing a garter and stockings. Putting them on without getting a run is a lot like Edward Scissorhands trying to put on a condom." She took her dress back from him, and went into one of the cubicles.

She heard Steve's chuckle as she closed the door, and mouthed along with him, "Ya'know Evie, I'll help you put your garter on anytime you need it. You just say the word."

Laughing, Evie flipped him the bird above the door of the cubicle, listening to him chuckle again as he left the bathroom. Their daily banter made her feel slightly better after her run-in with Jackson the Jerk.

Steve flirted with everyone—and she meant *everyone,* no matter their gender. Steve spent so much time jumping the fence that he could have been an Olympic hurdler. But he was a sweet guy. He was tall and well-built, in a down-home farm boy kind of way. His musculature was all from tossing hay bales while growing up. Not that there was much call for hay baling in L.A., but she assumed he still kept fit, because there wasn't an ounce of fat on the man and wow, did he fill out his tuxedo nicely. Coupled with his dark good looks, it made him look like James Bond.

Steve had tried to put the moves on her when they first started working together, but she had a firm "no dating anyone at work" rule. He'd respected that, so instead they'd become friends, and now he was one of her best friends.

She clipped up her garter, and rolled her silk stocking up over her thighs, holding her breath until they were clipped in. She really couldn't afford another pair. Each pair cost her seventy bucks, and it was her one luxury, other than Manny's burritos and a tub of Ben and Jerry's on Friday nights. She shimmied into her dress, the garment hugging her curves, and zipped it up as far as she could reach.

She was short, but Mexican food and ice cream aside, she had a healthy diet and ran every morning to keep herself in shape. She was always going to be curvy, but the early morning exercise kept everything nice and tight. The fact that she had to get into this dress four nights a week—and that her survival relied on tips from rich frat brats whose tipping habits directly related to the tightness of her ass—well, it provided enough incentive to keep her on track.

She brushed out her dark brown hair, letting it fall into its natural waves. Swiping on a few coats of mascara over her long, dark lashes made her brown eyes really pop. Red lipstick slid expertly across her full lips, completing her war paint. She pinned a large white silk flower in her hair to complete her uniform, then left the change cubicle.

Stuffing the dry cleaner plastic back into her locker, she pulled on the leather pumps that sat at the bottom. She tied on a lap apron—decorated with Casablanca's logo and surrounded by black and white lace trim—before loading a few pens and her notepad into the front pocket, and walking out of the locker room. She strode past the security guy, giving him a warm smile. She was pretty sure he was new.

She stopped at the bar, where Steve was double checking the stock for when they opened in fifteen minutes. There would already be a queue around the block. She whistled, and he came over and zipped up her dress the remainder of the way. They truly had a domestic arrangement going on.

She waved to some of the busboys, who were busy wiping down every visible surface, and ensuring the tables were set just right around the edges of the room. Huge palm fronds were stenciled on the walls behind real palm trees, giving the illusion of some subtropical paradise. The VIP area was all dark wood and red velvet couches, which were a pain to get vomit stains—

as well as other things—out of, and had to be steam cleaned weekly.

She walked across the black and white marble dance floor toward the back of house, loving the sound of her heels clicking in the near silence. The band was busy setting up on stage, and they'd play light jazz until the DJ came in at ten to take over.

Rick, the bar manager, came over and squeezed her shoulder. Evie wasn't sure if Rick was his real name, or just a persona he took on to run the place. Either way, he was dressed up like Humphrey Bogart, and he was the only man she knew who could pull it off. She'd seen him without the suit and fedora once and hardly recognized him. She preferred the illusion.

"I need you working the VIP area tonight, Evie. We have two private parties with over a hundred guests each—the daughter of some politician or another, and a trust fund kid turning twenty-one. It has the potential to get wild. I'll have Kate and Big Sammie up there helping you, but if you need more hands, give Steve a heads up and we'll figure it out."

Big Sammie lived up to his name. He was a three hundred and fifty pound Goliath of muscle. Once he'd shown her a picture of his dog, and she'd prepared herself to coo over some massive pitbull, but she'd been in for a big surprise. She'd sworn never to tell anyone that he had a chihuahua, smaller in size than one of Sammie's fists, with the super cute name of Pumpkin.

Rick liked to get worked up into a stressed out state; the nervous energy apparently helped him focus. But in all honesty, it was only going to be as busy as every other night at Casablanca's. It was a hotspot for the rich and famous, and if Evie had a dollar for every celebrity, sports star, socialite or playboy who came in and ended up puking their guts out in the corner, well, she could retire early.

As a general rule, the clients were obnoxious, and considered waitresses one step above street walkers, but they tipped well, so Evie had learned to grin and bear it.

She got to work, helping Steve stock the bar for the night. Casablanca's sold more high-end liquor than any other club in this part of town, which meant dropping a crate while hauling it up the stairs was like a whole month's worth of wages.

The bar was Evie's favorite feature of the club. It ran along one wall beside the entrance to the VIP area. On either end were heavy wooden doors with huge brass studs, looking like somewhere between a medieval castle's doors and the entrance to a BDSM club. Between the two big doors was a twelve foot long mirror, reflecting the shelves of liquor stacked neatly in front of it. Behind the mirror, they'd managed to get the name Casablanca's to glow like a neon red beacon. Even after all this time, Evie hadn't worked out exactly how they'd made that happen, but she loved the effect.

As the door opened, people started to pour in and she got busy taking drink orders, showing people to the roped-off VIP areas, and cleaning up spills. By the time things really got crazy, the DJ had been playing a set for forty-five minutes, and everyone was well and truly on their way to being drunk. The cool kids were just arriving fashionably late, and the normal folk danced down on the main floor, trying to sneak a look past Big Sammie into the VIP room to celeb spot.

Evie had just pointed out a paparazzi to Big Sammie, who'd stormed off in the guy's direction like a human thunderhead, when a hand tapped her lightly on the shoulder. She turned to see Jackson Harper standing next to her, dressed the same as this afternoon except for a black leather jacket thrown over his t-shirt. Somehow, as dressed down as he was, he seemed to fit in with the crowd around him.

"What are *you* doing here?" Evie blurted out. "How'd you even know I worked here? Are you stalking me?" She gave him a hard look, and tried to spot Steve or Sammie in the crowd to catch their eye.

Jackson just laughed. "No, I'm not stalking you. I remembered I'd seen you here before. Plus, your bag had the Casablanca's logo on it. Didn't take much detective work."

She was still suspicious, but he sounded legitimate enough. "Casablanca's isn't the kind of place the busking bums frequent very often," she said, probably unkindly.

He just shrugged. "I got lost one day meeting friends. Then I saw a beautiful woman in a red dress and decided to stay awhile."

He gave her a charming grin, but she shook it off. She'd been propositioned five times tonight by guys with grins just like that—guys who thought a fifty buck tip and nice smile would get her into the bathroom for a quickie.

She gave him her blankest stare, and he cleared his throat uncomfortably. "Look, I wanted to apologize for causing you problems. How about we have that drink sometime, and you could tell me how to be a better Venice Beach community member?"

Evie had to give it to him, he was persistent. She gave him a skeptical look, and he raised his hands in a placating gesture.

"Really. I'm eternally sorry for messing with your life. Maybe tomorrow night?" he asked.

Or when hell freezes over, she thought. Although, the reasonable part of her mind argued that she needed some of his space if she was ever going to get back more of her customers. Damn the logical part of her brain that worried about things like rent and power bills.

"Fine. I'm free tomorrow night. Though why you aren't busking after dusk is beyond me. Now, excuse me, but I have to work."

He gave her a sparkling smile, and butterflies fluttered in her stomach. "Okay, tomorrow night. I can't wait." He threw her a wink, and she forgot how to swallow.

Get a grip, she chastised herself. *It's business, not a date.*